THE MALTESE ANGEL

OTHER BOOKS BY
CATHERINE COOKSON

NOVELS
Kate Hannigan
The Fifteen Streets
Colour Blind
Maggie Rowan
Rooney
The Menagerie
Slinky Jane
Fanny McBride
Fenwick Houses
The Garment
The Blind Miller
Hannah Massey
The Long Corridor
The Unbaited Trap
Katie Mulholland
The Round Tower
The Nice Bloke
The Glass Virgin
The Invitation
The Dwelling Place
Feathers in the Fire
Pure as the Lily
The Mallen Streak
The Mallen Girl
The Mallen Litter
The Invisible Cord
The Gambling Man
Miss Martha Mary Crawford

The Tide of Life
The Slow Awakening
The Iron Façade
The Girl
The Cinder Path
The Man Who Cried
Tilly Trotter
Tilly Trotter Wed
Tilly Trotter Widowed
The Whip
Hamilton
The Black Velvet Gown
Goodbye Hamilton
A Dinner of Herbs
Harold
The Moth
Bill Bailey
The Parson's Daughter
Bill Bailey's Lot
The Cultured Handmaiden
Bill Bailey's Daughter
The Harrogate Secret
The Black Candle
The Wingless Bird
The Gillyvors
My Beloved Son
The Rag Nymph
The House of Women

THE MARY ANN STORIES
A Grand Man
The Lord and Mary Ann
The Devil and Mary Ann
Love and Mary Ann

Life and Mary Ann
Marriage and Mary Ann
Mary Ann's Angels
Mary Ann and Bill

FOR CHILDREN
Matty Doolin
Joe and the Gladiator
The Nipper
Blue Baccy
Our John Willie

Mrs Flannagan's Trumpet
Go Tell It To Mrs Golightly
Lanky Jones
Nancy Nutall and the Mongrel

AUTOBIOGRAPHY
Our Kate
Let Me Make Myself Plain

Catherine Cookson Country

WRITING AS CATHERINE MARCHANT
House of Men
The Fen Tiger

Heritage of Folly

CATHERINE COOKSON

— THE —
Maltese Angel

BANTAM PRESS

LONDON · NEW YORK · TORONTO · SYDNEY · AUCKLAND

TRANSWORLD PUBLISHERS LTD
61–63 Uxbridge Road, London W5 5SA

TRANSWORLD PUBLISHERS (AUSTRALIA) PTY LTD
15–23 Helles Avenue, Moorebank, NSW 2170

TRANSWORLD PUBLISHERS (NZ) LTD
3 William Pickering Drive, Albany, Auckland

Published 1992 by Bantam Press
a division of Transworld Publishers Ltd
Copyright © Catherine Cookson 1992
Reprinted 1992

A catalogue record for this book is available from the British Library

ISBN 0-593-02132-0

Typeset in 12 on 14pt Linotron Sabon by
Phoenix Typesetting, Burley-in-Wharfedale, West Yorkshire.
Printed and bound in Great Britain by
Mackays of Chatham PLC, Chatham, Kent

THE MALTESE ANGEL

BOOK ONE

1886–1888

PART ONE

I

It had taken him only half an hour from leaving Newcastle to reach the first gate of his farm. He had ridden faster than usual, yet all the while asking himself why, because once he got into the house, what would he do? He'd sit down at the table, put his elbows on it, droop his head into his hands and ask himself, and for the countless time, what his reaction would have been had the company at The Empire not been engaged for another week; and the answer he would give would be: he didn't know.

Things had moved too fast: he had never been in a situation like this in his life; he had never felt like this in his life; he had never even known what love was. He had known what need was. Oh, aye. And that had been a kind of torment. And so was this present feeling; but a different kind of torment . . . No, no; he couldn't call it torment, not this feeling of elation, of being taken out of himself; it was like being lifted on to some high hill . . . mountain; yes, mountain; and experiencing an exhilarating emotion flooding through him, more cleansing than frost-filled air in the early dawn.

He would then ask himself if he had gone out of his mind. Four times only had he seen the girl . . . no, the young woman . . . no, the beautiful creature that appeared to him as someone not quite human.

It couldn't be because he was unused to looking at turns on the stage: at least once a month over the past two years he had sat through a performance at The Empire or at one of the other theatres in the city; he had even sat through a play by Shakespeare, which, and he had to admit it, wasn't much to his taste; the twang and the rigmarole were hard to get into . . .

He pulled up at the second gate and, leaning from the saddle, unlatched the iron hoop from the stanchion; but his hand became still for a moment when he looked across the dark field towards the outbuildings of his farm and saw the movement of a lantern, not coming from the direction of the cow byres or the piggeries, or yet from the hen crees in the field, which might have denoted a fox on his rounds and Billy Compton after him, for there was no sound of barking from the dogs; nor was it coming from the floor of the old barn, but from the loft.

Having urged his mount through the gate, he turned in the saddle and replaced the hoop, then put the animal into a gallop towards the mud yard. There, dismounting, he patted its rump, and pushed it towards its stable, saying, 'Be with you in a minute, Betty,' before hurrying down the yard and entering an open-fronted barn.

Approaching the ladder that rose to the loft, he shouted, 'You up there, Billy?'

In answer, a head appeared above him, saying, 'Aye, Master Ward. 'Tis I up here all right; and a visitor. Better you come up and make his acquaintance like.'

When Ward Gibson reached the loft floor his eyes were drawn to a small figure hunched against the old timbers of the sloping roof, and he walked slowly towards it, saying, 'Aye! Aye! And who's this when he's out?'

'Can't get a word out of him, master. But he's in one hell of a state for a bairn.'

'What do you mean, hell of a state?' Ward's voice was low; and so was the old man's as he replied, 'He's been thrashed, an' badly; scourged, I would say. An' he doesn't seem to have any wits left him, he's so full of fear. Shook like an aspen when I first spoke to him.'

Ward dropped on to his hunkers before the very small figure and, kindly, he said, 'Hello there! What's your name?'

14

Two round eyes stared back at him. The lids blinked rapidly, but the boy's lips did not move.

'Come along, now; you've got a name. There's nobody here goin' to touch you.'

The old man, too, was now on his hunkers, and he held his hand out gently towards the boy, saying, 'Let the master look at your back, laddie. Just let him see your back. Come on, now. Come on.'

After a moment the boy slowly hitched himself round, and as slowly Billy lifted up the dirty grey shirt and so exposed in the light of the lantern the scarlet weals criss-crossing each other from the small shoulders down to the equally small buttocks, and that these overlaid older scars.

The elder man now spoke in a whisper: 'That whip had a number of tails, don't you think, master? An' take a look at his wrists,' and so saying he gently pulled the shirt down and turned the boy round again, and, taking up the small dirt-grimed hands, pointed to the wrists. 'Tarry rope, I would say. But look at the ankle! That's definitely a chain mark.'

The old man now looked at his master, waiting for him to speak; but it was some seconds before Ward, holding out his hand, said, 'Come along, son. Nobody's going to hurt you here. Come on.'

The boy did not at first move, but when he attempted to stand up he almost toppled; and instinctively Ward went to pick him up; but the child, as he proved to be from his stature, shunned back from him. And again Ward said, 'There's no-one going to hurt you here. Come on; walk if you can; otherwise, I'll carry you.'

The boy now walked unsteadily down the loft; but when he came to the edge of the platform and seemed as if he might be about to fall, without any hesitation now, Ward lifted him up and, holding him in one arm, made his way down the ladder.

Outside, and about to cross the yard, he said to Billy, 'Is Annie in the cottage?'

'Aye; she is, master; in bed this half hour. But there's your supper in the oven, and plenty of cold victuals. But if you think I should get her up . . .'

'No. We'll do what is necessary. . . How did you find him?'

' 'Twas the dogs. Flo was uneasy; even Cap kept runnin' back and for'ard. An' when Flo barked at the bottom of the ladder, well, I knew somebody was up there. When I shouted twice an' got no answer, I yelled I had me gun with me, and I pushed Flo up afront like. But as soon as she discovered the boy she stopped her yappin'. Funny, but he didn't seem to be feared of her.'

'Well, that's about the only thing in life, if you ask me, he isn't afraid of.'

It was nearly half an hour later. Billy had washed the boy's face and hands, and Ward himself had cleaned the boy's back as much as he could without causing him more pain than he was apparently already suffering, before applying an ointment that his mother had used on both humans and beasts for bruises and boils and every known skin ailment. Afterwards, they had watched the waif gulp at food like a ravenous animal, and when he had drunk a half pint of milk almost at one swallow, they had exchanged glances. But it wasn't until the lad was seated on the low cracket before the fire, a blanket about him, that the stiffness seemed to go out of his body and his tongue became loose for the first time.

When Ward again asked his name, he said, 'Carl Bennett.'

The name seemed ordinary enough to them both; but the tone of the voice was not one they would have termed local, nor would it have been recognisable for miles around.

When Ward asked how old he was, the boy at first said, 'Eight;' but then his head jerked and he had added, 'No; nine.'

Where had he come from? At this he had bowed his head before muttering, 'Farm.'

'Whose farm?' asked Ward. 'Which farm?'

The look the boy gave Ward was furtive before he muttered, 'A long way off, beyond Durham.'

'Beyond Durham?'

The old man and Ward seemed to repeat the words together.

16

'When did you leave?'

'Yesterday. No . . . ' The tousled dark head shook again. 'The day before. Not sure.'

'Why?'

There was no answer to this, only the look in the boy's eyes seemed to say, 'Need you ask?'

'What was the name of the farm . . . or the farmer?'

The boy now looked down to the wide hearth and seemed to focus his gaze on the huge black iron dog that supported the set of equally huge fire-irons; and he didn't raise his head again until Ward said, 'Well, don't worry; you're not going back. My man, here' – he nodded towards Billy – 'was saying only last week he could do with some help; that he's not getting any younger and was looking for a youngster to do the odds and ends. Weren't you?'

'Oh aye. Oh, yes. Aye, I was that, master. I was that. Definitely I was lookin' out for a youngster.'

The boy stared from one to the other and his voice held a note of natural eagerness when he said, 'I can work . . . work hard.'

'How long were you on the farm?'

'Two years.'

'Where did you live before that?'

The head made a movement as if about to droop again, but the thin bony chin jerked slightly as the words came: 'The workhouse.'

'Had you been there long?'

'Since being four . . . I mean, since I was four.'

Again they both noted the boy's strange way of speaking.

'How did you get there?'

'I am told that my parents were set upon on their journey. My mother had the sickness; she died, and my father, too.'

'What was the sickness?'

'Her chest. But I don't know how my father died. Joe said he knew, but he wouldn't tell me.'

'Who was Joe?'

'He was a boy in the workhouse, but he was taken to a farm before I was. He was older.'

'Is he still on the farm?'

17

'No, he ran away twice. He didn't come back the second time.'

'Is this the first time you've run away?'

Again the boy's head drooped and the voice was low as he replied, 'No; three times.'

'And you were whipped when you got back, and tied up?'

'Yes.'

'Well, why didn't you go back to the workhouse and tell them of the treatment?'

Both the boy and Billy stared at Ward now, and it was to Billy that Ward made the sharp retort: 'Well, there's laws, you know. They send inspectors to the farms; at least, they're supposed to do. Arthur Meyer has a workhouse boy. I think he's got two and the Masons have one. And as far as I understand they've got to be signed for and reports given as to progress.'

'Aye, well' – Billy's head wagged – 'there are workhouses an' workhouses, an' some folks would cut your throat for a back-hander. Anyway, master, where is he gona sleep the night?'

After a moment's thought Ward said, 'Put him in the boiler-house; it's nice and warm there; and we'll see about rigging up a room for him above the stables tomorrow.' He turned now to the boy and smiled at him, saying, 'How does that suit you?'

The boy did not immediately answer; when he did, his voice came as a thin mutter: 'You are not just speaking like this, sir, then tomorrow you will change?'

'No, son; I am not just speaking like this. And you will find that I don't say one thing at night and another in the morning. Go with Billy now, and he'll bed you down, and tomorrow we will talk. But I think, for the time being and for your own safety, you must not be seen abroad too much because, as the law stands, you could be sent back. You understand?'

'Oh yes. Yes, I understand, sir. And . . . and thank you.'

He stood up now. He was not more than four feet tall, and apparently he was a child of eight or nine – he had seemed uncertain of his own age – yet from the set look on his face and the expression in his eyes at this moment he could be taken for an adult; and this disturbed both men.

It was Billy who now said briskly, 'Well, come along, young man. If you're goin' to be any use to me you must get your sleep. Aye, you must that.' And with this he hitched up the blanket around the boy, put his hand on his shoulder and pressed him towards the door. But there he stopped and, turning towards Ward, he said, 'By the way, master, did you see to Betty?'

'No; but I'm going to do that now. Anyway' – Ward smiled – 'she's likely stuffed herself full of oats by now and taken her own harness off. I'm sure she's quite capable of it. So get yourself away to bed; the morning will soon be here.'

' 'Twill that, master. 'Twill that. That's one of the things you can be sure of: whether we're here or not, the mornin' will be.'

Ward did not immediately follow his man out and see to the horse, but he sat down with a heavy plop on one of the high-backed, wooden kitchen chairs; and now he did place his elbows on the table, but he did not droop his head into his hands. What he said to himself was, Funny, but this little business has knocked it clean out of my head. It's there though, and I've got to do something about it.

But what? Tomorrow is Sunday. I can do nothing till Monday night, when I can sit there again and face her. And how many nights after that am I going to be there without having a word with her? She knows I'm there; I'm sure of that. She looked at me tonight, and she smiled . . . she smiled at me, not the rest of them, she didn't lift her eyes over the stalls or raise them to the gallery. I'm not imagining it. No, no; I'm not. One thing, she isn't married. The doorman said she wasn't. His thoughts now took him back to the doorman, and he gritted his teeth as he said to himself, By, it's a wonder I didn't let go at him when he said, 'What d'you want to know for? And if she was, it wouldn't be to a yokel from the country.' A yokel from the country! And he was in his good suit, made of the best home-spun cloth. Of course, he'd had it these five years, and the neck was high. But surely that

19

wouldn't have stamped him as being from the country. He was lucky, that chap, that he left him still standing on his feet.

He went to rise from the chair; then he stopped himself, saying half aloud, 'What about tomorrow?' He had promised Parson Tracey that he would turn up for the choir . . . at least he had made the promise through Frank Noble, the curate, when he had called here only two days ago, and Frank, in his 'Hail fellow, well met' voice had exclaimed loudly how they all missed him; that the choir wasn't the same without him: all tenors and tremors, not a bass among them. 'You're being missed, you know, Ward,' he had added. 'You're being missed by everybody . . . everybody.' What he had meant by the second everybody was that he was being missed by one in particular.

Well, what had he to be afraid of? Daisy understood all right, by now, how things stood. She had been a pal since schooldays; she had been more of a pal to him than had either of her brothers, Sep or Pete. That was all she had been, a pal.

His rising from the chair was in the form of a jerk and as he made hastily for the door an inner voice checked his step. 'Stop kidding yourself, man,' it said. 'Face up to it. You know what she's always been after. Remember what Dad said to you the day before he died: "She'd make a good wife and she'd give you a family. Aye, a big one. But what else you'll get from her, you alone know. Just remember, lad: there's more in marriage than the bed, which you've got to get out of most times at five in the morning. And days are long, especially in the winter."'

His dad had been a wise man, a quiet, thinking, wise man; and he had picked right for himself. Which was why he had been unable to go on living without his partner, because she had given him more than was called upon as her duty.

Well, tomorrow morning he would go and sing in the choir, and leave the rest to God and common sense.

2

⌒⌒⌒

Part of St Stephen's Church dated from the early sixteenth
century; surprisingly, not the chancel and sanctuary section,
but the part of the nave containing the font.

Eight rows of pews were contained in this old part, the
rest, ten rows, were within the newer walls built earlier in
the century.

And, again surprisingly, a gallery was built to overhang
the font, and it was here the organ was housed and the choir
sang.

A huge wrought-iron screen stretched across the front of
the chancel, thereby cutting off the view of the altar and
sanctuary from the congregation, apart from those favoured
with the direct view allowed through the necessary central
opening in the screen.

However, the pulpit to the right side of the screen was in
view of all the congregation.

The screen had been given by a member of the Ramsmore
family in honour of his father, a general who had died in
battle.

Its immediate effect on the villagers had been one of
muted protest, muted because, for most of them, a man's
daily bread depended either directly upon the Ramsmores
or on their patronage. In those days, most of the village and
the surrounding countryside was owned by them.

However, nowadays, things were changed in all ways up
at the Hall. At one time, as many as sixty people would have

21

been employed in the house or on the estate, but, now, the fingers of two hands would have numbered them. Three farms had gone, as well as most of the immediate estate. Yet, they were still generally looked upon as Lords of the Manor, for the Colonel was a class man, and his second wife, Lady Lydia, was a lady in her own right, and she had given him a new son two years ago. Moreover, she was a woman who received respect without it being demanded, for she spoke her mind. It had even been whispered here and there that if she'd had anything to do with it, the screen would have come down, and without delay, and this might have encouraged a more open objection to it by the villagers, except that anyone daring to suggest such a thing would have had to face the wrath of Parson Tracey, and Parson Tracey was a power in the village. In fact, it was laughingly said he thought he had created the village, the church, and God.

From where he sat in the gallery, Ward gazed fixedly at the minister in the pulpit, and he asked himself for the hundredth time how much longer the man was going to keep yammering on about Job and his wrongs: poor Job had been stung by everything but a horsefly, but apparently God was now rewarding him in abundance with thousands of sheep, she-asses, and camels. My! My! He had heard it all before. How many times over the years? From when he was a boy he had pictured the sheep being chased by the she-asses, and the lot of them being chased by the camels. He had even made it his business to look out a picture of a camel. They were big and he had early come to the conclusion that thousands of them would soon have put paid to the sheep and the she-asses.

Parson Tracey had no imagination. He had six sermons, which he would vary from time to time. Even when they were boys, Ward would lay a bet with Fred Newberry, who was sitting next to him now, that he could repeat at least two of the sermons. The bet had always been his wind-up engine against Fred's pinching two meat and onion pies from his dad's bakery. The engine was still lying amongst the oddments up in the attic.

22

Fred dug him gently in the ribs now, and a whisper came from the corner of his mouth, saying, 'Bet you a tanner Old Smythe goes to assist Miss Alice from the pew, eh?'

Ward made an almost audible sound that could have been Huh! as he thought, Fred gets dafter. Of course the verger would go and offer Miss Alice his hand to assist her out of the pew as if she were an old woman instead of an eighteen-year-old buxom miss. The verger was a dirty-minded old swine. Perhaps he ogled the young ones because he had no children of his own.

Ah! There, it was over, the end being signalled, first by the scraping of feet as the four men on the choir bench and the three boys seated in front of them rose to their feet, and by the rising, almost as one, of those in the bare wooden pews just slightly before the more favoured ones in the three pews where the seats were padded, and the rustling of gowns seeming to accentuate further the difference of favour.

Sometimes as many as six gentry families would attend at the main service, but this morning the pews were occupied by only three: the Ramsmores, the Hopkins from Border Manor, and the Bentfords, who lived in the old Wearside Grange. They were a nice family, the Bentfords, so Ward thought; but they were under suspicion in the village as their daughter had married one of the Franklins who owned The Mill, and they were Methodists.

Ward drew in a deep breath, and looked towards the organ, which was now beginning to get under way as two young boys put all their strength into pumping its wooden handle. Then he glanced back along the row to where Ben Oldman, the shoemaker, who was honoured by the title of choirmaster, was now bending forward with his hand at shoulder height and seeming to pat the air.

They were away: Fred's voice in full flood, and Jimmy Conroy, the butcher's son, mouthing the words while thinking, so Ward was sure, not of his soul but of Susan Beaker down there at the end of the sixth row, her straw hat bobbing with the tune, and then, there at the end of the row Charlie Dempsey the blacksmith, as usual a note higher and a note in front of everyone else. But Charlie was a nice fellow, as were

23

his sons John and Harry an' all. But they shunned church, the pair of them, as he himself had been doing for some time.

> Jesu, Lover of my soul,
> Let me to Thy bosom fly . . .

Now why should he be looking at Daisy down there, because there was one thing sure, especially now, he didn't want to fly to her bosom. But had he ever wanted to fly to her bosom? No; no, definitely not. Not like that.

> While the nearer waters roll,
> While the tempest still is high;
> Hide me, O my Saviour, hide,
> Till the storm of life is past:
> Safe into the haven guide,
> O, receive my soul at last.

The hymn finished on the Amen being dragged out, the congregation sat back and with impatient patience, the outcome of practice, waited while the Reverend Bertram Tracey slowly made his way, followed by his two servers, from the altar, down the two steps, through the arch in the screen, and after turning right, disappeared into the vestry.

Ward did not hurry from the gallery; nor did Fred; and once they were alone, Fred said, 'Like to drop in home for a minute or so?' And leaning towards Ward, exclaimed, 'Home brew going. As good as what you'll get in The Running Hare or The Crown Head. I can vouch for it, 'cos this mornin' I had a head on me as big as the bell tower, with the bell in it goin' hell for leather.' He spluttered, adding, 'Eeh! let's get out of this.'

At the foot of the spiral staircase he nudged Ward, saying, 'Bet yer Daisy'll be at the gate . . . What d'you say?'

Ward made no answer: from experience he knew that Fred didn't require answers.

Outside, it was evident that they must be among the last to leave, for there was the Reverend making his way across the graveyard towards his extra large Sunday dinner and the following nap that could go on till four in the afternoon, or at least until his wife returned from taking the Sunday school.

Everything in the village had a pattern; and there was part of it standing outside the lych-gate. The Mason family had

24

mounted the trap, the father John, and Gladys his wife and Pete and Sep, their manly sons.

The occupants of the trap waved and called to him as they moved off, and Fred, too, bade him a jovial farewell, saying, 'You're not comin' then? Well, if I don't see you at the Harvest Festival, I'll see you on the Christmas tree,' and as if he hadn't been aware of her before, he now added, 'Hello there, Daisy. You get bigger and bonnier every week.'

'You're a fool, Fred Newberry. Always were and always will be.'

'Very likely you're right, Daisy. Very likely you're right. Ta-ra. Ta-ra, Ward. Happy days.'

'He talks the same as he did at school.' She was looking at Ward now, and he answered, 'Yes, I suppose so; but he's harmless, and I've never known him to come out with anything that would hurt another.'

'Huh! You got religion all of a sudden?'

He gave her no answer, but as she made to walk on and towards the village street, he stopped and said, 'I've got to get back; there's a lot to do.'

They were standing at the end of the cemetery wall, in the shade of a beech tree, and now, almost glaring at him, she said, 'What's up with you?'

'Up with me? Nothing.'

'You've never been to church for over a month.'

'Well, Daisy, if you keep count, you'll know that, for a time before that, I hadn't been for over a year. I have fits and starts in that way.'

'And in other ways an' all,' she put in quickly; 'and I say again, what's the matter with you?'

'Nothing's the matter with me,' he snarled back at her. 'What's the matter with *you*?'

'Now, don't you come the simpleton with me, Ward Gibson; you're not Fred Newberry. I've only seen you once in a fortnight.'

'Well, if you're reckoning on time, there's times when you've only seen me once in a month. And, if you recall, I've got a farm to see to, and I've only got one man to help

25

out. Your dad has the two lads and you, and your mother, besides the hired boy.'

As soon as he mentioned the hired boy his mind recalled the happenings at breakfast concerning their young visitor; he shelved it, the present issue being much more important, for she was saying, 'You've been four times to Newcastle in the week.'

'Ohoo!' He moved his head slowly up and down, then repeated, 'Ohoo! I'm being watched, am I? And everybody wants to know what I'm doing in Newcastle, I suppose?'

'I know what you did one night. You went to The Empire.'

'Yes. Yes, Daisy, I went to The Empire. But what did I do on the other nights? Haven't you found out?'

When she didn't answer, he said, 'Oh, that would surprise you. It would give you and your spies something to talk about, where I went the other nights.'

Her full-lipped mouth pouted before she said, and softly now, 'You're playin' fast and loose with me, Ward, and we're as good as engaged.'

He gaped at her. '*What! Engaged?* What are you talking about? I've never even mentioned marriage to you.'

'No; you've been crafty' – her voice was no longer soft – 'you've never mentioned it, but you've acted it. I mean, you've had me on a string, you've played about with me.'

'My God! Daisy. Played about with you? I've danced with you at the barn dances; I've taken you to the Hoppings, twice, if I remember rightly, and I've kissed you once or twice. But God in heaven! that doesn't signify I've asked you to marry me.' Even as he said this he was wishing he was like Fred and never hurt anybody by what he said; but then he must go on and say it, and for more reasons than one. Oh yes, for more reasons than one. And now he said it: 'I've never had any thoughts of marrying you, Daisy. I've known you since we were nippers, sat at school with you, ran the fields with you; we've climbed trees together. You were like one of the lads.'

He wished he could stop talking, for he couldn't stand the look on her face. And now he added in a subdued

26

tone, 'Oh, Daisy, I'm sorry. I really am. We were pals . . .
I mean friends.'

'*Friends! Friends!* I could have been married twice over but
didn't because of you. *Do you hear?* Arthur Steel wanted me,
him over in Chester-le-Street. He has a farm, a big 'un, he
could use yours for pig sties. He . . . he asked me twice.'

His voice was very low now and soothing as he said, 'Well,
then, Daisy, he could ask you again.'

He watched her lips move into a snarl, which issued
through her clenched teeth as she hissed, 'He's married!
You . . . you pig of a man! He's married.' She was audibly
crying now, the sound coming from deep in her throat. Then
gulping, she seemed to steady herself before pleading now,
'Don't do this to me, Ward. The lads expect it. Me dad and
mum expect it; everybody expects it. They have for years
while we've been walking out.'

He shook his head. 'Daisy, we've never been walking out,
not in that sense. Listen to me.' He now put his hand on her
shoulder and drew her along the side of the cemetery wall
into a narrow lane; and there he leaned towards her as he said
thickly, 'Have . . . have I ever tried to touch you? You know
. . . you know what I mean. Answer me truly: have I ever?'

'That makes no difference.'

'But it does. I'm a man. You know all about mating; that's
farming life. If I'd had marriage in mind I would have tried
something on. So there you have it. But well, I . . . I went
elsewhere, because I wouldn't insult you, or spoil what was
between us, which was a good friendship. We could laugh
together, joke together, make fun of them all . . . at least up
till the last year or so.'

She seemed not to have heard his last words, for she
muttered, 'You went elsewhere.' It was a statement, not a
question. Shamefaced, he looked away from her and said,
'Aye; yes, I had to. But it was nothing. She was married.
She wasn't a whore or . . . or anything like that, she was
. . . well . . . '

How could he find words to explain that a chance meeting
at an inn on the road to Durham with a woman who could, at
a pinch, have been his mother, could not lead to anything? She

27

must have been in her forties. But she had been nice, kind and understanding. His mother had just died, and it was as if, besides a lover, he had gained another mother. He had known her only a short time, and then she had said it must stop because her husband would soon be coming back from sea. At their parting, she had spoken words to him that he would always remember: 'It's been the most beautiful time in my life,' she had said; 'and I'll remember it till I die. But this is the time to end it, for even the most beautiful flowers fade.'

He had never known anyone talk as she did, and he had missed her. Even up till this last week he had wondered if he had loved her; and he knew he had in a way, but the feeling was something different; it could never happen again; it had been the birth of his manhood, and you can't be born twice, not in that way.

'What?'

'*You! You!* You heard. She's in Newcastle, isn't she?'

He couldn't answer this, not really; and so he remained silent. The next instant he sprang back in surprise and pain as her fingernails tore down each side of his face.

Instinctively, his fist came out and, catching her on the shoulder, knocked her back against the wall. But she didn't slide down to the ground; she just stood, pressed tight against the rough stone, her large breasts heaving, her face contorted.

As he put one hand to his face and felt it wet, he backed from her; and at this she pulled herself from the wall, and she stood there, staring at him.

There was no movement of any part of her body now; even her lips seemed not to part as she said, 'I'll have my own back on you, Ward Gibson. I swear before God I will; you and all yours. D'you hear me?'

He made no rejoinder; but now watched as her hands slowly went to her hat and straightened it, then down to her coat to button it over her heaving breasts, before she turned slowly away to walk back along by the side of the cemetery wall.

Now he, too, moved, but only as far as the wall; in fact, to the very spot where she had been standing; and he laid his

28

head against it and, taking a handkerchief from his pocket, gently drew it over his left cheek; then looked at it. It was covered with blood. He felt his other cheek. It was sore, but it was dry. He closed his eyes, and his body slumped.

How long he stayed like this against the wall, he didn't know; he only knew that for the first time in his life he was experiencing fear, for he could still see her face. He doubted if he would ever forget the look on it. He imagined it to be how a real mad woman might look.

After pulling himself up straight, he didn't make for the village street, but went down the narrow path that skirted the west wall of the cemetery, to lead into open pasture, then Morgan's wood. This way would take him twice as long to reach home; but he needed time to compose himself and to think.

Yet all he could think about throughout the whole journey was the look on her face and her threat, and the surprise, too, that the Daisy he had played with as a child, romped with during his boyhood years, teased, laughed and danced with, and kissed occasionally, should have in her what now appeared to him as an evil spirit, such as you read about in the Bible but never took any notice of, or, if you did, you thought of it as a fable. But Daisy Mason represented no fable. *No! No!*

'In the name of God!' said Annie. 'Where've you been? An' what's done that to your face? I thought you were at church.'

'Get me a drink, Annie.'

'Aye. Aye.' Her head wagged. 'Is it ale you want, or a drop of the hard?'

'A drop of the hard.'

She was only a minute gone from the kitchen before she returned with a glass in her hand, one third full of whisky; and after he had thrown it back without pausing she took the glass from him; then, her hand going out, she gently touched the two weals that were now covered in dried blood, and she asked quietly, 'An animal?'

For a moment he gazed up at her as if he were thinking. 'Well, it was like the act of one,' he said.

29

She now stood back from him, her face screwed up in enquiry; then, as if a light were dawning on her, she muttered, 'Not Daisy Mason?'

'The very same, Annie.'

She emitted a slow breath before commenting, the while nodding her head, 'I shouldn't be surprised. No, I shouldn't, because I've always thought of her as an untamed bitch in that great bulk of hers. But you've asked for it, you know.'

'I've never asked for it, Annie.'

'Oh yes, you have. There's half a dozen lasses round about you could have taken on jaunts, but who did you take? Daisy Mason. Now that must have made her think. But tell me what's made her think otherwise?'

'I told her I wasn't for marrying.'

'What brought it about?'

'Oh, she implied . . . No, she didn't imply, she said right out that we were as good as engaged.'

'And you said you weren't, and then she went for you?'

'There was more to it than that. I had to speak plainly. I'm sorry I had to do so, but there was nothing else for it.'

Annie turned from him and walked towards the oven as she said, 'Would there have been nothing else for it up till this last week?'

He stared at her bent back as she opened the oven door and took out a large dripping tin holding a sizzling joint, and she had placed it on the end of the table before he answered, 'Yes, Annie, it would have been the same. And what do you mean by . . . this last week?'

'Oh, lad; you're talking to an old woman.' She grinned now, and then said, 'Well, if not old, getting on, and as far as I can remember in this house, since the day you could toddle you've never made four journeys into Newcastle in a week, and I shouldn't imagine it was to the Haymarket, or to your solicitor man, nor anything else like that, an' going by the programme I found on your dressing table, I think I've got the answer.' She now pushed the hot roasting tin away from her, laid the coarse towel with which she had been holding it over the back of a chair, which she then pulled towards her and sat down on. Her knees now almost touching his,

30

she leaned towards him, asking, 'Is it the young lass on the front of the programme that's caught your eye?'

He stared back at her, his face and neck suffused red with embarrassment. 'It isn't just a fancy, Annie,' he said; 'I can't explain it. I'm drawn there, you know, like the saying is, as if by a magnet.'

'Well, lad, you know your own road best, but from what I understand and it might only be hearsay, but it's been said over the years that those bits of lasses on the stage are of light character.'

'Yes, Annie; I've heard all that.'

'But you think this one's different. What has she to say for herself? Is she well spoken? Is she . . . ?'

'I wouldn't know, Annie; I haven't met her.'

'*Oh! lad.*' She gave a chuckle now. 'If you had told me you'd jumped off one of the Newcastle bridges because you thought you could fly, I would have said, well, these things happen to daft individuals who haven't been well brought up and who haven't heads on their shoulders, but not to you, never to somebody like you. Ah, Master Ward' – she put her hand out and patted his shoulder – 'it's a sad dream. We all have 'em, you know. Women an' all. For meself, I never thought I'd marry a man like Bill; the fellow I was goin' to give me hand to wasn't goin' to do farm work. No, by gum. I was above that; I'd seen enough of it in this house, although there was nobody better as a master or mistress than your folks. But, in a way, I had taken a pattern from them and I wanted somebody better, somebody who wore a collar an' tie when he went to work, an' didn't smell of cow byres or pig muck.' Her whole body began to shake now as she went on, 'But then something hit me. I don't know what it is to this day; I only know if I hadn't him, life wouldn't be worth living; and he's a grumpy, impatient sod at the best of times.'

'Oh, Annie!' He closed his eyes and flapped his hand towards her, saying, 'Don't make me laugh. Please don't make me laugh; my face is sore; and at the moment my heart is sore, an' all. I've hurt somebody deeply, and what's more I've seen her character change so much that it frightened me.'

31

She stared at him and, seriously now, she said, 'She must have gone a bit wild to do that to you.'

'More than a bit, Annie; I would never have believed it of her. Anyway, I must go and clean this up.'

As he lifted his hand towards his face, she said, 'Sit where you are. I'll go and get some witch hazel and rose water, and wash it for you, then put the salve on. But I can see you're goin' to have a couple of marks there for some time. The other side'll fade . . . By! she did a job on you.' As she rose to her feet she added, 'It's been a funny morning all round. I got a surprise when I looked at that youngster's back; and then there was that salt business. That was funny, wasn't it?'

He nodded at her. 'Yes; yes it was funny.'

'I'll say it was. Fancy being frightened to touch salt! When I pushed it towards him, do you remember, and me saying, "Put salt on your egg now," he almost threw the cellar across the table, and at the same time shrank back in his chair as if it was going to bite him? Most odd, wasn't it?'

'It was, Annie. Yes, it was.'

As she once again hurried from the room he recalled to mind the incident of the salt and the look on the boy's face. It was full of fear, as it had been last night when he had first seen him. It was as if the salt had been a live snake.

The thought of the boy's fear recalled his own of a short while ago, because for a time he had been swamped with fear. It was a new emotion, almost as strong as the one he felt for the beautiful figure flitting from one side of the stage to the other, as light as he imagined a fairy would be; and when, at the end, turning into a bird by lifting her arms head high to expose wings of fine ribbed silk, before she was lifted and, the wings rippling like water, she flew from the stage to loud cheers and clapping from the audience, the feeling she left him with was so strong as to be painful, for she appeared more angelic than any angel his imagination had ever been able to conjure up.

But then, Daisy had expressed a fierce hate of him such as again his imagination had never been able to conjure up. Of a sudden he felt weak and fearful with the force of both.

3

It was a drizzling rain, and Annie remarked on it: 'It's in for the night,' she said; 'you'll get sodden.' She now raised her eyebrows, so stretching her longish features even further as she said, 'Have you got to go in?'

'Yes, Annie; I've got to go in. But as for asking me what I've got to go in for, well, I'll tell you shortly; and I might do it with a pleasant grin on my face or, on the other hand, looking at me, you'll know it's better to keep your tongue quiet and not ask questions.'

'Like that, is it?'

'It's like that, Annie. Yes, it's like that.'

'Well, I only hope she's worth it.' She was standing at the wooden sink and looking out of the kitchen window, and she exclaimed, 'You won't be goin' this minute, you've got company.'

'Who is it?' He went quickly across the room to stand by her side, and when he saw John Mason step down from his trap he bit on his lower lip, and before turning away, he said quietly, 'Show him into the sitting-room, Annie.'

'The sitting-room?' Her face stretched again. 'Well, all right, I'll do that; but he's always come straight into the kitchen afore; all of them have. But as you say . . . '

She went from him, leaving him again nipping on his lip, this time whilst waiting for Annie's welcome: 'Oh; good evenin', Mr Mason. Can I have your coat; you're a bit wet.'

'Is Ward anywhere about?'

33

'Yes; yes, he is. If you'll just take a seat in the parlour, I'll go fetch him for you.'

By the silence that followed Ward could imagine the man hesitating on the invitation to go into the parlour as if he were a stranger.

A minute or so later, on Annie's entering the kitchen, Ward held up his hand to silence anything she might say, then walked past her across the stone-flagged hall and into the parlour.

John Mason was standing with his back to the empty grate, and his greeting was, 'Hello, there, Ward. Oh . . . oh, I see you're ready for going on the road. Well, I won't keep you long.'

When Ward stood before him, the older man stared at his face, then turned his head to the side before saying softly, 'I'm sorry she did that to you. But she was upset. Oh, yes, she was upset . . . What's come over you, Ward?'

He didn't answer for quite some time, for what could he say to this decent man, a man he had always liked, because he was a fair man in all his dealings. Not so his two sons, at least not so Sep. He had never liked Sep; he was a big-mouth. And Pete . . . well, Pete didn't talk as much, but there had always been a slyness about Pete. Yet the father and mother were the nicest couple you could meet in a day's walk; and so, could he say to this man that he had become obsessed, because that word somehow fitted his feelings, and to a girl to whom he had never spoken and knew nothing whatever about except that she danced beautifully and was beautiful to look at, yet so fragile?

What he did say was, 'I never mentioned marriage to Daisy, Mr Mason.'

'No, lad; no. Perhaps you didn't mention the word, but all your actions over the past years have sort of implied that was your intention. To tell you the truth, me and her mother took it for granted that you would one day match up, because she would have made you a good wife. She knows everything about a farm that is to know; besides which she's a fine cook . . . Not much good with her needle.' A faint smile came on his face now. 'Not like her mother in that way;

but you can't have everything. I thought, though, she had everything that you needed, Ward. Oh yes. And I still do.'

'I'm sorry, Mr Mason. I am indeed. I'm sorry to the heart to upset you and your wife, because you've both always been very kind to me; and I shall never forget the help you were when both Mam and Dad died. But look at it from my point of view if you can. I've known Daisy all me life. We were like friends. She was . . . well, it's a funny way to put it, but she was like a mate to me, as neither Sep nor Pete were.'

'Well, if that was the case, Ward, why did you continue to keep company with her and not take up with some other girl in the village or hereabouts? No . . . no.' Mr Mason moved his head slowly now. 'Be fair, Ward, there only seemed to be Daisy for you. You took her to the barn dances, you took her to the Hoppings, Sunday after Sunday you used to drop in to tea. Well, that was some time back, I admit, before your people went; but, nevertheless, our house was like your second home.'

'That's it, Mr Mason,' Ward put in quickly, 'it was like my second home; you were all too close; too familiar; there was no . . . well, excitement. Oh—' He half turned away now, saying, 'I'm sorry about all this. I keep saying that, but I really am.'

'Tell me truthfully, Ward. Just answer me a simple question: have you found somebody else?'

Ward turned now and, facing Mr Mason again, he said, 'You could put it like that, Mr Mason; yes, you could put it like that.'

Mr Mason now walked slowly past Ward and towards the door, saying as he went, 'One could say, this is life, and these things happen; but that's from people standing apart. They are the onlookers, not the ones it's actually happening to. And it's happening to my Daisy, and she's hurt to the core.' He stopped, and he opened the parlour door before turning and saying to Ward, 'I haven't it in me to wish you harm because I've always imagined you becoming another son, but I would be lying if I said I wish you luck and happiness in your choice, because, in a way, you've ruined my lass's life. Yes; yes, you have, Ward.'

35

When the door had closed on him, Ward turned to the mantelshelf and, laying his arm along it, he drooped his head on to it, and as he muttered, 'God in heaven!' his fist thumped the wood.

After a moment he straightened up; and now he was looking into the iron-framed mirror above the fireplace, and his reflection was telling him Mr Mason was right: he *had* acted as if he had intended to marry Daisy. He had been utterly thoughtless, at least until a year or so ago when he guessed how things were with her. But still, in the end, perhaps he would have married her if this other thing hadn't hit him, for there would have been this same strong need in him; and it wasn't possible he would ever again come across such an obliging and understanding woman as Mrs Oswald.

And now he was in a fix, all because he had dropped into The Empire a week ago.

Was he mad? He must be. He had seen the creature only four times. God above! Why was he thinking of her as a creature now? Because she could be a creature: on closer acquaintance she could prove to be just a painted doll. Those bright lights bamboozled people. She could be a slut; most of them were; a lot of them sold themselves to men . . . old men, for money and big houses . . . or titles.

He turned from the mirror, and his gaze now focussed on the horse-hair sofa that fronted the hand-made rug set before the hearth, and he seemed to address it as his galloping thoughts said, Well the only thing to do to find out what she is really like is to wait till after the show's over and speak to her.

He had only once joined the crowd outside, and that had been on Saturday night. But she hadn't put in an appearance. The leading lady had come out, and made her way to the waiting cab; and the comedian and the juggler and six chorus girls had come out of the stage door; but she hadn't put in an appearance, and so, left alone on the pavement, he had surmised there must be another way out at the back of the theatre.

But tonight, stage door or back door, he must speak to her – and he would, so what was he standing here for?

When he reached the yard, Billy was coming out of the

open barn and, seeing him, called, 'I'm having trouble with the youngster.'

'Trouble? Why?'

'As soon as he saw Mr Mason come into the yard he scooted up into the loft, and there he is up against the timbers again as if he was glued. An' I can't talk him down. And another thing: I think his back should be seen to; one of those weals is running matter. Would you think about callin' the doctor on your way to Newcastle?'

'No, I wouldn't think about calling the doctor; unless you want the child to be whipped back to wherever he came from. What's the matter with your head, Billy? You should know Old Wheatley by this time, for, either drunk or sober, he's always for the law, especially where lads are concerned. Spare the whip and spoil the child. He wouldn't give youngsters the light of day until they were ready for work, of one kind or another, if he had his way. You know him. Anyway, I'll have a look at it when I come back . . . He seemed all right earlier on.'

'Oh, I think he was trying his best to show us he could work. But now he's a bundle of fear again. Could you give him a shout, do you think?'

Ward drew in a long breath. Already he'd be too late for the opening; and so he'd have to stay at the back. Anyway, it wasn't the show he wanted to see, it was her. But it was impatiently he marched into the barn and stood at the foot of the ladder shouting, 'Boy! Come down this minute!'

When there was no response, his voice louder and angry sounding, he cried, 'I am dressed for the road, and I am not coming up this ladder. If you don't put in an appearance before I count five you'll be on your way back tomorrow to where you came from. Do you hear me?'

He couldn't have reached three when the small head looked down on him; then the thin shanks stepped down slowly from one rung of the ladder to another.

Having reached the floor, he stood with his head down, and Ward, speaking slowly now, said, 'You know what I promised you last night: that you could be here for good, but I want a worker.' He now glanced sharply towards Billy

37

before going on, 'And not a lad that skitters into the barn every time a trap comes into the yard.'

The small head came up, and the boy's voice became a stutter as he said, 'I . . . I th . . . th . . . thought he had come for me. He s . . . s . . . said he would.'

'Who's he? What's his name?'

Again the head drooped.

Ward became impatient, saying, 'I'm not going through all this again tonight. Now, listen to me, and finally: nobody's going to take you back to that place. I promised you. Now go to the house and get your supper.'

As the boy now hurried from them, Billy put in flatly, 'He was right to skitter, for you could have the authorities round here if anybody gets wind of him. Well, I mean they would want to know where we got him, and all the rest of it. You know yourself you can't keep anything quiet for long, not round here. In the village your business is their business, at least, so it seems. So, in a way, the youngster was wise to make himself scarce. They all seem to know about what they call the Poor Law Contract; they know they'll be sent back, no matter where they're found, either to the same farm or to the same workhouse. You know yourself what the so-called guardians are like. Remember the business over at Burnley's farm a few years back?'

'Those boys were mental.'

'Aye. If I remember rightly they had escaped an' all; but Burnley kept them on. Then what happened when he was taken up for it? He said if the lads were mental then he was mental an' all; and they should never have been put away as children . . . They fined him. Oh, heavy.'

Impatient to be gone, Ward hurried from the barn and into the stables; and when presently he led the saddled horse into the yard, Billy called, 'She hates the rain. You'll get her under cover, I suppose?' And at this, Ward turned a look of disdain on the man for whom he had a deep affection, before putting the horse into a trot that turned into a gallop as soon as they left the farm yard; and Billy's remark to the wind and rain was, 'He's caught something a poultice won't help.'

*   *   *

38

He couldn't understand it. He was on the pavement outside the theatre looking at the rain-soaked poster on the wall. It was the same as last week's, except for one thing: there was no flying angel across the middle, but over it had been stuck a bill that read: Laugh With The Lorenzoes, the three side-splitting maniac acrobats from Spain. Above them and central was the picture of the soprano, with, to one side of her, the big fat woman and the little fat man with their four poodles, and, to the other side, the juggler. Below were the names of the 'lesser turns', the print getting smaller towards the end of the bill.

But where was the Maltese Angel? Gone too was her picture from the sandwich board that was positioned further along the pavement.

He did not go into the booking hall but hurried towards the stage door at the side; and when he saw the doorman standing in the passage-way, he gabbled, 'What's happened? I mean to the Maltese Angel? To . . . well, the dancer?'

The doorman looked him up and down, and grinned as he said, 'Oh! You here again? Not a night to come out and have your journey for nowt.'

'What's happened to her?'

'Oh, she had a bit of an accident. She won't be tripping the light fantastic for a few weeks, I would say. The wire gave way and she hurt her foot.'

'Where is she now?'

'Oh; back at her lodgings, I suppose. Yes, that's where she is.'

As the spout above him overflowed, Ward stepped quickly into the doorway, and from there into the hallway to where the doorman had retreated, only to be surprised by being sharply admonished by the man: 'Here! There's no entrance this way,' which succeeded in bringing forth an equally sharp reply from Ward: 'I'm not thinking about going in this way, but I'm not going to stand out in that while I'm asking you a question.'

The change of note in Ward's voice caused the man to back from him and again to look him up and down, then say, 'Well, the answer you'll get to your question will be no; I'm not at liberty to tell you where she's staying. An' you're not the only one this week who would have liked to know that.'

'I can understand your position; but I must tell you, I mean the lady no harm . . . none at all.'

'Aye; an' I can tell you, mister, that's what they all say, whether they're from the town or the country. An' you're from the country, aren't you?'

Before Ward could get over his indignation in order to make an appropriate reply to this observant man and demand how the devil he knew he was from the country, the man told him: 'Oh . . . Oh you needn't get on your high horse, mister,' he said; 'I've seen 'em all. But none of your townees would come four times in a week an' sit in the front row. No; by the second night they would have had a cab at the door an' flowers sent to her dressing-room. Oh, they're all the same, London, Manchester, or here. I've seen 'em all,' he boasted again; but then his tone changing, he said, 'Anyway, I'm sorry I can't let on where she's stayin', not even for a backhander.'

'I wasn't thinking about giving you a backhander. And seeing that you've weighed me up, and everybody else apparently—' His words were cut off by the opening of the swing door to his right and, through it the appearance of an enormous woman and a very small man, each of them carrying two dogs and each dog enveloped in a red flannel coat.

The woman, ignoring Ward, spoke directly to the doorman, 'That bugger won't do that to us again. Put us on in the first half. We know our place. We should be third from last by now. I'll have something to say to him at the end of the week. A year now since we first hit Newcastle, and it'll be ten before we hit it again.'

When one of the dogs in her arms moved uneasily and turned its head towards Ward while giving a sharp bark, she turned her attention to him, saying, 'It's all right, mister; as long as you don't touch her she won't bite you.'

But Ward had already put his hand out and was scratching the immaculate white topknot of the poodle, and the poodle, instead of biting him, was licking his wrist, the sight of which brought an exclamation from the small man in a voice that was so high as to seem to be issuing from the mouth of a young boy: 'Flora! Flora! Did you ever! Do you see what Sophia's doing?'

The large woman, looking straight at Ward now, said, 'You used to animals, mister? Trainer or something?'

He was forced to smile as he answered, 'No; no; but I have two dogs of my own.'

'Poodles?'

'No. Sheep dogs. I'm . . . I'm a farmer.'

'Oh. Oh.' She now said pointedly, 'Bitches?'

He was still smiling as he answered her: 'One of each.'

'Well, all I can say she must have got a sniff of something that pleased her, because she's very particular, is Sophia.'

Ward looked at Sophia. He recognised her as the clever one that pulled the little bottle out of the man's coat, withdrew the cork with her teeth, and then, standing on her hindlegs, put the bottle to her mouth; after which she staggered across the stage to the uproarious laughter of the audience, fell on her back and kicked her legs in the air, to be chastised by this woman, who picked her up, smacked her bottom and sent her off the stage, only for the dog to come slinking in the other side, supposedly unknown to anyone.

The woman was addressing him now: 'Have you seen the show, sir?'

'Yes; I've seen the show.'

She now leaned towards him, to peer in the dim light of the passage. Then, her mouth opening into a big gape and the smile spreading across her face, she exclaimed, 'Oh yes! The front row. The front row.'

Rather shamefacedly now, Ward nodded and said, 'Yes; the front row.'

'To see Stephanie.'

Before he had time to acknowledge this, the doorman put in, 'This . . . this gentleman . . . This gentleman came to see Miss McQueen the night, but was very disappointed that she wasn't on.'

41

'Oh. Oh.' The woman's head was now bobbing up and down. 'Well, I'm sorry you've had your journey for nothing, sir; but she had an accident, you see. Saturday night just gone. He let her down too quickly.' She now turned her head and addressed the doorman: 'He's a bloody maniac, that Watson,' she said. 'He's never sober. I'm not against a drink, you know that, Harry, but there's a time an' a place for it. And she's as light on her feet as a feather. But he bounced her down. She stotted off that foot like a rubber ball.'

'Is she in a bad way?' Ward's voice held an anxious note.

'Well' – the woman shrugged her shoulders and the flesh on her body seemed to ripple – 'not in a bad way, really; no life or death business. Yet, what am I talking about? It's her livelihood. Her feet are her fortune, you could say, and it'll be a week or two before she's able to go on the boards again. Yet she keeps rubbing it and declares she'll be all right for Sunderland next week. But she won't, will she, Ken?' She turned to the little man, who answered accordingly, 'No, Flora; 'cause she won't. But she's got pluck. Oh yes, she's got pluck.'

'Do . . . do you think . . . I mean, do you think I might see her? Sort of be introduced to her? I . . . I would like to make her acquaintance.'

The woman and the man looked at each other, their glances holding for some time before she, as if having come to a great decision, said with emphasis, 'I don't see any reason, sir, why you shouldn't make her acquaintance. Sophia here seemed to have a good opinion of you, so, animals having much more sense than humans, I've always said so, and I would trust them any day in the week to give me the right answer, I would say, no, I don't see any obstacle that need be put in the way. Have you got a conveyance?'

The word conveyance came out on a high note and with a change of tone; and when he had to confess that he was sorry he hadn't, only his horse, the woman laughed and her ah-la changed as she said, 'Well, we can't all get on that, can we? And so, as it's only a stone's throw from here, where we are residing, we could all walk the distance, couldn't we? Good night, Harry.'

She was nodding towards the doorman, who replied, 'Good night, Mrs Killjoy. Good night, Mr Killjoy.' And the little man answered, 'Good night, Harry.'

They were now in the street, Ward walking between the woman and the man, with the rain pelting down on them, and Mrs Killjoy wiped it from her face as she enquired of him, 'And what is your name, sir?'

'I'm Hayward Gibson, but I'm usually called Ward.'

'Ward. It's an unusual Christian name . . . Ward. Well, Mr Gibson, you know our occupation, so may I enquire if your farm is a large farm or a small one. You see, we are town folk, and the only thing we seem to know is that farms belong to estates where smallholdings don't.'

Ward smiled to himself at this diplomatic grilling, and he pursed his lip before he explained, 'Well, my farm isn't held on lease to one of the landowners, by which I mean it isn't rented; it is a freehold farm, much bigger than a smallholding, but much smaller than some other farms in the country.'

'Well, that is a fair answer.' She now turned towards him and smiled broadly as she said, 'We cross over here, and then we are almost there. But to get back to the farmers: you see, we are very ignorant of the country, we people who live by the boards, for entertainments such as ours are performed in the town, you know, aren't they?'

They were in the middle of the road now, and, halting suddenly, she held up a hand, as a constable might, to stop the approaching traffic. The astonished driver of a cab to one side of her and two boys pushing a flat cart to the other pulled up sharply, causing further astonishment from the drivers of the following vehicles dimly seen through the rain and gathering twilight as she led her company across the other half of the road and to the pavement, to the accompaniment of highly seasoned language from the cab driver and others and the ribald laughter of the boys. But as if this incident had not happened, she continued where she had left off, saying, 'So we must always enquire into the work, station, and habits of those who wish to make our acquaintance.'

He wanted to laugh aloud, he wanted to roar: here he was, walking between these two oddities and their four dogs and being questioned as to his character as if he were in a courtroom, and all the while there was racing through him a feeling of anticipation and excitement; he was going to meet her . . . not as the actress coming out of the stage door, whom he would not really have known how to approach, but he was going to face her in her lodgings.

For a moment the anticipation and elation were chilled by the thought: what if he didn't take to her? What if she were a hoity-toity piece and thought too much of herself; or, on the other hand, just plain common; but oh dear! what if she didn't take to him? Yes, that was the main point: what if she didn't take to him?

'Ah! Here we are. Home from home.'

He was standing in a street where every house appeared to be approached by three steps, guarded on each side by sloping iron railings. They were quite large houses. He wouldn't say this was the best end of the city, but it was no cheap street.

The front door to the house looked heavy and strong and was graced with a brass letter-box and door-knob, and when it was opened, the woman sailed in; and the man pressed Ward forward. And now he was being introduced to a woman who was apparently the owner of the house, for Mrs Killjoy was saying, 'This is a friend of ours, Connie. We have met him by chance this evening.' She turned towards Ward now, saying, 'Mr Hayward Gibson.' Then extending her hand to the flat bosomed middle-aged woman, she added, 'Mrs Borman, our landlady and the kindest you will find in a day's walk.' And now, with fingers wagging, she exclaimed, 'And I mean that, Connie. You know I mean that.'

Mrs Borman did not spread her gaze over his entire body as Mrs Killjoy had done; but she looked him straight in the face and in a pleasant voice said, 'Good evening, Mr Gibson. Any friend of Mrs Killjoy is welcome to my house.'

Nodding and smiling, Mrs Killjoy put down her small charges, as did her husband, and informed the landlady in the most polite terms, 'They have already done their number ones and twos, and Ken will give them their dinner as usual and put them to bed . . . Go along, my darlings. Go along with your papa.'

During this little scene Ward had been standing apart, holding his wide-brimmed hat level so that the rain wouldn't drip on to the polished linoleum of the hall floor, and not really believing what he was hearing and witnessing. It was as if he himself had been lifted on to a stage and was taking part in a play; and then more so when Mrs Killjoy asked in her assumed refined tone, 'And how is our patient faring? Has she behaved herself?'

'Yes,' replied Mrs Borman; 'I would say she has, as always, behaved herself. She is now in the parlour.'

'Oh, she has managed to get there! That is wonderful. And it has eased what might have been an embarrassing question, which I would have had to phrase very diplomatically in asking if our friend here would have been allowed to visit her privately. Oh, the parlour is very suitable. Would you come this way?' She inclined a hand towards Ward. 'But, ah' – she stopped again – 'before doing so, let me divest you of your coat and take that hat.'

He had to close his eyes for a moment whilst being divested of his coat. But then he was following Mrs Killjoy, a person, he considered, most definitely misnamed, into a room that seemed to be furnished entirely with chairs of all shapes and sizes, and there, sitting on one to the side of the fireplace, was a slim young girl.

As he walked slowly towards her, Mrs Killjoy was exclaiming loudly, 'I've brought a gentleman to see you, dear. He was so disappointed that you weren't on stage tonight. He was enquiring of your health. He is a Mr Hay . . . ward Gibson.' She split the name. 'He is from the country . . . How is your ankle, dear?'

As the girl answered, 'Much better, thank you,' she did not look at Mrs Killjoy, but at the tall man staring down at her, and she was recognising him, much more than at the moment he was recognising her, because he was looking down on a girl he imagined to be not more than sixteen, with her abundant brown hair lying in a loose bun at the back of her head. Her face was oval-shaped; her eyes large, and they were brown, too, but of a deeper brown than her hair. She had a wide full mouth and a small nose, and her

45

skin appeared to be slightly tanned. In no way did she fit the picture of the Maltese Angel.

'Good evening.'

'Good evening.' He bowed slightly; then he added, 'I . . . I was sorry to hear of your accident.'

'Oh, it was nothing. It will soon be better.' She put her hand towards where her foot was resting on the low stool. 'I'll be dancing again next week.'

'That you won't. I've never been a betting woman but I'll take a bet on that. Three weeks at the least. That's what the doctor said. And, by the way' – Mrs Killjoy now indicated Ward with a quite gracious wave of her hand – 'Mr Gibson is a farmer. And Sophia took to him, so that's a good reference, don't you think.' She smiled now from one to the other; then hitching up her large bosom, she added, 'Now, I'm away to tidy myself up and get ready for supper, although we'll have a good hour or more to wait, seeing that we're early in. He put us on in the first half.' She now bent forward, her finger wagging as if at the culprit who had done this thing. 'Would you believe that, Stephanie? The effrontery of it! Still, I'll tell you all about it later.'

At this, she turned about and sailed from the room, for, in spite of her bulk, her step was light.

Ward searched in his mind for something to say, but the only words it prompted were, 'It is still raining,' to which inane remark the girl quietly invited him to sit down.

He looked around as to which chair he would take, and her voice full of laughter now, prompted him, saying, 'Don't sit in the big leather one. It looks very comfortable, but the springs have gone. I think the safest would be the Bentwood arm.' She pointed to a chair a little to the left of her.

He returned her smile and, nodding, walked around her outstretched leg and seated himself in the chair which stood within a few feet of her own; and she turned to face him fully and said, 'It was very kind of you to come to the show.' She did not add, 'so often'.

He knew his colour had risen as he replied, 'You noticed me, then?'

46

'Yes. Yes, I noticed you.'

'I . . . I enjoyed your dancing.'

'Thank you.'

He sat looking at her in silence now. She had a nice voice, different from any he had heard, except perhaps that of Colonel Ramsmore's wife or of Mrs Hopkins, when either the one or the other opened the fair. Yet there was nothing high-falutin about it, like theirs; but it was different. Oh yes, it was different. She was different all round: different from her stage appearance; different from what he had expected her to be off stage; but she looked so young. He was slightly surprised to hear himself voicing his thoughts: 'You looked young on the stage, but pardon my saying, you look much younger off.'

She now leant back against the padded head of the high-backed chair, and she laughed as she said, 'I'm a very deceptive person. I shall be nineteen on my next birthday.'

He found he was so relieved that he, too, laughed back as he said brightly, 'My! no-one would ever guess it,' a remark which made her neither blush nor become coy, but divert any further allusion by asserting, 'Mrs Killjoy is a wonderful woman, a wonderful friend, but she is very bad at betting and I have proved her wrong so many times, for by next week I shall certainly be dancing again. But in Sunderland. That is our next booking.'

He did not wonder why she said this, but he repeated, 'Sunderland?' then nodded at her, saying, 'I often pop down to Sunderland. How long are you likely to be there?'

'Just a week, I think.'

'Oh. Only a week.' Another inane remark, he thought; then he asked, 'Where do you live . . . I mean your home?'

She turned her gaze away from him and looked towards her foot, and she seemed to sigh before she said, 'Wherever we are playing: I have no settled home.'

'No?' The syllable held a note of surprise, and she answered, 'My parents were on the stage too. My mother was a dancer, and my father sang. And so I've always been on the move. I think it was a year after my father brought my mother from Malta that we settled in Bristol, because I

47

wasn't born until the following year. And that was in York, and two days after Christmas Day.'

He did not remark on her Christmas birth, but asked, 'Your parents . . . they are . . . ?'

Her answer was without false sentiment: 'They are dead,' she said. 'My mother died of smallpox, and a year later my father was drowned. But that was almost six years ago. Since then Mr and Mrs Killjoy have been almost like parents to me.'

'I'm sure. I'm sure.' His head was nodding, but he could find no more to say; he felt utterly tongue-tied, all he could do was listen to his thoughts: she was beautiful, but of a different beauty to that which she showed from the stage. The word that suited her there, he supposed, would be ethereal, not quite of this world. But this girl was of this world. And she seemed at ease in it. There was a quietness about her. And yet her eyes were merry, and she smiled often. He wished he could see her standing up; he didn't know how tall she would be. She was very slim. Well, she would have to be very slim, wouldn't she, and of no weight to be hanging from that wire?

'Now you've heard all about my life, so may I ask about yours? Mrs Killjoy says you're a farmer. That sounds so interesting. It must be wonderful dealing with animals. I love the poodles.' She indicated a door at the end of the room as if that was where the dogs were.

He could answer her now: he gave a short laugh as he said, 'Not so wonderful when you have to get up on a winter morning around five, because you know, cows wear watches.' He actually pulled a face at her. 'And they don't like it if you're a bit late; they kick up a row.'

She was laughing outright now, as she repeated his words: 'Cows wear watches. Have you many?'

'Eighteen milkers and six youngsters coming on . . . heifers, you know; and three horses, one for the trap or riding. Her name is Betsy. And two Shires . . . you know, the big horses. I am sure you've seen them pulling the beer drays; well, mine pull the plough and many other things.'

48

'Oh, yes. Yes. And they are lovely. Have you got ducks?'

'Oh, yes; ducks, chickens, a few geese. And pigs, of course. All that you expect to find on a farm.'

'Have you always lived on a farm?'

'Always. And my father, and his father, and his father before him.'

She was staring at him again. Her face had been smiling; but now the smile slid away and her hand came out tentatively as if she were about to touch him; but she withdrew it quickly as she said, 'I . . . I noticed you've had an injury to your face.'

'Oh that.' He fingered the two thin lines of dried scab. 'I had a sort of accident.'

'With . . . with an animal?'

He could have replied, 'Yes, a bitch;' instead, he said, 'A wild cat got into the barn. I must have surprised her, frightened her. She sprang down from . . . a sort of platform that's found in some barns' – his hand wavered over his brow – 'and her claws caught me.'

'Oh dear! It must have been very frightening, and painful.'

His manner was offhand now as he said, 'The only thing is, it's a nuisance. I find it difficult to shave.'

'Yes. Yes, of course.'

At this point the far door opened and Mr and Mrs Killjoy entered the room. On Ward's rising to his feet, the woman exclaimed loudly, at the same time wagging her finger at the young girl, 'Now that's the action of a gentleman. You can always tell a gentleman if he'll get off his backside . . . I mean . . . er' – she slanted her gaze at him – 'rises from his seat when a woman enters the room.'

'Oh, Mrs Killjoy.'

The finger wagged again. 'Well, you know me by now, Stephanie: I say what's in my mind, and I can't stop it, because there's a leak there.' The large body shook with laughter, in which her husband joined. Then turning to Ward, she said, 'Would you like to stop and have a bite of supper? Mrs Borman says there's enough for all, and plenty of it.'

He did not immediately answer; then he said, 'I'm sorry; but I'll have to be going. Another time, though, if I am allowed to call' – he glanced towards the girl – 'I'd be very pleased to accept.'

'Oh, you'd be quite welcome to call again, 'cos there she is—' Mrs Killjoy turned to the now embarrassed girl, crying, 'Well, you're sitting there all day by yourself; you'll be glad of company.' Then to Ward, she ended, 'Yes, you'd be welcome. She's too shy to say so, but I'm asking it for her.'

It was to the girl he spoke again; 'Well, if I may, it would be in the evening,' he said.

She merely inclined her head towards him; and at this, he swung about and hurried from the room, with Mrs Killjoy endeavouring to keep pace behind him.

As she helped him into his coat she remarked in an under-tone, 'You weren't mistaken in your opinion, were you?'

He turned and looked at this surprising woman, and he said soberly, 'No, Mrs Killjoy, you're right, I wasn't. And I will call again at the first opportunity.'

'I'm sure, you will, son. I'm sure you will.' She patted him on the shoulder now; then handing him his hat and coat she opened the door and, with a wave of her hand, ushered him out.

It was still pouring, and he had the inclination to run, not from the rain, but just to relieve his feelings. She was right. She was right: he hadn't been wrong in his opinion. But the girl wasn't an angel. No, she wasn't an angel; she was a girl of nineteen, and she was sweet, lovely, beautiful . . . very beautiful. God send tomorrow soon.

Back in the parlour of the boarding house, Mrs Killjoy was sitting facing Stephanie McQueen, and she was addressing her as Fanny. 'Fanny,' she was saying, 'look . . . look at us . . . Ken and me. We're nearly on our last legs. I'm getting past falling flat on my face on those boards every night, sometimes twice nightly. Even without Charlie and Rose attacking me in the backside I could fall down many a night, for me legs an' me back are killin' me. Now, you know, we've got a little bit put by: and we're on the look-out for that little cottage with a patch of garden. It's been the dream of our life. It's forty-three years since I took over from my dad, and I'm nearing the end of the road. As for Ken, I don't know how he keeps going. Now! now!' She held up her hand. 'Hear me out. You've been like a daughter to us since your folks went. And I promised your mum I'd always keep an eye on you. And I've done that, haven't I?'

Stephanie's hands came out and gripped the podgy ones, and, her voice breaking and with tears in her eyes, she said, 'Oh! Mrs Killjoy. You know what I think about you, what I think about you both. I would never have got along without you. And I don't think I ever could . . . '

'Oh yes, you could, 'cos you've got an excellent turn. But how long is it going to last? That's what I'm worried about. Look at that.' She pointed to the foot resting on the stool. 'That can happen again at any time. And anywhere. And that's the point: if you're on your own, what's to become of you, with all the sharks about? And . . . and' – now she was wagging her hand – 'it's no use saying you can take care of yourself. No girl can take care of herself when she looks like you and she's in this racket. You've had some experience already, haven't you? But there hasn't been anyone like him before. Now, I'm going to talk plainly. He's a country fella. That's evident. And he's not of the upper class. That's also evident. But what is fully evident is he's certainly not of the clodhopper or farmworker class either. He's what I would call a respectable young country fella; and he owns his own farm . . . '

'Mrs Killjoy, dear' – the girl sighed – 'I've just met him for the first time. Yes, I'm aware I noticed him on the second night, and on the third and the fourth; but nevertheless, I've actually met him only a moment ago: I couldn't possibly think of him as . . . '

'Now listen to me. I don't expect you to think of him in any way yet; but he's going to call, and if he's come four times to the show he'll come four times here next week.'

'I could be back at work next week.'

Mrs Killjoy looked towards the slim ankle and she nodded as she said, 'Yes. Yes; I know you've been using those hands of yours, and I'm not saying you couldn't be back at work next week, because I also know the power you have in them

51

– you got Beattie on to her feet when I never expected her to be on the boards again – but I'm asking you a favour, and it is a favour: let your hands alone for the next day or so until you get better acquainted with him, then say what you think. Will you do that for me, Fanny?'

Stephanie hesitated for a moment; then she smiled and said, 'Yes. You know I will; I'll do anything for you; but don't count on the result, please. And stop worrying about me and think of yourself and Mr Ken more, and get into that cottage soon.'

'Well, let's put it this way: we'll think of the cottage once we've got you settled.'

'Oh! Mrs Killjoy.'

'Oh! Miss Stephanie McQueen.' And now the woman, shaking with laughter, hugged the slim body to her, whilst she asked, 'If you had to choose between Mr Harry Henley, that loud-mouth juggler, or the Honourable James Wilson Carter, so called, with his mimes, rhymes, and readings . . . educated idiot that he is, and our farmer, who would you choose?'

'No-one of them, at the moment, Mrs Killjoy. No-one of them.'

4

~~~~~

'Annie, I would like you to make something suitable for a tea in the parlour tomorrow.'

'Oh aye?' Annie took up a canister and sprinkled flour liberally over a large wooden board resting on the kitchen table before adding, 'And what would you have in mind?'

'As I said, something suitable for tea in the parlour, like you used to make years gone by for Sunday tea: scones, griddles, and little fancies.'

'Oh aye?' Annie lifted a large lump of dough out of a brown earthenware bowl and dropped it on to the floured board; and not until she started to knead it did she say further, 'And how many company are to be expected?'

'Only three.'

'Only three?'

'That's what I said, only three. But accompanied by four dogs.'

This last remark turned Annie from the board, flapping her flour-covered hands together, then wiping them on her apron, as she cried, 'Four dogs! People don't bring dogs to afternoon tea.'

'This company does.' He was smiling at her now, knowing he had her full attention. 'Don't worry; they're only little dogs . . . poodles.'

'Poodles?' She screwed up her face. 'Like Pekingese? Them like Pekingese?'

'No; larger; they're performing dogs.'

'Oo . . . h.' Her lips described the word, and she went on, 'Now I get it. Performing dogs. The guests are from the stage, aren't they?'

'Yes, you're right, Annie, they're from the stage. But you should have guessed that long before now.'

'I hope you know what you're doin'.'

'I know what I'm doing.' The banter had gone from his voice. 'And I would like you to be civil to them, because I might as well tell you, Annie, if I have my way one of them will soon be mistress of this house.'

Annie stared at him for fully five seconds before she turned back to her baking board, saying quietly, 'Well, it's your house and you're the master; but I've had concern for you since you were born, and so I can only say I hope your choice is the right one. But we'll have to wait and see, won't we?'

'Yes, Annie, just as you say. Anyway, they'll be here around three o'clock. I hope the table will look nice.'

He had reached the door leading into the boot-room, which gave way on to the yard, when he was stopped by her voice crying again, 'It's all over the place, you know, about your jaunting; and it's known to one an' all.'

'Oh. Is it really?'

'Aye, an' you needn't put that tone on with me, Master Ward. I'm just tellin' you for your own good: if anybody goes night after night to a theatre he goes for a purpose.'

'Well, Annie, I'll give you something to tell them, I haven't been once to the theatre this week. Now what do you think about that?' On which he closed the door none too quietly.

He made his way to the coachhouse, and there he saw the boy rubbing an oily rag around the hub of the trap wheel, and after making a point of inspecting the whole trap, he said to him, 'You've done a good job. Leave it now and go and clean yourself up; your meal will be ready soon.'

'Yes, sir.'

He stood watching the boy cleaning his hands at the pump at the end of the yard. He liked him: there was something about him, sort of appealing, fetching. Then his gaze returned to the trap and he told himself that for two pins he would put the horse into the shafts and ride in comfort to Newcastle, but Billy already had Betty harnessed.

He owned up to himself that he was feeling tired: he had come into the yard at half-past four this morning, as he had done every morning this week, in order to get through his share of the work well before evening, and to forestall any possible comment from Billy; although, and he gave him his due, it wasn't likely he would openly protest, which wasn't saying he wouldn't have his own thoughts about the matter, as assuredly as Annie had hers. Oh yes; she had made up her mind to be awkward. He could see that. Well, awkward or not, she would have to put up with it, because there was one thing sure, he'd have to speak to Fanny within the next day or so; if not she'd be on the road again.

He thought of her as Fanny because it was she herself who had stopped him addressing her as Miss Stephanie. 'Call me Fanny,' she had said. And so he did and he thought of her as Fanny now, even the while thinking that the name didn't suit her: it was too ordinary, too common, and in sound too near to Annie.

Billy was standing by the horse teasing its mane with his gnarled fingers as he said, 'Be all right, Master Ward, if I don't wait up for you the night?'

Ward stared at him. 'Of course it'll be all right,' he answered. 'Is anything the matter? Are you feeling off colour?'

'Me back's playin' me up lately.'

'Then why the devil didn't you say so? You don't want to find yourself flat out again, do you?'

'Oh, don't you worry. I won't be flat out; I'll still do me work.'

'Oh! you madden me sometimes, man.' Ward was mounting the horse, and the old man was on his way back to the stable, and he yelled at him, 'And don't you take me up the wrong way, Billy Compton. I'm having enough of it from indoors so, don't you start.'

He didn't wait for a response, but with a 'Gee up!' set the horse forward, but at a walk. And later, he defiantly brought it back to a walk as he passed through the village, where he answered one or two desultory hails from patrons making their way to The Crown Head.

He had passed the blacksmith's shop and was riding into the open country when he was hailed from the rising ground to his right, and there he saw Fred Newberry lolloping towards him.

Ward pulled up his horse and, as Fred slid down the grass bank to the road, he remarked, 'So you've been in the river again? They'll find you floating in there one day.'

'Oh! man; it's hot in the bakehouse.' Fred ran a hand over his wet hair; then, swinging the wet towel he was carrying in a circle about his head, he laughed as he said, 'Good job I kept me underpants on the day: two lasses came round the bend. Swimming like fish, they were. Never seen anything like it, 'cos none of the village ones goes in the river, do they? Well, not that I've seen. Have you?'

'No, I haven't, Fred.'

'They were cheeky pieces in all ways. By! they were. One of them waved to me. Out of the water, mind, she waved. They were on bicycles, of all things . . . Bicycles. I saw them lying in the grass, with their clothes . . .'

'Well,' Ward laughed, 'you read about the new-fangled lasses in the papers, don't you? You should have had a crack with them, man.' He laughed now and he was about to jerk the reins again when Fred spoke, and this time without the perpetual grin on his face. 'I'm on your side, Ward,' he said, 'no matter what they say. If you want to take a lass from the town, it's your business, nobody else's. It's as our John said, it's about time somebody brought fresh blood into the place. Of course, Will didn't like it, 'cos he's after Susan Beaker. So is Jimmy Conroy. There'll be hell to pay shortly. But anyway, Ward, you do what you want to do; there's bound to be some nice lasses among actresses. I only wish I had your spunk. I'm frightened of lasses, really. I always make me tongue go, but that's as far as it gets.' The smile slowly returned to his face now as he added, 'Me dad says I'll be hanging on me ma's apron strings when I'm sixty, 'cos she still thinks she's got me in the pram.' He covered up his self-conscious acceptance with an outburst of laughter, in which Ward could not help but join while affectionately pushing the flat of his hand against his friend's wet head and saying, 'It'll hit you one of these days, never you fear, Fred; and you'll wonder which cuddy's kicked you.' Then he urged his horse into a walk as Fred said, 'Do you think so, Ward? Well, you show me the cuddy and it can kick me with both back legs, and I'll welcome it . . . Will you be in church the morrow?' he now called.

And Ward, turning in his saddle, called back, 'No, not tomorrow, Fred. Tomorrow I'm going to give the village something to think about.'

'Aye? What's that?'

'Wait and see, Fred. You wait and see. So long.'

'So long, Ward.'

Some distance along the road, he muttered to himself: 'I'm on your side, Ward, no matter what they say.' So they must be saying a lot, then? and all in sympathy with her. And the words conjured up the face looming before him as he'd last seen it, and no will or strength in him could check an involuntary shudder. But then he attacked it with: to the devil with her! and them all. Gee up! there . . . As John had said, there was need for fresh blood in the place.

It was three o'clock on the Sunday afternoon when he drove the heavily laden trap through the last farm gate. He had skirted the village. He had not, at first, intended to, but when he saw Mrs Killjoy perched on one side of the trap, with the small man by her side, he who must appear to all who saw him, at least from his stature, like a fat boy with an old face, and each of them holding two be-ribboned and powdered white poodles, he knew that he had to save them the ridicule they would have evoked if he had driven through the village. Now, if he had been alone with Fanny . . . oh, yes, that would have been a different matter altogether.

They were in the yard and he was helping them down from the trap, having taken the dogs in turn from them and carefully put them on the ground, being thankful as he did so that the weather had been dry for days so that there were no muddy puddles: he gave a hand first to Mrs Killjoy; then

57

to her husband; and lastly, he held out both hands to the beautiful girl wearing a long blue summer dress and a large leghorn hat, the rim trimmed with a blue veil, so casting a shadow over her face.

Billy had looked on in astonishment throughout these proceedings, understanding fully now why he had been told to lock up Flo and Captain; for it was more than likely they would have swallowed these four yapping so-called dogs.

Ward was now apologising loudly as he led the party out of the yard and round by the side of the house, saying, 'This is a very odd house: the front door was put on the wrong side of it, and the hedge stops us driving up to it.' He pointed to the low box hedge that bordered the square of newly cut grass fronting the house. 'My father planted the hedge or I would have dug it up a long time ago. Anyway, here we are.'

The front door was open, and much to Ward's amazement, which he skilfully hid, there was Annie standing in the middle of the hall, wearing a clean white bibbed apron, and a tiny cap, which he had never seen before, resting on the top of her grey hair, and for a moment he felt qualms, thinking that she was about to bend her knee and turn the whole thing into a farce. But no: she stood waiting, as a housekeeper might have done, and he said, pointing first to the beaming woman, 'Annie, this is Mrs Killjoy. Mrs Killjoy, this is Mrs Compton, who has been with the family for years; in fact, she is one of the family, and she has looked after this house and me since my parents died.'

'How do you do, Mrs Compton?' Mrs Killjoy was at her theatrical best; she held out her hand, and, with a slight hesitation, Annie took it. Then Mr Killjoy was introduced, and, as Annie said to Billy later that night, 'How I kept me face straight, God only knows. Her like a house end and him only as big as a pea on a drum. And when he bowed over my hand . . . it was like a play.'

And now, Ward's voice was level as he said, 'This is Miss Stephanie McQueen, Annie.'

'I am very pleased to meet you, Mrs Compton.'

And what Annie said, as she took the thin hand in hers, was, 'And you, miss. And you.' And as she also remarked to Billy later, 'Well, I admit I was staggered, for anything unlike a stage piece I never did see or imagine.'

There were no outer clothes to be taken off, and as one wouldn't dream of taking off one's hat to partake of tea, they allowed themselves, accompanied by the four dogs, to be led by Ward to the parlour where, at a round table placed near the window, was set, on a lace hand-worked cloth, a tea surpassing anything that Ward had expected to see served to his guests.

Then a diversion was caused by Mrs Killjoy's directing her family to the hearth and informing them to be seated on the rug before the empty fire grate; admonishing them, meanwhile, to behave; and one after the other they lowered themselves, head on front paws, eyes directed towards their mistress, or their mother, as she termed herself, as whom, in their doggy world, they accepted apparently gladly.

Amid laughter the company were now seated at the table, and while Ward did his duty in handing round the plates of eatables, Annie stood at the side-table and poured tea.

What was surprising Ward more than anything at this moment was Annie's attitude towards the whole affair: she was acting as he imagined she might if in service in a big house as the housekeeper, or even the butler, and this, he knew was certainly not in her character. Was she determined to show the future mistress of this house where she stood? Ah yes, that was likely what was in her mind, for even during his parents' time she had never been relegated completely to the kitchen . . .

The tea over, and the dogs having been given their titbits, Ward now enquired if they would like to walk around the farm; and at this, Mrs Killjoy exclaimed in her unique way, 'No offence meant, Mr Ward, but if you were asking me what I would enjoy, I would say a nice sit-down and talk with the good lady housekeeper here, as would my husband. Wouldn't you, Ken?' and obediently Ken answered, 'I would.'

Ward slanted his gaze downwards: one up to Mrs Killjoy. She was a diplomat of diplomats, was this lady: she wasn't only getting into Annie's good books, but was leaving open the opportunity for him to have Fanny to himself. And this he took immediately by turning to her and saying, 'Well, would you like to see around my farm, Miss McQueen?' He stressed her name. And she answered in the same vein, 'Yes, Mr Gibson, I'd be delighted to.' And with exaggerated ceremony, he offered her his arm, and together, amid laughter, they walked from the room.

Ward showed her, first, the cow byres which, at the moment, were empty and pointed out the cow-stands, each bearing the name of an individual cow: Dolly, Mary, Agnes, Jessie, Beatrice, Flora, and so on; and she laughed gaily, saying, 'I can't believe it! Cows being named. It's so nice, though.' She shook her head, unable to find further words to describe the apparent treatment of his cows.

Then they visited the stables, the tack room, the boiler house, and the barn; and so to the round of the animals, from the sow and its litter to the two shires in the meadow; then he pointed out the cut hay that had been turned and was just about ready for gathering in.

Her amazement grew as they walked and he described the routine that went to the making of a farm year, season by season.

When they reached the stone wall bordering his land, he pointed beyond it, saying, 'Here begins the Ramsmore's estate, and over there, to the right lies the village church. You see the church belfry sticking up above those trees? It has one of the oldest bells in the country, so it is said. Old Crack, they call it.'

With her elbows resting on the top of the wall, she stood looking down over the slope, and her voice was low as she said, 'It's all very lovely, but not quite real.'

'What do you mean? Not quite real.'

'Well, all this.' She spread out her hand before turning to him and looking up into his face. 'And you, too, Ward,' she said, 'you're not quite real.'

'I am real enough, Fanny. Oh yes, I'm real enough. And you're real enough to me; and have been from the first time I clapped eyes on you and felt something stirring here.' He tapped his breast with his doubled fist. 'It was as if I'd known you from my beginnings, and I was just waiting for you to come to life. I can't believe this is only the sixth time I have spoken to you, although I have looked on your beautiful face nine times. You . . . you know what I feel for you, Fanny?'

'Yes, Ward. But I . . . '

'Don't finish it. Don't finish it; just hear me out. I love you. Dear God! How I love you. It surprises even meself. I wake up in the night and wonder what's hit me. I never thought to feel like this, never in me life. And now I ask you, do you like me?'

'Oh yes. Yes.' Her head went back and she gazed up into his face and she repeated, 'Oh, yes, Ward. I like you. I like you very much; but . . . but I must be fair, my feelings aren't the same as yours. You see, I've known you such a short time. Yet I am well aware you are a man of the finest character, and it wouldn't be fair to accept what you are offering . . . '

'Don't say any more, dear. Don't say any more. Just listen. I'll wait. I'll wait as long as ever you like, until your feelings change. That's if you want it that way. But—' Slowly he shook his head. 'What am I saying? I say I'll wait as long as you like. But who will I be waiting for? The week after next you'll be gone . . . where? I don't know. Travelling from one town to another; and you'll meet all kinds of men who will make you offers. And you've likely had them afore now.'

She now put her hand out and gently placed it on his shoulder as she said, 'Yes, Ward. I've had all kinds of offers but not one such as you are making me now, for I assume it is marriage you are suggesting?'

'Of course! Of course; nothing else. Why! who would dare . . . ?' He clutched at her hand.

'Oh' – she smiled gently at him – 'many would dare; they would call such an offer "protection". I have had offers to be protected since my people died. But the only protection I wanted was that of Mr and Mrs Killjoy. Now they are worried for me because they hope to retire soon and the thought of me being on my own troubles them. But I love to dance. You see, Ward, I cannot remember when I first walked, but I can remember when I first danced. My mother was a dancer, a beautiful dancer. She taught me all I know. As she said, she never, what they called, bounced me on her knee,

61

I stood up and danced from my earliest days; and this being so I could never imagine not dancing again. Yet, having said that, at times I get tired of the routine, I mean of travelling, of boarding houses and back-stage conditions, and, I must confess, of some types of audience, especially the Friday and Saturday ones.'

He now took her face between his hands as he said, 'I can understand that. Oh my dear, yes, I can understand that. To me, you are too fragile, too beautiful, too nice for that type of life; and if you want to dance, well, I'll take you to a dance every week. There's the Assembly Rooms in Newcastle; there's the . . . '

She laughed and, taking his hands from her face, said, 'I don't think I would care for that kind of dancing. I don't need people, you know, to enable me to dance. Oh . . . I am not expressing myself well. But look—' She turned and pointed to the field where the hay was spread and she said, 'I could very easily dance through your hay. But, of course, I should have to have slightly thicker shoes on than when on the stage.'

He laughed with her now, saying, 'Aye, that would be a sight; I would love to see it. But . . . but, Fanny' – again he had hold of her hands – 'if it's just dancing you want for your own pleasure I'd build some place.

'Look . . . ' He didn't continue, but quickly taking her hand, ran her along by the wall, round a copse of trees, and through a piece of woodland; and then, pulling her to a breathless stop, he pointed into the distance, saying, 'Look yonder. That's the back of the barns; but look there!' He now threw his arm out to the right and towards a strip of high stone wall as he said, 'That could be the very thing.' Still holding her hand, he drew her towards what she now made out to be some kind of glass-fronted lean-to. The wall was all of ten feet high and forty feet long. Fronting it was an eight-foot structure still holding, here and there, panes of glass.

'That,' he said, pointing to it, 'could be your own theatre. I'd have it done up. It used to be a vinery. My great-grandfather built it. Some say the wall was the end of a house that once stood there; but there's nothing in the deeds about it. Anyway, with the price of milk and meat changing so much in his early days, my father had to cut down on labour, and it was let go until it is as you see now. But the structure's fine. Come and look into it.'

He now beat a way with his boots through the tangled grass; and when they both stood in the doorless aperture, looking along the length of the building, the floor padded with the rotted foliage of years and yet still sprouting new growth, some of it reaching almost to the top of the wall, he said, 'It's a mess now, I admit, but I can see it being a fine place. There's a sketch of it somewhere in the house that my great-grandfather did when the vines were still covering the whole place, the grapes on it as big as plonkers.' He now laughed down on her, saying, 'You don't know what plonkers are?'

'No, I don't.'

'Well, they're what the lads call large marbles, the outsize ones.'

Her smile was soft as she stood gazing up at him without speaking, yet her mind was racing over the words Mrs Killjoy had spoken to her just before he had arrived to bring them on the journey here. 'Don't let him slip through your hands, me dear,' she had said. 'You're so young; you know really nothing of life. You've been on the boards practically since you could walk, but still you know nothing of life . . . and men, and I'm telling you, it is my opinion you'll not find a better. He's too . . . I won't say simple, because there's nothing simple about him; but he's too straightforward to be bad. His tongue is not false; nor is his face; and there are those, you know, who appear to be gentlemen, whose words are coated with butter; only something in the eyes gives them away. This I have learnt. And there's nothing in that countryman's eyes that warns me of any treachery one way or the other. What's more, he's no boy, he's a man of twenty-five, and looks older than his years. All right. All right.' Mrs Killjoy's voice was ringing in Fanny's ears now, repeating the words she herself had spoken. 'You say you don't love him, not as you would expect to about the man you intend to marry. But that comes, dear, that comes. It's

63

amazing how it springs on you, often brought to life by some little action or word. But it comes.'

Would it come to her with regard to this man? At the moment she couldn't say; what she did say was, 'I am not being swayed, Ward, by the promise of a long room in which I can dance, but rather because your sincere offer of marriage has made me hope that you could be right, that my tender feelings for you will grow into something stronger, and so with the hope that you will never regret having asked me, I promise you now to become your wife, whenever you wish it.'

She gasped as she was lifted from her feet and held so that she looked down at him, and as he slowly returned her to the ground, his hands, like his whole body, trembling the while, he muttered, 'I'm sorry. I'm sorry. That was enough to frighten you off altogether. I'm like a bear. But, oh Fanny! Fanny! You'll never regret those words ever, not as long as either you and I live.' And taking her face once more into his hands, he bent down and kissed her gently on the lips.

The action was restrained, and she was aware of this; and impulsively she reached up her arms and put them around his neck; and when her lips touched his cheek he remained still. His own arms about her, he held her as gently as if she were some ethereal creature; which in reality is how he saw her.

It was she who now said brightly as she straightened her hat, 'Let us go and tell them.'

'Oh aye . . . yes. But I don't think it will be any surprise. Well, it may be a surprise that you are going to take me on, but not that I've been breaking me neck for you over the past days. I know what Annie will say.'

'What?'

'Tell me something I wasn't expecting.'

Hand in hand now, they ran back up the field; then through another, and skirted the back of the barns and so into the yard. But in the kitchen they came to a stop: there was laughter coming from the hall; and she whispered to him, 'I know what's happening: the children are doing their turn. I . . . I mean the dogs. But that's how Mrs Killjoy sees them.'

When he opened the door into the hall, it was to see the surprising sight of Annie with her hand pressed tightly over her mouth, her body shaking with laughter, and Billy at her side, his head wagging like a golliwog; but more surprising still was the sight of the boy. He was smiling for the first time since he had come into the place; but more than smiling, he was gurgling as he watched the pretty white dog stagger down the hallway as if it were drunk; then fall on its back, its legs in the air, doing its turns as if on the stage; and when the little man bent over it, gently smacking its hindquarters as he scolded it, it rolled over twice before getting on its hind legs, its front paws wagging as it staggered down the room to where Mrs Killjoy was waiting.

Instinctively, Annie clapped; and so did little Billy; but the boy walked straight-faced across the hall to Mrs Killjoy, and said, 'May I pat him, ma'am?'

'You can that, son. You can not only pat him, you can put your arms around him. But "he" is a she. She's a drunken little no-good. Come here with you!'

She drew the dog towards her and, lifting it, put it in the boy's arms. And when the dog's tongue came out and licked his cheek, the boy actually laughed. But it was a strange sound, not like a laugh at all. But the sound changed quickly into a moan when Mrs Killjoy clapped her hand on to his back; and when his arms opened and the dog slid from him, she said, 'What is it, laddie? What is it?'

'He's got a sore back, Mrs Killjoy,' Ward explained, walking up the room. 'He's just new to us, but where he was last he was badly treated.'

'Never! Never! And him but a spelk of a child with no flesh on his bones.'

'True, Mrs Killjoy. But come into the parlour and I'll show you something,' Ward said, gently pushing the dog forward; and the company followed him, dogs and all.

There, saying to Carl, 'Lift up your shirt,' the boy did as he was bidden and exposed the rough bandage around his back; and when Annie took out the two safety pins holding it in place and so further exposed the suppurating weal, both Mr and Mrs Killjoy stood dumbfounded for a moment. Then

65

the woman demanded, 'Who did that to him? He should be in gaol. He should that. If I knew . . . '

'Only the boy knows, Mrs Killjoy, and he doesn't want to say; nor does he want this to go any further because, as he'll tell you, he's afraid of being sent back. And so I know you won't mention this matter.'

Mrs Killjoy now turned to Fanny, saying, 'Did you ever see anything like it.'

Fanny made no reply, but she went to the boy and laid a hand on his head and murmured something to him that caused his face to brighten and for him to say, 'Italiano?'

'No.' She shook her head. 'From Malta . . . And you? You are Italian?'

The brightness faded from the small face; and his answer was again muttered: 'I don't know. My mother was, I think. I can remember only odd words she said. It was long time ago. But my father, he spoke different, like everyone else. I did, too.'

She bent down to him and said slowly, 'I am going to touch your back; but you won't feel any pain.'

It was at this point Annie made a movement of protest, only to be stopped by Mrs Killjoy saying quietly, 'She knows what she's doing. Just leave her. She is like her own mother, she has power in her hands.' And she turned to Ward and nodded; and he looked from her to the slip of a girl who had promised to be his wife. He had hurried her here to bring the wonderful news, but now it seemed secondary to the needs of the boy, as he watched her place her hands across the suppurating sore. He watched her press hard on it, and the boy make no movement that might indicate he felt pain of any kind.

He now watched this beautiful girl, who had driven him half crazy over these past few days, close her eyes, bow her head, and talk as if to herself for a minute; then quickly taking her hand from the boy's back, she took out a handkerchief from her dress pocket and wiped it whilst smiling widely at the boy and assuring him: 'It will soon be better. Did . . . did you feel anything?'

66

He was smiling up into her face now. 'My back was warm, very warm, but nice. I mean comfort . . . comforting.'

She now asked him, 'Did you used to speak Italian?'

He shook his head. 'I don't know. As I said, my mother used some words. I can remember "bambino".'

She touched his cheek, then asked, 'What is your name?'

'Carl, ma'am.'

'Well, be happy, Carl. Be happy.'

'Yes, ma'am.' He turned now to look at Ward who, assuming now a stiff, almost angry front, exclaimed, 'You know what you have done, boy?' and the lad, somewhat apprehensively now, answered, 'No, no, sir.'

'You have stolen my thunder, that's all.' And Ward's hand went out and ruffled the boy's thick hair, while addressing the others, saying, 'And I mean that. I came tearing back to tell you my splendid news . . . our splendid news—' He held out a hand towards Fanny, and when she took it he drew her to his side and, placing an arm about her narrow shoulders, as he spread his gaze round from one to the other he said, 'This beautiful lady here has promised to be my wife.'

They all stared at him, and with the exception of the boy, it would appear from their expressions that they were dumbfounded. Then the exclamations came pouring out: and while Fanny was becoming breathless in being hugged to Mrs Killjoy's overflowing flesh, Ward's hand was being shaken, first by Mr Killjoy, then by Billy, and lastly, Annie stood there before him. She did not shake his hand, but smiling at him, she said jokingly, 'What a surprise! What a surprise!' and in answer he gave her a playful push in the shoulder. And then she pleased him by saying quietly, 'She's different from what I expected. You could travel far and fare worse. In fact, later on, when I come to think over it, I might even consider she's a bit too good for you,' and before he had time to reply, she added, 'Anyway, this calls for a drink, doesn't it?'

'Yes, Annie; I think it does.'

'Well, get them all into the dining-room and I'll see to it. But' – she paused – 'by the way, how about taking the little 'un in with you?'

He turned to look towards the boy whose face was bright and eager looking, only for his attention to be diverted to Billy who was now shaking the hand of his future mistress. However, he quickly turned back to answer Annie: 'Why not? Why not indeed! There's ginger beer there, isn't there?' And at this he thrust out an arm towards the child, saying, 'Come along, scallywag. Come and experience your first celebration. And remember, you'll never in your life be at a happier one.'

He now caught hold of the boy's hand and with his other arm he drew Fanny to his side and linked thus, like a family, it seemed to foretell their future.

5

The vicar's plump figure swelled with indignation: 'I never thought I should say this to you, Ward Gibson, but I find your suggestion utterly insensitive. You come here asking me to call the banns of your marriage to a person who has spent her life on the stage, and that would be questionable even if it were depicted in a higher form such as the noble prose of Shakespeare, or in the works of Mr Dickens; but not a dancer of the lowest type . . . '

'Be careful, parson! And let me tell you something: if it wasn't for your cloth you would now be stretched out on your vestry floor . . . Yes; you may well step back, for, let me tell you, I'm marrying a lady.'

'So you think. So you think. But what about the lady you've courted for years and have left desolate, slighted, and with a weight of disgrace lying not only on her but on her people, so much so that they cannot bear to come to church.'

'Oh. And you'll find that a great pity, won't you, parson? There'll be no more comforts handed out to you to fill that swollen belly of yours. You'll miss the suckling pigs, and the lamb carcass now and again, not forgetting your daily milk that you get free while your curate is called on to pay for his. Isn't that so, parson?'

The vicar's face was showing not only a purple hue but also an expression that revealed he was consumed with a blazing anger now as he cried, 'You're a wicked man, Ward Gibson. And you are bringing disgrace on the village. This is

69

a family community. And let me tell you, the general opinion of you is the same as mine.'

Ward's lips spread out from his teeth and his whole expression was one of disdain. 'That may be so, Parson,' he said, 'but have you any idea of what the general opinion is of you, and has been for as far back as I can remember? Well, if you don't know I'll tell you now. You're a sucker-up to those that have and you ignore those that haven't. It's left to your curate and others to help them. Aye, those who dare to be Methodists or Baptists, even those who belong to no church or chapel. What about the Regan family down in Bracken Hollow: they wouldn't turn their coats, would they, and go to St Matthew's down there, so you disputed whether the old man should be buried in the graveyard. You'd have left him on the moor if you'd had your way, 'cos there was a taint on them, wasn't there? They were Catholics. It was the same with the McNabs. But John McNab put you in your place, didn't he? He kicked your backside out of the door. And it's odd, isn't it, when others were getting poor law assistance a few years back, they would have starved if it hadn't been for a few unchristian people living in this village. Oh, Parson, you would know how you are thought of in this place and beyond if it wasn't that half of your congregation are afraid of opening their mouths, for fear that what they might say would go back to their employers when you are sitting stuffing your kite at their tables. Well, here's a member of the community, if not of the village, who's going to tell you how you appear to him, and that's as an overblown, unintelligent crawler . . . crawler, always crawling. So now you've got it.' And on this he turned from the infuriated countenance and strode out of the vestry and into the church, and there, standing by the pulpit, he yelled back towards the vestry, 'The next time I put my foot inside your church it will have to be for some very, very good reason. Aye, a very good reason.'

'I'll talk him round, Ward. Well, what I mean is, I'll tell him that I'll marry you down at St Matthew's. It's just about big enough to hold a wedding party. For myself, I prefer it to St Stephen's: more homely and . . . holy, I dare add. And it was built with love by the Ramsmore forebears. It was a better idea than that grotesque lump of iron cutting off the altar. Oh, that screen gets on my nerves.'

Ward looked kindly on the young curate, who called in at the farm the following day. 'Thanks all the same, Frank,' he said, 'but I've made up me mind, and Fanny is with me in this, it'll be a civil ceremony in Newcastle. Candidly, it doesn't matter a damn to me where it takes place, so long as it does and we are married.'

'She's a charming girl; I can understand your feelings for her. Anyway, what I've come to say is, Jane would like you to pop in for a meal. It'll be nothing special, for, as yet, I'm the recipient only of new potatoes. And these only at intervals. But I can have as many turnips as I care to store.'

'I heard just a few days ago that you were having to buy your milk from Hannah Beaton's shop in the village.'

'Yes; that is so. And Jane prefers it that way, unlike me, holding my hands out gratefully for scraps; but she wants no charity, she says. It irks her that our living itself is a charity.'

'Your living? What d'you mean, Frank?'

'Oh well; Lady Lydia, you know, happens to have a cousin, who happened to go to school with Jane's mother, and through the beating of the tom-toms it was discovered that dear Jane had married an impecunious and ailing curate, and that they were living in the most awful conditions, almost under the river itself in the lowest part of Newcastle. It simply could not go on. And as there happened to be a small church, and a so-called vicarage next to it, occupied by a very aged pastor who was incapable of even taking the service, and who was allowed to remain there only through the clemency of Colonel Ramsmore, the suggestion was to transfer the old fellow to a cottage and let the poor curate take over. His wife and child would at least have fresh air, if nothing else. And so that's how it came about.'

'What did you mean, Frank, ailing? Are you ill? You've never looked it to me, never spoken of it.'

Frank Noble now patted the left side of his chest, saying, 'A touch of tuberculosis. Just a little bit. I don't even cough

71

any more; I'm really fit. But, and this I'll confess to you, Ward, as I wouldn't even to Jane, I'd rather be back on that river front among many more who are in the same boat, some coughing their lungs out because, you see, the people are different there. I've always detested villages. I was brought up on the outskirts of one, very like the one here.' He inclined his head to the side. 'And there were so many irritations, apart from the marked division in class. There has got to be this division, I know; there always has been and always will be; but narrowness in both sets used to prey on my mind at times, and I had no sympathy with either lot. You know, I still haven't.' And now he bent towards Ward and whispered, 'I don't know why I'm in this garb . . . in this job, so to speak. I've asked God a number of times, but He never gives me a straight answer. But Jane, now, she's on much better terms with Him and gets a straight answer every time. You've made the biggest mistake of your life in your choice of a career, she tells me at least once a week. And you know something, Ward? If of a sudden I were to decide to leave and go and look for a job in a shipyard or a factory, or down a mine, she would jump for joy. I know she would.' He laughed before adding, 'Perhaps not as much now as she would have done three years ago, before the children came. Anyway, you're coming to supper. Which night?'

'Any night you choose.'

'Say Thursday. A quiet day all round, Thursday, don't you think? By Wednesday, the locals have chalked up so much on the slate in the inns that Thursday is a comparatively dry night. Friday, everybody's very busy getting ready for Saturday's market, to be followed by a swilling at night in the inn to finish off the week. Of course, that doesn't include our small band of Methodists. Decent lot, the Methodists. Always thought that.'

He was backing away now, laughing and waving at the same time, and Ward stood shaking his head and smiling broadly. Frank was a man after his own heart, and to his mind he certainly wasn't in the wrong profession: he should be in the parish; and he wouldn't be afraid to speak his mind from the pulpit; and he'd have more than six sermons a year to work on. It was good to feel he had one friend . . . What was he talking about? He had a number. There was Fred, over the moon about being asked to be best man. And his father, his brothers, John and Will, and Mr Newberry, who had promised to bake a wedding cake. It was supposed to be a surprise, but as Fred wasn't good at keeping secrets, he already knew it was to have two tiers and the best egg-white icing above an almond topping.

He stood and watched until the young parson had disappeared along the road, when he turned and hurried into the house.

In the hall he shouted, 'Where are you?' And Annie calling from upstairs, cried back at him, 'Where do you think?'

He bounded up the stairs two at a time, shouting as he went, 'What are you doing up there?'

Again he was given the answer, 'What d'you think?' And her voice led him to the room that had been his parents'; and there, Annie, standing on a chair, was taking down the curtains from the window.

'What are you up to? Get off that chair. With your weight, you'll go through it and break your legs. Get down, woman!'

'Don't rock me unless you want me to fall on top of you. And wait a minute until I get this pin out of the ring.'

When she had accomplished that task, she dropped the heavy curtain, half of it falling across his head. And now on the floor once more, she exclaimed, 'These should have been down years ago. Your mother liked tapestries. She picked these up at least . . . oh, twenty-five years ago; in fact, just before you were born, when they were selling off the things at Quayle Manor. It was beautiful stuff then; but now, I bet, it won't bear the look of water; it'll drop to bits.'

'What do you propose putting up then?'

'That depends on you and what stuff you buy. I think something nice and light; something that will tone in with the new carpet. Aye, aye.' Now she was poking her finger at him. 'Just look down at your feet. That's been down ever since I was in this house, and it must be claggy with sweat from your father's bare feet, for, you know, once in the house

73

he would never go round in slippers if he could help it.'

He stood back from her, saying, 'Well, that's a carpet and curtains. Now what about the furniture, Annie? You want all that removed?'

'You know, what I don't want now is any of your sarky remarks. And in taking this on meself I'm only pointing out your dimwittedness, for if you'd had any sense you would have had Miss Fanny up here and asked her what colour drapes she would like. And that's what you can do now. Are you going in the night?'

'Of course I'm going in the night.'

'Then I suggest you also go in first thing in the morning and bring her back, for what it must be like sitting in those lodgings all day, I don't know.'

He stared at her now as she gathered up the heavy dust-dispersing curtains, but said nothing, until she staggered past him, her arms full, when he suggested, 'How would it be if I brought her back tomorrow and let her stay in the house for the next three weeks?'

She stopped and, her chin stretching over the material towards him, she said, 'Wouldn't shock me.'

'No, I don't suppose it would, Annie. For two pins I would do it, too, for you know what? Old Tracey has refused to marry us in church.'

'*No!*'

'But yes. Frank though, he's offered to do it along at St Matthew's. But I said no, we'd have it done at the registrar's.'

'He's an old bugger, that, if ever there was one.' She humped the curtains further up into her arms, then said soberly, 'But perhaps it'll work out for the best, because whether you know it or not there's a civil war goin' on down in the village. Some are backing you, but others are backing Daisy Mason; in fact, things, I understand, have hotted up in that direction, stirred by the two Mason lads. What they're goin' to do, or what they would like to do to you is nobody's business, but like and actin' are two different things. That Pete is a big mouth. But Sep, he couldn't knock the stuffin' out of a feather pillow. Anyway, we'll only have to wait an' see which side comes off best, won't we? And by the way, I've

74

made an egg custard for her; take it in with you. She needs feeding up, and you don't want to marry a clothes prop with a frock on it, do you?'

Ward nodded his head, which then seemed to be in answer to her previous comment when he muttered, 'Yes, we'll just have to wait and see,' before he turned and moved towards the brass and iron bed, and he stood looking at it. He had been born in that bed; and his father had been born in it. But it had a different mattress on it then; two feather ticks, they said, and you sank through one into the other.

He looked about him. It was a large room. The furniture was good solid mahogany, but the walls could do with new wallpaper. Annie was right; it needed brightening up. The whole house needed brightening up; and yes, she must have a hand in it, so he would go in early morning and bring her here every day, and take her back in the evening, and they would plan the house together.

He stood holding the bed rail, in one part of him a feeling of joy wanting to lift him from his feet in a great leap, while in the other was a mixture of bitterness and regret, regret that he couldn't be married in the same church as his father and mother had been, regret that the whole village couldn't be one with him on the day, as he understood they had been on his parents' wedding day, regret that the barn down below would not ring to the sound of Harry Bates's and Jake Mulberry's fiddles, and Amos Laker's accordion, with laughter, merriment and high jinks rising as the spirits flowed.

His head shook as a dog does when throwing off water. What did the village lot matter? He still had friends there. The only thing that really mattered was, she would soon be here . . . and – his thoughts had rushed ahead – 'in that bed'. He warned himself now not to forget what he had learned from Nell: it was not as if it was Daisy Mason coming to that bed, oh no, but a young girl, fragile, like an angel. Yes, like an angel; but a laughing, kind, wonderful angel, and a different being from anyone he had ever known.

Yes – he paused in his thinking – different, so different. There was that business of Carl's back. The morning following the day she had laid her hand on him there was

75

no puss on the lint; in fact, although the strike marks all remained, the scars looked different, paler, as if in time they might disappear. He had been shaken by that, but when he mentioned it to Annie, he was surprised that she should accept it. She had heard of such things, she had said: people with healing hands. Oh yes, she had gone on to explain, at one time they used to burn them for witches. Thank God all that was in the past. At least, most of it, she had added.

He walked slowly towards the head of the bed and touched one of the pillows lying on top of the bolster, and he spoke aloud at it: 'I will never hurt you in any way,' he said. 'And may God forgive me if I should.'

6

It was done. She was his. And now the wedding party were piling into the brake. As Ward's farm only harboured vehicles such as the farm cart, the hay wagon, and the trap, Annie had voiced to Ward in Fred's hearing that he must hire a brake. It was following this that Mr Newberry had offered the use of his brake, which not only held ten people but also had a detachable cover.

There were nine guests in the vehicle, four of whom were connected with the theatre; and Billy in his Sunday suit and bowler was now shaking the reins and calling, 'Get up! there,' which set off Betsy into a dignified walk, because it was a heavy load she was pulling.

The journey back to the farm seemed long but merry. This was brought about by the cross talk between Fred and the juggler, and Mr Carter interposing the scraps of monologues; so no-one noticed that the newly married couple had little to say; nothing in fact, as they sat hand in hand, and it wasn't until the brake entered the farmyard that Ward gave vent to a surprised exclamation: 'Good gracious!' he cried. 'Look!' for there, awaiting them, was an unexpected number of people, and the next ten minutes were taken up with congratulations, handshakes and introductions.

Ward's heart was warm: here were people who weren't cutting him dead, who hadn't refused to take his milk. The cutting had started when the news of his forthcoming marriage was brought to the village. Billy was delivering the churn to Hannah Beaton's shop, as he had done for countless years, only to be bawled out by Hannah: 'You can save yourself the trouble, Billy Compton, an' tell him we won't be sellin' his milk any more. An' that goes for his eggs an' all.'

And she hadn't been the only one in the village to refuse his milk that day, for four others had done the same, and Annie's comment had been, 'Well, what d'you expect? Old Mother Beaton and Mrs Mason are cousins.'

But now, here was the whole blacksmith's family, not only Charlie Dempsey himself, but also their two young sons, John and Henry, and Phyllis, one of their married daughters from Fellburn; and there was Fred Conroy, the butcher, a quiet fellow, Fred, and a widower these ten years; but he had brought their Jimmy with him, he who was courting Susie Beaton; and surprisingly, there was Ben Holman the cobbler, go-between man or undertaker, which occupation he was following at this particular time. And lastly, which was no surprise to Ward, there was the Reverend Frank Noble and his wife Jane, and one of their two young children . . . and the boy Carl, smiling widely now as he gazed at the new mistress.

Ward stopped, and he turned and looked at Fanny. She was gazing at him, but not smiling: her eyes were large and moist.

As those from outside pressed in behind him, he gently guided her towards the top of the table, where Annie was standing beaming as if she had just conjured up all this out of thin air; and, impulsively, Fanny threw her arms about her and kissed her on the cheek.

For a moment Annie returned the hug, but then exclaimed loudly, her voice above the hubbub, 'I didn't do all this, ma'am; everybody pigged in. And there's a table full of presents next door an' all. Anyway, sit yourself down, ma'am; they're all dying to get started, 'cos they've never had a bite or sup across their lips since this morning.'

This caused a great roar of laughter, setting the pattern for the enjoyment of the meal which, between eating and toasting, and amid cries of goodwill, went on for the next hour or more.

Following this, the whole company crowded into the parlour where, to his regret, the juggler found there was no room to perform his act; but Mr Carter's talents didn't take up any space, and so he entertained the company with monologues, and to the surprise of those who knew him well, he never touched either on Shakespeare or on Mr Dickens. Nor did he mention the *Cornhill Magazine*, or any other erudite publication from where he had gleaned his knowledge, but he continually had them in gales of laughter when proving to be an admirable mimic of dialects from Geordie to Cockney.

And so the afternoon wore on, until it was time for the Newcastle party to take their leave. This they did amidst cheers and invitations to come again, not only to the farm but to the blacksmith's and the baker's; and, lastly, a somewhat macabre invitation from Ben Holman, who said, 'You can come any time to me and I'll fit you out with a nice box, brass handles thrown in free.' And so they departed in further laughter.

Others now began to make their departure, again amidst hilarious chaffing from Rob Newberry when he exclaimed in mock indignation, 'It's come to something, hasn't it, when me family's got to walk back home because I've been daft enough to lend me brake to those barmy actors.'

When the last trap rolled out of the yard with the young vicar and his wife waving their goodbyes, no-one remarked about the bride standing close to her husband and having her arm around the young lad, who was wearing a new knickerbocker suit and sporting a white shirt, for it had been whispered here and there that he was some relation to the bride: and had he not come on the scene at the same time as she? No-one had mentioned anything to Ward about the assumed relationship because Ward had been very touchy, and he would more than likely have told them to mind their own business. But that was before he had taken a wife . . . well, a man was always more approachable then, and the relationship to the boy would likely come out . . .

Fanny insisted on helping Annie clear the table and put things to rights, and although Annie objected, Ward did not, because what might have been a stumbling block for the harmony of the house between Annie and his wife did not after all exist. And so he walked out into his farmyard; but there was no-one to talk to now except the boy, and he said to him, 'Well, Carl, have you enjoyed your first wedding?'

And the boy, looking up at him, did not answer his question, but what he said was, 'She is so beautiful . . . bella, bella.'

At this Ward laughed and, affectionately rumpling the boy's hair, said, 'Yes, you're right. Oh, so right; she is bella, bella.'

At nine o'clock the house was back to normal, and Annie bade them a smiling but lower-lidded good night; after which Ward bolted the door. Then he carried his wife upstairs to bed.

He had definitely slept in, for the sun was up and shining through the new curtains. He turned hastily on to his side; and there she was, wide awake and smiling at him; and it was she who spoke first. Putting out her hand, she ran her fingers through the thick hair that was tousled on his brow as she said very softly, 'I still like you, Mr Gibson; but I must confess the feeling I have for you now is so strange that it might come under the heading of . . . love.'

'Fanny . . . Oh, Fanny. Fanny,' was all he was able to say.

PART TWO

I

〜

The first six months of their marriage was, for both of them, like a fairy tale. To Ward, each day was a joy to wake up to, and each night was a joy to go to their bed. To Fanny it was different types of joy: Ward had been as good as his word and had the vinery re-built and every now and again when she felt like it she would run down to it and dance, at times to an audience consisting only of her husband; at others she would be aware of Billy being in the background, but more often of the boy watching her.

As she had found her love for Ward, so she came to have most tender feelings for the boy. It was strange, she would tell herself, it was as if they were related; and perhaps they were, because he didn't really know who his people were. He had, though, definitely hailed from the same part of the world as her mother, for every now and again, spontaneously, he would come out with an Italian word that would surprise himself. But what troubled her about the boy was his nightmares, for Ward had often heard him yelling out from his bed in the loft.

But her joy wasn't only in her own dancing, for hardly a week passed but Ward took her into Newcastle. She had visited the theatre there, and had spent an hilarious evening at Balhambras, noted for its variety, much of it bawdy, and whose audience, Fanny felt, would not have received her type of act very well; and nor would Mr and Mrs Killjoy and their family have been as much appreciated as they had been at

The Empire. But the occasion she had enjoyed most was the dance at the Assembly Rooms. Yet Ward had said that was their first and last visit there, because she had attracted too much attention.

He had laughed when saying this, but she wasn't displeased that he had meant it.

Ward's consuming love seemed to have touched everything he owned, for his crops were blooming and his cows had never yielded so much milk; yet all the happiness seemed to be contained within the precincts of his land. It was a different story when he went into the village.

Within a few days of his marriage he knew where he stood there. He wasn't in favour in The Running Hare, because Sam Longstaffe and his little wife Linda were church-going. However, at The Crown Head he had been made more than welcome by Michael Holding and members of his family; not that he frequented the inn often, but on his return from Fellburn or Gateshead, he might step in for a pint of ale. He had laughingly said to Annie that as long as he had the barman, the baker and the blacksmith, and the shoemaker and the undertaker on his side, he would get by. Nevertheless, it annoyed him that most of the church folk could hardly bring themselves to give him the time of day. And yet it was because of this that it seemed he had found favour with Pastor Wainwright of the Methodist Chapel: he and his four sons would nod to him and bid him good-day. The two younger lads even raised their caps to him.

It was now the beginning of March 1887, and the month was living up to its reputation, with the wind raging and sending sprays of iced rain against the windows on the day when Fanny told him she was carrying his child.

The farmyard was a sea of mud and Annie was once again yelling at him, 'Will you take your boots off! I'm not getting down on me hands an' knees today again and scrubbin' this kitchen or that hall, so I'm telling you, Master Ward. And anyway, if you could lay a concrete floor in that dancing room for the missis, you could put one in that yard. They tell me that Bainbridge's farm is as clean as a whistle now that he's had the whole place laid with slabs cemented together.'

To this, he had said, 'Annie, if you say another word to me about mud or boots or wet clothes, either to get them off, or not put me boots on your floor, I'll take up the first thing to hand and I'll let you have it.'

After a moment of silence between them, he asked, and quietly, 'Where's the missis?'

'The last time I saw her she was up in the attics. She's taken it into her head to scour them out. I can't stop her, so see if you can. See if you get the same answer as I get. She must keep busy. If it isn't her feet going it's her hands,' saying which, she herself continued to be about her own business, whilst he padded across the kitchen floor in his stockinged feet, went into the hall and up the stairs, and on the first landing he called, 'Where are you?'

After a moment, her voice came faintly to him: 'I'm up among the gods, sir. I've got a good seat, and it's free.'

He took the steep stairs to the attics two at a time, and when he saw her on her knees before an open trunk and scattered around her, pieces of material and old albums, he said harshly, 'Now what are you up to? You're not thinking about washing out the trunks now, are you?'

'Yes; that's just what I am thinking about doing, sir.' She laughed at him, then added, 'Come and sit down.'

'I'm not going to sit down. You get up.' He pulled her to her feet; then held her at arm's length, saying, 'Look at you! Your skirt's covered with dust and . . .'

'Well, that shows that this place has never had a clean out for a long, long time, and' – she looked about her – 'you know, a lot of use could have been made of these rooms. There're three good size ones besides the small one along the passage.'

'I know the number of rooms that are up here, but we've got enough downstairs to see to.'

She now pulled herself from his arms and, going to an old basket chair that was propped against the wall, she sat down on it, then beckoned him to her, saying, 'Bring that box and sit down; I want to talk to you.'

When with a loud sigh he carried out her bidding, she caught hold of his hands, then began to rub them, saying,

'You're cold.' To which he answered, 'Of course, I'm cold: it's freezing up here, it's raining outside, the wind's howling. I've been wet through; Billy's in a temper; the boy's got a cough and has been in bed all day. As for Annie, no . . . no, don't let me talk about Annie. And now here's you.'

'Yes, here's me.' She nodded at him. 'And I, sir, I must confess, am . . . well, I think the word is devious, I'm a devious woman.'

'What are you talking about? What's the matter with you? Come on downstairs.'

'Ward—' Her voice checked him, because there was no banter in it now as she said, 'Not knowing about these things and having no-one to talk to, even Mrs Killjoy didn't discuss her personal matters, I . . . I had to be sure, and now I am. I am going to have a baby, Ward.'

He sat motionless; but when eventually he moved it was not to thrust out his arms and pull her roughly to him, but slowly to lean forward and to rest his head on her lap and as slowly to place his hand gently upon her stomach. There was no way he could speak, for at this moment it was impossible for him to express what he was feeling: he had been married six months and he had felt that his loving would surely have created a child long before now, and there had been times when she had lain asleep in his arms and he had wondered if there might be something lacking in his make-up: he himself had been the only offspring of his mother and father, and they themselves had each been an only child. And so he had asked himself, was the line running out? Did these things happen? But now she was carrying his child, this beautiful, beautiful girl, as he still thought of her, because sometimes he just couldn't believe that she was his wife, a young woman of twenty now. She was so slight, even ethereal. At times, when he watched her from a distance it looked as if a puff of wind would blow her away. All her movements, too, were quick and light. Often he was surprised by the way she spoke: her voice didn't match her body, or her face, and there was a surprising and unaccustomed depth to her mind.

As she stroked his hair, there was a strong desire in him to cry as any woman might. She didn't ask the silly question,

'Are you pleased?' but rather, with that practical side of her, she said, 'You *are* cold. Let us go down. I . . . I want to tell Annie, too.'

He rose from the box; and now he picked her up in his arms as he often did; but at the top of the attic stairs she began to laugh and shake in his hold, saying, 'You had better not try to go down there, because we'll get stuck.'

At this, he joined his laughter to hers and put her on to her feet. Still he hadn't spoken, not a word, and not until they were opposite the bedroom door did he push her slightly away from him, saying, 'Well, go down now and tell Annie.' And with this, he turned from her and went into the bedroom; and wisely and without murmur she went down the stairs to the kitchen.

The door shut, he stood with his back to it, his hand pressed tight across his eyes, and there was, at this moment, a deep shame in him, for he had never cried in his life; nor had he seen his father cry, not even when his wife died. He'd have to take a hold of himself, because this was an event that occurred every day to some man somewhere, and surely few men would react to such news as he wanted to do, and cry like a woman.

He must have a drink, and a strong one . . .

It seemed that from this glorious day the outside world began to impinge on Ward's happiness. On the day she broke the news to him, Fanny must have been two months pregnant. And it should also happen that a few days later Annie was seized with a pain in her side, and Ward called the doctor to her. While he was there, he spoke to him about his wife's happy condition and asked if he would see to her health.

Doctor Wheatley not only saw to her health and advised her cheerily to carry on as if nothing had happened, but he apparently informed someone in the village, and in his usual coarse way, that Ward Gibson had got results at last; he was beginning to think the young fellow had taken on a dud. When this was repeated in The Running Hare there was great laughter, except from the Mason brothers . . .

The first worrying incident occurred towards the end of March. The routine of the farm had been changed, though not to everyone's satisfaction, no. As Billy stated bluntly, he could neither read nor write, but the cows didn't take it out on him for that, nor did it interfere with his ploughing, or the gathering in of the crops, so he reckoned he had all the skills necessary for a farmhand, and that's what the young lad was going to be, wasn't he? And so he didn't see where readin' and writin' was going to help him. Besides which, it was taking an hour out in the morning, and another in late afternoon at that; and count that up for five days, and that was ten hours work lost a week. And hadn't he, the master, said himself that the lad was almost as good as a paid hand; better, in fact, than either one of the Regans or the McNabbs from the Hollow that could be called upon at times, for 'them two Irish lumps' liked work so much they could lie down beside it. But if it was the mistress's wish, well, he supposed he must put up with it. But to his mind, book learning was for them who hadn't the sense to use their hands.

Frankly, Ward himself had been a little surprised and taken aback by Fanny's request, which at first was that the boy should be sent mornings to the village school. And he had quickly pooh-poohed this, reasoning that they would want to know his particulars. But to this, Fanny had laughingly reminded him that if they were to believe the gossip brought to their notice through Annie, Carl was a relation of hers, for hadn't he appeared on the scene at the same time as herself?

No, no; Ward wouldn't hear of the village school, for that would have meant having to tell the boy he would have to pose as a relation, and that would be going too far. But all right, she could have him for a working hour at the beginning of the day and at any slack hour in the late evening. At this, she had rewarded him with some spontaneous kisses, and this openly in the hall with Annie passing, trying to look the other way. And then he was being told that she would need some books, one on arithmetic, another on history, and another on geography.

Privately, he was amazed that she was so learned when she had openly confessed that she had never been to school; but it appeared that her schooling had been very much of the same pattern as she was planning for the boy, for both her father and mother had taken a hand in her tutoring. They had not always been on the road, and had themselves both received some sort of education.

Fanny had fitted up a small room at the back of the house. It was sparsely furnished, and it had been used mostly for storing lumber. It now housed two wooden chairs, a small table, a shelf to hold the books she had requested, and two slates and lead pencils. But to her mind there was one book missing, and as yet she couldn't ask Ward to get it for her, because he would want to know what she meant to do with a book on learning Italian.

Her own knowledge of the Italian language was sketchy indeed because her mother had spoken the language only when they were alone together; apparently her father did not like the language, or, as she had come to suspect later, he was jealous of it, fearing that his wife might, in spite of all her protestations, be secretly homesick.

She was leaning across the table now and smiling at her young pupil while admonishing him: 'You must pay attention, Carl. Look at your book, look at your slate, you are doing a sum.'

The boy returned her smile as he answered, 'I've done the sum, mistress. The answer is twenty-two sheep.'

'Ah. Ah.' The smile went from her face now. 'That is where you are wrong, sir. The answer is twenty-four sheep.'

'Oh. I've missed something out?'

The boy looked from his slate to his book. Then said, 'Yes. Yes; I can see . . . twenty-four sheep. You are right.'

Fanny covered her eyes with a hand for a moment, before leaning across the table again, and now her voice held an earnest note as she said, 'Carl, you must pay attention to your school work. Or would you rather not have lessons? Would you prefer to work outside?'

Before she had finished the last word his head was wagging: 'Oh no, no, mistress. Oh n'n'no. I promise I will pay attention. I will look at the book more.' He could have added here, 'But I can't stop looking at you,' for this lady sitting across the table appeared to him really as an angel; no-one had ever been so kind; no-one had ever spoken to him as she did; no-one he had ever seen in his short life looked as she did. He would die for her; which is what he often told himself at night as he buried his face in the straw tick in the dark room above the stable.

'I . . . I promise, and I promise also to repeat the words I read at night. I can do it now: The cat sat on the mat. The dog barked at the cat. The cows give milk.'

She held up her hand, saying, 'That's splendid. That's splendid. Now you've got that far I will read you this little story. And then you will read it, eh?'

'Oh yes, mistress. Yes, mistress.'

She was checked as she took up the book to begin the story, for the door swung open and there stood Ward. His face looked grave. He spoke to her direct, saying, 'I want you a moment. Put your coat on, it's cold. I want you over in the shed. And you, boy, get about your work.'

As the boy scampered from the room, Fanny went hastily to Ward, saying, 'What is it? Something wrong?'

He pushed the door half closed as he looked at her, and speaking slowly, he said, 'Yes; very wrong, to my mind; and to any decent person's. Somebody's set two traps in the pasture. A cow . . . Maisie got her foot caught. She was bellowing; and there they were all standing round her. Billy heard the commotion, even in the yard here. I've never seen him run for years. I was in the bottom field.'

'A trap? What kind of trap? A man-trap? They've been abolished. It's punishable.'

'No; not a man-trap. These are home-made ones, on the lines of rabbit ones. You know—' He moved his hands as if to explain them. 'Some are just so big, enough to catch a rabbit's paw, but others are bigger.' His fingers spread. 'To get its neck. I've made them myself when I was a lad. We were swarmed with rabbits at times. But these were big enough to take a cow's hoof. Somebody knew what they were about. Anyway, come and see what you can do.'

For some time now, ever since she had healed the boy's back, he had accepted that she was one of these people who had healing in their hands. His mother used to talk about an old woman who had lived in the Hollow; and of the farmers who had come from far and wide for her services. Yet she was feared and held at arm's length by the majority of the villagers. However, she had never been known to cure any humans; it was just animals that responded to her touch.

As they hurried through the kitchen Annie, who was scrubbing the seat of a wooden chair, did not straighten her back, but commented to no-one in particular. 'It's started.'

As Fanny turned questioningly towards the woman, who now was not only the servant in the house, but a friend, meaning to ask the reason for the statement, she was actually pulled towards the kitchen door, then pushed through it.

The cow was in her stall. Billy was holding the animal's injured foot, and there was a large bowl of hot water placed on the box to the side of him.

Fanny did not immediately go to the back of the animal, but she touched its face and said, 'Hello, Maisie! That's a good girl. You're going to be all right. Do you hear me? You're going to be all right.'

Ward, standing to the side, turned his head away for a moment, for he did not like this side of the proceedings. It was all right her dressing a wound or holding it, but she had a way of talking to the creatures before she did anything. It was a bit off-putting . . . he did not use the word 'weird'. Still, she had marvellous hands. She was marvellous altogether; but . . . His voice was slightly terse as he said, 'Have a look at it.'

She stroked the cow's face twice before she turned away and joined Billy. Then looking about her, she said, 'Where's the stool?'

Almost instantly it was handed to her by Ward; and as she sat down on it, Billy straightened up, saying, 'Do you want to bathe it, mistress?'

For answer, she lifted the cow's hoof and looked at the cut made by the wire. It was deep, likely caused by the animal's struggles to release its limb. Her hands around the heel and without looking at Billy, she said, 'Would you please go and ask Annie for the bandage box?'

91

When Billy left her side Ward said, 'It's almost to the bone. She was nearly going mad; she could have snapped her hoof off.'

'Why should people do this to animals?'

He looked down on her head and found it impossible to say, 'I don't know;' and more so to answer, 'Because I married you.' He had never told her about Daisy Mason, but he knew that at times she must have felt something wasn't right between him and the village, such as when she expressed a desire to go to a service, he'd had to counter it with, 'Well, not in St Stephen's; we'll go to St Matthew's, Frank's place, one of these Sundays, when he has time to take a service there, when old Tracey's done with him. If ever there was a false minister of God it's that man, for to me he expresses the two main sins, gluttony and sloth.' What he said now was, 'Do you think you can do anything with it?'

She turned and glanced up at him, her hands still holding the animal's heel: 'I don't know; it'll be as God wills, not me.'

He felt his shoulders stiffening, his head going back on them. Why was the tone of her voice different when she was treating animals? At such times she was different altogether; she was like someone he didn't know, not his wonderful, warm, loving Fanny, his beautiful, beautiful Fanny. Sometimes he wished she hadn't this . . . whatever it was, for it was like a part of her that didn't belong to him; and he knew she was all his, entirely all his. Yet, no, not when she was doing what she was doing now.

Billy had returned with the box, and she now took from it a piece of linen and soaked it in the warm water before using it to clean the jagged ring of flesh and skin. Following this, she took some strips of linen, thickened one with ointment from the jar in the corner of the box, and placed it tenderly round the wound; then with more strips, she bandaged the heel and part of the leg, tying it top and bottom in place with a narrow strip of linen; after which she again took the now bandaged limb in her hands, bowed her head for a moment, then quite smartly got to her feet and, passing Ward, went to the cow's head, saying,

'It'll be all right, Maisie. Be a good girl, and I'll see you in the morning.'

She turned to look up at Ward, and he looked down on her. She was his Fanny once more: she was smiling tenderly at him, and she asked, 'Are you going to make sure there are not any more of them . . . I mean in any other pastures?'

He shook his head. 'I don't think there'll be any in the other pastures; this was the one that runs by the bridle path and leads into the wood on Ramsmore's estate. But the path starts in the village, and it's quite easy for anyone to pop over the wall alongside. But my God! I'll see they don't pop over again.'

'What are you going to do?'

'Shoot the first bugger I see standing where he shouldn't belong.'

It was the first time she had heard him swear; it was the first time she had heard him use this tone, especially so when he turned to Billy, who was standing to the side and said, 'I mean that, Billy. By God! I mean that.'

'And I don't blame you, master. Here's one that wouldn't blame you or anybody else. Anyway, if they were given over to the authorities, they would go along the line. It's punishable now; in any form, they're punishable . . . traps. Except, of course, when you set them on your own land for rabbits.'

As Ward marched out of the cow byre, Billy, after glancing at Fanny and nodding towards her, followed him. But she remained where she was for quite some moments. Shoot them, he had said. Yes, and perhaps he would. He had every reason in the world to be angry, but the man who had just gone out of the byres was a different man from the one she had come to love. She looked back at the cow who was now standing docilely looking towards her, and in her mind she spoke to it: There is more in this than meets the eye, Maisie, she said. There's something behind it. Why would anyone want to do him an injury through his animals? And why, when I go to the village, do some people pass me without speaking, while others are cheery? Why?

93

She went from the byres, across the yard and into the kitchen. Annie had finished her scrubbing, and had donned a clean apron. She had just banged the oven door closed, while exclaiming again as if she were talking to the air: 'This flue'll have to be swept; I'm not gettin' the heat I should. That piecrust in there is as pale as a reluctant bride.'

'Annie.'

'Yes, mistress?' Annie straightened up, dusted her hands and waited.

'Come and sit down.'

'There's no time to sit down; it's half past eleven in the mornin', ma'am.'

'Sit down, Annie. I want to talk to you.'

Reluctantly, Annie lowered her plump body down on to a chair she had recently scrubbed, and Fanny went on, 'At least I want you to talk to me. I want you to explain something, tell me something.'

'What do I know, ma'am, that I could tell you, you who are educated enough to learn the lad his letters an' such?'

'Listen to me, Annie. I am going to ask you a question, and it's this: what is it that makes some people in the village ignore me and others speak quite kindly to me? Is it because War . . . the master married me?'

Annie turned slightly and looked towards her oven, then lifted up the corner of the large white apron and rubbed it around her mouth before returning her gaze to Fanny and saying, 'He's never told you anything?'

'Told me about what?'

'Daisy Mason.'

When Fanny made no reply Annie gave an impatient jerk of her head; then casting her eyes upwards a moment, she explained, 'Men! Men! The silly buggers. They think they can hide behind their own shadows.' Then bringing her eyes back to Fanny, she said bluntly, 'Daisy Mason is a lass . . . oh, a woman, who expected to find herself in your place. Now that's the top an' the bottom of it. And don't look like that; these things happen. You hit him like a bull on the rampage. But anything further from a bull I'd like to find.' Her lips now moved into the semblance of a smile.

'You mean . . . he jilted her for . . . ?'

'Oh no, no!' Annie's head was being almost violently shaken. 'There was no jilting on his part, because the thickhead had imagined there was nobody to jilt. It's like this, ma'am. He and Daisy Mason went to school together in the village; an' with her and her two brothers, he romped about when they weren't working, as youngsters will; and as they grew, they still kept company . . . No, that's wrong, not company, because keeping company means courtship. And as far as I can gather I doubt if he has as much as kissed her over the years. I don't know, but I shouldn't expect so because, like most of his kind, he was blind, at least where a lass's feelings range from she's sixteen onwards. You know what I mean, ma'am. And he took her to one or two barn dances, set her home from church; an' sometimes he went and had tea with her people. Well, he had always dropped in there for a bite to eat at odd times – the two families were friends – that is, until about two years ago, when I think he must have smelt a rat, because he stopped going to church. I realise now it was really because he would have to set her home after. It was the rule to do so. And he started to visit Newcastle more; and Gateshead and the like towns, where there were good turns on. I'm sure he did it because he had seen the signal in Daisy's eyes; and he wasn't for marrying her, or anybody else at the time. Then, one night, he goes to The Empire, and there you were, the Maltese Angel, they called you. You were flying all over the stage, and dancing like a fairy, so he told me. And you were just the opposite in every way that God could think of to Daisy Mason. And you know the rest.'

It was a full minute before Fanny said, 'And that's what they're holding against him . . . and me?'

'Aye, in a way, you could say that. But it would have been the same whoever he had married . . . I mean the effect on Daisy and her family, because, you see, give them an' people their due, everybody expected it. To all intents an' purposes they had been courtin'. Well, I tell you, when you went about courtin' you kept to the same lass. And he had never bothered with anybody else over the years. And you know somethin', ma'am? If he had lived in a town it would have been different

95

. . . Oh! different altogether,' and she expressed the difference with a great wave of her hand. 'Nobody would have noticed unless the lass had taken him to the justices for breach of promise, which a lot of them are doin' these days, brazen hussies that they are. But in a village it's different. Well, in this one it is, anyway, 'cos it's like one big family: it is as if everybody was related to everybody else. And some are, you know, some are. They have intermarried for generations, some of them; and the results . . .' – her eyebrows went up – 'the results have left a lot to be wished for here and there. And the village isn't only the main street, lass; it spreads out . . . aye, even to the gentry, because you can keep nothing secret: everybody knows everything about everybody else. And if they think anything's been kept back they get the mud rakes out . . . That's a village, ma'am. They're nearly all alike; there's not a pin to choose atween them. But don't worry yourself. Just think of what you're carryin' and let them get on with it . . . But having said that, it's not saying that your man will, because once this kind of thing starts you don't know where it's gona stop. But one last thing, please don't let on that I've told you all this. There'll come a time when it's right for him to enlighten you about the whole matter. Until then, my advice, ma'am, is to plead dumb. You understand?'

'Yes. Yes, Annie, I understand. And thank you for making things plain to me. But nevertheless, I am saddened to think that I have been the cause of the division in the village.'

'Well' – Annie now rose from the chair – 'if it wasn't you doin' something, ma'am, it would be somebody else, because there's nothin' lies faller hereabouts. If it isn't some farmer knocking on the door in the dark, or high jinks at harvest time, it's somebody goin' off with the Christmas money from The Running Hare, like Sep Newton did three years ago. And he's never turned up since. Yet his mother still shows her face at church on a Sunday, I understand. And them's only scraping the surface of things. So don't worry, ma'am, just carry on with your life, and continue to be a nine-day won-der to your man.' She now grinned widely as she added,

96

'And that's what you are, you know. He still can't get over having you.'

'Oh, Annie.' Fanny moved impulsively forward and put her arms around the sturdy body, and for a moment she rested her head on Annie's shoulder, saying, 'What would I have done without you? I thought when I parted from the friendship of Mrs Killjoy I would be alone here, but from the moment I stepped in the front door you took me under your wing. I shall always remember that, Annie. And I thank you.'

'Oh, go on with you, ma'am. Go on with you. Besides having dancing feet you've got a dancing tongue,' and at this she pushed Fanny gently from her and turned her attention quickly to the oven, saying again, 'They've got to sweep this chimney, and soon, unless they want cold porridge set afore them on the table.'

Before the day was out the village was made aware of Ward Gibson's reaction to the planting of the trap. The term 'tearing mad' was putting it mildly. First, he visited the blacksmith's shop, and there, showing the trap to the blacksmith, he said, 'What d'you make of that, Charlie?'

Charlie Dempsey grasped the iron spike to which was attached a piece of wire with a loop on the end, and he fingered it for a time, pushing one end of the loop backwards and forwards; then looking at Ward, he said, 'Crude job, Ward, I'd say, but very effective. It's on the lines of a rabbit snare, but bigger. I don't know what they'd hope to catch with it. Nothing like a man-trap, 'cos as I see it, you would have to step into this. And it's a pretty big loop.'

'Big enough to take a heifer's foot?'

Charlie looked at Ward before he said, 'Aye. Aye, yes. It could step into it, but being silly bitches they wouldn't step out, they would just pull it and it would tighten. Aye.' He now pulled on the main piece of wire and repeated, 'Aye. Aye. What's it about?'

'It's about crippling my herd, Charlie. That's what it's about.'

97

The blacksmith made a gesture of almost throwing the contraption away from him, saying, 'No! No, man. Who'd do a blasted thing like that? I mean, it's never been heard of. Rabbits, foxes, badgers, aye, but never cows . . . Is it badly seared?'

'Almost to the bone in one part.'

'Good God! Well, I'll be damned! This is something I've never known afore.'

'But you've likely seen those spikes; they're all of nine inches, and it takes some knocking into the ground.'

'Yes, I've seen those spikes, because I made them; and I think I've supplied them to every farmer in the district, and to every farmer for miles around; an' you yourself. But they would have had to be knocked fully into the ground else they could have been spotted.'

'Yes, if they were on bare ground; but they were placed cunningly in some lush grass, near one end of the field. And there's another thing: bairns cross that field, those that come from the school. The lads, in particular, climb the wall. Amos Laker's two young 'uns often do. I've yelled at them more than once because the little devils go scattering the cows and disturbing the milk. What if one of them had been caught in that, because their clogs would have dropped off and some damage would have been done before they could have got their foot out of the infernal thing.'

The blacksmith now picked up a pair of tongs, took a piece of iron from the glowing forge and hammered the end of it flat before he spoke again, saying, 'You've got to face up to it, Ward; there's them round about that's got it in for you. It's like a lot of bloody fools in this world, going fighting other people's battles, because, you know, I don't think the Masons themselves would do anything. There's not a nicer couple than him and her; and I've had a drink with the lads now and again, and they never utter a word against you. No; it's some of them like the Conway lot, or Ted Read and his pal Jock MacIntosh. Oh, he gets under my skin, that fella. Why doesn't he go back to Scotland among all his brave countrymen, those who he shoots his mouth off about? Likely one of that ilk. Of course, we mustn't forget them down in the Hollow. There's good and bad among all kinds, but there's one or two that smell down there; like Riley, for instance. I know where I'd like to stick a hot rod in that one . . . sly, smooth-tongued . . . crawler. He'd spit on his Pope for a tanner.'

This tirade had been going on between bangs of the hammer; and now, dipping the piece of bent iron into a bucket of water, Charlie Dempsey waited until the sound of the sizzling had died away before he said, quietly now, 'Anyway, there's another side to it: you've got good friends among us; and I can tell you this, the more I see of your little wife the more I understand your situation.'

The leather apron around his stomach now began to wobble, and he bent his head and rubbed his sweat-covered face with his blackened hand as he muttered, 'You should have heard my missis the other night when I was talking about your young lass. And you know what I said? I said, we all had regrets in life, and it was a pity that I hadn't clapped eyes on that dainty piece before Ward had, because he wouldn't have had a look in. And do you know what? She brought her hand across me ear; and her hand's not delicate, it's a mitt, I can tell you.'

Ward did not smile. At this moment he couldn't appreciate his friend's trend, which was an effort to lighten his humour, so that when he turned slowly and went towards the open door of the forge, Charlie said, 'Where you off to?'

And Ward's reply was short: 'To both of them: The Hare and The Head; and I won't be drinking in either. But I'll tell Sam Longstaffe of The Hare and Michael Holden of The Head in no small voice so that their customers can hear me, that I'll not rest until I find out who did this.' He now shook the trap that was hanging from his hand. 'Then God help them.' And with this, he walked down the street in the direction of the two inns.

In bed that night, holding Fanny in his arms, he said to her, 'Don't go walking round the fields by yourself. Do you hear me? And don't go into the village again, unless Annie goes with you.'

'But Ward, my dear, that won't happen again . . . I mean what's happened today.'

'No, it mightn't happen again; and yet it might. But other things could happen; and don't say "Why?" just do as I ask. Do you hear?'

'Yes, Ward, I hear.'

'I love you.'

'And I love you, too, Ward, so very much.'

2

The weeks wore on; the months wore on; the weather remained favourable, the crops were good; the prices in the market were moderate, but healthy enough to allow Ward to make improvements. Not only did he have the yard stone-paved from the open barn right to the yard gates but he had the house painted and, what was more, he didn't engage Arthur Wilberforce, cousin to the verger, but a Mr Percy Connor, painter and decorator, who had a business in Fellburn. The village didn't like this at all: even his friends felt he was going too far, because everybody knew the village tried to be self-sufficient, and likes and dislikes were forgotten when they touched on a man's livelihood; even the gentry round about rarely went farther afield than the village for either victuals or inside and outside work. As Hannah Beaton confided to one of her customers, 'That little dancer up there has wrought havoc in this place.'

As for the little dancer herself, she no longer felt little: she was carrying inside her a weight that grew heavier each day. She was almost on her time. Annie told her she had carried well: she hadn't been sick at all, and she had been blithe in herself, which wasn't always the way with the first one.

It was now nearing the end of August. During the months past they'd harvested two crops of hay; and now they were stooking the last of the corn. Ward, Billy and the boy had been working from early morning, and during the day Annie and Fanny had brought out three meals to them; and to eat the last one they had not sat propped up against the hay cart, or seated in the shadow of the hedge. Instead, Fanny had laid a check cloth on the stubble, and they had all sat round and drunk of the cool beer and ate shives of bread and cheese and veal pie, and a great deal of laughter had ensued, mainly over Annie's chatter.

However, as soon as the meal was over, Ward and Billy rose and were away to resume work; but Carl, his mouth still wide with laughter, continued to stare at Annie, and she shouted at him, 'Don't you laugh at me, young man, else I'll come over there and skite the hunger off you,' and at this, Carl, still laughing, enquired, 'What does that mean, Mrs Annie, skite the hunger off you?'

Annie paused before replying, 'Well, I don't really know, lad. Me mother used to use it. I suppose it's sort of saying, "look out or I'll box your ears".' Then she cried, 'Mind where you're going!' and thrust out her hand as Fanny stumbled a little on the rough ground and, grabbing the basket from her, she said, 'Give me that here! You've got enough to carry with that lump of yours. Have you been having any pains?'

'Not pains exactly, no; just a feeling.'

'Well, from what I gather, you've got another week to go. But then I might have gathered wrong.'

'Oh, I'll go another week. I mean to' – she nodded at Annie – 'because I'd love Mr and Mrs Killjoy to be here . . . You won't mind them staying for a few days, will you, Annie?'

'Oh, my goodness me! girl,' and Annie let out a long slow breath. 'It isn't my house. I've told you afore, you've got to know your place, like I know mine. You can have who you like: the old Queen if you like, or that juggler friend of yours and his pal; you can do what you like in your own . . .'

'Annie, I know, I know; I am well aware of that, but I hold you in such regard that I don't want to put on you with more work, or displease you.'

They had now reached the yard and Annie walked on without answering. She pushed the door open so that her mistress could precede her through the boot room and into the kitchen; and there, dropping the basket of crockery on to the table, she bent over it before she said, 'You know, sometimes, ma'am, I think you're too good to be true, and it's just as well I am who I am else you'd be taken advantage of up to the hilt.'

'Oh, no, I wouldn't Annie! I'm not as simple as it might appear.'

'Oh, ma'am; there's nothing simple about you. Funny thing is, you've got a head on your shoulders; but you get too soft about people, you could be taken in.'

'Annie.'

'Yes, ma'am?'

'I am now going to say to you what I have heard my husband say so often in his way of appreciation . . . Shut up!'

She now lumbered round the table and walked out of the kitchen, leaving Annie biting on her lip to stop herself from laughing; but as she saw the door close on her mistress, she said to herself, 'Just think what this house would have been like if he had taken that big hulk. Dear God in heaven! I should go on me knees and thank God for big mercies, not little ones.'

She was on the point of scooping up the dishes from the table to take them to the sink when she heard her name being called, but in a way she hadn't heard before, for this time it was in the nature of a cry.

Within seconds she was in the hall, there to see Fanny clinging to the stanchion of the parlour door.

'Lord above!' Annie almost carried the bent form towards the couch, and there she exclaimed, 'It's coming?'

Lying back, and her eyes closed, Fanny made a slight movement with her head as she muttered, 'Bad pain.'

'Lordy!' Annie straightened up, looked about the room as if waiting to be directed what to do, then said, 'Not a soul in the yard. Now, do I go for them? or do I get you upstairs?'

The answer came from Fanny who, sitting forward, said, 'It's eased off; but if you would help me upstairs, and then . . . get Ward.'

'Yes. Yes, that's the best thing. Come on now.'

A few minutes later, in the middle of undressing, Fanny was again brought double with pain; and with this, Annie exclaimed, 'You're not going to wait for Mrs Killjoy then?'

The spasm passed, and Fanny breathing heavily muttered, 'Go and get Ward, please Annie . . . now.'

And to this Annie replied, 'I think it's Billy who's more necessary than your lord and master at this minute, lass. He'll have to get the midwife an' Doctor Wheatley, that's if the old sod's sober enough, yet I hope he isn't, so the young 'un can come. Will you be all right?'

'I'll be all right.' Left alone, Fanny finished her undressing and climbed into bed; and there, lying back amidst the pillows, she closed her eyes, and now, as if appealing to an unseen but present force, she said, 'Help me through this and bring my child into life,' then lay quiet.

Presently she nodded her head twice and, as if in reply to a suggestion, she let her body sink into the depths of the feather tick.

'It isn't seemly; you can't go in.'

'Seemly bedamned! I could do something. It's gone on too long.'

'You're not talking about a cow. What d'you think you could do? Put your arm in up to the elbow? I tell you it'll come in its own time, as Doctor Wheatley said.'

'Doctor Wheatley. Where is he now? He should be back here.'

'Master Ward' – Annie put out her hand and rested it on Ward's shoulder – 'I know how you feel. It seems it's always the same with the first, the man gives birth an' all; but it eases off with the second and third and fourth . . . at least so they tell me.'

He stared down into her face, then muttered, 'Oh! Annie, I'm frightened. It's been going on since seven last night; now it's half-past two in the morning. And . . . and she's not the heifer type, is she?'

'No. No, she's not, lad. But it's amazing how calm she keeps in between times. But you go on downstairs and get Billy to make another pot of tea.'

'It's no time since the last.'

'I know. I know. But it's hot work in there; and Kate must have lost a couple of pounds already in sweat, I should think.'

She made an attempt at smiling as she pushed him away.

When he entered the kitchen he realised, by the way he pulled himself to his feet, that Billy had been nodding in the chair; but even so the question he would ask of Ward was plain enough in his eyes, and for answer Ward shook his head; it was the boy, who had been sitting on the low cracket at the other side of the fireplace, his arm around Pip, the poodle Mrs Killjoy had brought as a present for Fanny, who spoke. 'I . . . I rubbed Delia's stomach. I kept rubbing it and she stopped whingeing,' he said.

Both men now looked at the boy, and it was Billy who said, 'What d'you mean, you kept rubbin' her stomach? She must have had it in the middle of the night, around two o'clock?'

Carl hung his head now, saying, 'Aye, I know. But . . . but Delia . . . she knows me.' He now glanced at Ward. 'And so . . . and so I came down and sat with her.'

Three days previously, one of the cows had calved somewhat before its time. She hadn't been too well and they had been dosing her. She had been placed in the rest box, as they called the section that was railed off at the end of the byre.

The two men exchanged glances, but it was Billy who said, 'No wonder you were dozy an' asleep on your feet t'other day. The beasts know what to do without your help, young man.' But the chastising words did not carry any harshness, rather a note of kindness and understanding. Ward now walked slowly to the window through which the moonlight was streaming.

It was like daylight outside. A wind was blowing and he could see wisps of straw being lifted here and there as if they were dancing . . . Dancing. He drew his lower lip tightly between his teeth. If anything happened to her he would go mad. Yes; surely he would. He wanted a child, but not at her expense. Last night, while holding her as the pains increased, he had thought, I shall soon have a son, and he had felt elated. But no longer.

He turned towards the boy. The dog was making that thin whining sound as he strained from the boy's arms to go towards the door. That dog loved her. It had never willingly

105

left her side since the day it had arrived. And that boy loved her, too. And he was a good boy; a boy who would stay up half the night to comfort an animal was a good boy. He could hope if he did have a son he would grow up like this youngster. There he was again: it didn't matter whether it was a son or a daughter; the only thing that mattered was that she should come through this alive.

He turned from the window, remembering why he had come downstairs, and said to Billy, 'They want more tea up there.'

Almost before he had finished speaking Annie's voice came to them from a distance, and at the sound they all three dashed to the kitchen door and into the lamplit hall, to come to a stop at the foot of the stairs and look up to Annie who was shouting down to them, 'It's come! the bairn. It's a girl.'

There was a split second of disappointment before Ward leapt to the stairs, only to be checked by Annie's strong arms and her saying, 'Now look! Hold your hand a minute. Hold your hand. You can't go in there yet. She's in a bit of a mess, and she'll want to be cleaned up. But I'll bring the bairn out in a minute. She's big and bonny.' She laughed outright and pushed him none too gently in the chest, crying, 'She's like you. Got your hair already.'

He made no further protest, but stood now with his back against the landing wall, his head dropped almost on to his chest. She had come through and he had a daughter. Well, he had a daughter . . .

It was almost a half hour later when he saw his daughter; but it was to his wife he went first. And after standing for a moment looking down on her almost deadly white face, he dropped on to his knees by the side of the bed and laid his head on her shoulder while his hand stroked her face; and as Kate Holden said later to Hannah Beaton in the grocery store, 'You never did see anything like it: on his knees he was, as if she was the Queen of England who had just delivered. Although that would have been a miracle at her age, wouldn't it? Still, talk about excess and palaver. Not like a man at all, he wasn't, but like some daft lad. And what he gets out of

106

her two pennorth of nothing beats me, because she's hardly a bit of flesh on her bones. Talk about being bewitched.'

And at this moment, Ward felt bewitched: his angel, as he thought of her privately, had come through and given him offspring.

Presently, he lifted his head, rose from the bed, and walked round the foot of it to where a wooden cradle stood, draped in white lace. And he looked down on his daughter for the first time.

The face was wrinkled; the eyelids were opening and shutting; the lips were moving in and out; and there was a tuft of hair, almost black, like his own.

Well, well! So this was his daughter. But he hoped she wouldn't grow up to look like him, like her mother, yes. Oh, yes, she must look like her mother.

'Satisfied?'

He turned and looked at the midwife. As he put it to himself, he had no room for her; besides being a blowsy piece, she had a very slack tongue. Nevertheless, she was good at her job, so he understood; and although it had taken a long time, she had been good at this one. And so he answered her, 'Yes, you could say I'm satisfied.'

'Not disappointed because it wasn't a lad?'

He was quick to reply, 'No; oh no; as long as my wife is all right, that's all that matters to me.'

'Aye, well, she's come through; and not many squeaks out of her, which' – she now turned and looked towards the bed – 'when you come to think of it is odd, because she's not as big as two penn'orth of copper. Still, she's done it. It doesn't really surprise me, though, because I meet all kinds in this line of business.'

Then with a sly grin, she said, 'Seeing how you've suffered in this lot, are you for trying again?'

His countenance darkened, and she did not wait for what would have been a brusque reply, but went out laughing.

He returned to the bed, and sitting down on the edge of it, he leant over and placed his lips gently on hers. Then, his face hanging over hers, he whispered, 'This must never happen again. It has been torment.'

She closed her eyes while saying, 'Oh, Ward. You can be very funny at times.'

'I'm not being funny, Granny Shipton,' he said and gently tweaked her nose; but when she smiled and sighed, then closed her eyes, he said, 'You're tired, my love. Go to sleep.'

Without opening her eyes, she said softly, 'I have been thinking of names, and I wonder if you would mind Flora, because, as you know, Mr and Mrs Killjoy have, in a way, become as dear as parents to me. If it had been a boy, I should have liked Kenneth, Mr Killjoy's name.'

He, too, had been thinking of names, but those of his father and mother, John and Jessie. He liked the name Jessie. He simply said, 'Whatever you wish, my dear; I only know if it had been a boy, I would have been dead against Hayward.'

He watched her smile widen; yet her eyes still remained closed.

Slowly he rose from the bed; then quietly he walked around it again and looked on the child.

Flora Gibson. It was a nondescript name somehow. Flora Gibson. He'd much rather have Jessie ... He'd put it to her later.

Only the very necessary work was done on the farm that day. The weather was still very dry: the stooks could remain for a day or two before being gathered in. What was more, Ward was definitely needed at the house to receive the number of visitors. The first was Fred Newberry; and he took hold of Ward's hands and shook them up and down, much to the new father's embarrassment, for it happened in the yard, and not only Billy and the boy were there looking on, but Annie was, too, from the kitchen door; and they all listened to Fred gabbling, 'Oh, I am pleased, man. I am pleased. And the lass ... a girl. Mam said straight away you'd be calling it Jessie; and Dad's got a great idea for a christening cake. Mam's coming over later. She's bringing some sugar dollies. Dad's baking them now. Eeh! I am glad you've got it over.'

At this Ward was forced to let out a bellow of laughter in which Billy joined, and the boy too; but Annie from the kitchen door cried, 'You're a fool, Fred Newberry. Always were and always will be. Why aren't you surprised that the father isn't in bed with a binder on?'

At this, it was her husband who let out a bellow of a laugh, in which Fred joined as he answered Annie back, saying, 'Well, I only know that Dad says he suffered twice as much during Mam's carrying the three of us than she did. And he had to get drunk each time to help him get over it.'

'Oh you're an idiot, all right.' Ward thumped Fred on the back, then urged him towards the kitchen door, saying, 'Come in and have a drink.'

Maisie Dempster was the next visitor; and she cooed over the mother and baby. Then Jane Oldham, the shoemaker's wife, called. But she wouldn't accept the invitation to go upstairs to see the mother and baby: she had been unable to have children of her own, and it was known that this brought on dark bouts in which she might weep a lot. However, she called to pay her respects and to leave a basket of fruit, all picked from their garden.

Frank and Jane Noble were the last to call; and Frank was already talking about the christening. But it was as they were leaving and he was helping his wife up into the trap that he saw Carl. The boy was carrying a bucket of swill from the boiler house towards the pig sty, and he called to him, 'Would you like to come to the magic lantern show this evening, Carl?'

The boy stopped, put down the bucket, and he was on the point of expressing his delight, but he looked towards Ward, who was standing near the curate; and Ward answered for him, saying, 'Get your work done, and you may go.'

The boy picked up the bucket again, and without having said a word, hurried away, and Frank Noble, turning to Ward, said, 'You've got a good boy there. And Fanny has done a wonderful job on him. He can read whole passages of the Bible, as good as myself.'

At this, Ward put on a mock serious expression as he replied, 'I'm not interested in what he can do with the Bible, but how quick he can carry that swill.'

109

'Go on with you!' Frank thrust him aside; then mounted the trap, and Jane, from her seat, called to the boy, 'We start at seven, Carl,' and Carl answered, 'Yes, ma'am.' Then stood still while watching the trap leave the yard; that is until Ward's voice caused him to jump: 'You'll get your work done standing there gaping, won't you?'

Carl did not immediately turn and run; but he stared at Ward, saying, 'Would . . . would you let me have a look at the baby, master?'

Ward pulled a long face as if he were listening to an impossible request; then shaking his head as if addressing company, he said, 'And he's going out to a magic lantern show? It doesn't matter to him about the evening chores. Oh no. And now he's asking for more time off in order to see the baby.' He adopted a false glare as he stared down on the boy; but then quickly he thrust out his hand and, laughing, grabbed the thin veined arm as he said, 'Come on. Come on. You'll see the baby.'

However, their hurried progress was checked by Annie emerging from the bedroom and demanding, 'Where do you think you're going?' And she looked from one to the other, then ended, 'Eh?'

'I am taking this young gentleman to see my daughter. Is there any harm in that?'

'Could be. Could be,' said Annie. 'Stay there till I see if they're ready to receive you.'

She pushed open the bedroom door, put her head round, saying, 'You've got more visitors; are you up to it?'

If there was an answer it was inaudible, but Annie stood aside and allowed them to pass her, Ward still holding the boy by the hand.

'Oh! Hello, Carl.'

'Hello, ma'am. Are you better?'

'Yes. Yes, Carl. Thank you. You've come to see the baby?'

'Yes, ma'am. Please.'

'Well, there she is, in the cradle.'

They both watched the boy now walk towards the cradle and stand looking down on the child. Then his hand, in

110

the act of moving downwards, wavered, and he looked across the bed towards them, saying, 'Me hand's clean,' and immediately returned his attention to the child, resting his forefinger on the tiny fist, and when it was grabbed his face became alight and he actually gurgled; and turning to them again, he whispered, 'She's got my finger.'

Ward glanced at Fanny, and she at him, and the look they exchanged was soft with understanding: the boy was experiencing, next to suckling, one of the first natural instincts of a baby, but the impression on Carl's face was as if it could never have happened before; and it hadn't, not in his world.

When his finger was released, he lifted his hand and looked at it; then his lips were drawn in between his teeth as if to suppress some inner emotion connected with either tears or laughter, but with something new and strange springing from the depths of his growing and groping mind.

He now left the cradle and, walking to the side of the bed, he said, 'She is beautiful . . . lovely, ma'am. Thank you.'

He did not look at his master, but turned and went from the room, across the landing, down the stairs, and into the kitchen where Annie said, 'Well, what d'you think?' But he gave her no reply; he did not even stop, leaving her gaping after him and saying aloud, 'Well, I'll be jiggered! That was a response and a half.'

The boy now made his way across to the stables, but not into the cowshed or into the barn, but up the ladder and into his room. And there he sat on the side of his shakedown bed, his eyes fixed on the sloping rafters above as he questioned his feelings: he had felt wonderful when the baby was holding his finger; then of a sudden when he had looked at his mistress that nightmare feeling had attacked him again, not of being flailed, or screaming out when the salt was thrown on to his back and hearing Mr Zedmond's drunken, insane laughter. No; it wasn't that feeling, but another, not unlinked with the past. Of the fearful dread of Mr Brown, the workhouse master? No, it wasn't that either, but a fear of some sort. He couldn't understand it because it had come upon him in that happy room, and in that happy house. Perhaps something was going to happen to himself that would make them get rid of him, send him away? Oh, that was silly thinking. He would never do anything to upset either the master or mistress, or Mr Billy, or Mrs Annie. They had all been so kind to him. And he knew that the master liked him. Well, otherwise he wouldn't have kept him from the beginning, would he? Sometimes he bawled at him; but it was mostly in fun; and he could always tell.

Why was he sitting here? The master wouldn't be joking if he found him up here at this time of the day. What was the matter with him? Was he going wrong in the head?

He sprang from the pallet; but paused a moment to stick out his forefinger and to look at it. He started to smile: she had gripped it, hadn't she? and really tight.

Then in a rush he made for the ladder.

3

〰

There were only ten children at the magic lantern show. Apart from Carl, they were the children of the families from the Hollow. If the show had taken place in the schoolroom most of the village would have been there, but not those from the Hollow, and Frank Noble had purposely set up the apparatus in the little church to give the Hollow children a treat. It did not matter to him that the parents seldom attended his services, and he understood: in any case, a number of them were Catholics in whom the feeling of hell-fire was strong, and any Catholic would be bound straight for that place were he to enter a Protestant church. But the children were different, and the parents seemed to think this way too. Perhaps they considered their offspring would only go to Purgatory for committing what would have been for them a mortal sin.

Anyway, the children enjoyed the show immensely. Carl, with the rest, rocked on the form when the donkey kicked the man with the stick into the air. And the following plate was better still, because the donkey was now chasing the man with the stick. Then there was the lovely one of the bird feeding its young. But the one that the Reverend kept on longest was that of Jesus sitting among a group of children. He had a lovely face. He hadn't a beard, and his hair was fair and fell on his shoulders, and he was dressed in a white gown.

But Carl wasn't exactly familiar with this particular picture. In the workhouse, he had heard a lot about Jesus and

113

how kind he was, especially to children. This was from the preacher, yet none of the staff or the master seemed to have heard of him. They knew a lot about the devil, though, and what he could do; and when he was farmed out he was to find that there was no doubt about the power of the devil.

The Reverend had made the show last for more than an hour, for he had given a commentary on each slide, his remarks being amusing enough to keep the children laughing heartily.

After the show, sweetmeats were distributed by Mrs Noble, then the children quickly dispersed to their so-called homes, which were little more than hovels.

Carl was the last to leave; and as Frank and Jane stood with him at the church door, Frank said, 'You're going to be blown about on your walk home, Carl,' and pointed to where the tops of the trees were swaying. 'The moon's on a wild rampage tonight. She doesn't know whether to stay in or come out. But you know your way back, don't you?'

'Oh yes, sir.'

'Well' – Frank Noble pointed again to where the scudding clouds were blocking out the moonlight – 'I would run when she's out and walk when she's in.'

Carl laughed and said, 'I'll do that, sir. 'Tis good advice.'

'Oh, I always give good advice, Carl.'

'Yes, you do, sir.' Carl was still laughing; then he added, 'Good night, sir. And good night to you, ma'am. And thank you for the evening. It has been wonderful.' Then with a touch of humour, he added, 'I hope the donkey caught that man and kicked him hard.' And with this he hurried away, Frank and Jane Noble's laughter following him.

He was feeling pleased with himself: he had made the parson and his wife laugh.

The moon was riding through a clear patch of sky now. It was a lovely night, in spite of the wind. Well, it had been dry and warm for ages. Tomorrow, they'd get the last of the corn in. They would have had it in today if the baby hadn't come.

He skirted the woodland, for although the moon was bright, he did not know how long it would stay that way

114

and he didn't want to be caught in the dark among all the trees. He didn't like the dark. The cellar on that farm had been black, pitch black. Two whole days . . . No, he mustn't start thinking about that again . . . He would take the bridle path that led to the village, and half-way along he would climb the wall with the help of the old oak whose roots went under the wall and the lower branches over it. This way he would drop into the corn field where they had finished stacking the stooks yesterday.

It was as he reached the bridle path that once more the clouds obscured the moon; but he was on a path he knew, and it was only a short way to the tree. The wind seemed to be getting stronger, for it was bending the hedge growth almost into the middle of the path; at one time a branch whipped his cheek.

When he reached the oak the clouds were clearing just the slightest. He lifted his arms and gripped the lowest branch and pulled himself up to the top of the wall. Astride it, the position was very uncomfortable, for the top stones were angled. But instead of lifting his right leg over and dropping into the field he became perfectly still as, further along on the field side of the wall, he watched the dark bulk of a figure swinging a can. He knew it to be a can, for he caught the glint of it. When the can stopped swinging the widening of his mouth and the intake of breath were but the precursors to the loud yell he emitted when the flames shot up from the grass and rivulets licked their way towards the stooks.

When he was gripped by the shoulders and hoisted upwards he was still screaming, until his face was bashed against the tree trunk, when all went quiet.

How long he lay on the edge of the field he didn't know, but he was brought into startling life by the realisation that his hair was on fire; also his coat. His reaction was to stagger to his feet and to break into the war-dance of a dervish. With one hand he frantically tore at his hair the while dancing on his coat in an endeavour to put out the flames.

As yet he wasn't aware of what was happening in the field; but when with startled and unbelieving eyes he saw the flames licking hungrily at the dry stubble and climbing one stook after another, he was again screaming, but running drunkenly as well.

The moon was again clear of the curtain of clouds; and his throat was sore and his step almost flagging when he reached the yard. But his screaming penetrated the bedroom and brought Ward down the stairs and into the yard, to see the boy grabbing at Annie's apron and yelling, 'It's the field. It's afire! Afire! All of it.'

'What are you talking about, boy?'

Before the lad could answer Ward, Annie cried, 'Look! His hair's all singed, and his coat, look! Dear God in heaven!'

'Buckets! Buckets! master.' The boy was staggering towards the boiler house.

Ward himself was now running frantically after Carl and yelling, 'Get Billy! Get Billy! He's in the cottage.'

Carl was running again, but so muddled was he in his mind that he hammered on the door of the empty cottage next to Billy's. But this brought Billy out of his own door, crying, 'What's up, lad?' He was dressed only in singlet and trousers, and when Carl yelled at him, 'The cornfield! It's afire . . . blazin',' Billy paused only a second before leaping forward, Carl behind him now.

From the boiler house door Annie threw two pails at her husband's feet, while she cried to the boy, 'Run to the Hollow an' get the men! Look at that sky!'

The moonlight was now tinted by the delicate flame flush that seemed to be borne on the wind; and as Carl went stumbling off behind Billy, she screamed at him, 'Don't go empty-handed!' and a milk pail came rolling to his feet, and her voice hit him again, crying, 'And put a move on!'

When he reached the field, he brought himself to a sudden halt: at the sight before him, Billy himself too had become stock-still, and he was whispering in dismay, 'Oh my God! My God!' But then a cry from Ward brought them both running again, and he yelled to Carl what Annie had said, 'Go to the Hollow! Fetch the men.' He hadn't said the village, but the Hollow. And to Billy he cried, 'Get to the rill, Billy. Hand me the buckets, I'll douche the hedge, else it'll get into the bottom field.'

Carl had jumped the tiny stream that ran between the two fields, and when he reached the hill which formed one side of the Hollow he stotted down it like a ball, crying, 'Mr Riley! Mr Read! Mr Mackintosh!'

As he banged on the first cottage door, others along the row opened and voices cried through the darkness. 'What's it? Is it a fire or something?'

And in answer to this usual first reaction, Carl yelled, 'It's master's cornfield. All ablaze. He wants you.'

More doors opened to cries and statements such as:

'My God!'

'Jesus in heaven!'

'Can you believe it?'

Then someone cried, 'Look at that sky! God, it's a fire all right. Let's away! Eeh! let's away.'

Eight men and seven young boys, not one older than twelve, scampered along the Hollow, then up the hill; but strangely, Carl made no move to follow the yelling mass that had disappeared into the darkness, for the moon had momentarily hidden itself again. There was something wrong with him: he couldn't make his legs move, yet they felt light. All his body felt light. It was as if he were about to fly. But of a sudden it wasn't into the air he went but deep into the ground.

'The lad's collapsed. Well, I never did! An' look at his hair! It's been on fire. And his shirt's singed an' all. Poor young 'un,' said a large woman.

'Will I throw some water over him, Ma?'

'I'd throw a barrel full over yersel if I'd one near at this minute. An' don't hang over him, you lot.' She pushed the children and two other women aside. 'Move your hides till I lift him.' She gave a wiggle of her wide hips, and two children suddenly sat down on the mud road; then she stooped and picked up Carl in her arms and, stepping over her youngest, she went sideways through the door into the cottage, and laid her burden down on a wooden bench covered with a straw tick, saying to her daughter in an aside, 'Bring the lamp nearer. Then wet the small coarse towel in the bucket and let's have it.' The nine-year-old girl did not run immediately to do her mother's bidding, but muttered under her breath, 'You always bring me da round by douching him.'

'As sure as God's in heaven this night, Patsy Riley, I'll douche you with your own blood if you don't do this minute what I'm askin' of you. An' you lot back there! Settle down, else I'll scud your hides one after t'other. An' you know me, I waste neither spit nor words.'

Five small but interested spectators, three boys and two girls, scuttled away towards the open hearth where a fire, built up with slack coal, was endeavouring to show a glow. They sat all close together and watched their mother wrap coarse towels round the visitor's head; and they listened to their sister Patsy saying, 'He's Mr Gibson's lad. He's got a cushy job there, an' he knows it, 'cos he never gives you the time o' day when he passes you. You'd think his nose was smellin' a midden. He's comin' round. He's blinkin'. An' I bet when he wakes up he won't thank you for landin' him in here.'

The children hunched their shoulders when their mother yelled, 'Will you shut that wobblin' gob of yours, Patsy Riley, or else I'll shut it for you, an' with such a bang you'll think a cuddy's kicked yer.'

During the short silence that followed this exchange, Mrs Riley looked down at the blood-stained face: the nose was caked with dried blood, and blood had been running from a cut in the lad's brow. Someone had given him a right bashing. And for why? she would like to know. But all in good time.

'Hello there,' she said. 'Are you feelin' better then?'

Carl lifted his heavy eyelids but he couldn't really make out the face hanging over him, yet he knew who it was; at least he knew it was one of the Irish women from the Hollow . . . He had come to the Hollow for the men.

He tried to rise, saying, 'The fire.'

'Lie yersel back, lad. Lie yersel back for a minute. They've all gone. 'Twill likely be out by now.' She again spoke in an aside to her daughter, saying, 'Go and get me the bairn's flannel.'

'The bairn's flannel? His face'll mucky it up. You won't let any of us use it.'

118

Mrs Maggie Riley's voice was still low as she said, 'One of these days, Patsy Riley, I'll use a hammer on you, as sure as God's me judge, I will that, I'll use a hammer on you.' With a swift movement, she now turned and barked, 'Get me the flannel!'

The sound of her raised voice startled Carl, and he made another effort to get up; but Mrs Riley's voice was once again calm and soothing: 'Lie still, lad. Take no notice. The storms are always risin' an' fallin' in this house. But would you like to tell me who did that to your face?' She stretched out her hand to the side now and took the piece of wet flannel from her daughter; and when she applied it, and gently, to Carl's cheeks, he winced and whimpered, 'No! No!'

'All right. All right; we'll leave it.'

'I must get back to . . . to help.'

He now managed to pull himself upright from the bench, and after slowly sliding his feet to the floor he put his hand to his head and held it there for a moment, saying, 'Thank you very much, ma'am, for your kindness.'

'Oh, 'tis nothin', lad. 'Tis nothin' at all. But I don't think you're goin' to make it on your own back to the farm.'

The suggested inability of his walking back to the farm brought him to his feet, and for the first time he took in his surroundings. Although the image was hazy he made out the group of children by the fire, the kale pot hanging on a chain over smouldering coals, the clutter in the room of boxes and bedding. There seemed to be only two chairs. The table was littered with pots and pans.

At the door, he held on to the stanchion for a moment; and it was then that Mrs Riley said to her daughter, 'Go along of him, Patsy, an' see that he gets there.'

The girl having made no objection to this command, and Carl none to her accompanying him, they had nevertheless walked in silence until, having emerged from the wood and on to the bridle path, Carl stopped and, putting a hand out, supported himself against a tree for a moment. It was then that Patsy, her voice as soft as her mother's could be, said, 'Let me give you a hand.'

And so for the first time, Patsy touched him, and they were both to remember this.

When they reached that part of the wall which, with the help of the oak tree, he had climbed a short time before, he now leant against it and peered over the top. To him, a haze of smoke seemed to be still covering the field with a red patch here and there breaking through; and he could just make out a dim line of dark figures. They seemed to be standing still looking towards him. Then he imagined them to be all running towards him, and he was rising from the ground once more and about to fly.

As he slid down by the wall Patsy Riley shook him by the shoulders, crying, 'Come on, man! Come on!' But when he made no attempt to move, she did what he had done earlier: she pulled herself up and on to the wall with the help of the long branch and, with its support, she stood on the coping and yelled, 'Somebody come! Hi! there. Hi! there. Somebody come! He's passed out again.' Then finally, she screamed, 'Da! This is Patsy. The lad's conked out!'

There was a break in the dim line of figures, and when three of them reached her, she pointed down to the other side of the wall, saying, 'It's Mr Gibson's lad. He's been battered, and he's conked out.'

It was Ward, hardly recognisable from his two companions, one of them being Fred, who clambered over the wall and dropped to his knee beside Carl.

Lifting him, he handed him back to Fred, saying, 'God above! Look at his face.' Then looking wildly beyond Fred at the men, all of whom were now gathered together, he cried, 'I swear to you on my oath, when I find out who has done this, not only to my field, but to the lad, I'll kill him, even if I have to swing for it.'

The men remained silent, for each knew that if Ward Gibson were to find the perpetrator within the next few hours he would likely do what he said, and swing for him. But they also knew that the one who should swing was he who was so low he would set fire to a man's field, the work of a year, his livelihood; for one of the worst crimes against a farmer was to set fire to his barns or his fields. And no man

120

standing there this night could recall it ever having happened, not around here, anyway. Accidents, yes, would happen; and there had been fires of sorts; but nothing ever deliberate.

They all knew that this had been a deliberate act, and all because he had married someone other than Daisy Mason; and here and there the thought passed through a man's mind: God help those two Mason lads if it could be laid at their door.

Ward clambered back over the wall, and taking the boy from Fred Newberry's arms, he paused a moment to look at the smoke-blackened faces of the men who had helped him; then he said quietly, 'Thank you all. Thank you very much. Without your help, the hedge would have gone and the other field an' all. I'm grateful.'

There were grunts and murmurs, but no-one made any rational reply as Ward stumbled away, the boy hugged to him.

The men dispersed, some making their way along the bridle path towards the village; while those from the Hollow moved away in the opposite direction.

As Patsy's father held her by the hand, he did not ask why she had come to be there with the boy, the one she would often speak about as being the stuck-up skit from Gibson's farm. He loved his daughter and he knew why she talked about that particular lad; it was because she was wise enough to know that from where she was placed now she could never hope to link up with someone like him . . . even the farmer's boy that he was.

You could have said that the field had looked almost pretty in the moonlight, with a flame here and there spitting through the haze of smoke. Everything last night had looked pink or silver grey, only the men had looked black. But as Ward gazed on the devastation of his land in the early morning light, the dirty blackened sight of the charred stooks that yesterday had been golden pyramids fanned the rage that was still boiling in him.

When he first saw the licking flames the name that had sprung immediately to mind was the Masons; and while

121

battering the ground with a sack between grabbing the buckets of water and drenching the hedge, his mind had dwelt on the name. And it did so until Fred, who came back later, happened to say, 'I don't know who did it, Ward, but you can count the Mason lads out,' at which Ward had swung round, growling, 'Why count them out?'

'Because from six o'clock onwards, they were in The Crown Head. I saw them go in meself. And when I dropped in later, they were still there. And they were playing dominoes when I left. And it was only ten minutes later when I came out of the bakery and saw the weird light in the sky from over here. At first, I didn't take it for a fire, but me dad did. He was just coming out of the house an' we both took to our heels . . . And as for Daisy. Well, she went into Fellburn this afternoon to stay with her cousin. Now you'll ask how I know that. Well, she dropped into the shop. She wanted half a dozen rice dollies, because she said her cousin liked them. She was chatting to me mam for a time. So you've got to look elsewhere, Ward. And in a way I'm glad of that, 'cos you know, there's not a nicer couple than John and Gladys Mason, and they wouldn't let their lads do anything like that. He would die of shame, would John Mason, if people thought that way.'

It was then that Rob Newberry, who had also come back after cleaning up, put in, 'You'll likely get your best lead from the lad later, because by the looks of him he must have come across whoever it was actually doing it, and they battered him. The poor lad's face is in a state, and I wouldn't be a bit surprised if his head's been hurt an' all. You've said yourself he's asleep again.'

Well, if it wasn't the Masons, who was it? The family had many friends in the village. But would friends feel a bitterness as members of the family would feel; and if they did, enough to do a thing like this? Kids might start a fire, but no kid had started this fire. This one had been paraffin fed. The quart can lying against the wall proved that. Whoever was carrying out the work must have retreated in a hurry.

And now there was the worry of Fanny. When Annie had gone back into the house it was to find her sitting slumped

122

on a chair near the landing window from where she could see, if not the actual field, the smoke and the flames at their height. And she had hardly stopped crying since, blaming herself that this had happened. And in a way it had. Yes, in a way it had. But he wouldn't change things, not for one minute. That didn't mean, though, that when he found the culprit he wouldn't throttle him with his own hands. Last night he had been stupid enough to say those very words to her, and it had made her worse.

He turned about and hurried quickly back towards the house. That boy must start talking.

They had had to call the doctor to Carl, for he had been unable to keep awake. Doctor Patten was a young man who was now noted for looking at and listening to patients, but had little to say himself, which made the villagers wonder if he actually knew anything about medicine, for he was altogether different from Doctor Wheatley. After examining Carl he had said simply that he was badly concussed and needed rest.

But Ward could not wait until the boy was fully rested, because he meant to go and put the matter in the hands of the justices; and besides the evidence of the fire itself, he wanted to know from the boy what he had seen before he had been attacked.

Carl was now lying in the storeroom beyond the kitchen, because Annie had stated flatly she wasn't going to climb that ladder in order to see to him. And so his pallet bed had been brought down and a space found for it. And it was to there that Ward now made his way.

The pallet bed was headed by an old chest, against which was placed a sack full of some commodity, and two pillows; and Ward had to drop on to his hunkers in order to come face to face with the boy. As he looked at him he gritted his teeth, for the lad could not possibly see out of his eyes. The flesh around them was purple and his nose was swollen. He did not say to him, 'How are you feeling?' but, 'You feeling bad?' and at this Carl muttered, 'Sore.'

'Oh aye, yes, you would be sore. Now listen, Carl. Try to tell me what happened.'

123

Try to tell the master what happened? Between sleeping and waking he could still see the flames licking at the stubble, and then the great black thing springing on him. But the master wanted to know what happened. He said slowly, 'He was a big man . . . very big. Cap on.' He lifted a hand to his brow to indicate the peak; then muttered, 'Big cap . . . He had a big cap I . . . I think.'

'Didn't you see his face?'

'No. No; 'twas dark. 'Twas dark . . . well, nearly.'

'And you think it was a big man?'

'Oh yes. Yes . . . strong. He lifted me by . . . ' He now patted his shoulder before saying, 'Up, and crashed me against the tree.'

'He didn't hit you with his fists then?'

'No. No . . . just the tree . . . I'm tired, master.'

'All right. All right, Carl.' Ward now put his hand upon the boy's head where the thick hair was standing up in tufts; then he straightened his back. He did not, however, immediately leave the room but stood looking down on the boy's face. He had said 'a big man'; and it would need a big strong man to lift that boy up by the shoulders and bang his head against the tree, because the boy, although thin, was no lightweight, and, too, the bole of the tree was only visible above the wall. Of course, there was that low branch, but that came over at an angle. A big man. A big man. Who were the big men in the village? The blacksmith, or his lads John and Henry? No, they were more broad than tall. But they were his friends; as were the Newberrys. Hannah Beaton wasn't; but then she had no man behind her. The verger? Aye, there was a big man. But pot-bellied and bloated, and he doubted that he had lifted anything heavier than the Bible in his life.

He went through others in the village. They were all men of medium height, from the shoemaker up to Parson Tracey. But there were some big men in the Hollow. Some of those Irish Paddys could lift a horse; but all of them had, at some time or other during the year, done jobs for him, and they all seemed to like working for him – they had told him so, more than once – for when times were hard he had taken one or other of them on when he could easily have done without

124

them. No; it had not been anyone from the Hollow.

Then who? His mind swung back to the Masons. As Fred had vouched, the brothers had been in the inn; and Daisy was away from the place. That left only Mr Mason.

Well, he would just as easily blame God for setting light to his fields as he would have John Mason.

But he wasn't going to let this matter rest, for likely the same one who had caused the fire had set the trap for the cattle; and once having started, God knew what he would do next. So he was going to the Justice.

In the kitchen he said as much to Annie; and she agreed with him, saying, 'Aye, well somebody wants bringin' to boot. Apart from the field, there's that lad's face. To my mind, somebody got a big gliff when they were doing their handiwork, and thought to finish him off. And they could have, an' all. By the way, I've had to burn his clothes; and the bit of hair he's got left was running with them.'

'Running with what?'

'Dickies, of course. He had lain in that hovel of the Rileys, hadn't he? Well, you only need to put your nose in the door of one of those shanties and the dickies, lice and bugs come out to meet you. You'll have to buy him a new rig-out, at least coat and pants. But when you're at it, you could throw in a couple of shirts, 'cos as he stood he had only one on his back and one off it.'

'Anything else you can think of?'

'No, not at the minute, but you owe him that.'

'Huh!'

He walked from her, out of the kitchen and up to the bedroom.

Fanny had the child at her breast; and he pulled a chair to the side of the bed and watched his daughter feed; and he didn't speak until Fanny, laying the child to her side, said, 'What do you intend to do?'

'I told you. I'm going to the polis. Let them deal with it, because I've racked my brains and I can't think of anyone I can lay it on, not round about, anyway.'

'Have you thought of the boy?'

'Yes; yes, I have; and that's why I'm doing it.'

125

'When you mention his name they will likely question him.'

'Of course.'

'What if it should reach the papers, Ward, and that man from whom he ran sees it? The local papers probably get as far as Durham, and it was from some farm near there that he ran away.'

'I see what you mean.'

'You could change his name, and instil into him why you're doing it. It's for his good. And yet he once said to me that that was all he had, his name.'

'Well, what shall I say it is?'

'You could give him mine . . . McQueen. Anyway, from what I understand, Annie tells me that some people think we are related, because we came on the scene at the same time.' She did not smile when making this statement; and he, taking her hand, patted it as he said, 'I'll say it's Carl McQueen. Sounds a good name, one he shouldn't object to.'

When her eyes moistened, he said quickly, 'Now stop it. You are not to cry any more. Think of her' – he pointed to the child lying on the patchwork quilt – 'and remember, the more you worry the longer you will have to stay in bed.'

She now brought the hand that covered hers up to her breast and, pressing it tight, she said, almost in a whimper, 'I'm afraid, not for myself, but for you. What will they do next?'

'Nothing. Nothing, my dear. Once they know it's in the hands of the polis, that will scare them. You know, in a way they are sort of proud of the village and its good name, and so they don't like intruders, and for them the polis are intruders. Probably we all have something to hide.'

There was a pause before she said, 'No; no, they certainly don't like intruders, not of any sort.'

He could give no answer to this, but he bent forward and kissed her; then he went hastily from the room, thinking, Yes, she is right. They don't like intruders of any sort. Someone was determined to make him pay for the one he had brought in.

*　　*　　*

126

Two days later there was a report in the *Newcastle Journal*. It was headed: Outrage on farmer. And the journalist went on to prove his powers of imagination in describing the blazing cornfield and the intruder who must have been intent on killing Farmer Gibson's young farmhand, Carl McQueen, who was now suffering from severe concussion and with his face utterly distorted, having been banged repeatedly against a tree trunk. And this wasn't the first time that Farmer Gibson had been the recipient of village spite: not so long ago his cattle had been nobbled. There must have been a reason for these actions, the journalist went on; but as yet he had not been able to fathom it, as the villagers themselves were all tight-lipped.

The villagers were not tight-lipped in the inns, nor in the grocery shop, the butcher's, the cobbler's, nor the baker's. Even Fred said it was a mistake to call in the polis; in the end they would have found out who it was. As for neighbouring gentry, Colonel Ramsmore had suggested it was the outcome of a lad tampering with matches and tobacco, having a sly smoke behind the wall. When the state of the boy's face had been pointed out to him, he had blithely come back with, Oh, that could be explained by the young fellow's climbing the tree; then slipping and falling on to the top of the stone wall. Those copings were pretty sharp. Perhaps it was indeed Gibson's own boy who was the arsonist.

When this version was spoken by the man who was in all senses Lord of the Manor, well, said the villagers here and there, there could be something in it. And wasn't Ward Gibson's wife called McQueen before he married her? Now that was funny, wasn't it?

However, the overall version was, let them wait and see what the polis did. But those friendly towards Ward Gibson hoped that the polis would get the fellow before Ward did, for if they didn't, then the village would definitely be in the papers; and not only the local ones, because they remembered what Ward had said on the night of the fire.

As it happened, nothing emerged from the enquiries, and Ward soon found he had other problems to deal with.

4

Fanny was slow in regaining her physical strength, and so it was two months later when the baby was christened Jessie Flora Gibson: Jessie, after Ward's mother, and Flora, after Mrs Killjoy. Frank Noble had taken the service in the little chapel in the Hollow; and the children of the Hollow had waited outside to receive the christening piece. The contents of the christening piece, so named, held whatever the family could afford, be it sweetmeats, a piece of silver, or even just a copper. It should happen that Patsy Riley had placed herself determinedly at the head of the queue and so received the bag from Ward. And, as primed, she said, 'Health an' wealth an' all things good fortune bring to it.'

Present at the christening tea were, except for the actors and Mrs Boorman, those who had sat round the table at the wedding feast. Mr and Mrs Killjoy were present, and of course their family who, on this occasion, had been relegated to the barn under the care of Carl, and following the tea, they weren't brought back into the house to show off their tricks. There were two reasons for this: first, Mr Killjoy was not at all well; and secondly, an unusual altercation took place at the end of the tea between Charlie Dempster and the Reverend Frank Noble. It came about when Jane Noble happened to remark that she was glad to see Patsy Riley get the christening piece, and Charlie came back promptly with, 'Well, here's one that wasn't glad to see her get it, missis, for she's a scamp, that one, leading the others rampaging around,

128

picking up things they oughtn't to. Been round my backway. If I'd caught her I'd have wrung her neck. She should be where her dad is at this minute, doing time,' which caused Frank to come back at him with: 'Now, now, Charlie, be fair. Riley got into a fight, and, after all, he was just defending his own.'

'Got into a fight, you say, Parson? Are you for them? Those Feenians comin' over here blastin' an' bombin' an' murderin' the gentry; all under orders from that man Parnell. Scum he is, lowest of the low. Riot-rousers.'

'Now! now! Charlie; you've got your facts wrong.' He didn't add, 'again', but went on, 'Parnell, let me tell you, is of the gentry, born and bred; all he is doing is fighting for the Irish poor, and if he was an Englishman fighting for the English poor, such as the factory workers, the miners and such, he'd be praised as a hero.' Frank was tactful at this point not to mention farm labourers.

'You're damn well on his side; and on theirs an' all, that lot in the Hollow. Of course, you live next to 'em, that's why, likely.'

'It isn't because I live next to them,' said Frank quietly now; 'it's simply because I read history: I see two sides of this question. Have you asked yourself why so many Irish come over to this country? It's because they're starving; and they were brought low through the rents and taxes of the English landlords over in their country. And I would add this,' said Frank, getting a little heated now, 'if this was just a matter of politics it would soon be settled, but the main trouble is religion and bigotry. Yes, bigotry, believing that, there being only one God, He is for you, and you alone. Bigotry, I say again. And you needn't go any further than your own village, which is rife with bigotry.'

Seeing the look on Fanny's face, Ward put in quickly and on a false laugh, 'I'll always remember this day, and we'll talk about it to Jessie when she's grown up, won't we?' He reached out and took hold of Fanny's hand. 'We'll tell her that our two friends, the parson and the blacksmith, almost came to blows, and it was a good job the argument didn't take place in the forge, else you, Frank, would have been a gonner.'

129

This caused general laughter around the table, and Frank, looking now at Charlie, said, 'I'm sorry, Charlie. I lost my head. And as Ward's just said, I could, couldn't I, literally have lost my head had I been in the forge.'

But Charlie wasn't to be placated so easily and, his big head wagging from side to side, he said, 'I still don't know, Parson, how you can be on their side after Mike Riley busting that fellow's jaw.'

'Well,' said Frank, with a broad smile on his face now, 'what would you do if someone called you a pig-nose Paddy? and to that added, "Do you push the pigs out of your bed to let your wife in?" I can tell you what, Charlie, I'd have had a go meself if that had been said to me.'

'Sticks and stones may break me bones, but words won't hurt me.'

At this childish retort, Fred and his father and other men at the table laughingly shouted him down.

Mr and Mrs Killjoy were the last to leave; and it was while Mr Killjoy was outside gathering up his family ready for the journey back to Newcastle in the brake that Mrs Killjoy, already dressed in hat and cape, suddenly took Fanny by the hand and led her unhurriedly back into the sitting-room, and there in a mumbling whisper she said, 'I must tell you. I promised him I wouldn't, but I must. He's not long for the top. We did our last turn a fortnight ago. My heart is heavy, Fanny, so heavy.'

'Oh my dear. My dear.' Fanny was now embracing her friend as far as her arms would go around her, and exclaiming rapidly, 'Why didn't you tell me before? Oh, you must stay, you mustn't go. We can look after him. There's plenty of room. There's . . . '

'Quiet, dear. Quiet. Now we've been through all this, Mr Killjoy and I, and it is his wish that we stay with Mrs Boorman. She has been good to us all over the years, and she understands us. And, of course, our family. We had intended to stay there in any case while we were looking around for the cottage. But he'll never live in a cottage now. Don't . . . don't cry, my dear, else he'll be angry. No. No, I mustn't say that; he has never been angry with me; nor even

130

vexed. Everything I have done has been right in his eyes, for he was so grateful that I chose him, and I was more than grateful that he chose me, because we were two oddities, despised in different ways for our bulk, or lack of it; but no two people have been happier than we have. And for this I thank God; and now we both say His will be done . . . Oh, please, my dear, don't . . . don't. As he said, when he goes I will still have the consolation of the family and you, though Biddy and Rose are getting on, and their death, too, has to be faced. But from the moment we are born a day is regularly knocked off our life, whether the number is written long or short. Oh, there he is now.' She gently pushed Fanny away from her, saying briskly now, 'Dry your face. Come, dry your face. Oh dear! If he sees you like that he'll know in a moment. Go on, fetch the baby down; and you can hide your face in hers. Quickly now.'

She had already turned and was walking towards the door, calling loudly, 'I can hear you, Mr Killjoy. I can hear you. And my family too.'

In the yard, Billy was in the driving seat of the brake, and behind him the dogs were barking their heads off while jumping up at the door of the brake to receive Carl's last patting.

When a strict word came from Mr Killjoy, they scrambled on to the seat and sat quivering with pleasure as Ward helped their mistress up beside them.

Annie now called to Mrs Killjoy, 'Come back soon, please,' to which Mrs Killjoy replied, 'I will. I will, me dear . . . with pleasure.'

As for Mr Killjoy, he looked towards Fanny, who was slowly approaching him across the yard and, hurrying towards her, he kissed her on the cheek as he said, 'Bye-bye, my love. Be seeing you soon.'

She could not answer him, but she took one hand from holding the child, and gripped his; then she stayed where she was, not joining with Ward, Annie and the boy in waving goodbye; but as soon as the brake had disappeared from sight, she turned hurriedly to go into the house; and there, Ward and Annie found her sitting in the kitchen on

131

a straight-back chair, rocking the child back and forth, the tears once again running down her face.

'What is it? What is it?' Ward was on his hunkers before her, and Annie to the side of her.

After a moment, haltingly, she told them what she had learned about her dear Mr Killjoy.

When she had finished, neither of them made any immediate remark; but presently Annie said, 'When he goes you must have her here, 'cos as you've always said, ma'am, she's been like a mother to you.'

When Ward made no comment on this suggestion, Annie looked at him, and she said, 'She needn't stay in the house. Well, you wouldn't want that tribe of dogs in the house; but there's always the cottage next door to us. It's been empty these many years, but it's still dry; just wants airing. It's got a good flue. I remember that much about it: it doesn't smoke like ours. Well, what do you say?' She was looking straight at Ward; and his non-committal answer was, 'We'll see.' Then taking Fanny's arm, he said, 'Come on, dear, and put the child down and rest a while. It's been a busy day.' And as he left the kitchen he would not have been surprised had Annie called after him, 'I can read your thoughts,' because he was recalling the look on her face when she had put it to him with the words, 'Well, what do you say?'

He liked Mrs Killjoy; he'd always feel indebted to her, for if it hadn't been for her, Fanny wouldn't be his now. But that was not the point: Fanny was his, and his only, and the thought of her sharing her affection at close quarters with anyone else was at the moment unbearable to him. He knew that she loved him, but how could he measure her love against his own? His feeling for her was more than just love, it was a burning passion that he had to control. And there were times when he was even jealous of the attention she gave to the child, which, he knew, was a kind of madness. But there it was, he wanted her for himself, for himself only: he wanted her every thought, every feeling to be directed towards him; and even then it wouldn't be enough.

There were times when he questioned his feelings for her. Was this possessiveness normal? He could give himself no

132

answer, because he had no-one or nothing with whom or with which to compare it; he only felt sure that for as long as he lived the feeling would not lessen; nor would it increase, for he couldn't see any other form that it could take: she was the centre of his life and the pivot around which he revolved. Yet never, never, not once did he wish that this thing had not happened to him. Even when they had maimed his cattle and burned his crops, no thought of his had touched her with blame for having come into his life. But now that she was in it, there was in him something that demanded her entire devotion. Her attention to Carl had more than once annoyed him and had made him sorry he had ever taken on the boy. But when the same feeling had been directed against his own child he had said to himself, Steady on! But the command was equivalent to trying to curb a stallion with a donkey rein, for the stallion in him was out of control, except in one way: he never roughly overrode her body, for in his arms she appeared a fragile thing. Yet he was constantly aware there was a strength in her beyond his control. It was a spiritual strength that at times made him fearful, because he could never understand it. Nor could he face up to the fact that what he lacked was sensitivity.

After he had made her comfortable on the couch, she said, 'What do you think about Annie's suggestion?' to which he could, or would, only answer: 'Well, we'll have to leave it to Mrs Killjoy, won't we?'

It happened that, after all, Ward had no need to worry about Mrs Killjoy's coming to live with them, or near them. Mr Killjoy died on 2 January 1888, and was buried three days later amid a storm of sleet, snow and piercing wind.

It was the custom that no woman should attend a funeral; therefore, besides Ward and Billy, only Harry Bates the fiddler and Mr James Wilson Carter the Shakespearian actor, who happened to be engaged in the town at the time, were in attendance, Mrs Killjoy and Fanny meanwhile awaiting their return with Mrs Boorman in this lady's sitting-room.

From the moment the coffin left the house, Fanny had been unable to suppress her tears, and Mrs Boorman, too,

133

had cried, but Mrs Killjoy's face remained quite dry. As Mrs Boorman later remarked on the quiet to Fanny, how strange, indeed very strange, it was that she had never shed one tear since Mr Killjoy had breathed his last breath, not one sign of it; but very likely, she had added, she had cried inside.

It was some time after the four men had returned and been warmed with glasses of whisky, and had sat down to a hot meal of beef stew and dumplings, that Ward found himself alone in the sitting-room with Mrs Killjoy and Fanny, and Mrs Killjoy was saying quietly but firmly in answer to Fanny's statement that she must come and live with them, that everything was already arranged: the idea of a cottage now was out of the question; nor had she any intention of imposing herself on her two good friends; but there had been an arrangement struck between her third friend, Mrs Boorman and herself. Mrs Boorman was alone in the world, except for her fleeting visitors, and over the years an understanding friendship had grown between them, and she had now offered to share her home with her, and of course her family. And she had added, 'Where would I get anyone else who would understand my family as Mrs Boorman has done?' And when Fanny put in, 'Oh, my dear Mrs Killjoy, we would. You know we would.'

'Yes, I know you would, my dear,' Mrs Killjoy hastened to assure them, 'but have you consulted your cows and your own dogs, not forgetting your sheep?'

At any other time this would have been the cue for loud laughter, but neither Ward nor Fanny smiled; but Ward, looking at Fanny, said, 'She's right, you know; she's right.' Then turning to Mrs Killjoy, he added, 'But that won't stop you visiting us often, will it?'

'Oh no, my dear. I shall make it my business to come and see you as often as possible.'

As Fanny again embraced the bulk of her dear Mrs Killjoy, Ward gave vent to a long slow breath of relief, the while feeling satisfied with himself for having told Fanny only a few hours earlier that he would fall in with whatever plans she had for Mrs Killjoy's future.

It was as if, for him, a giant pair of arms were about to release their hold on his wife, that from now on she would continue to be all his. He conveniently forgot, as if it had never existed, the jealousy he felt for her attention to his own child, and, too, the irritation caused by the interest she showed in Carl.

Life would be plain sailing from now on, he told himself.

5

~

It was in March 1888 that their second child was conceived, and Fanny told Ward in May; but his reception of the news was not as she had expected.

'I'm sorry,' he said. 'You're not fit yet; you were just getting on your feet.'

'Don't be silly. And as for fitness, don't go by my height or weight; I feel strong inside.' She could have added, 'Spiritually,' but she didn't, because she knew that Ward did not understand that part of her; in fact, she was aware he was a little afraid of that in her which he couldn't reach. And so, smiling now and holding his face between her hands, she said, 'This time it will be a boy. And that will be a good thing, because Billy is getting on, you know, and you'll soon need another hand.'

'Shut up!' He held her to him. 'I don't care what it is, but what I care about is your health. And what is more, you have your hands full with that bouncer along the corridor there.' He nodded towards the bedroom door. 'She's going to be a whopper; she must put on a pound nearly every day.'

'Well, I said from the beginning she looks like you and takes after you.'

'God forbid!'

'Oh Ward. She's beautiful now, and she'll grow more so. You'll see.'

'What if it *is* a boy,' he said, 'and takes after you and isn't able to lift a pitchfork, never mind carry a bale of hay?'

136

'Well, in that case I'll send Jessie out on the farm and I'll keep the young Master Gibson in petticoats for as long as I can.'

They fell together, laughing; then, when softly he laid his lips on hers the kiss was broken by Annie's voice outside the door, saying, 'You've got a visitor, ma'am.'

When Ward opened the door, Annie said, ' 'Tisn't for you, 'tis for the missis.'

'Who is it?'

Annie was suppressing a broad grin as she said, 'She says to me her name is Miss Patsy Riley and she wants to speak to the missis. That's what she says. But she said it outside the back door, because I wouldn't let her in; I want to walk home to me cottage the night, not to be carried there by livestock.'

Fanny had now come on to the landing and she looked at Ward and said, 'Patsy Riley? The girl from the Hollow? What would she want?'

'I'll come down with you. We'll soon see.'

But just before they arrived at the back door, Fanny put her hand to stay Ward, and in a whisper said, 'Let me talk to her. Stay back.' And this was meant, too, for Annie.

When Fanny opened the back door, both amusement and pity rose in her at the sight of the young girl: the heart-shaped face with the deep black eyes had been washed in a style; the hands joined in front of her, they too had been washed in a style, for the nails were showing rims as black as her eyes; the hair beneath the grey straw hat that had once been cream-coloured and had likely adorned some prim miss showed the ends of her straight black hair. She was wearing a coat which also, originally, had been made for some child of a bigger stature and better class. The skirt of the dress, which fell just below her knees, had evidently seen many rough washes, and her thin bare legs disappeared into a pair of heavy boots which, from their size, indicated they must be cramping her toes.

Fanny leaned forward towards her, saying softly, 'Yes, my dear? You wanted to see me?'

'Do ya want any help, missis?'

'Help?'

'Aye. Mindin' the bairn, an' such. I'm good at mindin' bairns. I've seen to our squad. But me da cannot get set on; an' me ma's tried the fields, but they've got their own crews. An' so I thought, you see, missis . . .'

'But aren't you going to school?'

'Oh . . . Only half days now and then. Johnny, Mike and Shane go to keep the school-board man quiet; but Rob, he's stone pickin'. Not that that brings in much. You couldn't wipe your nose on what he earns.'

Fanny's lids were shading her eyes; her head was slightly drooped; she said softly, 'My baby is very young, and as yet I see to it myself.'

'I'm not nitty now. I've cleaned me hair. Look.' The hat was lifted with both hands from her head as far as the elastic band under her chin would allow. 'I did it with a small toothcomb an' washed it in the stream. It's not alive.'

What Fanny was saying inside herself now was, Dear Lord. Dear Lord. That a child has to come to this. She swallowed deeply, then asked, 'How old are you?'

'Nine. I'm the eldest now. There was three others, but they went with the cholera; an' there was another atween Rob 'n me. She hadn't the cholera; she was just puny.'

When a voice behind her said, 'Fanny,' she thrust a hand backwards and flapped it at Ward; then she said to the girl, 'Stay there a moment now.' She did not close the door on her, but, hurrying past both Ward and Annie, she went into the kitchen, and there, turning, she confronted them saying, 'I know what you're both going to say, but I'm going to say this: I mean to do something for that child. I don't know what, so you tell me.'

'I don't want her in this kitchen, ma'am.'

'Oh, Annie. She's desperate; she's in need of help, she's trying her best to be decent. You heard what she said.'

'Yes, ma'am, I heard what she said; but I know that lot. Let her in here in the daytime and she'll go back to that mucky kip at night, and she won't be able to keep herself clean. Don't you see, ma'am? she won't be able to keep herself clean.'

Fanny looked from Annie's straight face to Ward. 'Is there anything she can do outside; anything?'

'Oh, Fanny. What can she do outside, a lass like that?'

'Scrub. Sweep up. Help feed the animals . . . anything.'

'There's Carl to do that, and do you think he would put up with a lass in the yard?'

All of a sudden it was as if Fanny had put on inches: her back stiffened, her chin went up, and, looking straight at Annie, she said, 'You've been on for some time, Annie, about the old dairy. When it's been hard to place the milk, you said that if a hand could be engaged they could make their pay, and more, through butter and cheese.'

'Oh my God!' Ward turned from her, shaking his head. 'A dairy is the cleanest place on a farm, or should be, and you're proposing to put that lass in there? It's madness. No! No!'

'Yes, it's madness, ma'am. As he says, it's madness. Another thing: that churn needs some handling; it would take a young ox to turn it at times.'

'Well, let me tell you both' – Fanny looked from one to the other now – 'need makes people as strong as oxen. And she wouldn't go in there dirty; I would see to that myself: I'd strip her and clean her and dress her.'

'No, by God! you won't do any such thing, Fanny. You're forgetting what you told me not fifteen minutes ago, you're carrying another within you.'

'No. No.' It was Annie now who was shaking her head as she looked towards Fanny. 'You're carryin' again, ma'am, and you're proposin' to take on that thing outside? Oh, you must be mad indeed.'

Fanny's voice was low now, and even had a sad note in it when she said, 'Yes. Yes, there's part of me quite mad. But it's a madness I mean to carry through. Ward, I've never asked anything of you for myself; but now I'm asking this: I'm begging you to let me do this for that child.'

For answer, Ward went towards the fire, put his hand up and gripped the mantelshelf, then lowered his head, and all he muttered was, 'Oh, Fanny. Fanny.' And through the tone of his voice she knew she had won.

Turning now to address her other opponent, a much harder nut to crack, she said, 'Help me, Annie. I won't be able to carry it right through without your help, for I know nothing

139

about a dairy, or butter or cheese-making. But you do. And so that I can promise you she won't go home every night and come back lousy, I'll tell you what you could do. It's like this: you were willing that Mrs Killjoy should have the cottage next to you, so why not let Carl go into there; there's enough odds and ends in the attic to furnish a room. The girl could then sleep in the loft.'

'Dear Lord in heaven! I've never seen anything happen so quickly, not even a miracle. You've got it all cut and dried, ma'am, haven't you? Talk about a quick thinker.'

'When you want something very badly, Annie, and you know it's right, you know inside yourself that you've got to help that person, then God helps you to think quickly.' She glanced towards her husband's back; then back to Annie, before turning and almost running out of the kitchen.

In the yard, the girl was still standing as she had left her, and saying, 'Come with me,' Fanny led the way across the yard.

She pushed open a weather-beaten door next to the cowshed, and stood aside, indicating to the girl to enter, which she did with some caution, looking around her in a half-fearful, half-defiant manner.

It was a square room, with a long stone slab attached to one wall; along another was a table holding buckets and bowls and platters, and from their lack of brightness the utensils showed that it was some time since they had been used.

But in the middle of the room stood a large wooden churn, its wheel as big as that of a small dog-cart.

'This is a dairy,' said Fanny, 'where butter and cheese are made. Now, my dear, I cannot offer you a position inside the house, but I would like this room cleaned up and made very bright again.' She pointed to the utensils. 'Then we might start making butter and cheese. But, you see, to achieve this, everything must be very clean, spanking clean, and the person who will work in here must also be clean.' She paused, and looking down into the dark staring eyes and unsmiling face, she emphasised this: 'Very clean. You understand me, dear?'

'Yes, ma'am, I understand. An' I said me hair's clean, an' I'll wash.'

Fanny turned her head away for a moment before looking back at the girl and saying, 'I must be truthful to you: the persons who would do such work as required must be scrupulously clean . . . very, very clean, and must not be in contact with anyone who is . . . well, not so clean. If my husband employed you, I would have to see to your well-being and clothes and such; but the main thing would be you would have to sleep on the farm.'

The girl's voice came brisk now, saying, 'Not go back at night?'

'Yes, my dear, that's what I mean: you would have to stay here and only visit your people on leave days.'

'No, no. I couldn't do that, missis. Me ma wants me at night; the bairns are fractious. Nights? No, no, I couldn't.' The head was shaking violently now. 'An' me da. Well . . . well, we go rabbit . . . in'.' The word trailed off.

'In that case,' said Fanny, 'I'm sorry, my dear. But you go home and talk it over with your mother.'

At this, the girl looked round the room, and it seemed for a moment that she might be about to change her mind. But turning, she darted out of the door, leaving Fanny standing with her head bowed for the moment. When she did go into the yard it was to see the girl running into the distance beyond the farm gate . . .

'Well, that's a good job,' said Annie. 'You must have been mad, ma'am. I can tell you, if you had taken her on she wouldn't have got into my kitchen, 'cos if she had, I would've walked out. Have you ever seen those hovels they live in, ma'am?'

'Yes, I have seen them, Annie, and that is why I felt I must do something for that child.'

Ward's relief was the same as Annie's, although he didn't express it so plainly: 'And there was the school, you know. They have been on her to go to school. And yet from what I hear, they keep the whole tribe from the Hollow to one side of the class, and the other bairns are told not to play with them. There's been mothers up there complaining before today.'

141

As Fanny tugged at some straw poking out from a bale Ward had just stacked, she muttered, 'I could have seen to that, the same as Carl.' Then she almost jumped at the sound of her husband's voice, for he barked at her, 'By God! no; you wouldn't have seen to that. I put up with the lad and the time wasted; but I'll draw the line at another, and such another. If you had your way you'd have a school running in here shortly.'

As they stared at each other, his mouth opened and shut twice before he turned from her and beat his fist against the stanchion of the barn, saying, 'I'm sorry, dear. I'm sorry.'

She did not answer for a moment; but then going to him, she placed her head on his shoulder, saying, 'It's all right. I understand. And it's not the first time I must have tested your temper with my silly ideas.'

He turned towards her and, taking her by the shoulders, he repeated, '*I am sorry*, my love. I am. I never imagined anything could make me bark at you.'

She was smiling at him now, saying, 'Well, you have been proved wrong, and you were right.' But although she thought them, she did not add the words, 'I suppose.'

At this he bent his head over her until his brow touched hers and he whispered, 'I would do anything in the world for you, anything.' To which she answered, 'I know, dear. I know.'

It was his statement that was put to the test the following morning . . .

Ward, Billy, and the boy had been up since before five o'clock lambing, and Annie had left her cottage shortly after five to get the fire blazing and to attend two orphaned lambs that had been dumped into her kitchen. And she had just finished serving a number of long thick rashers of bacon, six eggs, dabs of white pudding and slices of fried bread on to the three plates which she now laid before her master, her husband and the boy, when Ward asked, 'Has she had her cup of tea?'

'Had her cup of tea!' Annie shook her head. 'This hour gone. And what's more, she's had her bite. But I wish she ate like you lot.' She now flicked her hand across the table. 'Anyway, for the last hour she's been at her books, preparing stuff, I suppose, to knock into that one.' And with her thumb she indicated Carl, and he, his mouth full, turned and grinned at her.

There was no more conversation until they had almost cleared their plates, when Billy said, 'Another night like this 'un and we'll need an extra hand. What do you say, master?'

'Oh, I don't know. And yet ... aye, perhaps yes. We'll see.'

At this moment came a knock on the back door. They all looked towards Annie, who spoke for them, saying, 'And who's this at this time in the mornin'?'

'Well, until you go to the door you won't find out, will you?' Ward said to her. And she flounced out of the kitchen, only within seconds to flounce back again and to go and stand close to Ward, her face almost near his ear, and to say, 'You've got two visitors instead of one, an' they'll both be alive.'

He stared at her for a moment before rising; then he turned his gaze on Billy as if to confirm his thinking, before slowly walking from the kitchen and through the boot-room, where stood Mike Riley and his daughter Patsy.

'Mornin', master.'

Ward's voice was a low mutter as he answered, 'Morning.' But then in a clearer tone he asked, 'What can I do for you?'

'Well 'tis like this, master: your good missis, she gave this one here' – he nudged his daughter with his hip – 'the chance of a lifetime yesterda', an' the silly little bugger, what did she do now but turn it down 'cos she thought her ma couldn't do without her. Well, her ma's of the same mind as meself, she could do without her fine if it means a new life for her.' His voice now dropping to a low tone as if his daughter wasn't present, he said, 'Just for one of 'em to be given a chance, master, just one of 'em, 'twas like as if the good God hadn't forgotten us after all, for it seems to have been empty bellies an' cold nights ever since we settled here. But as I said to her, me missis, 'twas as if God was relentin' an' pullin' open a door in hell an' lettin' one of 'em out. I'm an ignorant man, master, like most of us down there, an' that

143

life suits some of 'em, but not all. Nothin' can alter for us elders, but for the youngsters, well, as I said, master . . . ' He now hunched his shoulders and spread his hands out, and as Ward stared at him, for a moment he saw the whole situation through Fanny's eyes, but only for a moment. He had a farm to run; he had two good servants who were more like faithful friends; taking on this strip of a girl who looked all bones and eyes would surely bring discord into the place, and hadn't he enough discord flooding in from the village?

'Good morning, Mr Riley.'

'Good morning, Patsy.'

Mike Riley looked at the slight form of the woman standing beside her husband and he smiled widely at her, saying, 'Good mornin' to you, mistress. A very good mornin' to you. I've just brought this 'un.' Again he indicated his daughter by a movement of his hip. 'She sees now that you are right, she should stay on the job. And, ma'am, it's up to you how often you let her home. If it's once in a month for an hour or so, or once in six, I'll understand. An' I'll say this, ma'am, you've got me thanks from the bottom of me heart. An' there'll come the day when she'll bless you an' all, won't you?' His hand went out and was placed gently on his daughter's shoulder, but she made no response, she just continued to stare at Fanny, and not without defiance in her look. Then her father, putting on his cap and pulling the peak to the side, addressed a definitely bewildered Ward, saying, 'If there's anyt'in in this world I can do for you, sir, I'm your man. 'Tis at liberty I am at the moment, so if you should need a helpin' hand, just call on me, sir. Anytime, night or day, call on me.' And with that he took three steps backwards before turning his glance on his daughter and in a soft voice saying to her: 'Ta-ra, girlo. Behave yoursel'. Remember the crack we had.' He stared at her one moment longer and it was evident that his lips were trembling before he turned and walked smartly away, leaving the girl looking after him, and Fanny and Ward looking at each other.

It was a week later and there was tension in the house, and it had touched every member of it, not least Carl.

The boy had been delighted with the news that he was going to have a cottage to himself; at least he was until the reason for it was put to him, which had been immediately after Mike Riley's departure.

'But she's dirty, mistress. They're lousy, all of them. They could keep themselves clean, but they don't, they're lousy.'

'It isn't their fault, it's the conditions. It's those awful hovels that they live in, and they haven't any money.'

'There's a stream; they could still be clean.'

She had taken his hand, saying, 'Carl, do this for me. Be kind to her. She needs the work: her family are in desperate straits; they go hungry.'

'The master gives them turnips, and he sent two sacks of taties.'

'People cannot live just on turnips and potatoes. And what your master sent them wouldn't have lasted long.'

'They all gang up down there and they steal.'

'Well, Carl, you've never been in a position where you had to steal. I don't want to remind you but I must now. If it hadn't been for the master's kindness when you were in dire need, where do you think you would have been now? So, I'm asking you to extend the same kindness to the girl by way of repayment in part. Because, you know, we can never repay a good deed, but we must keep trying.'

'Is . . . is she coming into the kitchen?'

'Oh, no, no. Her meals will be sent out to her. She'll eat them in the boiler room, where it is warm or in the barn or up in the loft, wherever she chooses. But no, she won't be coming into the kitchen.' She said this emphatically as if Annie were prodding her.

When she had told him what work she intended to give her, he was amazed and he brought out, with a wrinkled nose, 'She smells.'

'She won't smell when I'm finished cleaning her. And' – she had smiled – 'I'm not much bigger than her, am I? So she will adjust to my clothes.'

That was the first battle over. However, that had left two still to be won. One concerned the newcomer's wage. Ward had said a shilling a week.

Couldn't he make it two?

No, he could not. And it had been only by a great deal of self-control that he had not bellowed at her once more.

Even so, they had both known that the heated discussion with regard to the wage was but a small matter; it was the presence of the girl herself and the reason why she was there. This butter and cheese business; hadn't he enough to contend with?

But the third battle had been the hardest – this time coming in the form of a verbal attack from Annie, who made her feelings plain, not to Fanny but to Carl.

'I've told the mistress I'll not go near that girl to learn her anything: I'll pass on what I know to her herself, and then she can please herself how she instructs that one. In any case, by the time any butter comes out of that dairy it'll be rancid. An' to think of the mistress cleansin' that one, stripping her bare. I can tell you this for nothin', 'cos afterwards she'll have to do some cleansin' of herself on the quiet. She's tried to keep it dark, but different fuels give off different smells an' that what came from the boiler house was singed cloth, if I know anything. Oh, I've never in all me born days experienced anything like this; an' it all goes back to Parson Noble's door, if you ask me, because they would have been hounded out of that Hollow years gone if he hadn't come an' put his nose in, with his live an' let live patter. I'm all for live an' let live meself, but where is another question. And you, young Carl, keep your arm's distance from her. Her clothes might be clean and her body too, but you can't get nits out of her head in one, two, or three goes. They are stickers, are nits. Oh, I never thought I'd see the day when the mistress of this house got mixed up with that lot down there. Now the master's mother was the kindest body you'd ever come across, but would she have done a thing like that? No; no way. Send them down taties and such, but that would have been the limit. I don't know where it's gona end. I really don't.'

It didn't end, but it began for Annie two further weeks later. The dairy now spotless, she showed Fanny how long the milk should be left in the big trays for the cream to rise to the top; how to use the skimmer; then how the handle of the churn should be used, not jerked, but in a steady swing. And she had immediately exclaimed, 'But *you're* not turning it. It'll have you dead in a day. If that 'un's here to be a dairymaid, then let her be a dairymaid an' get at it.'

The progress made by the new dairymaid was related to Annie each evening during the respite between supper and the last round. At least it was brought out of Carl by tactful questioning. At first he did not seem reluctant to tell of . . . that one's progress. Then one evening, having taken her seat at the side of the fireplace, Annie said, 'Well lad, what's your news today?' But no answer was forthcoming. Carl simply bowed his head, which made her lean towards him, saying, 'Ah-ha! you've got something bad to tell me, haven't you?'

'No, no!' His head jerked up. 'Well, not really bad, no.'

'What d'you mean, not really bad? 'Tis about her, isn't it?'

'Yes; but . . . '

'Come on, no yes, buts. What's she been up to? I knew she'd get up to something sooner or later, and the mistress would be covered with shame for makin' a stand on her behalf. Oh, I knew it.'

'No, no; it isn't like that, Mrs Annie.'

'Well what is it like then?'

'She ain't eating.'

'What? Ain't eating? I send her a good heaped plateful out twice a day. I haven't been spiteful like that, no matter what I think. If she's got to turn that churn, she needs somethin' in her belly. I've sent out two good . . . '

'Yes; yes, I know you have, Mrs Annie. Well, it's like this. I took her dinner over one day during the week and I went back a few minutes after and her plate was clean.'

'She gollops, then?'

'No. No. I watched her the next day. The same thing happened. I'd seen her taking bits of paper from the waste heap and I wondered why. But I found out this morning. You know' – he looked down again – 'the mistress said she hadn't to be roused before six. And when I shout up the ladder, she generally shouts back, "All right", but this morning I was on

147

me way to the new piggeries. It must have just turned half-past and it wasn't really light, but the moon was still out and I felt sure I saw her going round by the big wall, and when I went to see I made her out running like a hare across the fields. And . . . and I followed her, near as I could, like, without her knowing. She went right over the bottom field an' all, and I stood at the side of the glass house and I could just make her out bending down at the railings. Then the next minute she came flying past. If she had put her arm out she could have touched me. And I waited until she was well away, then I went to the place she had been and I saw the little bundle of newspaper.'

He stopped now as if he were thinking, and his voice jerked his head up as he went on rapidly, 'I opened it: it was the meat and some of your carrots and taties, that was the day's dinner, and there was some crackling and a bit of pork, that was from yesterday. That's as much as I could make out. I bundled it up quick.'

They were now staring at each other in silence, and he watched her lean back in the rocking chair. She didn't rock herself, but her head fell back against the top bar and she bit her lip. Then she again startled him by bending forward and gripping his shoulder as she said, 'Now don't you repeat a word of this to the mistress. Do you hear me? Not a word, else she'll be clearing this kitchen to feed the whole tribe. But I've got to think about this. She can't do her work if she doesn't eat. And anyway, have you thought that she must have been in contact with one of them?'

'No' – he shook his head – 'I don't think she'd be in contact, I mean, she wouldn't be close. She's likely told one or other of them, likely the brother who's next to her, that if she got any bits she would leave them somewhere. I don't know. But now that she's clean I don't think she'd go near them . . . well, I think she would know better, because if she got dirty again even the mistress would give her up.'

'Oh, I don't know about that. The mistress is a very stubborn lady underneath that gentle skin of hers. And look what she's been asking you to do now, 'cos the master won't let her do it herself: pass on your lessons to her, hasn't she?'

'Yes, but I don't mind.'

'Well, you should mind; you're not paid to waste your time.'

'I don't waste me time, Mrs Annie. And anyway, the mistress said . . . '

Annie got to her feet now, saying, 'I know what the mistress says; she says more than her prayers and she whistles them. Oh, what am I saying? Look, I've got to think. I'll see about this matter later. Now, as I told you, not a word to anybody, else I'll ring your ear for you, both of them, until you think there's two bells in the church steeple.'

It was from this time that the discord in the house eased, and no-one other than those directly concerned knew what took place on the day the master drove the mistress into Newcastle and Annie confronted the dairymaid for the first time. The only result of this meeting was made plain to Carl when the slop buckets for the pigs were not so full of table scraps, and the dogs were given fewer meaty bones to chew upon.

The day came when the first ivy-leaved pat of butter was put on the kitchen table and Annie, reluctantly, pronounced it not bad.

So one more strand was worked into the pattern of their lives. And not only one, for on the day Billy took the first few pounds of butter into the market, a round of it was bought by Colonel Ramsmore's housekeeper. A fortnight later a note came from Lady Lydia of Forest Hall to say she would be obliged if they could supply her with two pounds of butter weekly, and also if they were disposing of any suckling pigs, could she be informed.

This benevolent order made even Annie say, 'Well, well! We're going up in the world, aren't we? 'Tis the country folk now coming to our door.'

But whatever Ward really thought, his only comment to Fanny was, 'This is Lady Lydia's doing, not the old fella's. He's of the type, know your place, man, and keep it. But as far as I can understand, she's go-ahead, and a very genial woman. I've glimpsed her a number of times and she looks as pleasant as her character. But there' – he had tweaked her nose – 'your butter business, my dear wife, is going to make a name for itself in the end.' And to this she had answered, 'Thanks to Patsy,' only to have him come back scoffingly, 'Oh yes, thanks to Patsy;' and then he added, 'You know something? That girl has never opened her lips to me in all the weeks she's been here. But her eyes speak for her.'

'And what do you think they say?' asked Fanny.

'Oh, I wouldn't know, but one thing I do is, she'll take some mastering when she grows up, that one.'

And Fanny, looking away from him, said softly, almost dreamily, 'Yes, she will . . . she will.'

On the 20th December 1888, Fanny's second child was born. It was a daughter and on looking down on her for the first time Ward exclaimed, 'She's the image of you . . . absolute image.' And his face bright, he picked up the child and held it to him and repeated, 'Just like you, the spitting image. We'll call her Angela. What about that? Angela.'

Fanny was too weary to make any comment, but she could see that her husband's reaction was different altogether from that which he had shown at the sight of his first child.

Jessie was now a bouncing and loving, happy child; but she had never seen Ward look on her as he was looking on this, his second daughter. And she was too weak at the moment to reason why she felt pained at the sight.

BOOK TWO

1896–1914

PART ONE

I

He was six feet tall, well-built and he carried no spare flesh. His hair was fair almost to whiteness and this was emphasised by his weather-tanned skin. His movements were lithe, as he unconsciously demonstrated when he jumped from the high seat fronting the farm wagon.

The farm wagon had built-up detachable sides, and so he bent over the tail-end of the wagon and lifted from it a basket full of shopping, two parcels, each wrapped in thin brown paper, and a slim book which he now pushed into the inner pocket of his coat. Then calling to the horse, 'Stay a while; I'll be back in a minute,' he hurried across the yard and into the farm kitchen.

And as he went to drop the packages on to the table, Annie's voice came from the scullery, crying, 'Don't put them there! I'm just about to bake. Leave them on the saddle.' Then she added, as she came into the kitchen, 'How did things go?'

'Quite well considering; butter and cheese holding, and the vegetables up quite a bit because of the drought. Where's the master?'

'Down in the lower field, I should imagine, seeing that the two Irishers do a better job on the fencing than they did afore.'

'Oh, they were put up all right; it was somebody in the farming business knew how to take them down. That was no kids' work.'

155

'Aye, I'm with you there. An' there's another thing I'll tell you, Carl, if the nigglin' business starts again in any quarter, it'll drive him round the bend. Since Mrs Killjoy's dog got it, I don't think he's had a complete night's rest. It's affecting the missis an' all. And Jessie's had one of her crying bouts again.'

'What for this time?'

'You ask me, I don't know. Oh yes, I do. What am I sayin'? But we won't go into that now. You had better get yourself changed and get your hand in, because I think it's going to be a heavy night for you. Billy's back went again this mornin'. And you know something? I never thought to hear my man say this place needs another hand. But he's right, it does, you know, 'cos you're doin' practically the work of two.'

'Oh, don't worry about me, Annie. I could go on for forty-eight hours; you know I have, without sleep.' He paused and smiled to himself as he said, 'Funny, that. If I have three hours straight off I'm as fresh as a daisy. But give me five and I wake up with a thick head as if I'd been on the beer the night before.'

'Did you get my wool?'

'Yes; I got everything you asked for.'

'An' I suppose, the lasses' taffy? Well, if I were you, if you can spare a minute, I would find Miss Jessie and give her hers first for a change.'

'What d'you mean, give her hers first for a change, Annie?'

'What I say, lad. Because she doesn't get put first much in this house nowadays. Perhaps you haven't noticed. He's not unkind to her. No, no. But he doesn't treat her like he does the young one. Right from the beginnin', from the first moment he saw her there was nobody else, because she took after the missis. He had a full-grown one and a young one and his first born was put aside. What am I talkin' about? Look, lad, you open parts in me that haven't any right to be spoken of.'

'I haven't said a word.'

'It isn't what you say, it's what you look, an' just standing there. Look, get out of my sight, will you?'

156

He went out, but not on a laugh. Annie was right about the master and the child, his first born. He himself had never seen him lift her up in his arms, or open his arms wide for her to run into, like he did with Angela. It was hard to believe that Angela was nearly eight years old, for she still had that elfin, babyish way and look about her; whereas Jessie, coming up nine, was sturdy, tall for her age but well built. And although she was quite pretty, she had none of the appeal of her sister. He unharnessed the horse from the wagon and put her in her stable, saying as he did so, 'Have a feed. I'll brush you down later.'

He now pushed open the door of the dairy and, taking a small paper bag from his coat pocket, he threw it towards the young woman who had turned from the bench, a wooden patter in each hand. Her face was bright and she smiled at him, crying, 'Oh, thanks, Carl.'

'Houghhound candy. It was a new batch, just made. She sells it out so quick. 'Tis a month since I managed to get any.'

Again she said, 'Thanks.'

'All right?'

There was a hesitation before she said, 'Yes; yes, all right.'

He stared at her over the distance, then hurriedly closing the door, he walked towards her.

'Something wrong?'

She turned her head to the side, her dark eyes shadowed as she said, 'I've had a do with Miss Jessie. I found her crying an' went to comfort her and she turned on me.' She pointed to her chin, saying, 'Her claws went in.'

Slowly he took her face between his hands and he said softly, 'Oh, Patsy. I'm sorry.'

She stared into his face, the image of which never left her mind day or night: his kindly eyes, his thin but shapely mouth, his beautiful hair. He was beautiful altogether to her. Never once since she had been in this service had he said a harsh word to her. The mistress was kind, the master was tolerant. Billy, too, was tolerant, even more tolerant, and Mrs Compton put up with her. But Carl, here, had been kind, understanding and thoughtful; and he had taught her so much, more than any of them in the house knew. The midnight hours with the books and the candle, learning not only how to spell, but where tea came from, and what happened to the coal when it went from the mines hereabouts. And she had even learned the name of the last prime minister, Mr Gladstone. And she remembered crying over the story of the babes in the Tower of London. She would have known nothing about these things if it hadn't been for Carl.

When he said, 'Do you know ... why she did it, I mean?' she answered, 'Oh yes,' and nodded her head. 'She was splattering that nobody loved her, and I understood how she felt.'

'Oh, Patsy.' His fingers moved up and down her cheek, but he didn't say, 'I love you, Patsy.'

Yet she felt that he loved her, but she also felt that she understood why he wouldn't speak: he had his way to make. He was well in with the family: he ate with them; he also sat in their sitting-room and talked to the mistress about what he called books, things that farmer's wives don't usually talk about. But then, the mistress wasn't an ordinary farmer's wife. In no way was she like a farmer's wife. She was delicate and learned and, as her da said, she was fey. Her da said she was the nearest thing to the Irish wee folk he had come across in this country: wasn't it proved when she could heal an animal? Yet she hadn't managed to heal the fat woman's dog last year. But then she hadn't much time, for the woman had whisked it away. Oh, that had been a day.

There was now making itself felt within her that strong feeling, that independent feeling, that feeling that told her at times not to bow her head to anyone. And she didn't, except to Carl. But he was different. Yet the feeling made her step back from him now, causing his hand to fall from her face, and it gave her tone a dignity as she said, 'Thank you very much for the candy.' Even to him, the feeling told her that she must never cheapen herself.

Carl was aware of this feeling. There were times when a cloud would fall between them, when he could neither

158

understand her nor reason why this should be. So now he turned about and went out of the dairy, saying, 'I'd better get changed. I've got a night's work ahead of me.'

On opening his cottage door he stopped abruptly, for there, sitting in his one easy chair, was Jessie.

She did not get up as he closed the door behind him, but said, 'I know Mammy said I hadn't to come into your house, but I don't care if I'm scolded: I feel awful; I've been awful all day.'

'Look, Jessie,' he said softly, 'I'm in a hurry. I've got to get changed for work. There's a lot to be done. Now if you'll go over to the house and . . . '

She was now on her feet, her voice high, and crying, 'Don't be like all the others, telling me to go some place else. Everybody else tells me to go some place else. Nobody loves me. Nobody. Nobody.'

'Now that's silly. Of course people love you.'

She was standing close to him now, her head back, looking up at him as she demanded, 'Do you love me?'

'Of course I love you. I love you both. I've told you all along I love you because you were the first baby I held. Of course I love you.'

'Not like you love Patsy Riley though, do you? Not the same as you love her.'

'Now, Jessie, stop that. I don't love Patsy Riley, well what I mean is . . . '

'You don't love Patsy Riley? She thinks you love her. I scratched her face, do you know that? I scratched her face. I told her I would do it again if she didn't stop pestering you.'

'Patsy doesn't pester me.' His voice was harsh now. 'You are the one who pesters, Jessie, not Patsy. Now look—' He stopped as her head drooped and the tears flowed down her face, and he watched them drop from the end of her nose. He sighed deeply, then went and put his arm around her shoulders, saying, 'There now, there. You must get this silly notion out of your head that nobody loves you. We all love you.'

Her shoulders shaking, her head wagging from side to side, she gulped out, 'Oh no. No. Daddy doesn't love me. He doesn't know I'm here. The only one he sees is Angela. It's always Angela. He cuddles Angela. He throws her up in the air.'

'Well now, well now, he'd have a job to throw you up in the air, because you're a big girl.'

She pulled herself away from him and, almost shouting now, she said, 'Yes, I'm a big girl, and I'm ugly, and she is dainty and like Mammy. And Daddy loves them both, but he doesn't love . . . me! Do you hear? He doesn't love . . . me!'

Carl was silent. This was no eight-, coming on nine-year-old girl he was looking at; she was no child; her awareness of the lack of parental love had made her into an adult.

He put out his hand towards her, about to lie yet again to her, when she shrank back from him and stepped towards the door, saying, 'I know what you're going to say and I don't believe you.' And with this, she pulled open the door, only to give vent to her surprise through an audible gasp as she was confronted by her father.

Ward's voice came deep from within his throat, almost as a growl, as he said, 'What have I told you about pestering? You're in for a spanking, my girl.' And he grabbed her by the shoulder, swung her round and brought his hand across her buttocks in no light slap; in fact her feet almost left the ground; then he thrust her forward, yelling after her: 'Get into the house this minute!'

Turning angrily on Carl, he cried, 'You've got to stop soft-soaping her. She's not a little child any more. She's getting out of hand.' Then, without waiting for any defensive reply, he went on, but in a lower tone, 'How did things go?'

'Very well. Prices held, vegetables went up; but that's because of the scarcity.'

Ward stepped over the threshold and into the cottage and there he dropped wearily into the chair so recently vacated by Jessie and as though he were having to force his words through his teeth now, he said, 'It's starting again.'

'More railings down?'

'Worse than that. Mike Riley just told me. He found two rabbits last week. They had been poisoned; their bodies were bloated.'

'Where did he come across them?'

'Just on the borders of the Hall grounds, next to our bottom field. But rabbits don't die instantly. And anyway, there's nobody going to do anything against the colonel.'

'Oh, I don't know so much. There's a couple of the fellas down in the Hollow could have it in for him, because he's threatened them with the gun.'

'Yes; but that lot down there wouldn't go in for poisoning. Don't you see? They'd be killing off their source of meat?'

'Yes. Yes.' Carl nodded now. 'There's that in it. Do you think we'd better move the flock up?'

Ward rose to his feet now, saying, 'I don't know what to think. If it isn't trouble outside, it's trouble inside. I must go now and see to that daughter of mine. She's causing her mother distress, and I won't have it.' And he looked straight at Carl while he added, 'And don't let her in here again.'

'I didn't let her in; she was here when I got back. And . . . and master, I'm going to say this, I feel bound to. She . . . she acts as she does because . . . well, she needs comfort.'

'Comfort? She has every comfort in the . . . '

'Not that kind of comfort; she needs loving as . . . as much as Miss Angela does. You see, she's different.'

Ward's head was nodding now. 'Yes, of course she's different from Angela. She's been a trouble since she was a baby, if she ever has been a baby. Can you recall the time we had with her from she was two years old, crying and slapping out? Oh, don't talk to me about caring and love.' He now stamped out of the room; but then called from the road, 'Put a move on! Bill's back's gone again. He can't see to the milking.'

Carl stared at the open door for a moment; then he went to it and actually banged it closed. It was the first protest in any way he had made against his master . . .

Fanny was sitting on the edge of her elder daughter's bed in the girls' room in the attic. She was holding her close and saying, 'There now, there now. He didn't mean it. But you know, you've been told you mustn't pester Carl. Nor be rude to Patsy.'

'He . . . he thrashed me.'

161

'Your daddy wouldn't thrash you. He smacked your bottom. I smack your bottom, and Angela's too.'

'Oh no, you don't, Mammy.' The tear-drenched face was lifted now defiantly. 'You smack me harder than you smack Angela. You never smack Angela, only in play.'

Fanny sat staring at her daughter, and thinking much the same as Carl had done a short time earlier, when he had been confronted with someone who should have been a little girl but was a little girl no longer, at least in her mind. But in her own defence Fanny knew that all the love she could give this child would not compensate for that lost through her father and the complete absorption which he shared between herself and her young daughter. Oh, how she had wished over the years that Angela hadn't been born a replica of herself, not only in looks but in disposition, too. And in her mind, she still wondered in amazement at Ward's constancy towards her, and for which he'd had to pay dearly over the years; just as she herself had paid, too, in the loss of the deep friendship and love of her dear Mrs Killjoy. The scene in the yard would never be erased from her mind. Mrs Killjoy had lost two of her family, Beatty and Rose, one of them through advanced age, the other through no known reason except that it had been while on a visit here. And she had mourned them as much as she had Mr Killjoy, perhaps more, because they were her children. On this particular day, she had brought Charlie and Sophia on a visit, and when they were ready to go only Charlie could be found. Everyone joined in the search and it was Patsy Riley who found her. Her pitiful whining had attracted her to a shallow ditch out of which the little creature was trying to climb on three legs.

When Patsy had carried her back into the yard it was found she had two pellet shots in her thigh, and, in the words of one of the Hollow men, 'The fat woman howled like any banshee at the sight of her wee creature.'

Fanny still remembered holding the soft little body of Sophia, aiming to alleviate her pain, which she apparently succeeded in doing, for the little dog ceased whining as Ward extracted the pellet from its leg. Then to her amazement, when the dog's leg was bandaged and it once again

162

lay in the arms of its mistress, Mrs Killjoy not only ceased her wailing but addressed her in a voice that all could hear, crying, 'I rue the day I was the means of bringing you to this house, for there's evil in it, and all about it. And I might tell you that Mr Killjoy said the same thing. He prophesied to me that Ward would have to pay for you till the day he died. That was after you found your dear Pip missing. And what had happened to him? Shot dead. Yes, there is evil about this house.' And in the ensuing shocked silence she had mounted the trap. And so she had gone out of their lives.

She recalled now the scene when they had found Pip. He, too, had been shot with an airgun, but in the head. However, what was worse, he had been found by Phil Steel, one of the colonel's yardsmen. And Ward's reaction had been to tear over to the Hall and accuse the colonel of shooting his wife's dog. The colonel, of course, always peppery, said he hadn't been out shooting for days; but if Ward didn't get off his land he would start immediately.

This altercation had resulted in a surprise, for the following day Fanny had a visit from Lady Lydia herself. She had called to say she was so sorry that the little dog had died and also to assure Mrs Gibson that neither the colonel nor any member of the staff had been out shooting for days. She had gone on to praise Mrs Gibson's two fine daughters, and how like her mother the younger one was. And wasn't it strange, the characteristics of children? There was her own son whose features were like those of his father, but whose character was more like her own: he didn't like shooting of any kind. And confidentially, she had added with a smile, this angered the colonel, for being an army man, shooting was his business, so to speak. But having a son who didn't enjoy killing of any kind caused a clash of temperaments.

Fanny recalled how she had agreed on the last point with Lady Lydia. And after she had thanked her Ladyship for being kind enough to call, that lady had assured her she had been desirous of making her acquaintance for a long time, and she hoped that now she would be permitted to call, and they had drunk a cup of tea together in the sitting-room.

163

And so it might have been thought that when the news got through the village that Lady Lydia was visiting Ward Gibson's wife, it would have been the signal for all further petty irritations to cease. The reverse, however, was the case. If anything, they increased: gates were opened, cattle strayed, stays were pulled up, even gaps were made in drystone walls, the incidents always being perpetrated at night time. It was impossible to keep watch on every yard of fencing or walling all round the place. And when Ward exploded his chagrin to Fred or to his father, or to the blacksmith, demanding almost if one or the other could give him an inkling who was at the bottom of this, he would be answered simply by a silent shaking of the head. It was as if they were tired of his ranting, or, as he put it to Billy, they knew who it was and they wouldn't let on. And to this, Billy had replied quietly, 'Aye, likely.'

At times Fanny had great difficulty in hiding her concern from Ward, for not only was she physically weak, but also her spiritual resistance seemed to have lessened. Especially since the episode with her dear friend, because Mrs Killjoy's last words were forever in her mind. She, too, was being made to wonder if it would have been better for all concerned had she never come to this house, had never met Ward, and so had never experienced a man's overpowering love, and for some time now she had faced up to the fact that it *was* overpowering. Her returning love, measured against it, was as something minute; and she knew it wasn't good or healthy to be held in such high esteem and made to feel that she was incapable of any mean thought or action. To be put on such a plane caused her to feel less than human. However, she knew she could never make her husband understand this, for he saw her as being apart from all others.

'Daddy doesn't love me, not even a little bit.'

Fanny's voice was stern now as, wagging her finger at her daughter, she said, 'You must not say that, Jessie. It isn't true.'

'Oh, Mammy.' The girl now rose from the bed and, standing with her face on a level with her mother's, she leant towards her and asked pointedly, 'Why do you lie like Carl?

164

He lies all the time. He says he loves me but he loves Patsy better. Although he says he doesn't love her, he does.'

'Be quiet, Jessie. Be quiet this minute. All this silly talk about love. Now it has got to stop. Let me tell you something.' She now reached out and gripped her daughter's arm. 'If Carl loves Patsy and Patsy loves him, it is quite a natural thing, because they are grown up. This happens when people are grown up. But you are not grown up and you shouldn't be talking like you do.'

'He said he didn't love her.'

'What did you say?'

'Carl, he said he didn't love her. I asked him.'

'You had no right to ask him. I am finding you a naughty girl today, Jessie, and it is upsetting me. How do you expect people to love you when you are so naughty?'

'I am naughty because nobody loves me and never has.'

Fanny closed her eyes. That the child should be thinking like this, talking of love in this way, was worrying. It was as if she were grabbing at it, wanting to tear it out of people. She herself had always shown her love. But then it wasn't her love she needed, it was her father's love, or Carl's, a male love. She would have wished to refute any such thought connected with her daughter; yet, she knew that, deep within her mind, it had been born some time ago.

2

~~~

It was a week later and there was no sign of the irate, love-starved girl as Jessie forked some of the last hay upwards to her father, near the top of the haystack at the end of the yard. She didn't even seem to notice that Patsy was working near Carl, straightening out the ropes attached to the tarpaulin that would eventually cover the stack. The change had come on Thursday evening after her father had said to her, 'How would you like to stay off school tomorrow and help me get the last of the hay in?' He had not said, 'Help us,' but 'Help *me*.'

For a moment she had been unable to answer, but then she had said, 'Oh yes, Daddy. That would be lovely.'

And so on the following morning there was no need for either Billy or Carl to drive the sisters to school, or later in the day, to meet them coming out, which had been the protective procedure since they had started at the village school. So, all day yesterday Jessie had raked and carried hay. Angela had been there, too, but not accomplishing half the work her sister was showing she could do. And later, it had been a merry evening meal.

This morning she would have gone out before breakfast if Fanny hadn't insisted that she eat a good meal, reminding her that there was a hard day's work before her, the while thinking how simple the solution had been with regard to her daughter's state of mind: her appealing to Ward to show his daughter a little personal attention, which he could do

166

unobtrusively by suggesting the girl should have a day off school in order to help in the hay field. She knew he would not immediately see the point of it all, but he complied with her wishes, even acting the part he didn't feel. Yet, last night, he had to admit that the effort he had made had brought results, for it was a long time since he had seen his daughter so merry and talkative, at least in his company.

It was when the work was completed that Annie came into the yard, saying, 'You all look like dustbins and it'll be another half hour, I should imagine, afore you get yourselves cleaned up an' ready for a bite to eat, so why not have it like you are, outside, eh?'

It was the two girls who cried at once, 'Oh, yes! Annie. Yes. We can have it in the meadow.'

'Oh, that's too far to carry the stuff,' said Annie. And at this Ward shouted back to her, 'Well, you don't expect us to sit on the yard or in the stubble fields, do you?'

'That's up to you,' she said cheerfully. 'And it'll be all hands to the pumps. I'll pack the baskets; but you're not getting me across there, for me legs are worn off to the knees as it is.'

'Aye, poor soul, it's her age,' and this coming from Billy caused a gale of laughter.

And there was more laughter when the girls went through the unusual procedure for them of washing under the pump; at least, sluicing their faces and hands.

In the kitchen the baskets were handed out to Carl and Patsy and the girls carried the cans of cold milk and equally cold beer; Ward brought the rugs from the blanket-box in the hall and a large cushion from the sitting-room, the latter for Fanny's benefit.

As he was passing through the kitchen, Annie said, 'Here! they forgot the cloth,' and loaded him further with a large check tablecloth.

'Sure you'll not join us?' he asked her, and when she answered, 'Me head would like to but me feet are contrary,' he said, 'Well, that's your fault; you should put them up more. And don't tell me you haven't got the time. All right. All right.' He shrugged away what remark she was about to make and went out and followed the small cavalcade along by the side of the barn, down by the field that had been turned into a vegetable garden, past the glass house that Fanny had not used for the past two years and which he had now turned into a forcing shed for plants, and into the field that had lain fallow for a year and now should have been covered with lush green grass. But the heat had yellowed it, except where it was shaded by the wood that marked the beginning of Colonel Ramsmore's estate on this side of the Hall.

When Jessie's voice came to him over the distance, calling, 'Shall we lay it in the shade, Daddy?' he shouted back, 'Yes, of course, unless you want to cook. But wait, I've got the cloth.'

It was Patsy who, kneeling, spread the cloth and emptied the victuals from the basket; Fanny filled the mugs with either milk or beer, all but the last when, looking at Patsy, she asked, on a laugh, 'Milk or mild for you, Patsy?' And Patsy, smiling back at her, said, 'Mild, mistress, please; I've seen all the milk I want to today.'

'Oh, sour milk and rancid butter we'll be having from now on,' put in Billy, 'now she's taken to ale.' And with this he pushed Patsy none too gently so that she toppled on to her side, and Jessie, laughing, helped to pull her upright again, so that Carl was made to wonder at the change in the girl. What a difference from this time last week, for she looked so happy; it was like a small miracle.

After they had eaten bacon and egg pie, hard boiled eggs, crusty bread thickened with their own butter, and all had quenched their thirsts, in their separate ways they lounged in the cool shade of the trees: Ward lying stretched out alongside Fanny, who was sitting on her cushion, her hands joined round her knees and looking almost as young as her daughters who, too, were lying flat out on the grass; Billy had his back supported by a stake of the boundary fence, while Carl was resting on his elbow looking towards Patsy, who was sitting upright, her feet tucked under her. She was pulling a round stemmed grass between her teeth, her tongue licking at the white sap, looking to Carl like a picture he had seen hanging in one of the galleries in Newcastle. It was of a young Spanish girl in a red flowing gown. Patsy had no red flowing gown, but she was beautiful.

It was an idyllic scene. It was one of those moments they were all to remember, broken not by a human voice only by the sound of nature, a rustling of leaves from the wood and a drone of bees, with the 'zimming' of midges high up, portending still further fine weather. Then came a sound as if a small line of bees were parting the air and which ended on a cry from Fanny as something struck her temple and caused her to fall across Ward.

'What is it? What is it?' He was holding her as the others were rising to their feet.

She did not speak for a moment; then on a gasp, she said, 'Something . . . something struck me.' Her fingers were pressing at her temple, and Ward, on his knees now, raised her into a sitting position again.

It was Patsy who said, ' 'Tis a stone. Look!' She pointed to Fanny's skirt where, lying near the hem, was what appeared to be a large pebble.

Ward examined it as it lay on his palm. It was pointed at one end, flat at the other.

' 'Tis a catapult stone.' It was a whisper from Billy.

'What? God!' Ward thrust the stone into the pocket of his breeches, then looked along the fence that bordered the wood. And Carl was doing the same as he cried, 'They must be in the wood.'

'Get your mistress back to the house, Patsy. Help her, girls!' ordered Ward; then he was racing alongside the fence, with Carl running in the opposite direction, each looking for a place where he might get over the barrier of wired palings that fenced the boundary of the Hall, for in many parts the wire had become entwined between the many saplings, so forming an almost impregnable tangle.

Ward had to go to the very end of the field before he found a place over which he could climb. Then he was running through trees, zig-zagging here and there and stopping now and again to listen for running footsteps.

The woodland opened out abruptly into a narrow field, crossing which was the path leading, in one direction, to

169

the village and to the Hollow in the other, and bordering it on the far side was Morgan's Wood. Presently, while he was standing still, two running figures appeared on the path. One was swinging a can, the other had something dangling from his hand, something he could not make out from this distance. But they were the culprits, he'd bet, Michael Holden's grandsons. He'd had trouble with the young scamps before, jumping the walls and crossing right through the middle of his corn. By! when he got his hands on them. But he checked his thinking at this moment; surely, they couldn't have got that far in this short time; they would have had to cut through the Hall's private grounds. Well, they could have done that, and come out on to the path before it turned to the Hollow. Just wait till he got his hands on them.

He now turned as Carl's voice hailed him: 'Seen anybody?'

He returned to the fence, shouting, 'The two Holden youngsters.'

As Carl put his hand out to help Ward over the fence, he said, 'Oh, those two! They can use a catapult all right.'

Billy now arrived on the scene, saying, 'You said the Holden youngsters? Where did you see them?'

'Running down the path near Morgan's Wood.'

'That far? They'd have to be goin' some to have got from here to there in that short space of time, don't you think?'

'Those two rips have got wings on their heels. But by God! they'll need them if I get hold of them; another half inch and that stone could have put her eye out.'

The thought seemed to act as a spur for he now started to run, with Carl at his side . . .

Fanny was sitting in the kitchen holding a damp cloth to her temple and the girls and Patsy and Annie were standing around her. But she said immediately to Ward as he entered the kitchen, 'Now, now, it's all right. Don't make a fuss. Only,' she smiled now, 'I'll likely have a black eye in the morning.'

'You could have lost your eye.'

After a pause, she said, 'Well I didn't, and don't take it so seriously. It was someone's prank.'

'Someone's prank, be damned! And look, don't sit there. I think you should get upstairs and rest.'

'Oh, Ward.'

'Never mind "Oh Ward". Come on.' He pushed the others aside and drew her up, and as he led her from the room, Annie said, 'Nice end to a picnic party, if you ask me.' Then turning to Patsy, she went on, 'Does your lot down there use catapults?'

'No, our lot down there doesn't use *catapults*.' And the word was emphasised as if it had been fired from the instrument itself.

'Don't you speak to me like that, miss.'

At this, Patsy tossed her head and went from the kitchen with Annie's voice following her, saying, 'It's coming to something. By! that it is.' Then she, too, went from the kitchen and up the stairs and, after tapping on the bedroom door, she opened it, to be greeted by Fanny saying, 'Will you stop this silly man from making such a fuss, Annie?'

'If you can't stop him, ma'am, how d'you expect me to.'

'Shall we send for the doctor, Daddy?'

Ward turned to answer his daughter, but any derisive remark was checked by Fanny, saying, 'No, my dear. I don't need a doctor. Look, you and Angela go downstairs and see if there is any way in which you can help Patsy and Carl. You could get the chickens in; being so hot, they won't want to roost inside and who knows but Mr Fox may be passing by.'

Reluctantly, it would seem, the girls left the room, and as Annie followed them Ward pulled a chair up to the bed and sat down, saying, 'First thing in the morning I'm going into that pub, not for ale, but to tell Mike Holden to take his hand to those two devils of his.'

'But it may not have been them; surely, all boys use catapults.'

'Not with pointed flints as ammunition.'

'Well, tomorrow's Sunday, so leave it to the beginning of the week . . . Please.'

The look he gave her and his silence told her he would comply.

*   *   *

171

But at seven on Monday morning, well before he would have made his way to The Crown Head, he was shouting down from the landing window into the yard, 'Carl! Billy! Carl!' and when they appeared, from different buildings, in the stockyard and peered up at him through the early morning light it was Billy who shouted back, 'What is it, master?'

'This . . . my . . . it's the mistress. I cannot waken her. When I left her at half past five I thought she was still asleep. You, Carl, ride in for Doctor Wheatley as fast as you can go. Now!'

Carl made no comment but immediately ran to the stables, and Patsy, who had appeared outside the dairy, ran with him and helped to saddle the horse. And it was significant to their understanding that neither of them spoke a word.

Doctor Wheatley's house lay at yon side of the village, and the shortest way to it was through the village. Carl had galloped the horse as far as the cemetery wall, and was just pulling her into a trot when from a side road there appeared a small gig, which he recognised immediately and he pulled up to the side of it, crying, 'Oh! Doctor Patten. 'Tis well met. I'm on my way to fetch Doctor Wheatley to the mistress; the master can't get her wakened.'

Philip Patten leant from the seat, saying, 'Can't get her wakened? What d'you mean, Carl?'

'Well, she was hit by a catapult – 'twas a sharp stone – on Saturday when we were all eating in the meadow, and she's been in bed since. And now 'tis as I said.'

Hit by a catapult stone and now can't wake up? The Gibsons were the old man's patients and he was very touchy about trespassing, as he termed it, unless one was invited for consultation, and then who dare express an opinion that went against his. But what young Carl was describing was very like a coma, and by the time his superior could manage to get to the farm after the load he had on him last night, it might be too late to do anything that would be of help. After four hours at The Grange, he wanted nothing but his bed at this moment, having endeavoured to bring Drayton's grandson into the world, which he had done, although without thanks, for the poor mite was a mongol.

172

'Ride on. I'll follow.'

As soon as Philip Patten looked down on Fanny he gnawed at his bottom lip before he asked Ward, 'Has she been moved at all?'

'No.'

He now gently pulled back the bedclothes and began to examine her while Ward stood at the other side of the bed, staring at him as if to extract from his expression the reason why his beloved Fanny was in this state. He watched the doctor go to his bag, open it, then close it again before turning to him, saying, 'Go and tell Carl to ride for Doctor Wheatley and request him to bring some leeches with him and make it as quick as possible.'

'What is it? What's wrong with her?'

'I don't really know yet, Ward,' Philip Patten lied. 'I would like another opinion. Go now and get him away.'

Ward didn't respond straightaway to the command, but remained for some seconds looking down on Fanny, his lower jaw moving as if he was grinding his teeth.

A few minutes later Annie entered the room and was surprised to hear the young doctor talking away to the mistress, which she thought was silly, because if the poor thing could hear him she would have made some sign, wouldn't she? Tommy Taylor went like that, but he tapped a finger.

It was only half an hour later when Doctor Wheatley entered the room, which indicated he had indeed answered the call promptly; not so much, perhaps, because of the patient's need, but because the young snipe was not only on his preserve but had sent him an order, a veiled order maybe, but nevertheless an order, to bring leeches, which suggested he had already diagnosed the trouble. So it wasn't unusual that he should ignore the young know-all and go straight to the inert figure in the bed.

'Well! Well! What have we here, Mrs Gibson, eh?' He took the limp hand and wagged it; then let it go so that it dropped back on to the coverlet, and he turned to Ward and said, 'How did this come about?'

173

'She was hit on the temple by a stone from a catapult on Saturday.'

'Saturday! It's now Monday. Why didn't you inform me before?'

'She seemed all right until this morning.'

The old man now pursed his lips, looked down on Fanny, then again lifted his head sharply towards Ward, and as if he had made a decision he said, 'Go down and get them to bring up a bowl of very hot water and towels.' Then he took off his coat as if he meant business.

As soon as Ward had left the room, however, the urgency went out of his actions, and now addressing his partner, he said simply, 'Coma? What do you think?' and Philip Patten replied, 'Yes; through a clot on the brain, I would say.'

'Would you?'

They stared at each other; then Doctor Wheatley said, 'She should go to hospital.'

'I doubt if she would make it.'

'Would you now? Well, perhaps for once you're right and so we will try your other notion with the leeches, for what it may be worth in this case. And you know something, Patten? She is one problem, but there's a bigger one looming up in him, should she go.'

'Yes, I'm aware of that.'

The old man again stared at his younger associate; that's what he couldn't stand about the fellow, that bloody cocksure manner of his.

They had bled her. They had wrapped her in hot, then cold towels, but to no avail; and so the day wore on and it came to six-thirty on the Tuesday morning. Annie was dozing in a chair at one side of the bed while Ward sat close to it at the other side. He was resting on his elbow, his back half bent as he held the limp hand. When his head nodded he gave a slight start and blinked rapidly. Then, his eyes wide, he stared down at the face on the pillow. It had changed. There was no colour in it; it had changed into that of a wax doll. He was now on his feet, muttering, 'Annie. Annie; come here.'

174

When Annie reached his side she muttered, 'Oh my God! No!' and he echoed her last word, but as a yell: 'No! No! Fanny! Fanny!'

When the door was thrust open and Jessie's frightened face appeared, Annie cried at her, 'Tell Carl to ride for Doctor Patten. He's nearest.' Then she almost fell on her back as Ward thrust her aside and, throwing back the bedclothes, lifted Fanny bodily into his arms and rocked her as he would have a child, the while moaning, 'Love. Love. No, you can't! You can't leave me. No! Fanny, don't go. No! No! I can't go on. Wake up! Wake up!'

He was still walking the floor bearing her limp body in his arms when Philip Patten hurried into the room and exclaimed, 'Oh, dear God!' Then putting out his hands, he checked Ward's flagging steps and said softly, 'Come; lay her down . . . Come.'

As if in a daze, Ward allowed himself to be led towards the bed and to let his beloved slip from his arms, but remained looking down on her, and Annie whimpered, 'All through a catapult.'

'Catapult,' Ward took up the word; then he repeated the word: 'Catapult! That's it! That's what killed her! They killed her!' And with his arm thrust out towards the doctor, the fingers stretched accusingly, he cried, 'Bear witness, you! she's dead! They killed her, and, by God! I'll finish them.'

The sudden movement of his body as he sprang towards the door startled them all and motivated Philip to run on to the landing crying out to him, 'Wait! Hold your hand a moment. Wait!' and then to step quickly back into the room and to address Annie: 'Who does he mean, they? Who was he referring to?'

As Annie shook her head it was Patsy who answered him: 'He thinks it was the young Holden lads.'

'The Holdens? Dear God!' And on this he dashed from the room; and on reaching the yard, he shouted to where Billy and Carl were standing on the road outside the gate, 'Go after him! He's making for the Holdens and their lads, and the state he's in anything could happen. I'll follow on.' Then he rushed back into the house and up to the bedroom again . . .

Ward entered the village from the church end, and as he ran alongside the cemetery wall and so into the street, William Smythe, the verger, paused while putting a large key into the vestry door, which he then left in the lock and hurried down the gravel path and into the street to watch Ward Gibson in his shirt sleeves racing along it. And he wasn't the only one to be surprised by the sight: Fred was loading the van with the early baking and he could not at first believe his eyes. Instead of running after Ward, however, he rushed into the house, shouting his news.

Jimmy Conway was heaving a carcass from the back of the cart. He, too, stopped in amazement; then he shouted across to Hannah Beaton, who was humping a sackload of potatoes up the two steps into the shop: 'Did you see what I've seen? Or am I seeing things? Where's he bound for?'

Ward soon reached where he was bound for, and it wasn't for the front of The Crown Head but round to the back of it.

At the kitchen door he stopped for a moment, his chest heaving, and he gulped in his throat before banging on the door, and which he continued to do until the voice from behind it cried, 'All right! All right! What is it?'

The door was pulled open; and he stood staring at Holden for a full ten seconds before bringing out on a growl, 'You satisfied then? You've let your breed act for the village, eh? You meant to do her in one way or another, didn't you?'

'In the name of God! What are you talking about, Ward? Are you drunk or daft? What's up with you?'

'Don't tell me you don't know. They came running in, didn't they, after they had shot their bolt? Well, it's the last catapult they'll use. By God! they'll pay for this, or you will through them.'

But as Ward's hands came out to grab him Holden struck out at him, the while he yelled, 'You're mad! That's what you are.'

'What is it? What's the matter?' Winnie Holden was now standing beside her husband, and Ward answered her: 'The matter is, you've spawned two murderers, missis. Your devils have killed my wife,' he cried at her.

176

'*Oh my God!*'

He watched the big woman put her hand over her mouth, and then turn and look back into the room before saying, and quickly now, 'Come in. Come in, Ward.'

He seemed to need no second bidding: he almost thrust them aside because he had caught sight of the two lads who had been sitting at the table but who were now standing against the far wall of the room and close together, and he was himself now thrust aside by the Holdens and held against the wall, all the while hearing the older man shouting, 'They never hurt your wife! Listen to me, Ward! but I know who did.'

'Shut up! Mike. Shut up!' It was his big brawny wife yelling at him now.

'I won't, woman, I won't. It's our lads he's trying to get at, as if you didn't know.'

They were talking now as if they were alone in the room together and not struggling with a man who was behaving like a maniac.

Again Holden cried at Ward, 'Stop it, man! Stop it! Quiet! Listen to me, and I'll tell you who it was. The same one as set fire to your crops, and crippled your cattle, the one you threw over for your wife.'

Suddenly Ward became still. His face was close to Holden's and he whispered a name: 'Daisy? No.'

'Aye; Daisy Mason. Well, what did you expect, lad? What did you expect? Haven't you ever given it a thought?'

Slowly Ward pushed their arms from him and straightened up; but a doubt still remained and he continued to stare at the two boys who were crouched close together, until their father said, 'Sit down, lads, and finish your breakfast.'

As Ward watched them come slowly, even furtively to the table, some part of him was saying, 'I'm sorry. I'm sorry.' Then he muttered as if to himself, 'It couldn't have been her, not the fire. She was away at the time in Fellburn.'

It was Winnie Holden who now spoke, and quietly: 'She was wily,' she said. 'She had it all planned out, like everything else. She's been goin' mad these last years, but nobody would let on 'cos John and Gladys are a decent couple, and they've

177

had enough on their plate trying to keep her under lock and key most of the time. But everybody in the place seemed to know who was the culprit for your misfortunes, except you, and we've often wondered why it hasn't dawned on you. And on Saturday gone the lads were in the Hall wood. They shouldn't have been there, but there's some good bleeberry bushes and that's what they were doing, gatherin'. They saw her. She had a catapult, they said, and through the bushes they saw her fire it. She caught sight of them and whether she meant to chase them or not, they were so scared they took to their heels and didn't stop running until they reached this kitchen.'

There was silence for a matter of thirty seconds, and it was broken by George Holden saying in a fear-filled voice, 'Don't tell me, Ward, that your wife's dead!'

Ward didn't answer him, but he moved from the wall, then turned and looked towards the fire. There was a pot on the hob with porridge bubbling in it, but he wasn't seeing it: he was back near the cemetery wall and her hands were coming out and clawing his face. Why hadn't his suspicions touched on her? They had on one family after another in the village: the Longstaff twins, Mike and Adam. He had never frequented The Running Hare, which seemed, in his state of mind, reason enough to feel they had it in for him. Or it could have been one of Kate Holden's lot? His suspicions had even touched on the McNabs in the Hollow. Then there were the Wainwrights. They were Methodists, and they had four sons, all married and scattered round about the countryside. No; that was daft thinking: just because he was the Methodist pastor. Why! he had always spoken to him, he had even bought his milk. No; he had been blind, stupid, not to put his finger on Daisy, after her parting shot. He remembered her actual words.

'I'll have my own back on you, Ward Gibson. I swear before God I will. You and yours. Do you hear me?'

And she had carried out her threat. She had killed Fanny, his beloved Fanny. Oh! Fanny, Fanny. There was a strange feeling in his head. For a moment he felt as though he might burst into tears like a woman, or howl like some animal, such

178

was the pain of her loss. And he realised that this was only the beginning . . .

He turned his gaze from the fire towards George Holden, who had caught his attention with the words, 'You and yours will never be safe, Ward, as long as she's about. She should be put away where she cannot do any more harm.'

You and yours. These were her words again. He had two girls, he had two daughters . . . you and yours will never be safe as long as she's about.

He swung round as if he were going to leave the room, but, turning again, he said simply, 'I'm sorry.'

'That's all right, Ward. That's all right. We understand.' And they moved to the door with him, and on its being opened they were as surprised as Ward to see, standing in the long dray yard, Philip Patten, Carl, Fred and his father, and a number of other villagers.

It was the doctor who moved towards him, saying, 'Come on home, Ward.'

Ward looked at the doctor and around the small crowd and when he spoke to Philip Patten his voice gave no indication of the rage that was rising in him, as he said, 'I'm going home, Doctor; just leave me alone for the time being . . . Come, Carl.' And with that he walked through the villagers, seeming not to notice Fred's outstretched hand.

Ward did not now run back through the village, but his step was quick and firm, as was Carl's. Once past the church and well out of sight of any of the villagers, however, Ward stopped and, looking at Carl, said, 'Go back home and see to things.' And before Carl had time to put any kind of question to him, such as, 'Can't I come with you, master?' Ward had jumped a ditch to the side of the road and was once more running across his field of stubble . . .

The work so far at Beacon Farm had been carried out according to the usual daily routine: the first milking had been done, the byres swilled out, and Seth Mason had just finished harnessing the two shires and was leading one from the stable, when the sight of Ward Gibson stopped him in his tracks. And after glancing swiftly about him as if looking for someone, he left the horse and began to run to where Ward was nearing the kitchen door, crying as he ran, 'Here! Wait a minute. Don't go in there. What d'you want, anyway?'

And to this Ward answered grimly, 'You know what I want,' which impelled Seth to spring forward and confront him, the while yelling, 'Pete! Pete! Here!'

As Ward's forearm thrust Seth staggering back against the wall of the house, Pete Mason came racing across the yard, and as he barred Ward's way to the kitchen door, he cried at him, 'Get yourself to hell out of here, and quick!'

Again Ward's arm came out, straight this time, but the blow just grazed Pete Mason's cheek, and now he retaliated with his own fists, only to be stopped by the kitchen door being dragged open and his father's hands on his shoulders pulling him back, as he yelled above the mêlée, 'Stop it! For God's sake! What's come over you all?'

The two combatants were now glaring at each other when Mr Mason again spoke. 'What brings you here, Ward?' he demanded. 'You're not welcome; you know that.'

'Huh! In the name of God! listen to the man: I'm not welcome. And what brings me here, you ask? Well, I'll tell you, Mr Mason, what brings me here. Just a small matter of having your daughter put away for murdering my wife. That's all. That's all.' The last words seemed to rattle in his throat, and the three men looked at him aghast and in silence. Then Pete and Seth Mason turned to look at their father, who first put one hand to his head, then with the other felt, as if for support, for the stanchion of the door, and there was a note of both fear and disbelief in his voice as he said, 'No! No! What d'you mean? What d'you mean?'

'Just what I say. My wife died this morning from a catapult shot that carried a flint.'

It was a thin voice that seemed to pipe in as Seth Mason said, 'People don't die from catapult shots.'

'No?' The bark made Seth Mason retreat a step and he muttered, 'Well . . . well, I mean . . . '

'She . . . she wouldn't do that. Mischief, yes, mischief: she gets up to mischief, but not that, not that.'

'Mr Mason—' Ward's voice seemed strangely calm as he now went on, 'that flint burst a blood vessel in my wife's

180

brain. And I have only this morning been awakened to the fact that all my ill-fortune over the past years: fires, maiming of my animals, shooting innocent little dogs, and all other irritations I've had to put up with, have come from the hand of your daughter. Everybody seems to have known this, but they have been protecting you. Well now, murder cannot be protected. If I had my hands on her this minute, there would be another one. This I promise you. But that would be letting her off lightly. What I've come to tell you is, I'll have her certified before this day's out.'

'No, no. Oh Ward, no, no.'

The voice caused them all to turn and look at the frail figure of Gladys Mason; and when her husband gripped her shoulders crying, 'Go back! Go back!' she answered him, 'Leave me be, John. I must speak to Ward.' And she pressed herself from his hands and, moving to the threshold of the door, she looked at Ward and pleaded, 'Please, don't do that, Ward. I beg of you. I'll . . . I'll see that she causes you no more trouble.'

'What more trouble can she cause me, Mrs Mason? She has killed my wife. Didn't you hear? she has killed my wife. Your mad daughter has killed my wife. You say she can cause me no more trouble. I have two girls, remember, and she'll not rest until she gets them an' all, if not me before that. Can't you take it in, woman? She's mad; and she won't stop at one.'

'Don't you speak to my mother like that.'

Before Ward had time to respond, John Mason cried at his son, 'Shut up! you. Shut up! If you had kept your eyes open and done what you were . . . ' He again put his hand to his head; then, as if a surprising thought had struck him, he said sharply, 'What proof have you got, Ward, that Daisy has done this thing? There's hardly a lad in the village that hasn't got a catapult.'

'Granted. But George Holden's sons, young Peter and Alan, saw her.'

'Oh, those two.' It was the thin voice of Seth Mason piping in again. 'They are noted liars, and thieves into the bargain. We caught them raiding our chicken run only a few weeks ago. Didn't we, Pete?'

181

'Aye, we did that. And either of them would say anything to save their own skin.'

'She was in the wood. They saw her. She chased them.'

'Aye, she could have, likely because they were using the catapult. Ward' – John Mason's bent shoulders seemed to straighten – 'she's been up to mischief, I admit, and there's something to be said on her side, as you only too well know. What you did turned her brain. But murder? No. No. I won't have it. Anyway, she hardly ever leaves the room up above, except to go for a short ramble now and again. And then one or two of us keep an eye on her as much as—' He stopped . . . then he pointed to Seth, saying, 'Go up and tell her she's wanted downstairs.'

As Seth was about to pass his father to enter the house, he paused for a moment, saying, 'What if she won't . . . ?' Only to be cut short by his father's voice crying at him, 'Bring her down!' Then turning to Ward, he said, 'Come indoors a minute, will you, and we'll clear this thing up one way or another. There's one thing I'm sure of, she won't lie to me.' And he stepped back, at the same time pressing his wife aside to allow Ward to enter before them.

It seemed to Ward that the kitchen hadn't changed in any way since the last time he had sat at the long, white kitchen table and had eaten a good meal amid laughter and joking about different members of the church community. The breakfast crockery was there on the table now.

He stood some distance from the end of it, waiting, as were Mr and Mrs Mason and their son, their gaze directed towards the door at the far end of the room. No-one spoke and the silence became eerie until it was suddenly pierced by a high female voice, crying, 'Leave me be! will you? Leave me be!'

When the far door opened it seemed that the bulky figure had been thrust into the room and that it was about to turn round again in protest, when it stiffened. Ward saw the head slowly turn to look at him, and the expression on the face seemed to be no different from the one he had looked on at their last meeting all those years ago, except, as the body had, so it had swollen to almost twice its size: for the figure now walking heavily towards the end of the table was enormous.

Her father checked her, saying, 'Sit down, Daisy. I want to talk to you.'

It was as if she hadn't heard her father speak, for she took no notice of him. Instead, putting her two hands flat on the table, her fingers began to tap out a regular beat.

When her mother said sharply, 'Don't do that, dear. Sit down. Do what Dad said,' she again made no response; nor did she when her brother Pete barked at her, 'Do what you're told and listen to Dad, or you'll find yourself in hot water.'

When his father reprimanded sternly, 'Pete!' his son cried back at him, 'Well, get on with it. Ask her the question you brought her down for.'

Putting a hand on his daughter's shoulder, John Mason said, 'Look at me, Daisy. Did you take a catapult and fire it at Mrs Gibson? I want the truth.'

She glanced towards Ward, then looking back at her father and a sly smile coming over her face, she answered him with, 'You never let her out, do you?'

Mr Mason's head dropped on to his chest for a moment before again looking at his daughter and demanding, 'Did you fire a catapult? Did you take a catapult out?' then attempting to shake the large solid body as he demanded further of her: 'Answer me truthfully! You know what can happen to you if you don't behave. Now, have you been out these last few days and taken a catapult and fired it at Mrs Gibson, causing her to die?'

The bulky body seemed suddenly to come to life, normal life, and in a voice of enquiry, she said, 'She died?'

'Yes. Yes she did, Daisy. Mrs Gibson has died from a catapult shot.'

Mr and Mrs Mason and their two sons watched Daisy turn and look fully at Ward; and a thread of despair ran through each of them as the habitually dull expression on her face turned to one of glee, her voice then expressing this feeling as she cried, 'I got her, then. I knew I would one day. Payment. Payment. I said I'd make you pay.'

'Oh, dear God!' As Mrs Mason dropped on to a chair and John Mason turned away for the moment from the sight of his daughter, she cried at Ward: 'By way of payment, eh? By way of payment.'

It was at this that Ward found his voice, and he cried at her: 'And you'll pay, too, you mad hussy, for I'll have you in the asylum before the day's out.'

'Asylum? Asylum?' and she shook her head. Then again she was shouting at Ward and in a voice that sounded normal now, 'Oh no! you won't. Oh no! you won't.'

What happened next came so swiftly that not one of the three men could have prevented it: grabbing up the bread knife that was lying across a wooden platter on which lay half a loaf of bread, and with the artistry of a knife thrower, she levelled it at Ward's face.

Whether or not he saw it coming, he never knew; but his body instinctively stretched upwards and to the side which took his face and neck away from her blade, to be conscious that it had found a target when he realised he was pinned to the side of the delph rack against which he was now leaning. In the confusion he was aware that the long wooden handle was weighting the blade down. Then, as his body bent forward, the knife slid to the floor, leaving him standing in a daze, watching the blood soak into his shirt sleeve where it was rolled up above the elbow, then stream down his forearm.

There was a queasy feeling in his stomach; then he became aware that the kitchen was empty except for Mrs Mason and himself and that the yelling and squealing were coming from a distance.

Mrs Mason's words came out on a trembling stutter: 'It . . . it isn't deep, Ward; it . . . it's ju . . . just gone through the top.' She had torn his shirt sleeve apart, and now she was wrapping a towel around the wound, saying, 'Ke . . . keep the end under your oxter, Ward, and . . . and the lads will ge . . . get you to the doctor.'

He pressed her away from him, and as he turned towards the door to go out, she muttered, 'Oh, Ward. Ward. I'm sorry. I . . . I'm s . . . sorry for us all.'

His left arm pressed tight to his side and his right hand holding the towel on to the top of his shoulder, he walked

184

across the farmyard. And he wasn't surprised at all as he was about to enter the first field to see Carl standing in the shadow of a hedge. And Carl's greeting to him was, 'Oh! master. Good God! What's happened?'

And the strange reply he received was, 'Run on home. Harness the trap. I want it straightaway.'

'You . . . you're sure you can manage? I mean . . . '

'Do what I say.'

As Carl sprinted from him Ward told himself that it was as well this last incident had happened, for it would help to put her where she should have been a long time ago.

Twice he leant against a drystone wall, not because there was a weakness in him, but because he was pondering as to why he himself hadn't suspected the source of his misfortunes: everybody had seemed to know the culprit but himself. One thing he could have understood was that his friends had kept quiet because they feared the result of his knowing.

He reached the farm gate to see Carl leading a horse and trap into the yard, with Billy tightening the horse's girth as he moved. Annie was there, too, with the girls one on each side of her, and Patsy standing apart, her forefinger nipped tight between her teeth.

On seeing her master, Annie pushed the girls to one side and, hurrying towards him, said, 'Dear Lord in heaven! Come away in and let me see to that. Oh, this is surely a day that God didn't make.'

As she made to take Ward's free arm, he pressed her aside, but he did not speak; nor did he look at his daughters as they cried to him, 'Oh, Daddy! Daddy!' But with a heave he pulled himself up on to the trap, where Carl was already seated, the reins in his hands, and with a muttered, 'Get going,' they rode out of the yard.

It wasn't until they had gone some distance that he again muttered, 'Make for Doctor Patten's;' and within five minutes the trotting horse brought them to the doctor's cottage, which lay just outside the village at the church and cemetery end.

When Carl jumped down and ran up the path towards

185

the door, it was pulled open before he got there by the doctor's old housekeeper, who exclaimed, 'Oh; I thought it was himself. He's out. But he should be back at any time. He hadn't sat down to his meal when he was called again. With one thing and another, he's done a day's work already. What is it you will be wanting?' Then she looked beyond him, and after a pause said, 'Oh. Oh, yes; I see,' only to exclaim louder now as she looked along the road, 'Speak of the devil! Here he comes, and it looks like he won't be sitting down to his meal again.'

When Philip Patten drew his horse to a stop alongside Ward's trap, he stared at the blood-soaked arm before asking quietly, 'How did that come about?'

'A knife. She aimed at my throat. I want you to come back to Doctor Wheatley's with me; I'm having her put away if it's the last thing I do this day.'

Philip Patten made no comment, but he held Ward's gaze for some seconds before he jerked his horse forward and turned it in the road, by which time Carl had taken his seat again and set the horse at a trot in the direction of the village.

Again many of the villagers stood and gaped as Ward Gibson, his arm covered with blood, was driven through the village, followed by the young doctor on horseback.

It was evident that Doctor Wheatley had not gone without his breakfast, which never varied: no matter what he had imbibed the night before, he was ready for his steak topped with two fried eggs and also for a mug of tea into which a raw egg had been beaten. It was said in the village that it was his plain diet that had prevented his indulgence in raw spirits from eating away his innards.

One of the rooms of his well-equipped house he used as a surgery, and there he was confronted by the three men, towards not one of whom he had any kindly feelings.

'Well! What's this? Been getting yourself shot?'

When Ward made no reply but just stared at the bloated face and figure before him, the doctor bawled, 'Come on! Come on! Out with it!'

And Ward did come out with it, and right to the point: 'I

want you to come back to the Masons' farm and certify the Masons' daughter,' he said.

'What!' The doctor looked towards Philip Patten, then back to Ward, before he said, and very quickly now, 'You do, do you? And on what grounds?'

Philip Patten came out with one word that seemed to speak volumes: staring at his superior, he said simply, '*Doctor!*' And in return, the older man yelled at him, 'Yes? Doctor! What were you going to say?'

'You know what I was going to say, what Mr Gibson here is going to say: she should have been seen to some time ago. You knew the way things were going.'

'I knew nothing of the kind, fellow! The girl . . . woman was under stress. Do you lock people up because of that?'

It was now Ward who answered: 'Stress that killed my wife, sir!' he cried. 'That maniac laughed when she knew that her catapult had done the trick. She gloried in it. Then she did this.' He pointed to his shoulder and went to pull the towel away, but winced as it brought the torn skin with it.

They all stood for a moment staring at the bared arm with the blood oozing down both the back and front of his body. Then Ward muttered: 'She aimed for my throat. And she'll do it again. And remember, I have two daughters. She won't rest until she finishes them. She's raving mad.'

'And who's to blame for that, Mr Gibson? Do you ask yourself who's to blame for that? You turned her brain when you threw her over.'

'I did not throw her over. There had been no talk of marriage.'

'No; not talk, but action.'

'Do you intend to do what I ask, or have I to go for the police to assist you?'

The older man now stood glaring at Ward. Then, his voice muffled and sounding ominous, he said, 'You brought distress on this good and respected family the minute you married your cheap dancing piece.'

Philip Patten and Carl reacted simultaneously by stretching out their arms to prevent Ward from attacking the doctor, who had fearfully stepped back towards the open door, but was nevertheless determined Ward Gibson should take heed of his words: for they were, 'I may not live long enough to see it, but what you are forcing me to do will have its repercussions on you a thousandfold, for the family that you have destroyed will eventually destroy you.'

PART TWO

I

Carl watched Patsy coming down the side of the stubble field. She was walking in the shadow of a short line of trees, where the March sun had not been strong enough to thaw the heavy frost of the night, so that her feet seemed to be treading a silver path; but even as his thought presented the image to him he discarded it, for Patsy's life had always been devoid of silver paths.

As she emerged into the light it was as if he were seeing her for the first time as a young woman, a young beautiful woman who carried herself straight, head bowing to no-one, while still having to be subservient.

When she reached him, where he was standing by the stile, she took his outstretched hand and before he had time to greet her she said, 'Will you kindly tell me, Mr Carl, why you never come up this field to meet me?' to which he answered, 'For the simple fact, Miss Riley, that I like to see you walk. You walk proud, a different walk altogether from what you walk inside the farm.'

The smile left her face as she said, somewhat soulfully, 'Yes, yes; it's a different walk, for there I am running or scurrying to someone's bidding.'

He helped her over the stile, saying, 'It won't always be like that, Patsy. Believe me.'

'No?' It was a question; and now, she leant against the wooden stanchion as she said, 'I am twenty-five years old, Carl. Ma reminded me of it the day. "Breeding time will soon be past," she said. She does not mince words, does Ma. And she was right, Carl: I want a family; but most of all, I want you.'

He put his arms about her and pulled her tightly to him, saying, 'Not more than I want you, Patsy. Oh, no; not more than I want you. I ache for you.'

'Then why can't we just go to him and put it to him? It should be so simple. You have the cottage; I've just got to move from the loft. Oh my dear.' She put up her hand and touched his cheek. 'I know the situation; that was a silly thing to say. But on the surface, it seems as simple as that. The truth is, he looks upon you as a son; but me, I'm still Patsy Riley from the Hollow. Oh . . . oh, I know.' She patted his lips. 'I know he's been good in other ways; in letting Da take Billy's place; and taking Rob on too. Oh, I know I said it was good, but, in a way, it makes matters worse for me. There's Da, a feckless Irishman, and Rob following in his footsteps. They're good workers when they're being governed, but like all the Irish, except perhaps me' – she twisted his nose – 'who will work without being overlooked. But what they are besides this is, they're loyal. And of course' – she now drew herself slightly from him, yet not out of his embrace, as she added, 'There is Miss . . . there is Miss Jessie.'

'Oh dear me! Patsy, as I've told you before, time and again, for my part she's like a sister. I've told you: I held her as a tiny baby; and I'm ten years older than her. She's just a silly girl.'

'Oh no.' Patsy shook her head, and a knowing look came into her eyes as she said, 'Miss Jessie's no silly girl. When I first came into that yard sixteen years ago she made it plain who owns you.'

He now actually thrust her from him and angrily he said, 'Nobody owns me, neither her nor her father, nor anyone else. But I owe them a debt; at least, her father. He took me in and saw to me when I could have died. He could have sent me back to that farm. He took a risk in keeping me. He's been good to me.'

Patsy closed her eyes and slowly turned from him, saying, 'It's like an old fairy tale, Carl: I've heard it so many times;

192

you keep repeating it.' And now she swung round to him. 'I'm going to ask you something. Is your debt so great that you're going to repay him with your life? You're not bonded; nor am I. We could up tomorrow and go and get work elsewhere.'

'Where? Where? Tell me.'

Her head to the side now, she kicked the toe of her boot into a stiff tuft of grass. But he was holding her again, and both his eyes and his voice held a plea as he said, 'Believe me, Patsy, there is no other in my life but you. The master had a feeling for his wife which, at one time, I couldn't understand. I used to think it was a mania. She was a lovable creature, but his feelings for her were more like adoration. Well, I've come to understand a little how he must have felt, for, Patsy, the very sight of you warms me and wakes such a stirring in me that I want to throw everything to the wind and do as you say, get away . . . run with you into a life that is entirely ours, free from duty or guilt or being ungrateful. And so I ask you, Patsy, to wait just a little longer. I've got the feeling that things are coming to a head in one way or another. Yes, believe me, I have. A strong feeling tells me that I shall be forced to come into the open. And so then, if we can't marry, we'll leave. That's all.'

She stared at him again, but softly now; and then in a quiet voice, she said, 'He'll never let you leave, Carl. Apart from any feeling he has for you, you run that place. He's never taken a real hand in it since the missis went. He makes decisions, oh yes, but only when you put them to him. Oh no, he'll never let you go.'

'Well' – he nodded at her – 'if he wants me to stay so badly he'll let me take the wife I want to have. So that's all about it. Come on!' And with his arm around her shoulders now, they walked down the narrow field path that would give on to the bridle path about a quarter of a mile distant. But before they reached it, he pulled her to a stop again and, putting his arms about her, he kissed her long and hard; and her returning the pressure of his body caused them to sway together for a moment before she withdrew herself from him. But as they walked on, it wasn't with her head held high, it was with it leaning against his shoulder . . .

And that is how Ward saw them as he entered the field path. He had sat on his horse on a bank some distance from the path, and had kept them in sight ever since they left the stile. He had known there was a liking between them, but he had never thought it would come to anything: surely the boy, as he still named Carl in his mind, would have more sense; had he not, over the years, imbued in him a feeling of class through his treating him as a member of his household? No; but he had thought he would never let himself down to the level of any member of the Hollow tribe. They were workers of the lowest class, all of them. The fact that Patsy's father was the cowman and her brother the yard boy should have emphasised the plane to which he was stooping.

His Fanny had always maintained that the boy was well bred; and his growing had seemed to prove it, for in voice and manner and intelligence, he was far above the ordinary. He had become a great reader, a talent with which he had been imbued by his dear Fanny and which, he thought, should have helped.

Well, he wasn't going to let any little Irish chit from the Hollow alter the plans he'd had in mind for some time now. He had always looked upon Carl as a son, and a son he determined he should now become . . .

But what if he left? He was a free man.

He wouldn't dare; he owed him too much to walk out.

But the question persisted: what if he did? How would he ever replace him? He realised he had left almost the entire running of the farm in the boy's hands for this long time. Eight years? Was it eight years since he had lost his beloved? What had he done in that time? His eyelids blinked rapidly as he thought back. It seemed that he had spent the time erecting fences around his land and keeping a watch on the girls. He had taken them to school and brought them back. He had trusted no-one else to do this; and when the time had come for Jessie to leave he made Angela leave too for, as he told himself, he couldn't be in two places at once. And now he would allow them to leave the farm only on a Saturday, when he would take them into town. Carl always accompanied them and saw to the delivery of the produce to the wholesale trader. On the odd occasion he had allowed Patsy to accompany them. But not during this past year.

His daughters had never been to Newcastle. As for attending a play or a variety show, they never knew about such things. And what was more, he had stopped them dancing.

One day he had found them, with their hands joined, doing the steps their mother had taught them. Perhaps it was because, compared with her, their actions looked cumbersome. Yet, had that been the truth it would have applied only to Jessie, not to Angela, who was so much like her mother that, at times, even now, he found it painful to look on her; at others he would hold her close, hugging her tightly to him, trying to recover the essence of his beloved Fanny.

He pressed a heel against the horse's flank, and it began to move down the hill. By the time he reached the farmyard there was no sight of either Carl or Patsy; but coming from the direction of the front door and accompanied by Jessie and Angela was Frank Noble, and the curate hailed him in his usual smiling way, calling, 'Oh, I'm glad I've caught you. I just dropped in to say I'm looking for an audience for tomorrow night: I'm putting on a real good show. A friend in Newcastle has brought me two dozen ... mark you, two dozen new slides; with what I've got, they'll run for an hour and a half, or more.' He now looked from one girl to the other, saying, 'I think I'll have to charge an entrance fee, don't you?'

Laughing, Jessie answered him: 'Well, I can promise you I'll pay with left-over pies from Annie's last baking.' Then bending forward to look round the curate at her sister standing now by his side, she said, 'What'll you pay with, Angela?'

'Acorns.'

'Do you hear that?' said Frank Noble.

Ward had dismounted and his reply was, 'It's far too much, to my mind.'

'May we go, Daddy?' Angela had now taken her father's arm, and as he answered her he looked at Frank Noble. 'I don't see why not,' he said, 'although the man's whole show is so inane I'm surprised you waste your time looking at it.'

'It's the way of the world' – Frank was nodding seriously towards Jessie now – 'ingratitude. Ingratitude. I'm so used to it that I no longer retaliate. I only hope the good Lord chalks it up in my favour.'

'Have you had anything to eat?'

'Oh yes. I've had two shives of Annie's treacle tart; I've had a slice of her currant bun cake, lathered with butter as thick as the cake, and I've had three cups of tea with real cream in it. To tell you the truth, that's all I come for.'

'Oh, I've known that for some time,' said Ward. 'And by the way, hasn't Annie given you anything to take back for the children?'

'She offered, but I refused.'

'You had no right to.'

'I have every right to; my children are being spoilt. Every time they come here they go back laden, and when they know I've been here they expect me to come back with my pockets stuffed. Well, I've put a stop to it. Speaking seriously now, Ward, I just had to: there is a limit to receiving as there is to giving. Well, now' – his voice changed – 'after that little sermon, I must be off; but I'll see you ladies tomorrow night, eh?'

'Yes. Oh, yes, we'd love to come.'

'I'm going over now to Forest Hall to see if I can persuade Lady Lydia to come; or failing that, get the young master to persuade her. He's a great ally, is Mr Gerald . . . Well, see you tomorrow night.'

Ward now looked round the farmyard, then said, 'You haven't walked? Where's your horse?'

'He's slightly lame. Anyway, it's Sunday and he needs a rest; and the walk does me good.'

Ward shook his head, then stood beside his daughters watching the ailing parson stride out of the gate, and as he wondered how long was left to him, he experienced a tinge of envy for the serenity that emanated from this proven friend . . .

The girls had gone to the sitting-room: Angela was seated in the corner of the couch, her feet tucked under her, and looking like an outsize doll, her shining, straight black hair

196

drawn back into two thick plaits, emphasising the alabaster tint of her skin. She could really have been a replica of her mother, except that her eyes were a clear grey, not a dark brown.

Jessie was placing some pieces of coal on the fire with a large pair of tongs, and Angela was saying, 'I wonder if the Lord of the Manor has grown out of making sheep's eyes. It must be over a year since we saw him.'

'Don't be silly.' Jessie dusted her hands one against the other; then took a handkerchief from her dress pocket and proceeded to wipe her fingers, before taking a round tapestry frame from a nearby table. Then she sat down at the other end of the couch, saying, 'That's a silly term . . . sheep's eyes.'

'No sillier than you saying, "Don't be silly". You're always saying that to me, you know, Jessie, "Don't be silly".' But then she laid her head back into the cushions before adding, 'Perhaps I am silly after all, because I think silly things, fairy-tale things, things that could never happen, and things that might happen, frightening things. Do you think frightening things, Jessie?'

There was a pause before Jessie answered quietly, 'Yes, sometimes. I mostly dream them.'

'What about?'

'Oh, I couldn't tell you.' Jessie now thrust the needle into the canvas, pulled it through, then thrust it back again before going on, 'Dreams never really enter into reality; dreams are outrageous things, fantastic, impossible things.' Her hands slowly laid the frame on her knee, and she sat staring towards the fire until she was jerked back into an awareness of her sister by Angela saying, 'Don't you think we lead a very restricted life here, Jessie? I sometimes feel that the walls of the farm and all those fences are like bars.'

Jessie's mouth was agape. She could not have been more startled if her sister had used obscene language, and she was only fifteen and a bit: to her mind, she was feather-brained; yet here she was daring to put into words the thoughts that had for some time been tormenting herself. Then she was more amazed as Angela went on, 'Daddy is too caring for us, don't you think? Do you think that he is still afraid that that

197

woman will break out of the asylum and do us an injury?'

Angela turned her head now and must have seen the startled expression on her sister's face, but she still went on: 'We never go anywhere. You remember the girls at school? Well, we never invited them here, did we? And do you remember Bella Scott? She used to talk about the family going to the pantomime at Christmas; and she once went to a play and saw a famous actress in Newcastle. You remember . . . ? We never go anywhere, do we, Jessie? Only to the dear Reverend Noble's magic lantern show.'

When she stopped speaking, they continued to stare at each other. Then in a mere whisper and with a tremble in her voice, she said, 'I feel lost at times, Jessie . . . lonely. And I want to do things which I know I mustn't, such as dance. Oh, I do want to dance. You remember, Mummy danced so beautifully? Sometimes I think I'm her: in my dreams I dance. Oh, Jessie.'

Almost with a spring, Jessie hitched herself along the couch and enfolded her sister and, as if she were the mother, she was patting Angela's head, saying, 'There, there. Don't cry, dear. I know what you mean. I, too, feel it. We must talk to Daddy; at least, I will. I shall ask him if he will take us to the city, and let us buy some clothes from the shop. Mrs Ranshaw has a poor idea of dress. All our clothes look home-made. Yes; yes, I shall talk to him.'

Angela raised her head. Her face was running with tears. 'Oh, if only you would, Jessie,' she said. 'Anyway, if he says no, it won't matter so much, for now you understand me.'

'Yes; yes, my dear; I understand.' And again Jessie's arms went around her sister; and again she comforted her and felt a strange feeling as she did so; she could almost say she felt happy, until Angela whispered, 'I feel so guilty, Jessie, because – I want to get away. I dream of, of . . . someone coming and, and' – the words became fainter – 'taking me away and into a wonderful life . . . different.'

It was around ten o'clock the next morning when Ward entered the kitchen and, looking at his daughter where she was rolling out some pastry on the floured board, said to her, 'Leave that, and go and tell Carl I want a word with him in my office. You'll find him likely in the second paddock.'

Jessie paused a moment and looked across the table towards Annie, who was sitting peeling the last of the apples from the previous year's crop. And she, noticing Jessie's hesitation, said, 'Well, leave that; it won't walk away.'

It wasn't until Jessie had left the kitchen, after washing her hands in the wooden sink, then drying them whilst looking out of the window, that Ward's voice came at her harshly, saying, 'You don't need to titivate yourself to walk to the fields, Jessie; and I haven't got time to waste.'

After the girl had left the kitchen through the back door and Ward was about to leave by the far door, Annie spoke again, saying, 'She has a light hand with pastry, has Miss Jessie.'

He turned and looked at her, saying, 'What?'

'I said she has a light hand with pastry. She'll make a good housekeeper.'

Ward stared at her over the length of the room before going out hastily and closing the door none too gently after him. And Annie, continuing to peel the apples without snapping the rind, muttered, 'He'll appreciate her one day. But then, perhaps, it'll be too late; you can't keep birds caged if you leave the gate open.'

Meanwhile, Jessie had reached the bottom of the second field where Mick Riley and Rob, with the assistance of Carl, were patching a drystone wall bordering the bridle path on that side of the land.

Mick and his son greeted her as they always did with exaggerated Irish courtesy: 'Mornin' to you, Miss Jessie,' with Rob's voice just a little behind that of his father, but he left the rest to Mike as his father said, ' 'Tis a grand day, isn't it, miss? Can't ya hear it singin' "Spring's on its way"?'

Jessie did not answer, but she smiled, then turned to Carl who was now saying, 'You want me, Miss Jessie?'

Jessie looked at him. His blond hair looked to be almost silver; his face, as always, appeared beautiful to her; and his straight body was something on which she must not let her thoughts dwell; and she could have answered, 'Yes, I want you, Carl. I always have; but you don't want me; you want the daughter of this rough man, don't you? I wish I hated Patsy, like I used to, but she won't let me, for she, more than any other, has understood how I have felt, and in her own way she has been kind to me. She it was who would put her arms around me after Mother died, not Annie, and oh, not Daddy. No, the only one who's ever felt his arms since then has been Angela. Yet his love doesn't satisfy Angela. Angela would fly away tomorrow and forget him if her fairy prince were to come riding along, whereas I, who have never had his love, could never forget him.'

Carl was saying, 'Is anything the matter, Miss Jessie?'

'What? . . . No. I'm sorry.' And she gave a little laugh. 'I was thinking of something else for the moment; as Mike says, it's a bit of a Spring day . . . Father would like to see you in his study.'

'Now?'

'Well' – she shrugged her shoulder – 'he sent me for you.'

Looking at Mike, Carl said, 'I won't be long,' the words implying, And so you had better keep going; no sliding down against the wall and lighting your clay pipe . . .

They were walking side by side across the field when she said, 'Will you be going to the magic lantern show tonight?'

He laughed as he replied, 'No; I don't think so. In fact, I've seen it so many times I could give you the show without the slides.'

'But the parson tells us he has twelve new slides.'

'Oh well, I suppose that's something to look forward to. And he's always obliged to you when you go. It makes his efforts worthwhile. He's a good man.'

'Yes. Yes' – she nodded – 'he's a good man. It's a pity he's so sick. But I feel he'd improve somewhat if he'd only move out of the Hollow. It's a damp place at the best of times.'

'Yes, you're right there. But those down there are his flock; although half of them' – he refrained from saying, the Irish – 'don't pass over the church steps; but nevertheless he treats them all alike. They would all have known even harder times if it hadn't been for him.'

200

'But Daddy's been kind to them.' Her voice sounded on the defensive now, and he confirmed quickly that he recognised this by saying, 'Yes; yes, of course. No-one kinder. With his taties and turnips, and all the odd bits, and giving Mike half a pig at Christmas. Yes, you're right.' But again he had to stop himself from saying, It's easy to give when you've got plenty, but when you've got as little as Parson Noble, it's like his name: it's a noble deed he does every time he shares the little he's got. Instead he said, 'You say your father's in his study?'

'Yes. Yes, Father's in his study.'

When they reached the yard, she left him to go into the kitchen alone, and there, looking at Annie, he said, 'I'm wanted in the study. What's afoot? Do you know?'

'Now, why ask me that? What would I know of the inner workings of the master's mind?'

He smiled and pushed her gently in the shoulder, saying, 'More than the next, Annie.'

'Are your boots clean?'

He looked down at them, saying, 'Yes; yes, they're clean; the ground is as hard as flint.'

A minute later he was knocking on the study door, and when Ward's voice called, 'Come in!' he entered the room, which was small, although it was lined with bookshelves, the only other pieces of furniture being a desk and two chairs, in one of which Ward was sitting, the other one being placed near the window.

Pointing to it, Ward said, 'Draw it up; I want to talk to you.'

They sat for a moment looking at each other; then Ward, running his fingers through the front of his greying hair, said, 'I've asked you here because this is a private talk. It will be the one and only, I suppose, we'll ever have along these lines. How old are you now?'

'Oh . . . Oh. Well, you know, master, I wasn't sure whether I was nine or ten when I came to you, but I reckon I am now twenty-seven.' And he was in such a position in this household that he could add, 'I wouldn't have thought you would have to ask that.'

'Oh, perhaps not. But I just wanted it to be emphasised that you are twenty-seven; you are no longer a youth, not even a young man, you are a fully-fledged man. And now I am going to ask you if you have thought of your future.'

'Oh yes; many a time.'

'Have you ever thought that one day you could own this house and farm?'

Carl moved slightly on the chair, which caused the legs to squeak on the polished boards; then emphatically he said, 'No! No, never!'

'Well, well; you surprise me, because any onlooker, any close onlooker, that is, would have said you have been running this farm for a good few years now.'

'Oh no . . . no.'

Carl was shaking his head, when Ward put in, 'But yes; I don't want to hear any false modesty: you know you've been carrying the weight of it since I lost my' – he had to gulp in his throat before he could bring out – 'wife. I haven't been the farmer I was before. My mind has been centered on protecting my daughters; and yes . . . and yes, myself, too. I have enemies in that village, strong enemies. I'm only too well aware of it; and because of this, I've left you to carry on, for you've not only helped to grow the produce, you've seen to the marketing of most of it. I've taken the profit and paid out the bills and wages, and in a way, I am still master here, but I haven't been running my farm. You have. So, what would you say if I offered to make you my heir? But wait!' He lifted a hand. 'There is a condition. And the condition has weighed heavily on me for some time. I am going to ask you a straight question: do you like Jessie?'

Carl sat perfectly still for at least ten seconds; then he closed his eyes and bit on his lower lip before he said quietly, 'Yes; yes, of course, master, I like Jessie. Apart from yourself and Annie, I was the first to hold her. She is like . . . '

'Don't . . . don't say she is like a sister to you, because she is not your sister; and she has never felt that she was your sister. Jessie is very fond of you.'

Carl drew in a deep breath before he said, 'Yes . . . yes, I know that, master; and I am fond of her . . . '

202

'But what you are going to say is, fondness isn't love; you don't love her.'

'Yes; that's about it, master.'

'But let me tell you, Carl, that after marriage fondness very often grows to love, a lasting love. There's more to marriage than a burning flame that attacks you.'

It was at this point that Ward sat back in his chair and closed his eyes. What was he saying? More to marriage than a burning flame. Had *he* not been consumed with the flame? Were not its embers still burning within him? It wasn't only protection of his daughters that had filled his mind all these years, it was the constant ache for his loss, for his love had been a mania; there was nothing reasonable or logical about it. And here he was telling this young fellow, whom he already thought of as a son, that love grew out of fondness.

He was actually startled when Carl said, 'I'm afraid I can't agree with you, sir. And anyway, now that we're speaking openly, I love someone else, and I am sure you know who that is. And I've often felt, sir, that as you loved your dear wife so I, in a similar way, love . . . '

'*Don't say it! Don't speak* of Patsy Riley in the same breath as my wife, or of my feelings for her. What is she? She is not even a village girl, but springs from that Hollow where pigs are cleaner than some of their owners. And don't say to me that she is different, for breeding will out. Just look at her father and her brother. Do you want to link yourself with that lot? You will either marry Jessie or you will no longer remain here.'

Carl was now on his feet looking down on the man whom he had loved as a father, and his heart was sore for him as he said, 'I would do anything in the world for you, sir, because I owe you a great debt, but if I did what you ask I would make two people very unhappy, not to mention a third, for I don't love Miss Jessie as a man should love a woman, and she would suffer for that. Then the woman I love would suffer, too. And yes, she is from the Hollow, but she is an intelligent woman; she is a fine woman. You, sir, have never spoken more than half a dozen words to her in all the years she's been in your employ. And now I am going to say this: your

203

wife valued her; she lent her books, and she talked with her on the side when you were out of the way so it wouldn't annoy you, because she realised that the little Irish girl who came to your door, pointing out that she had washed her hands and her hair in the river, was worthy of better treatment than that meted out to a pigswiller or dairymaid.'

They were again looking at each other, each in deep sorrow now.

When Carl stepped back, he asked one question: 'Do you want me to leave now, sir?'

It was noticeable to them both that he was no longer using the word master; and with averted gaze Ward answered, 'You may work your month.'

When Carl passed through the kitchen, Annie turned from her seat and, looking at him, asked, 'What is it, lad? Something wrong?'

'Yes, Annie. Yes, you could say that, something's wrong. I'll . . . I'll talk to you in a short while.' And with this, he hurried out into the yard, where he stood as if in a daze, until he saw Patsy coming from the open barn.

He ran towards her and, taking her arm, drew her back into the barn, into the corner where some bales of hay were stacked but where the sunlight streaming in through the shrunken old oak slats dappled them both in light and shade as they stood looking at each other.

Patsy did not question, 'What's the matter? What's happened?' for from the look on Carl's face she guessed something vital to them must have taken place; and when he suddenly moved from her to lean back against a supporting beam, his head touching the wood as he muttered, 'We're free!' she sprang towards him, her hands on his shoulders now, her voice rapid as she said, 'You've told him? You've told him? And he said we can? Oh Carl! Carl!'

He brought his head down to the level of her own now, and quietly he said, 'No, he didn't say we can, he gave me the option: he offered me the house and the farm if I married Jessie.'

'No.' Her voice was a whisper. 'He made it as plain as that?'

204

'Yes, my dear; he made it as plain as that. But I told him I couldn't make her unhappy and myself at the same time because I loved you.'

When she fell against him, her head on his shoulder, he placed his arms gently about her; and as he held her he said, 'It was awful, Patsy, really awful. Although I felt I owed him so much, the price he was asking was too much for me to pay.'

'It's my fault.'

And to her almost inaudible mutter, he replied, 'No, it isn't your fault; it's nobody's fault. Anyway, we've got a month to find another place. And we'll be together, in the open. That's the main thing, because it's been a long time' – he raised her face to his now – 'overlong. It's odd, you know, but I was thinking about it this morning, that it was overlong already. Now we're going to be like Jimmy Conway and Susan Beaker. By what is said in the village they had been going together since he was nineteen and she eighteen, but he had to stay with his father until he died, and she had to stay with her mother until she died. And there they are now: she's thirty-six and he's thirty-eight, almost twenty years' courtship; and I could see ours being the same, because we've known each other for nearly sixteen years. Anyway, they are being married today. That's what made me think of it.'

She turned from him, yet retained a hold of his hand as she said, 'Strange that you should mention them; that was the first thing I thought of, too, this morning. I thought it was because Ma said yesterday that there would be high jinks in the village tonight, for both inns were stocking up, and Da said there would be free drinks all round because the butcher's business has been thriving and he had been the closest of men, and so Jimmy would be very warm. And he said the Beakers would be, too. Strangely, though, I didn't think about their wedding, I just wondered if we would have to wait almost twenty years, and if could we last out.'

They turned together to look at each other.

He bowed his head and, his lips in her hair, he said, 'For my part, I doubt it.' Again they were in each other's arms;

and now tightly holding, he added, 'We can make it as soon as you like.'

'Oh, Carl; as soon as ever you like.'

After they had kissed again a gentle, warm gesture now, they separated from each other and walked side by side into the yard.

But beyond the farther side of the barn, Jessie did not move, only, just as Carl had done, to lean her head back against the wood as she pressed her lips into an indrawn thin line in order to prevent the tears from spurting from her eyes. She hadn't meant to listen. It was as she walked along the back of the barn towards the hen pens to gather the morning eggs that she heard their voices, and stopped for a second to look through a cleft in the wood. And so she saw and heard almost all they had to say to each other.

Now she was saying to herself, 'Oh, Daddy! Daddy, why had you to do it? I could have borne it. But never to see him again. I might have been able to change my feeling into that for . . . a beloved brother. Yes. Yes, I could, because I am not a silly girl; I never have been; I have been made old by my feeling for both of you, you and him; and soon there will be only you, and you don't know I exist.'

2

'Look, Mummy! You promised. And you know it gives old Noble a kick if you're there. You're always saying he's a saint and should be supported.'

'Yes, I know, Gerald; but I made that promise before your father came in an hour ago and said Percy and Catherine would be popping in, and so I can't possibly leave the house. And Alice and Nell will be with them, and so you should be here, too' – she now wagged her finger at him – 'you should stay and *support me*.'

'The very sight of Nell terrifies me, Mummy; you know that. I shouldn't be surprised if she were to bring her horse into the drawing-room one of these days. She smells of the stables.'

Lady Lydia Ramsmore gave a girlish giggle, then put a hand over her mouth as she said, 'She does rather reek a little of the horseflesh, I admit; but Alice is nice, different.'

'Not different enough, Mummy. Anyway, I'd rather sit through a night with Captain and Mrs Hopkins and their *two* eligible daughters.'

'Your father will be annoyed.'

'I can't help that, Mummy; it'll only add one more annoyance to the list I create.'

'You're still of the same mind, dear?'

'Yes, Mummy, I'm still of the same mind. And always will be.'

'But literature, dear, is all very well; and you know how

I like reading. As far as I can judge it will be very difficult to make a career out of writing poetry and such. And another thing, dear: I just cannot understand why you are so against entering the Army, because you know you must have inherited something from both sides. You know, my ancestors, too, were involved in the battling business, oh, far back. And you know, dear, your father can't help getting annoyed when he hears Percy Hopkins rattling on about his boys fighting in the Boer War, and who will be sailing for India shortly. Don't you feel any remorse? I mean . . . well, not actually remorse, but . . . Oh, I don't know what the word is.'

'The word is guilt, Mummy. No, I don't feel any guilt in not going to shoot someone I have never seen in my life before. And let us state plain facts, Mummy: they are men who are trying to protect their own way of life and that of their families.' He bent over her now, where she was sitting on the couch, and his face close to hers, he said, 'I'm a changeling, dear; and at times I feel that you've had a hand in it. Now tell me, just between ourselves, did you not, in your gay days, fall in love with somebody like me, a literary man? A classics scholar, perhaps?' he teased.

'Oh, you are impossible.' She slapped him lightly on his cheek; but she was laughing as she pushed him away, saying, 'No, I didn't! But I have an idea from where you might have sprung, and from your father's side, too, for there was one of them more than a bit odd: he would eat nothing but greenstuff, and he lived for the last twenty years of his life in the end of the hall here, the part that was first built, and he never left it. I understand he sewed himself into his clothes.' She laughed outright now as she said, 'What he must have smelt like would certainly have put Nell in the shade. Anyway, he didn't waste his time, it must be admitted, and apparently he translated things from the ancient Greek language; but what it was he translated nobody seems to know. I think it's quite possible that the following generation wanted to forget him.'

'Where did you hear that, Mummy?'

'I didn't hear it; I read it one day when I was browsing

208

among the tomes in the library. I came across a sort of diary in which there were a few sentences about him, and when I mentioned it to your father his response was, 'Oh, him!'

'Well, Mummy, I can promise you that there's a chance I might follow the old fellow, and within the next forty, fifty, sixty years translate something from Latin or Greek, but I can also promise you I shall never do anything that will make me smell. By the way, you said he ate only greenstuff. I suppose that means vegetables. Odd that, don't you think? Because I'm not very fond of meat, am I? I'll have to look up that old fellow and get to know more about him. But now to the present. You won't come to the show?'

'We've been through it, dear. I can't come to the show. I have to live with your father, remember, while you can jaunt off, to Oxford or London or wherever your fancy takes you. Where's your fancy going to take you for the remainder of the vacation?'

'I've been invited to Roger Newton's in Shropshire.'

'Oh well. I'll miss you, dear. I always do.'

He now dropped down on to the couch beside her and, putting an arm around her shoulders, he said, 'I needn't go to Roger's; it was to be for only a short spell. They're having a hunt ball, and you know how I love hunting and shooting.'

'Then why are you friendly with him at all if he loves hunting and shooting?'

'Simply because we have like ideas. And fortunately for him he isn't plagued to take up arms. His people are in law . . . Oh, look at the time!' He pointed to the gilt clock on the mantelpiece. 'I must be off.'

He bent down and kissed his mother's cheek, and then, pulling a face at her, he said, 'Give my love to the girls, won't you? Have a nice evening.'

She again laughed at him, then said, 'Are you riding in?'

'No; I'm going to walk; it'll be a lovely evening, for there'll be a full moon.'

She watched him striding down the room, but before he reached the door she called to him, 'Your father will have something to say to you, remember.'

He paused and looked over his shoulder at her, and his

voice was flat now as he said, 'Yes, I suppose he will, dear.'
And with this, he went out, and she lay back on the couch
and sighed. He was such a lovely boy. No; not a boy any
more, a young man. But she wished, oh how she wished he
didn't annoy his father.

The magic lantern show was over and Frank Noble was
showing the children of the Hollow out of the door. One
by one he spoke to them as he handed to each child a square
of barley sugar, and they, in turn and each in his own way,
assured him it had been the best show ever.

It had been a poor audience tonight. In the past, there had
been as many as twenty children, but tonight there had been
only four from the outlying farms apart from the children
from the Hollow: a wedding tea had been held in Farmer
Green's barn earlier on, and at this very moment a dance
was being held there which would likely continue into the
small hours if the patrons from the inn should decide to join
them. There would be some sore heads tomorrow and, as
Jane had said in her forthright way, other results, too, if she
knew anything about barn weddings.

He turned now to his last three guests. His young friend
Gerald was gathering up the slides while Jessie and Angela
seemed to be wiping their eyes. 'Oh, I'm sorry,' he called to
them; 'it does give off a fug, doesn't it, that coke stove.' He
coughed, then said, 'It gets me, too; but I wouldn't have an
audience without the stove, now, would I?'

When they smiled at him, he said, 'Carl should be here
shortly. But we did finish earlier than I expected.'

'It was the dogs running, I suppose,' said Angela. 'It made
the time go quicker.'

He laughed at her joke, saying, 'I shouldn't be surprised.
It was a funny bit, that, wasn't it?'

'Yes. Yes.' Angela nodded at him. 'You would actually
think the dogs were running. You made them go so quickly;
and it was so funny when the little one hung on to the
policeman's trousers.' She paused before ending, 'I like the
funny ones.'

'Then I'll have to see if I can get some more . . . Do you like the funny ones?' He looked at Jessie, who answered, 'Yes, I do. But I also like the ones showing the black children. They all look so merry.'

'Yes. Yes, they do.' He did not add, 'some of them,' but turned to speak to Gerald who had joined them, saying, 'I am not going to ask you if you enjoyed the show, for I am sure it must be a penance to be behind the screen.'

'No, no; not at all. I think I get more fun watching the reactions of your audience, because, you know, I think some of them must groan, for they've seen the old ones so often.'

'No, they don't. Now! now! You can't get too much of a good thing. What do you say, girls?'

The girls said nothing, and there was a moment's embarrassed silence before Gerald said quietly, 'You're waiting for Carl to fetch you? But there is an awful fug in here; it's getting in my eyes, too. May I escort you along the road, until you meet him?'

As if she had been stung, Jessie took a quick step to the side, and taking hold of Angela's arm she turned her about, saying, 'No, thank you. You're very kind, but no thank you. And it's bright moonlight outside. Carl should be here any minute. We'll just walk along to meet him.'

As the girls made their way towards the door, Frank Noble looked at the face of the young man who had definitely been snubbed and whose expression was showing it; then he hurried outside, and there he stopped for a moment and drew in a deep breath of the cold air, as the girls were also doing.

Another time, knowing the feelings of their father, so protective as to amount almost to a mania and which to his mind was cramping their lives, Frank would have said to them, 'I do think you had better wait;' but tonight, the moon was giving out a light almost as bright as daylight, and although the show had finished early it was almost time for Carl to appear, being a few minutes off eight o'clock, so he said, 'You're bound to meet him within a very short distance; he's always on time, isn't he?'

'Yes; yes.' It was Angela who answered him. 'And I did enjoy the show. Thank you so much.'

211

As they were walking away he called to them, 'Oh, and don't forget to thank your father for that parcel: he is too kind.'

No answer came to him, but he watched until they were beyond the bend in the path and should be mounting the hill out of the Hollow.

The girls didn't speak to each other until they reached the brow of the hill and were on the path leading to the junction where one branch led off to the valley; and it was Angela again who spoke, saying, 'Why didn't you let him escort us? He's very nice.'

But when she received no answer, she added, 'And yet it's nice, too, to be able to walk alone, isn't it, Jessie?'

'Yes; yes, it is.' Jessie now caught hold of her sister's hand, and as she did so, they both turned their heads towards the sound of laughter and shouting that was reaching them from the village.

'That must be some of the wedding . . . party, and by the sound of them, they appear to be drunk.'

Their steps seemed instinctively to slow until Jessie said, 'They're likely on their way from the barn to the village inn.'

The laughter died away, and they resumed their normal pace until they were within a few yards of the junction; and here, emerging from the village path they saw three men, and over the distance they could see that the men were laughing, but silently. Angela pressed herself close to Jessie's side, and they stopped.

The men, too, stopped within a short distance of them, and one of them exclaimed, 'Good God! See who we've met up with?' And another one called out, 'Aye. Aye. An' we thought it was Mary Ellen and Cissie. But it's the Angel's daughters; he's let them out, and unprotected. Do you see, lads? Unprotected.'

Neither of the girls knew the man who stepped towards them and who, bowing low, said, 'Good evenin', missis. Are you lost?'

For a moment Jessie stared at the man she didn't know; then she appealed to the one she did know. He was the

212

verger. 'We are waiting for C . . . C . . . Carl,' she stammered.

The verger's fat belly began to shake, and he turned to his companion on to whom he was hanging, and in a thick and fuddled voice he said, 'Did you hear that, Pete? She's waiting for Carl.'

Without answering the verger, Pete Mason pushed him aside and, swaying, stepped towards the girls; and looking from one frightened face to the other, he muttered something under his breath; although his next words were just audible. 'The time has come,' he said. 'I knew it would one day.' And with this, he thrust out an arm and grabbed Angela, meaning to drag her towards him. But Jessie's hands tore at him, her screams joining Angela's, but only for a moment for Angela's were now being smothered: with an arm around her neck and the hand across her mouth, Pete Mason's other hand tore at the front of her cloak.

Meanwhile Jessie had been clawed away from Mason by the third man and was being thrust against a tree. There was a mighty scream within her which couldn't escape through the hand over her mouth; but it activated her limbs, as did the cold air that hit her chest when her blouse was ripped down the front.

Clawing at the man's face, she lifted a knee and brought it upwards; then she was free, with the man staggering back before doubling up. When she forced herself to move, she too staggered and not until her feet left the grass verge and hit the rough path again did she regain her bearings; and then she was screaming, 'Angela! Angela!' But there was no answering cry from Angela, only a rustling in the thicket to the side of the road telling her that the men were there; and her fear gave wings to her feet as she flew back towards the Hollow.

At the top of the bank she almost fell into Gerald Ramsmore's arms. Her hands gripping the lapels of his coat, she gasped, 'The men! They've got Angela.'

For a moment he was unable to take in what she was saying, for her whole appearance staggered him: her hair, which must have been piled up under her hat, was now

213

hanging down her back and part of her bosom was bare.

'It was the verger,' she was saying. 'They are drunk. They . . . ' She screwed up her face. 'He . . . one tried. Oh, please! Come! Come now!' She was pulling at him, and he was running by her side.

When they reached the place where Angela had been dragged from her, she pointed, crying, 'Look! There they are,' and he was able to make out three figures reeling drunkenly across the open field.

'Where is she? Where is she? Have they taken her? It was here! It was here! It was here!'

Gerald jumped across a shallow ditch and rounded a small group of bushes, only to come to a stop when he saw something that was to impinge on his mind for the rest of his life. This delicate, fairy-like girl whose beauty alone had always touched on his artistic sense and drawn his eyes towards her, lay sprawled, her arms outstretched, her hands at each side gripping the earth, the bottom of her skirt half covering her face, her lower limbs exposed; and he shut his eyes against the sight, and gripped his face tightly with one hand while he groaned. Then he spun around as he heard Jessie stepping over the ditch; and he cried to her, 'No! No! She's here; but she needs help. Get Carl. Go to your people quickly! Go and get help!'

'I must see . . . '

'Please, she's in distress. Go and get help.'

As she turned from him and leapt the ditch again, calling out as she ran, 'Carl! Carl!' he walked slowly to the side of the prone figure and, pulling the skirt down from her face, he slid an arm under her head, saying, 'It's all right. It's all right,' even though his mind was yelling at him that it would never again be all right for this child, never; and he went on, 'Your people are coming. Dear Miss Angela. Oh, dear Miss Angela.'

When she made no movement whatever, he thought, Dear God! She's dead. Then he dared to put a hand where he thought her heart was, and after a second or two he heaved a deep sigh. And now his hand was stroking the hair, that beautiful, seal-shiny black hair, from her face.

He was not aware of Carl's approach until the bending body over him blocked out the moonlight and the exclamation, 'O . . . oh!' preceding words which could have been said to be blasphemous, and then the loud and despairing, '*No! No! This can't have happened. No! No!*'

Gerald looked up at Carl and said quietly, 'But it has. We must get her home.'

Carl, too, was now kneeling by Angela, patting her face and saying, 'Come on, love. Come on. This is Carl here. Come on. Don't be frightened any more. Come on, love. Come on.'

But receiving no response, he muttered, 'Oh dear God!' Then looking across at Gerald, he said, 'He'll kill them for this; there'll be murder done. He'll kill them surely.'

'Do you think we could carry her between us?'

'Aye. Yes. But I can carry her myself.'

'There's some way to go; I'd better help you.'

After gently pulling up her ripped drawers and straightening her limbs, Carl picked her up bodily; and Gerald said again, 'Let me help,' and laid her legs across his arm, and together they started towards home.

They were about a quarter of a mile from the farmhouse when they were aware of Ward tearing towards them; and when he met up with them he stopped for barely a moment to look down on the white face of his child. Then thrusting out his arms, he relieved them of their burden; and without uttering a word he turned and hurried back to the farm.

Gerald followed on with Carl, and as they entered the yard, he said, 'If I could use your horse I could ride for the doctor.'

Carl turned to him. 'Yes. Yes, by all means, yes. But wait! I should see what the master says.' But then shaking his head, he said, 'No. She'll need a doctor. Oh yes, she'll need a doctor.'

Patsy could be seen standing in the light from the open door. Her hands were joined at her throat, and Ward called to her, 'Go and get Annie!'

After the evening meal, because of the condition of her legs, Annie usually returned to her cottage, leaving the washing-up

215

and the preparation for the following morning's breakfast to Patsy. And Patsy had been attending to these duties when Jessie, like a wild woman, had dashed through the kitchen, calling for her father.

She now took to her heels and ran to Annie's cottage and, banging on the door, she cried, 'Are you in bed?'

Annie's answer came back to her, 'I'm getting ready for it. What's the matter with you now?'

When the door was pulled open, Patsy gasped, 'The master . . . he's just carried Miss Angela in. She looks dead. And Miss Jessie's been attacked, the clothes torn from her back.'

'Dear God! What are you saying, girl?' Annie demanded, at the same time reaching out to lift her shawl from the back of the door and putting it around her shoulders. Then she was shambling as fast as her legs would carry her towards the house . . .

Fifteen minutes later she and Patsy gently drew the last of the clothes from Angela's bruised body. They were both crying, and it could be said they were both frightened of the master, and for him. Ward had not spoken a word until he saw that they had been about to wash his daughter's limbs; and then he said, 'Leave them until I get the doctor.'

Patsy now muttered quietly, 'He's been sent for, master. Mr Gerald from the Hall, he's gone for him.'

At this, Ward stood back and waited for them to put her into a nightdress, when he said simply, 'Leave her,' which they did. Annie went down into the kitchen where Carl was waiting; Patsy went to the bathroom where she knew Jessie would be. However, receiving no answer to her knock, she gently pushed open the door, to see the girl sitting on a stool. She was in her nightdress, her clothes lying in a heap on the floor; she turned her white and scared face towards Patsy, and her lips trembled as she muttered, 'Oh, Patsy, Patsy.'

Kneeling by the girl's side, Patsy put her arms about her and brought her head on to her shoulder, and as a mother would, she comforted her, saying, 'There, there, dear. There, there. It's all over.' And when Jessie murmured, 'No, no; never will be, never will be,' she countered, 'Yes; yes, it will. It'll fade away with time. I know. These things do.'

216

When Jessie's sobs shook them both, Patsy didn't say, 'Don't cry, my dear,' she murmured softly, 'That's it. That's it: get it out of you,' at the same time hoping that the death-like figure in the bedroom along the landing would soon wake up and that she, too, would cry. Perhaps, too, she would have something more to cry about. God help her. Oh, yes, God help her. Three of them! Oh Jesus in heaven! For such a thing to happen, and to a child such as Angela, so fragile, so light and airy as was her mother. As Annie had said, it would seem she was a twin fairy. Oh, this house. She'd be glad when she got out of it . . . when they both got out of it. But what was she talking about? Would Carl leave the master now, being able only to guess what his reactions would be to this outrage? And could she leave this girl, leave the pair of them with Annie, who could hardly trot now? Oh, and she had thought . . . she shook her head . . . enough of her own wants at the moment, for there would be more tragedies afore another day was out, if she knew anything about it.

'Come,' she said now; 'dry your eyes. There you are. And lie yourself down in the spare room. If Doctor Patten comes, he'll likely see you and give you a draught.'

Jessie pulled herself up from the stool, saying, 'I want no draught. I must go to Angela.'

'No. No, dear; your father's with her, and he sent us out. Leave him be until after the doctor's been. Come; do as I say now, and lie yourself down. I'll get you a hot drink, hot milk with nutmeg in it, the way you like it. It's very soothing.'

Jessie allowed herself to be led out of the bathroom and to the end of the landing; and in the spare room, Patsy said, 'The bed'll be still aired: you both slept in it not two weeks ago when I turned your room out. You lie down now, and I'll be back directly.'

As Patsy made to move away Jessie stretched out her hand and, gripping her wrist, spoke in a voice that held a plea and a question. 'What'll happen? What'll happen to her?'

'I don't know yet, my dear. I don't know yet.'

'Men are dreadful, aren't they, Patsy? Dreadful, dreadful.'

'Not all, dear. Not all. Lie down now. Lie down.' And

217

Patsy unwound the fingers from her wrist; then went quickly out of the room and stood on the landing for a moment, her hands gripped tightly against her neck as she was wont to do when agitated or worried.

As she went to go down the stairs, so the doctor was about to come up; and on sight of her, he stepped back and bade her descend; then without a word he passed her, and she continued to the kitchen, there to see the young master from the Hall talking to Carl; and she was surprised to hear his voice almost breaking as if he were on the verge of tears as he said, 'I'll never forget this night. I'll call in the morning to see how she's faring.'

'Yes; do that.' Carl was nodding at him.

The young man inclined his head towards Annie, saying now, 'Good night,' and she answered, 'Good night, sir. And whatever happens, you are to be thanked for your help.'

He made no response, but stared straight at her for a moment before turning and going out.

Looking at Annie now, the while pulling a chair forward, Carl said, 'Here, get off your feet,' and she obediently sat down. Then he asked of Patsy, 'How's Miss Jessie?'

'In a state. I'm going to make her a hot drink. I think the doctor should see her and give her a draught,' which brought the immediate response from Annie, 'Oh, I'd better go up and tell him then. And he might need assistance.'

'Stay where you are,' said Carl; 'Patsy can go and wait outside until he finishes what he has to do. She can tell him what is needed. And he'll have something to tell too. My God! he will at that. But speaking of draughts, I think it's the master who needs one; I'm fearful for him.' . . .

It was a full half hour before Philip Patten finished what he had to do. Even before he began his examination he had been aghast, and when, in a small voice, he had ventured to say, 'I think I should have Annie here,' Ward had come back with, 'What help you need, I'm here.' And so it had been.

Now that it was completed, Ward asked him in what appeared a deceptively calm voice, 'Will she live?' And Philip answered, 'I hope so: her heart is strong; but this will depend upon her will.'

218

'Her will?'

'Yes. Yes, I said her will.'

'Why doesn't she open her eyes? Is she unconscious?'

'She's in shock; and she might be like this for . . . well, two or three days. I can't tell you how long. On the other hand she might awaken tomorrow morning after the draught I have given her has worn off.'

Philip Patten watched Ward look down on his daughter, and what the man said next and how he said it sent a shiver through him. 'She is fifteen. Her woman time began last year; there could be results,' he said; then turning slowly to confront Philip, he stated rather than questioned, 'Even with the damage that's been done, there could still be results, couldn't there?'

Philip Patten gulped in his throat, and he had to look away from the eyes that were staring into his before he could say, 'That's to be seen; only . . . only the future can say yes or no to that.' And on Ward's next words, he had to turn his back on both the bed and the man, for Ward said, 'Three of them couldn't miss, could they?'

Philip made no reply, but then almost jumped when the voice barked at him, 'Could they?' and he swung round to face the distraught man, saying, 'We don't know if there were three. I mean, there were three men there, so I understand, but . . .'

'Then I ask you, doctor, could one man have done that damage?'

'Yes. Yes, he could.' Philip Patten's head was bobbing now and his voice was loud.

'But three could do more harm, couldn't they?'

'Ward. Ward.' Philip's head was drooped almost on to his chest, and there was a plea in his voice as he said, 'We don't know.'

'You don't know? You didn't see Jessie when she came in, half mad, the clothes torn off her back. She managed to escape; so, would that one be satisfied? No; he would take his turn.'

'Oh, for God's sake! Ward. You've got to stop this way of thinking, else it will drive you to do something that can only bring disaster. You must let it be dealt with by the authorities. I will contact the police myself.'

'Oh no! O . . . oh! no; you'll do no such thing, doctor!' And besides shaking his head, allowed his body, too, to follow the movement as if to emphasise his request: 'I'm asking as a favour, don't go to the police.'

'What! But those men must be punished. *And you mustn't, Ward. No, you must not* take it into your own hands. That will mean murder; and what will happen? You'll swing. Putting it plainly, you'll swing. And how will your girls be left then? What protection will they have?'

'Who's speaking of murder? I am not going to murder them. After what I intend to do, their own consciences, and the village, will murder them in their own way; just as they have murdered me over the years.'

Definitely puzzled now, Philip said, 'What . . . ? Well, I mean, what do you mean to do?'

'What do I mean to do?' Ward looked to the side. He had seen what he meant to do from the moment he had looked down on his daughter's ravished body. Although the method of its accomplishment was not wholly formed in his mind, in one part it was indeed very clear; but he had as yet to work out how to bring it about, and so he said, 'Just leave things for a few days, will you, doctor? I'll come back to you in, say a week.'

'A week! But they'll think they've got off with it. And what about Doctor Wheatley, when he gets wind of it?'

'I would think that if I don't make any move your superior won't. What do you think?'

What Philip thought was: Ward is right, for if a scandal such as this were to break it would scar his village, for just as it was usual for the parson never to think otherwise, he too considered it to be his, and far beyond the village. 'My patients,' he would say. 'Do not interfere with *my* patients.'

He said now, 'All right, I'll do as you wish. But don't forget that the young man from the Hall was the first on the scene, so I understand, and by now I should imagine he has informed his parents; he was greatly affected, you know.'

'Well, we shall have to take that chance. Being the

220

gentleman he is, he will likely call tomorrow to see what has transpired; if so I shall ask him what I have asked you, to remain silent for a few days more.'

'Oh, Ward.' The doctor put out his hand and placed it on Ward's shoulder, saying, 'Don't do anything that's going to bring retribution on you. I beg of you.'

'If there's any justice in the world, it won't; but is there any justice in the world?' Ward said vehemently and through his clenched teeth; but then added more calmly, 'Has any justice been dealt out to me and mine over the years because, as a young man, I was silly enough to be pleasant to a young woman whom I had no intention of marrying? Justice is blind, Doctor. I thought you would have become aware of that in your profession. The young and innocent die, while the no good, Godless, wrecking, raping villagers survive. But how they'll survive after this is another question . . . oh yes.'

Philip could find no way to refute Ward's original request, but the implied intent in the last words, spoken with such a look in the man's eyes, made him shiver, and so without further words, and not even a nod of assent or goodbye, he picked up his bag from the table, glanced once more at the bed and left the room.

In the kitchen, he looked from one to the other and said, 'He'll likely sit up all night with her, but I think somebody should be on the alert.' And Carl said, 'Don't worry about that, Doctor. I'll be up, and Patsy, too.'

'Good night then,' he said; and as an afterthought added, 'I imagine the running of the place will now have to be shared between you for a long time to come.'

3

The village was uneasy. A strange tale was being circulated.
Some believed there was some truth in it, others denied it
flatly, saying it had originated from Rob Riley in the Hollow,
who with his father worked for Ward Gibson. Part of the
rumour was that the young daughter had been frightened by
some drunks from Jimmy Conroy's wedding. Some said that
the young girl had been interfered with. But how could that
happen? She was never let out without a guard. A disgrace,
it was, the way the lasses were hemmed in. But there was
something wrong, and Fred Newberry said so to his parents.
It was the first time he had been in that house, he said, and
had not been offered a cup of tea or some such; and when he
asked of Ward's whereabouts, he was told that he was busy
upstairs. And that was that. He had come away thinking
they were all close-mouthed about something, and it must
be to do with the rumour that was going round the village.
It wasn't like Ward not to have a word with him, although as
everybody knew he had been acting strange ever since he had
lost his wife. All he now seemed to think about was building
his walls and his fences higher and not letting the girls out
of his sight.

It was Fred's mother who had said, 'Perhaps he's afraid of
Daisy escaping again, because she has become sly enough,
you know that. By! she was sly. I was always thankful
she didn't pass her spleen on to us for being friendly
with Ward.'

The patrons of the two inns were asking similar questions. Was there any truth in the rumour? And who were the three fellows who were supposed to have shocked the girls? It would be hard, it was said, to pick them out of all those who danced in the barn and had drunk deeply from the barrels that night, for it had been classed as one of the best wedding receptions that had been held in the village for many a year, if you could rate it on the liquor drunk and the food eaten. Nevertheless, it was generally agreed there was something afoot. But what? And look what had happened to Parson Noble from the Hollow when he called at the house: he had collapsed and had been taken home to bed. Oh yes, there was something fishy about the whole business.

It was on the Wednesday morning that Angela opened her eyes; and the first face she saw was Jessie's, and she made a moaning sound as she lifted her hand towards her. Gripping her sister's hand, Jessie cried almost joyfully, 'Oh! Angela. Angela. You're better. Oh, that's wonderful. How are you feeling?'

Even as she said it she knew it to be a silly thing to ask; but she waited for the answer.

When her sister's mouth opened and shut and no words came, she said, 'All right, dear. Just rest. Don't trouble yourself. I'll go and get Daddy,' and she ran from the room and to the landing window that looked on to the yard, and shouted down, 'Patsy! Patsy! Carl!'

When Patsy came running from the dairy and looked up at her, Jessie called, 'Get Daddy! Angela has come round.'

'Oh, good! miss. Good!' And Patsy ran the length of the yard and round by the woodstack and into what was called the box-house, used for stacking timber and cutting staves, where the master had been for the past two days doing things with binding twine and shaving poles as long as clothes-props. What he intended to use them for, she didn't know; and neither did Carl, who had said they were much too long for fencing. He had also cut yards and yards of binding twine into strips. In a way, it was frightening. She did not enter the place, but stretched her arms across the opening

223

to grasp the stanchions and leaned forward, crying at him, 'She's come round, master! She's come round!'

Almost before she had time to move aside he had rushed past her and was in the house and up the stairs.

When he thrust open the bedroom door and saw his beloved child looking towards him, he hurried to her; then stood aghast when her mouth widened as if she were about to scream; then shrank back from him, her hands spread wide against her shoulders as if pushing him away. And at this, Jessie cried, 'It's Daddy! Angela. It's Daddy!' And she stepped aside so that he could come further up the bedside.

Bending over her, he said softly, 'It's me, my love . . . Daddy.'

When he took hold of her hand, she tried to withdraw it; which elicited from him the plea, 'Look at me, dear. See? It's your daddy, who loves you. Angela, look at me.'

Her eyes were now tightly closed, and as if in despair he turned to look at Jessie, and she said, 'It's all right, Daddy. It's as the doctor said, she's still in shock. She'll know you shortly.'

He straightened up and turned slowly from the bed, and he whimpered, 'Oh, my God.' He had seen a look of horror in her eyes because she was looking at a man. What if she didn't recover? The thought was so unbearable that he turned quickly again and, taking hold of Jessie's hand, pulled her towards the door, and there, bending down to her, he whispered, 'Keep telling her, will you, Jessie? Keep telling her that I'm her daddy, I'm not the—' He jerked his head to one side, breaking off what he was about to say.

And she, holding his hand in both of hers, pressed it tightly as she said, 'It's all right, Daddy. It's all right. I'll make her understand. Don't worry. Please don't worry.'

He nodded at her, and said, 'Yes, you do that, Jessie. You do that.'

'I will, Daddy; so please, don't worry. Try not to.'

The fact that he did not withdraw his hand from hers, that she was the one who let it go, caused her to experience a feeling of warmth. For the first time in her life she felt needed, and by the one who mattered most to her. But oh, if only it

224

hadn't happened this way. Her hand went to the front of her dress and gathered the material into a bunch as if she were once again being exposed and that not one, but two, three men were tearing at her. Last night she had woken up screaming, and Patsy who had been sitting with Angela had hurried into her room and comforted her. Patsy was like a mother to her. What would happen to her when she left? She didn't mind any more her having Carl because what she really wanted now was a mother to comfort her. As Angela did. Oh yes, Angela needed a comforter.

She went hurriedly to the bed now, and bending over her sister, she said softly, 'It's me, dear. It's me. Open your eyes.' And obediently Angela raised her lids and her mouth opened again as if she wanted to speak. But no sound came; and Jessie said, 'It's all right, dear. Don't try to speak yet. But that was Daddy. And Daddy loves you. You know Daddy loves you. He is not one of those wicked men. Try to understand, darling. Do try to understand he is not one of those wicked men. And don't close your eyes again. Look at me.'

When Angela's eyes opened wide again, Jessie went on talking to her: 'You know what I was thinking, dear? That when you are better I am going to ask Daddy to take us on a holiday to the seaside. You would like that, wouldn't you? We have never been on a holiday, have we?'

When the head on the pillow was slowly turned to the side and towards her, she reached out and pulled her chair closer to the bed and in such a position that she herself could lay her head on the pillow and in much the same position as they had done since they were children, except for the times when one or the other would flounce about after some petty upset.

However, now Jessie knew that never again would there be petty upsets between them; nor ever again would she be jealous of her sister's beauty or of her father's love for her. Life had changed for them both, for good and all.

4

Philip Patten called every day. When, by Thursday, Angela still had made no effort to speak, and when Ward asked tersely, 'How long do you think this will go on?' he was given the blunt answer: 'It could go on for ever, as long as she lives, as could her fear of men. Such cases have been known. She's afraid of me, and of you; but I don't know how you are going to break that down. You'll have to be very, very gentle with her. That's all I can say. But of one thing I must warn you with regard to the future, unless something untoward happens, enough to overcome her present condition, and I really can't see that coming about, well, in that case, there is little hope of her leading a normal life. But' – he let out a long slow breath – 'you never know; we are not masters of our destinies. God, if you believe in Him, seems to take a hand now and again.'

'*Be quiet! man.* What are you saying?' Ward's words were not tersely spoken now, they were growled out.

Philip did not come back with any sharp retort, but in softly spoken words, he said, 'Yes, I'll be quiet, for I know so little; my training has left great gaps; I can only follow my books and common sense. And so, at times, you have to leave it to the Deity. That's all one can do. Well, I'll be off now; but' – he hesitated – 'before I go I will dare to say one more thing to you. It's a piece of advice: I think you must remember you have two daughters, and that Jessie, too, is in a state of shock. I think

226

she's coping admirably, but only because of the potions she is taking.'

Without further words, he turned towards the stairs, leaving Ward to stand looking after him, his teeth gripping his lower lip; then he turned to glance towards the bedroom door: leave the rest to the Deity, he had said. Well, some things had been in the hands of the Deity too long; from now on he would play God, and see what came of that.

On this thought Ward hurried down the stairs. He did not, however, pass through the kitchen, where he would no doubt have to re-encounter the doctor, who would assuredly have been plied with a hot drink; instead, he opened the glass door that led into a small flower garden; then skirted the back of the house and made for the grain store where, just a short while ago, he had seen Mike Riley enter, two large scoops in his hand. He knew from experience that, being on his own, Mike would take his time to fill them; and he wouldn't be surprised to find him sitting at rest among the sacks.

In this case he was wrong, for Mike was about to emerge from the store weighed down with the two large heavy scoops. On seeing Ward, he put them down on the ground, saying, 'You looking for me, master?'

'Yes, Mike, I was looking for you.' And he pointed to the two skips, saying, 'Pull them to one side, I want to shut the door.'

Mike did as he was bidden and in the dim light afforded by one narrow window he watched his master close the door, then walk between the racks of the narrow room, before seating himself on a box a little distance from the window. As he followed Ward he had to wonder at such unusual behaviour, but he was indeed surprised at the question now put to him: 'Can I trust you, Mike Riley?'

Mike's eyes narrowed, and his big, broad face screwed up for a moment before he said, 'If you were to ask me, master, what I think of that question, I would say it was unnecessary, for you should know if you could trust me or not. I've nivvor taken a grain of corn from this place, although I have chickens of me own. I've nivvor asked Pattie for a bit of butter or cheese . . . '

227

Shaking his head impatiently, Ward said, 'I'm not meaning that kind of trust, Mike; I'm meaning, would you stand by me in trouble?'

'Trouble! Oh aye, aye if you're in trouble, master, I'm your man. Aye, I'm with you there.' The tall middle-aged Irishman now nodded as he repeated, 'Trouble? You'll have no better beside you, if it's trouble you're in, than meself.'

'That's good enough for me. What about Rob?'

'Well now, Rob's from me own bone an' breed, an' being as big as meself, an' only half me age, he'd be on the other side of you.'

'How many Irish families are there in the Hollow?'

'Seven of us. But that's not the lot of 'em down there. Counting them of a different colour, bein' Protestants, there'd be sixteen families all told.'

'Are there any among your lot . . . I mean the Catholics, that I could rely on as much as I can on you . . . I mean, who wouldn't shirk me in a tight corner or in taking a risk?'

'Oh, well now, there's Tim Regan an' Johnnie Mullins; there's a pair of them that I'd bet me life on. An' there's another; but he's a Scot, an' not of our colour; but he's a grand fella. That's Hamish McNabb. He's a great talker, a bit of an agitator, I'd say, but there's nothing wrong in that.'

'Which one of the lot has been along the line for break-in and entry?'

'Oh . . . ' Mike now tossed his head slightly as if throwing off any aspersion on his friend as he said, 'Oh, that was Johnnie, master, but it was some long time ago . . . five years or more, an' he's nivvor had to look a polis in the eye since.'

'Do you think he could still pick a lock?'

Mike's face stretched, his eyes widened, and he said, 'You want somebody to pick a lock, master?'

'It's one of the things I want.'

'Oh well, now. Well, now' – Mike's face spread into a beam – 'Johnnie's the boy for you. He could pick the teeth out of your head, an' you wouldn't know they'd gone. He makes locks, you know; a sort of pastime. He makes 'em out of any old bits of iron and tin. An' keys. Give him a bit of wire and a file an' the Bank of England would be open to you.

But' – and the smile went from his face now – 'he looks after his family, he does. And he's a hard worker, he is, when he can get it. You've had him around here, master, when you've needed more in the fields, an' he's not like some that only go when they're pushed.'

Ward passed over this comment, and what he said now was, 'You have a gun?'

Again Mike's expression changed; but this time he didn't speak, and Ward said, 'It's all right. It's all right, I know you're not licensed; but you shoot, don't you?'

'A rabbit now an' then. Not so much lately; it was when things were tough.'

'But you can still shoot?' The words came out with force now.

'Oh aye . . . yes, master, I can still shoot.'

'And straight?'

'Aye, master, an' straight.'

'What about Rob?'

'Oh, Rob. He could shoot the pom-pom off a Scot's glengarry an' the fella wouldn't know it was gone. Oh, Rob's a . . . ' He stopped, knowing he had said too much; but then he added offhandedly, 'Well, I put him in the way of it from he was a lad. An' it was only rabbits or rooks and crows; an' the Colonel's keeper turned a blind eye 'cos he was glad to get rid of the vermin. You see, they haven't got the staff up there to see to things as they used to . . . '

Ward's upraised hand stopped the flow; and now he put a hand to his brow and squeezed his temples tightly for a moment before saying, 'The main thing about this business, Mike, is a closed mouth. Can you count on your friends keeping their mouths shut for forty-eight hours?'

'Aye, master; I'll stand for them. It all depends upon how many you want; but however many, they'll go along with what I say.'

'Besides yourself and Rob I'll want another two, perhaps three. How many guns are there in the Hollow altogether?'

Mike looked a little sheepish now as he said, 'Well, Rob's got one, but it's an old shot-gun. The pellets fly all over the place. But when he uses mine his aim's as straight as

229

a die. There's only the two; but now an' again I lend Tim mine 'cos he's like family. As for Johnnie Mullins, well, he seems to manage without guns. He doesn't need suchlike implements, he says. 'Tis the locks that . . . ' He was stopped again, this time by the look on Ward's face; and now Ward said, 'Listen to me carefully. Bring the men you choose here to me tomorrow night round eight o'clock, and I will tell them what's required of them; at least, some part of it. But now bear this in mind, Mike: if one of them opens his mouth that they've been here, or even gives a hint that something's afoot, there'll be nothing afoot, and what is more neither you nor Rob will put a foot in this place again. D'you get my meaning?'

'I do that, master. Yes, I do that. An' let me tell you as man to man, so to speak, you have no need to tell me to keep me mouth shut.' He did not add, 'Nor that of my son,' for what he had done to his son on Tuesday after he found he had opened his mouth about the happenings to the lasses would be nothing to what would happen to him if he dared to let his tongue pass between his teeth about this new business, whatever it was.

Ward rose from the box, saying, 'One last thing: don't mention any of this to Carl;' and in some surprise, Mike said, 'He's not in on it? Carl?'

'No; he's not in on it.'

Mike thought it best at this point not to ask why; he simply followed his master to the door and picked up the scoops and went about his work, his mind in a questioning whirl as to what the master was up to. Whatever it was it was some funny business that required guns, and somehow he felt shy of guns himself.

It was early evening on the Friday that Ward spoke to Patsy, who was now helping in the house. 'Go and tell Carl to come to my study.'

Although he knew that the house, in a way, was now depending on her services, for Jessie hardly ever left her sister, he could not bring himself to be civil to her, for he still saw her as the one who had frustrated his plans

230

for the future, which concerned this house and the lives of those in it.

When for the second time within days Carl stood at the other side of the desk, he was not this time bidden to sit. Ward addressed him immediately, saying, 'You haven't changed your mind?'

Looking pityingly at the man before him, Carl did not pause before he said, 'In one way, sir' – there it was again, the sir instead of the master – 'I am very much of the same mind. I mean to marry Patsy. After you dismissed me I made it my business to have a word with Parson Noble. He is putting our first banns up on Sunday. But having said that, sir, I must tell you that right from' – he paused a moment – 'this terrible thing happened, we knew we couldn't leave you as long as you needed us: Patsy, too, is strong on this point and ... '

Ward cut him off here saying, abruptly, 'Later on this evening some men from the Hollow will be coming to see me. I am using them for something I have in mind, and you are not involved in it.'

Carl's voice was stiff now when he said, 'And may I ask why?'

'Yes, you may. And the answer is, I may return here after the event, or I may not be long at liberty ... Whichever way it goes, I may not remain long at liberty. And in that case, I' – he wetted his lips now – 'I would need you to carry on, as you always have done, and to see to my daughters until such time as I return.' He looked down at his desk now, and asked himself on what counts would they be able to take him? And the answer was, on two. But there were extenuating circumstances, surely? Here, however, his line of thinking was sharply interrupted by Carl's action of leaning across the desk, his hands flat on it, and himself appealing to him. 'Sir, for God's sake! don't do anything rash. I mean, anything that might have you put away. They need you. The two girls, they need you. And what's done's done: retribution is not going to help them.'

'If you were in my place, would you let those men go free?'

Carl drew back slightly. His head was drooping now, and he thought, No. Oh no, for he, too, would have sought revenge.

Slowly he straightened up, then quietly he said, 'Whatever happens I am with you for as long as you need me; and no matter how long or short you might be away, we' – he did not say 'I', but 'we will see to your house and land and family as long as it is necessary.'

Ward did not say, 'Thank you,' but his head drooped and he looked down on his desk again; and on this, Carl went slowly from the room . . .

The men were assembled in the barn. Besides Mike Riley and Rob, there were Tim Regan, Johnnie Mullins, and the Scotsman, Hamish McNabb. Of them all, this last man stood out, for he was the tallest, standing about six feet, but of bony frame and with a long unsmiling face, whereas Tim Regan was of the same sturdy build as Mike and Rob; but the one who seemed not to belong to either the Irish or the Scots clan was the one called Johnnie Mullins. He was small and thin, but was wiry.

They had all risen to their feet when Ward entered the barn; and he now stood surveying them. All except Rob were middle-aged; but he knew from experience that at least four of them were strong; of the small thin one, he knew nothing.

Ward looked at him now, saying, 'Your name?'

'Johnnie Mullins, sir.'

He stared at the small man for a moment. Then he glanced towards Mike before addressing him again, saying, 'Could you open a vestry door?'

Now Johnnie Mullins narrowed his gaze and peered along the line of men as if to say, That's a damn silly question, isn't it? Then looking straight up at Ward, he said, 'I could that, sir, any time you like.'

'You're sure?'

'Oh, I'm sure.' The thin face was unsmiling now. 'But to prove it to you, sir, I could take you back there this minute; in fact, I'll do it as we're passin' the church, and Mike there can give you the verdict in the mornin'.'

Ward, now looking towards Tim Regan and the Scotsman, said, 'You're both used to guns?'

Tim Regan looked slightly sheepish, but Hamish McNabb answered, 'If I had the pleasure, sir, of havin' one in me hand, then I could use it. No man better. 'Twas in the Army I spent my early life; an' travelled I am. There's nothin' I wouldn't do, sir, to help a man in trouble.'

He was about to go on when Ward put in, 'Yes. Yes.' He hadn't met up with this man before, but from the sound of his voice and volubility of his talk he was surprised he was still living in the Hollow. But then he recalled something: he hadn't actually met up with him personally, but he had seen him. Yes, he it was who had led a pit strike and was now likely blacklisted. He had been in the Army, and had come into the mines later in life and so did not possess the miners' inbred tenacity to put up with such unremitting toil. He said briefly, 'You will have a gun. But there's one thing I would like to know first. There was a third man in the assault—' He wetted his lips before he added, 'on my daughter. I don't know his name. The verger was one.' And now he had difficulty in uttering the second name, 'Pete Mason was the second. But I would like one of you to find out who accompanied these two when they reached the barn on . . . that particular night.'

It was the Scot who spoke up again, and quickly. 'Oh, I can name him for you, sir, right away. If he was with Will Smythe and the farmer Mason, then 'twas Smythe's relative. His name's Wilberforce. He lives on Walker's Bank, not five minutes from the inn. He left along with the others. I was there that night. Free drinks there were.' He turned to look from one to the other now and smiled. 'They were all very merry. I can say that for them. Not blind, nor mortallious, they could stand on their feet; but they were on their way to finish up the night at the barn dance. Oh, it was Wilberforce. There you have it, sir.'

In the ensuing silence, the five men looked at Ward, who was staring down towards the straw-strewn floor; then they watched him put his hand to his inner pocket and bring out a four-folded piece of paper, and after looking round as if

233

for some place on which to lay it, he went towards a broad standing beam that supported the roof; and here, unfolding the sheet, he said to Mike, 'Bring the lantern.' When he seemed satisfied with its position, he called to the others, 'Come here!' Then to Rob, 'Put your hands on the top and bottom of this sheet,' and after Rob complied, he began his explanation: 'This is a drawing of the screen in the church,' he said. 'I am giving you instructions what to do in order that I can fulfil my intentions, at least, in part. And this is what I wish you to do. But before going into detail I must ask you to be prepared to be here at six o'clock on Sunday morning, and everything done as quietly . . . ' and he repeated, 'as quietly as possible.' He paused now, then said, 'Who of you has a young son who could run an errand?'

It was Tim Regan who answered: 'My youngest is ten. He's a good lad an' he's quick on his feet.'

'Then I'll want him to run two errands. Don't tell him anything beforehand. Bring him with you on the morning. Now these are your positions.' He indicated a position to each man in turn. 'And this is what you must do.'

As the men listened, their eyes, without exception, widened; and when the expression 'Holy Mother of God!' escaped the lips of Tim Regan, Ward turned on him sharply, saying, 'You're not getting cold feet?'

'No . . . No, no, no, sir. I've never had cold feet in me life.'

'Well, you might all have when I tell you that if you're recognised you could be in trouble. *I'm* prepared for that; but as for you, I think you should cover your faces in some way.'

'Oh, master.' It was Mike now, laughing as he spoke. 'We could cover our faces till the cows come home, but once we open our mouths they would know; if not us individually like, then from where we hail. The trouble you refer to, sir, means the polis; we could be run in?'

'Just that,' said Ward briefly.

'Well, here's me; I'm for me plain face. I don't know about the rest.' He looked from one to the other of his neighbours, and it was the Scot who said, 'I've never covered up in the face of any foe, an' I'm not goin' to

234

start now, sir. In for a penny, in for a pound. That's what I say.'

'An' . . . an' so say I.' Tim Regan was nodding now.

'Thank you. Well, in that case I will leave it in writing that should any of you be detained with me for a long or short time your families will be seen to.'

'Well, you can't say any fairer than that. Englishman that you are, you can't say any fairer than that.'

Ward turned a sharp glance on the Scot. He knew he was dealing here with a man who would neither bow his head nor touch his forelock to any master, and although he knew it stemmed from the same pride as was in himself, nevertheless, he didn't like it. He said now, 'Anything more I want you to know I shall pass on through Mike.'

He had actually stepped out of the barn and into the dimly lit yard when he turned back and, facing the men, who were now gathered in a bunch, he said, 'As for yourselves, you will be well paid when this is over, whichever way it goes.'

They replied in chorus, 'Thank you. Thank you, sir.'

Once in the house, Ward went straight upstairs and to his own bedroom, and there, taking a chair, he sat by the head of the bed and put his hand on the pillow where once her head had lain, and he spoke to her, as he did every day.

'Am I mad, Fanny?' he said. 'Am I mad? What put this idea into my head?' And it was as though he did receive an answer from her, for he said, 'Yes. Yes. The minute I saw her, I knew what I intended to do, but didn't know how to accomplish it. But now I know.' He stared at his hand on the pillow for quite some time, and then he said, 'You are not for it. I know . . . I know you are not for it, my love, as you are not for Carl going. What's done's done, you say, as he said too, but I am me, Fanny; I am still me. Even your soft tongue and guiding hand could not keep me from dealing out this retribution.'

Again he waited; and then he said, 'Well, Carl will be here; and he's going to marry that girl. And you understand that, too, don't you? You have always said she is for him; but I don't see it like that, my love. Anyway, come what may, he will look after the girls . . . What do you think will be the outcome, my love? Oh, don't fade away. Please don't

235

fade away.' He now leaned over and laid his face on the pillow. 'And don't ask why I can't let you go. I've told you I thought I could, because Angela was you re-born; but now, you see what's happened: she shrinks from me. I can't stand the agony of it, Fanny. Fanny, don't go. Don't go.'

When there was a tap on the door he sprang up, straightened his neckerchief, stroked his hair back, and said, 'Yes?'

Jessie entered, saying, 'The doctor has come. He's sorry he couldn't get here earlier.'

'I'll be there in a minute.' He made small movements with his hands as if waving her away. And he stood now staring towards the door before turning slowly again and looking at the bed and the dent in the pillow where his head had lain; and he asked himself again if he was mad, while appearing sane on the surface, and the answer he gave was: well, if he was he had been mad for some time, and he couldn't see himself returning to normality, because she was with him in this room. He knew she was. She was always waiting, because he willed her to be here. But at times he was made to wonder if it was the sane patches in his mind that made her cry out, 'Let me go!'

Where was it going to end? In a like place as the mad bitch who had willed disaster on him? Yes, there was the word 'willed'. You could will things to happen. He had willed Fanny's spirit from the grave, and now he was willing infamy on the village. What he would make happen would cause that village to stink for generations to come. The pride of the hypocrites would be ground into the dust. As he saw it, in justice he owed it to himself.

236

5

∽

As soon as the first two members of the congregation, Mr and Mrs Napier from The Lodden, entered St Stephen's on this Sunday morning, they not only sensed, they knew something was wrong. Miss Steel, the new assistant teacher at the village school, who had taken over as organist when John Silburn had given it up because of cramp in his hands, was not doing her weekly duty, and they knew that playing the organ was in her contract, for the school was under the patronage of the church. And then, what was the matter with the screen? Had something happened to it? The left hand side was completely covered over with what seemed to be a hayrick sheet held away from the top of the screen by poles, but kept in place at the bottom by three large stones.

But why? They hadn't heard that there was anything wrong with the screen. If some idiot had defaced it, it would soon have been made known around the village.

So too thought the rest of the congregation as they took their seats. And there were murmurs here and there as people leaned forward or back over the pew and whispered, 'What do you think's happened to the screen? And there's no-one in the organ gallery, I notice.'

The tolling of the bell seemed to be the only sign of normality in the church.

As was usual, the gentry were the last to file into their pews. There were six of the Hopkins' from Border Manor, an indication that they must have someone staying for the

237

week-end. These days, there were only two of the Bedfords, for their daughter had gone over to the Methodists years ago. Then there were the Arkwrights. They were comparative newcomers to the village, having been here only six years. They had moved into Whiteberg Farm; Mr Arkwright was what was called a gentleman farmer. And lastly this morning, there were the Ramsmores.

The colonel, it was noted, really was getting doddery, and his son just managed to prevent him from falling as his foot caught the end of the pew.

After the bell stopped tolling there was an eerie silence in the church. At this point it was usual for the vicar, followed by his servers, to emerge from the vestry, the choir having already assembled in the gallery; but this morning there was no emergence, no swishing of surplices; the only procession being that of the Youngston family entering the church and being quickly ushered into a back pew, the mother and father admonishing, as usual, the four children to be quiet.

But then a series of very unusual events began to occur.

First: the church door was closed with a bang; and when heads turned towards it, they saw a strange man standing there grasping something by his side. Here and there, those near enough to him thought it to be a gun; but that was surely not the case.

Secondly: the congregation's attention was swung to the opening between the screens and to the two men who had appeared. One of these was certainly carrying a gun. This man walked down the steps and to the far side of the covered screen. *His* gun, however, wasn't being held by his side, but in a position that left no doubt as to what he meant to do with it.

The astonishment of the whole congregation had so far kept them silent, but now there was a concerted gasp as the first man made his way towards the pulpit, for even those at the back of the church, as well as those straining their necks to see beyond the pillars at the left side of the main aisle, immediately recognised him as being the farmer, Ward Gibson.

All through his young days and well into his twenties, Ward had watched Parson Tracey climb the steps of this pulpit, and now here he was, standing in it, gazing on the sea of faces and gaping mouths. All the week he had known what he was going to do, and at times he had wondered whether he would falter in his purpose; of how he might react when he was forced to speak of his daughter and of her ordeal. But now, he found he was possessed of a strange calmness, albeit a smouldering calmness, for he must go beyond telling them, he must drive home into the minds of these staring faces something they would never in their lives forget.

For a while he allowed his gaze to roam over them; then he spoke, and quietly. 'Some of you may not know why I am standing in this pulpit, here in place of your hypocrite of a vicar. Well, I shall tell you. I am standing here because there are three men, all church-going, God-fearing citizens, who are so vile that they do not deserve to live.

'As you all know, I have two daughters, and I have tried to protect them since that mad woman, Daisy Mason, killed my wife; but although she was put away, the threat hanging over myself and the children did not abate. Your opinion, as a whole, was that I deserved all I had got because I dared to marry someone other than that mad bitch, to whom I had never offered marriage in the first place. The girl I married . . . the woman I married was superior in all ways to anyone I am looking on now. She was an intelligent, cultured woman. Yes, she was a dancer; but that was her career, as it had been that of her parents before her. They were artists, of which profession you, neither the high nor the low among you, would know anything.'

He now passed his glance over the front rows as he went on, 'It should happen that last Monday night I allowed my daughters to attend Parson Noble's lantern show. I had them escorted there, and my man was on his way to fetch them, but it being a bright moonlight night, they did not wait for him, they dared' – and now he leaned over the pulpit – 'they dared to walk alone on the outskirts of this village. Do you hear me? They *dared* to walk alone. And the first time they walked alone they were confronted by three men.' He drew himself up now and took in a deep breath before going on. 'My daughter, Angela, a replica of her mother, but even

239

smaller—' his voice now faltered a little as he said, 'has just turned fifteen, and therefore had already reached her womanhood.' Now he again bent over the pulpit, but further this time and, his head swinging from side to side, he allowed his gaze to rest on different women, and he repeated, 'She had just come into her womanhood. Well . . . she was torn from her elder sister and dragged into a field while her sister was also being attacked and the clothes torn off her back. She, thankfully, managed to escape. *But what of my little Angela?* Many of you, in fact, all of you, have seen her at some time or other. She is tiny, fragile, no semblance of a fifteen-year-old village girl about her. She was from another sphere, as was her mother.' He stopped now, and there wasn't a murmur in the church, not a cough, not a movement. And then, his voice became so loud, so high-pitched, almost a scream, so that many of the faces were screwed up against it as he cried, 'She was raped by three men! Not one . . . not two, but *three*!' His head was now bowed and he was gripping each side of the pulpit. When he raised his head he wasn't a little surprised to hear women crying. But it did not touch him in the least; and he went on. 'She was found by a young man who was so shocked at the sight of her that he said he will never forget it to his dying day. And this young man helped to carry her home.' He now looked down to where Gerald, his face white, his lower lip drawn tight between his teeth, was staring at him. And he went on, 'She did not open her eyes for two days, and from the moment she was laid on the bed until this very morning she has not spoken a word, and Doctor Patten can give me no hope that she will ever recover normality. What is more, she is terrified to death of the sight of a man . . . even of me' – he now thrust his finger into his chest – 'I who love her as I did her mother daren't go near her.'

Again bending forward, and in a rising voice he said, 'But this is not the end, is it, ladies? This is not the end. We will not know for two, or perhaps three months, will we, what her body holds, if anything but the feeling of torture.'

A man now stood up and cried at him, 'Enough! Enough!' then looked down on his wife who was bent double: and

240

Ward answered him, 'No, not yet,' and when after a moment he added, 'I have only just begun,' an actual shiver passed through all those present.

He now took one step back as if he were about to leave the pulpit, but then stopped and said, 'I would advise you, every one of you, not to make any move at all,' and he pointed now to the man at the church door, then to the one standing by the screen. And then he did turn and descend the steps of the pulpit.

Having walked across the front of the screens, he knocked on the vestry door, all eyes having followed him. When it opened and there stepped out another man with a gun and, following him and almost tottering on his feet, there came Parson Tracey, the whole congregation gasped when it could be seen that his hands were bound behind his back and that he was gagged. Behind him came four servers. They were all young boys, and they cast pleading glances towards their parents in the congregation, bringing forth cries of, 'Oh! Oh!' from here and there. Then followed seven members of the choir, and the lady organist.

The men looked sheepish, but it was noted that she held herself straight and looked defiant. Lastly came the bell-ringer. He was an oldish man and he was actually smiling as if he considered the whole thing a joke; that was until a few minutes later, after they had been lined up along the steps at the foot of the uncovered right-hand side of the screen when, as did everyone else, he watched two of the men go behind the screen.

It soon became evident that they had loosened something, for the great heavy sheet began to slip, together with the poles that had prevented it from hanging straight down and close to the front of the screen. The men quickly reappeared and were just in time to gather up the sheet and the poles as they fell. These they laid aside in a tumbled heap . . .

What was revealed now caused, first of all, a horrified, blank, utter silence, then a great combined gasp, followed by cries of loud protest; and here and there a moan. Some women actually collapsed in their seats or on to the floor, *for there*, strapped to the screen by their ankles, their arms,

241

waists and their necks, and their mouths gagged, were three naked men. Their heads could not hang in shame, so tight were they held against the ornamental ironwork, but their eyes roamed, wild with fear.

Great shouts and cries now came from different parts of the church, some calling on God, others, mostly from men, shouting that enough was enough. But when the latter cries came to Ward's ears he yelled back at them, 'Not yet! Not quite,' and with this he leapt up the steps and put his hand behind the screen, and when he brought it forth he was holding a splay tailed whip, and on the sight of which a great roar came from the colonel. But when he stepped into the aisle with the intention of making for Ward, Mike Riley's voice rose into a shout above the mêlée, crying, 'Stay where you are!' He too had stepped forward, with his gun at shoulder level; and fixing his gaze on the colonel, he said, 'Another step, Colonel, an' I'll splatter your knees with so many pellets you'll be pickin' 'em out for months.'

Whether or not he was deterred by this, or by Lady Lydia preventing his further movement by putting her arms around him and pulling his wavering body back into the pew, it did not prevent him from yelling at Ward, 'You'll pay for this, my man! I'll see to that.'

'No doubt. No doubt, Colonel. As I always have done, I'll pay for this but I'll do it gladly.'

He now motioned towards Mike, indicating he should step back; then he went and stood before the verger; and he looked into the man's fear-filled and cringing face for a number of seconds before he brought the whip viciously twice across the bloated loins, and the fat repulsive-looking body jerked within its tight bounds, and the screen seemed to shudder.

Seemingly taking no heed of the cries of the women and screaming children, he now stood in front of Pete Mason, and his gaze remained longer on the hate-filled eyes before he meted out the medicine again, with three lashes this time.

He did not hesitate when he came to the third man, for this one had offered no fight when he was trapped: he was a cringing individual, trying to put the blame on the other two; and so he did what he had to do. Then he walked to the opening in the screen again, before turning and looking at the congregation, some crying, some shouting, others just standing utterly mute. He went now to where a man and woman were undoing the vicar's bonds. They had taken the gag from his mouth, and he was gasping for breath as Ward addressed him, saying, 'It's all in your hands now, Vicar. When the police come they know where to find me; so we'll take it from there, shall we?'

The vicar's response was to cry out: 'You'll . . . you'll pay for this day, Ward Gibson. God . . . God's house will not be mocked.'

Ward's reaction to this was to motion to the man standing at the back of the church, and to the one who was still holding the gun at the ready. Two other men then emerged from behind the screen and rolled up the sheet that had covered it. And then they all followed Ward into the vestry.

When the door had banged closed behind the men the hubbub in the church died away for a moment, but there was no immediate rush to release the men from the screen. But then, as if of one mind, a number of men rushed forward, some to stand in front of the trussed figures in order to hide their nakedness, while others went behind the screen and endeavoured to undo the knots of the ropes binding the men firmly to the framework.

When a lone voice cried, 'They'd better have a doctor,' another drowned it by screaming, 'It's the polis we want, and now, for it's no use trying to explain what has happened; they'll want to see it for themselves. I'll ride in this minute.'

'No. No.'

It was the vicar now, clinging to the lectern for support, and he repeated loudly now, '*No! No! I say*. Listen . . . listen, all of you. *That is what he wants*. Don't you see? He wants the polis brought here. He wants this to be taken to court and blazoned in every paper in the country, because he's out to defame this village. Don't you see? Don't you see?' His arms stretched wide, he was swinging his body from one side to the other in an endeavour to influence them all.

It had its effect, for, apart from the continued moaning of some women and the crying of children, the commotion

243

died down, and the vicar again shouted his warning: 'If this is blazoned in the papers, this village will never again be able to lift up its head; but what will happen? It will become notorious: people will even come from a distance to see the screen that has been defiled by these men, who themselves have defiled nature. God forgive them, because I never can. My . . . your church, God's house, will become a peep-show. I can see it all as clearly as if it is happening now. This place would attract young hooligans from the city because a maniac of a man has taken justice into his own hands and tied three naked men on a holy screen before scourging them. *Can't you see? Can't you see the headlines?*' He paused again; then, dropping his arms and joining his hands together, he pressed them outwards, beseeching his congregation now, 'Let us suffer this together. Let us not even discuss it among ourselves. The three men who have committed this outrage will suffer from it for the rest of their lives; they will be ostracised by all good folk.' And now his voice rose as he ended, 'As will the perpetrator who has dared to commit sacrilege in the house of God this day. That man has been a bane on this village for years, and has wrought havoc on a good-living family; he has been the means of incarcerating one of that household, and through sorrow causing the early death of the mother. Ward Gibson is an evil man and . . . '

Suddenly, not only the minister was now startled but also the occupants of the first rows of the select pews, as young Gerald Ramsmore almost sprang into the aisle and, facing the parson, cried, 'He is not an evil man; he is a man who has been wronged. Your narrow-mindedness, sir, has helped to turn the villagers against him. Yes, you're afraid of bringing in the police because it would show up your hypocrisy and that of many more who attend this church. And why do they attend? Let me tell you: not for the love of God, but for the fear of where you might place them in the so-called society of this community.'

A voice suddenly barked, 'Be quiet! Hold your tongue, sir! I order you. Come here this minute!'

Gerald Ramsmore turned and looked at his father's florid face, and to him he said, 'I am going to speak my mind.

Remember, Father, I was the one who came across that child after she had been savaged by those three evil individuals.' He pointed towards the men now being led into the vestry, and then flinging wide an arm, went on, 'If anyone here had seen the state they left her in, they would never . . . as I shall never forget the sight till the day I die.'

He looked at his father again and cried, 'I'll tell you this, sir: I only wish I had been asked to take a hand in what has transpired this morning. Yes, right up to the use of the whip.'

Gerald was drawn now to look at his mother, whose eyes and voice were beseeching him; her arms were about his father, steadying him, and for a moment he lowered his head. He knew he had gone too far: his father was an old man. But anyway, he had said what in justice had to be said; and now, bringing up his head again, he marched past his people and up the aisle and out of the church, leaving behind him another kind of amazement.

Those of the congregation who were now moving out of the pews, many women being helped by their menfolk, turned once more as the vicar addressed them.

In a shaken voice, he said, 'There is confirmation of my words for you: evil has the power to bring discord into the best of families. And you know from where this particular evil springs.'

6

'How could you do such a thing, Gerald! And to your father. And in front of the whole village – to defy him like that! Oh, I know, I know that poor man has had a lot to put up with; and now his poor little girl. And those men deserved to be punished. Oh, yes. Oh, yes. And I would have gone along with him, all the way, no matter what your father said; but I would have had the sense to keep it to myself. What came over you?'

Gerald looked at this woman whom he loved, she whom he could never understand having married his father. What on earth had she seen in this stiff-necked, narrow, ageing, opinionated man who thought that the Army was the beginning and the middle and the end of life. Although they had been married for twenty years, he couldn't imagine he had ever been much different from what he was now.

He said gently, 'I'm sorry if I upset him so much, but it had to be said. Mr Gibson is a good man – you yourself have always said so – also that he had been misjudged from the time he married his pretty little wife.'

'Oh yes, I know . . . I know.' She flapped her hands at him. 'Personally, I like the man, but you cannot get away from the fact that it was because he married that pretty little wife, and having rejected a young woman with whom he had been friendly for years; and really, the truth is he must have deceived not only her but her parents into thinking his attentions were other than serious, and that was very wrong

246

of him, and consequently he has wrought havoc in the Mason household. And now, Gerald, whether you want to believe it or not, he is causing havoc in this house. And your career is at stake now, for your father says he will no longer support you at Oxford, and you must know, in any case, he has found this difficult, for our finances are stretched to the very limit. He has already had to sell a cottage and another stretch of land in order to meet your expenses. Just think, too, how I have had to cut down on the household, and in the yard also.'

She turned from him now, saying tearfully, 'It was inexcusable of you, Gerald, inexcusable.' And with this, she turned from him and hurried out of the breakfast-room, along the corridor and into the small drawing-room. And after closing the door, she stood just within the room and put her hands over her face.

Her whole body was shivering, not only from the coldness of the room, but also with anxiety and fear of what was now going to happen to her son, for she knew that unless he went into the Army his father would wash his hands of him. And she also knew in her heart that there was no threat strong enough to drive her son into the Army.

She now walked further into the room and sat on the edge of a chair, asking herself just what was the matter with her son? her beloved son, her only son, her only child. Why was he so different?

She would never forget the night, which was the forerunner of what had happened in the church today. She had left her husband in the billiard-room. She liked a game of billiards; but having been brought up in the diplomatic world, she knew it was policy to give way to the other side more often than one would normally do, and she did this often when playing her husband at billiards, for now neither his hand nor his eye were as steady as they once were. She had found out very early in their married life that he *had* to win in most everything he undertook: if battles were lost it must never be his fault; and that evening she had left him happy again as he knocked the balls here and there on the table, and as she entered the hall she had said to Roberts, 'Has Mr Gerald come in yet?' And he, looking up the broad staircase, had answered, 'Yes, madam. Just a few minutes ago. And—' he paused before adding, 'he seemed in some distress, madam.'

At this she had hurried up the stairs and, after knocking on his door and receiving no reply, she had pushed it gently open, there to see her son sprawled across the bed, his shoulders heaving.

She had hurried to him, saying, 'What is it, Gerald?'

When she placed her hands on him and he did not turn to her, she couldn't believe, for she did not want to believe, that her son was crying, actually crying. And it shocked her, and in that moment she thanked God that his father was not present.

She had been brought up in a family of four brothers and three sisters. Now and again the sisters would cry, as Ann had when she received news of her young husband having been killed in battle; but when her brother Harry had lost the girl he was going to marry just two days before the wedding when her horse had rolled on her, he had remained dry-eyed, even at her burial. Men didn't cry. No; men didn't cry. *No, men . . . did . . . not . . . cry.*

Her voice had been curt as she pulled him around, saying, 'What on earth's the matter with you, Gerald? What has happened? Why are you in this state, crying like . . . ' She did not add, 'a girl?' nor 'a woman?' because he had now swung himself around to the edge of the bed and, his head bowed, he had taken a handkerchief from his pocket and dried his eyes before looking up at her and saying, 'I am crying, Mama and, as you were going to add, like a woman, because tonight I have witnessed something that will be imprinted on my mind for ever: I have looked on the ravished limbs of Mr Gibson's young daughter, the small one who was the image of her mother, after she had been raped, Mama. *Raped, Mama, raped,* and by three men! Yes, apparently, three men. I don't imagine just one could have wreaked the havoc on her body as I saw it. She was unconscious when I found her; but at what stage her mind closed up will never be known. The elder sister, too, had the clothes torn from her breasts. When she came running to me she was like a mad thing; she had just

248

escaped from one of the fiends. I had seen both girls just a few minutes earlier. It was a moonlight night, so they wouldn't accept my company because Carl was to meet them.'

He had then leant forward and gripped her arm and, his voice choking, he had said, 'You know how I hate shooting, shooting anything, but I have longed to go after those men, at least the two that Miss Jessie recognised, and blast them to hell.'

When she had muttered, 'Oh, Gerald, Gerald . . . How awful!' she didn't know whether her horror was against the crime that had been committed on the girl, or the fact that her son had been so affected by it that he would actually have done what he said, or because he was crying his eyes out.

And then she had been further shocked a few minutes ago when he had said, 'I have waited all the week wondering why her father was making no move; but the retribution he must have been planning was more effective than anything I could have thought up. And I was elated. Do you hear, Mama? I was elated by the outcome of his plan and, as I made clear, my only regret was that I couldn't join him in the infliction of the punishment he was dealing out.'

It was from that first painful scene that she knew she had, in some way, lost her son, for the man that had been born in him that night was of a stronger and more determined nature than any military training could have achieved.

Yet he had cried. She would never be able to forget that he had cried; and in such an abandoned way.

7

~

They waited for the coming of the police, those in the
farmhouse and those in the Hollow. And when by Monday
evening neither a police constable nor a reporter acting on
rumours had made his appearance, Annie said to Carl, 'It
couldn't be they are going to let such a thing as this drop;
you know, besides the flailing they could be had up for
levelling guns.

'And then there were the fights they'd had afore they could
get them stripped. They say it was Pete Mason who left his
bootmarks on Johnnie Mullins. His shin was split. But both
he and the Wilberforce fellow must have been scared in the
first place when they assumed that the notes were from the
verger; as Mike said, they came skittering into the vestry like
rabbits. But whereas Mason put up a fight, the other one was
as cringing as a beggar. Well, they got their deserts. The only
thing I'm sorry about is I wasn't there to see it.'

Raising his eyes to look up at the ceiling, Carl said, 'Patsy
says there's no improvement whatsoever,' and to this Annie
replied, 'And if you ask me, there never will be; she's gone
far away into another self, and it's filled with terror. One
thing I do know, if her fear of a man doesn't soften a little,
himself will wither away inside. You mark my words. And
God knows, there might be still more torment for him to
come. But this we won't know for a time, will we?' She
looked at Carl, who was sitting at the end of the table, and
she added, 'There's one good thing has come out of all this:

250

he can't do without you; in fact, he can't do without you both, for Miss Jessie must have somebody to relieve her or shortly she herself will end up in bed. But 'tis odd' – Annie nodded her head now and repeated, ' 'Tis odd, really it is, for that young lass has come into her own with this business, an' there's no gettin' away from the fact that himself, though he be her father, didn't even seem to notice she was there. It was Angela, Angela, all the time; but of course, being so much like her mother, you could understand that. Still, now that he's got no solace in that direction, he's havin' to look at his first-born. Although he's seeing her without any real feelin' for her, he will, nevertheless for the future, I should imagine, have to rely on her.'

Annie now turned to the stove, her voice trailing away as she said, 'Funny that. And all she ever wanted from him was a kind word, a loving word, which she never got.'

It was on the following day that Fred paid a tentative visit to the farm. Their boyhood friendship and that of their early youth had been strained somewhat over the last few years as Ward had grown more and more into himself. But now he was knocking on the kitchen door, and when Patsy opened it, he said, 'Hello there,' and she answered simply, 'Hello,' and looked back to where Annie was at the table cutting raw meat away from a bone, and she said, 'It's Mr Newberry,' and Annie called, 'Come away in, Fred. Come away in.' And then she added, ' 'Tis some time since we've seen you.'

'Aye, Annie, aye. Business has been brisk. How are you?'

'Fine, Fred, fine; at least down to me waist, the rest of me is rotten.'

He grinned at her; then straight-faced again, he said, 'Me mother . . . I mean, we all were upset about the latest business, Annie. And poor little Angela . . . Is he about?' And to this she answered, 'No. He's along the corridor, in his office, where he seems to spend more than half his days. He's in a state. You can understand.'

'Oh aye. Oh aye. D'you think I should pop along and have a word?'

'Yes, I would do that, Fred; an' I'll have a drink ready for you when you come back.'

'Ta, Annie. Thanks.' He walked around her cautiously as if he were unused to being in this kitchen, and he smiled at Patsy before going out.

When he tapped on the study door, there was no answering voice calling, 'Come in,' but the door was pulled open, and Ward stood there, looking surprised for a moment, and when Fred said, 'I thought I would just pop in, Ward. Hope you don't . . . you don't mind,' Ward stood aside, saying, 'No; come in, Fred.' And after Fred had passed him, he closed the door, then pointed to a seat, before again seating himself behind his desk. 'I suppose you're surprised at finding me here?' he said gruffly.

'No; no, man, no. I'd have been surprised if I hadn't found you here. That would have meant that all had gone against him.'

'Gone against him! What d'you mean, gone against him? Who do you mean? What are you talking about?'

'Well . . . well, you know, Sunday. Me meself, I've never set foot in the church for years. You know that. But it seems some of them wanted to get the authorities straightaway. It was then the young master from the Hall jumped up and what he didn't say wasn't worth listenin' to, so they tell me. And the old man, the Colonel, yelled at him, an' he yelled back. He said he'd stand up in court and tell . . . well' – Fred now lowered his eyes – 'just how he came across poor, dear Angela . . . ' Then looking directly at Ward again, he went on, 'That seemed to put the seal on it. Anyway, they have all taken heed of what Tracey said, that the village would attract hordes of all kinds, so they had to keep their mouths shut.' He now leant forward towards Ward, adding in a low voice, 'And I know this: almost everybody in the county would have been with you.'

Ward made no comment, and there followed a silence for a few moments, before Fred, his tone changing, said, 'Charlie and his lads were a bit peeved, you know, Ward, that you hadn't let him and us in on it. He said he would have liked nothin' better than puttin' some iron into his fire an' shaping body-belts for the three of 'em; and similar things have been said in the village here and there. You won't believe it, Ward; you never would; but there's a lot over there that are for you. Always have been. And they've always objected to old Tracey making out that the village was his. And you know somethin' else, Ward?' Fred's voice dropped a tone: 'Yesterday, me dad had me drive over two big baskets of stuff to the Hollow, and it wasn't all week-end stuff, stale. No; some was freshly baked yesterday morning. But it was just to show that if they went along the line their womenfolk would be seen to.'

Ward lay back in his chair and looked at this kindly simple man, this innately shy man, one who was never likely to marry and so experience the heights and the depths of such a state, but who could only find his happiness through supporting and being supported by his close friends. And at this moment he felt a tinge of guilt at never having appreciated Fred; in fact, he had despised him for his simplicity. But now he said quietly, 'Thank you. Thank your dad and your mother, too. Tell them . . . that I appreciate what they did, and their support.' And he added, 'And yours, too, Fred. Yes, and yours.'

'Oh' – Fred's head now wagged from one side to the other – ' 'Tis nothin', man. 'Tis nothin'; we just want you to know we're with you, always have been. And my mum told me to say if there's anythin' she can do, you know where she is. Night or day. An' she says she could put her hand out to half a dozen others who would say the same. Women are handy at these times, you know, Ward.'

It was too much. Ward could stand no more at the moment, not of this kind of emotion, such sympathy tore at him.

He now rose so quickly to his feet, saying, 'Have you had a drink?' that Fred almost fell backwards with his chair as Ward passed him, and he laughed as he stumbled and said, 'You'd think I'd had one of the hard stuff already, wouldn't you? But Annie said she would have a drink ready for me.'

'Good. Anyway, thanks for coming, Fred. And, as I said, thank your dad and mother, and—' He nipped on his lip before he could add, 'Charlie and the rest.'

'I will. I will, Ward. I'll tell them.'

In the hall, Ward placed a hand on Fred's shoulder and gave him a gentle thrust towards the kitchen, saying, 'I'll be seeing you.'

'Aye, Ward, aye. So long then.'

Ward stood for a moment watching this friend making his way to the kitchen. Then he hurried up the stairs to his daughter's bedroom. But after entering the room, he stood looking towards where his beautiful little Angela was sitting propped up in a chair to the side of the bed, her eyes wide and staring. To her side sat Jessie, the book she had been reading aloud from now lying on her lap, and she turned to look at her father and said one word that was hardly above a whisper: 'Slowly.'

And he obeyed. Walking almost on tiptoe, he crept towards the chair. And he looked at his daughter, and she looked at him; but this time she did not shrink back into her pillows. And Jessie now smiled at him and nodded her head, and he nodded back at her, and when she made a small flicking motion with her hand he stepped back from the bed and walked softly towards the door again.

When it had closed on him, Jessie, leaning towards the still figure, said, 'That was Daddy, dear. He came to see how you are. Do you understand?'

The face was turned towards her; the lips opened slightly but no sound came from them, and Jessie said, 'You're not afraid of Daddy; he loves you very dearly. Never, never be afraid of Daddy. You see, I'm not afraid of him.'

It seemed that the slight chest heaved as if a long breath were being drawn into it; and Jessie said, 'You liked this story, didn't you? It's about the little match-girl. At one time it used to make you cry, didn't it?'

As Jessie now lifted the book to begin reading again, she thought, Oh, if only it could make her cry again. But they were making progress. Oh, yes; they were making progress because she no longer shrank into her pillows when their daddy came into the room. His next step must be to sit at the very foot of the bed. A thought now crossed her mind, which was startling: she was giving her father orders, and he was obeying them. It was like being imbued with a strange power, and she recognised that it was this feeling that was keeping her going and enabling her to see to her sister, for at times she felt strangely ill: her nightmares were not abating, and whenever she fastened her bodice she could feel that man's hands on her.

But her father had avenged her, avenged them both; Angela more so, of course. Oh yes, Angela especially. If it had happened to her alone, would he have gone to such lengths as she had heard had transpired in the church on the Sunday morning, when naked men were strung on to the screen and lashed? When her mind aimed to conceive the picture of its happening she brought the book nearer her face and began to read, her voice over-loud as if to drown her thoughts.

8

~ ⚭ ~

It was six weeks later when Angela indicated that she was
about to be sick. Patsy happened to be sitting with her at
the time. She had, by now, persuaded the young girl to sit
in a chair by the window. There were two windows in the
bedroom, one overlooking the yard; the other, at the back
of the house, had a view of the garden.

It was to the latter that they would lead her, Jessie and
Patsy between them, as if the small slight girl were an old,
enfeebled woman.

The routine repeated itself day after day. First, they would
wash her, then place the breakfast before her, which by this
time she would manage to eat, at least in part, although
never quite finishing it. They would then wrap her in a warm
dressing-gown and sit her before the window. She was, however, never left on her own. And this was tiring for the two
girls, although Annie, when her swollen limbs would allow
her to climb the stairs, would occasionally give them relief.

Patsy no longer had time for the yard work, and so
another dairymaid had been engaged by Carl. She came
from Fellburn on the carrier's cart, arriving at nine in the
morning, leaving at six in the evening. It was soon apparent
that she knew her work well; and this lessened any objection
Ward might have felt, for the dairy produce supplied a good
portion of the profits.

But this morning the daily routine was to be altered, for
Angela, for the first time, was sick.

256

When Patsy saw this, she did not exclaim as Annie might have done, 'God in heaven!' or call on the deity in any way, for her feelings were too deep, in fact, too frozen with the horror that this sign portended.

The effect on Jessie, however, was different: she exclaimed loudly, 'Oh no! No! Please, Angela, no! No!' Then she turned to Patsy beseeching her now to deny what she was saying, 'Is this a sign? It is said that . . . Oh Patsy! Patsy!'

'Hush! Hush! What will be, will be, miss. Yet she ate more than usual last night; and fish has a tendency that way.'

'Oh please! Please say it is the fish.'

'I can't, miss, not yet; we'll have to wait a day or two to see if it is repeated.'

'But Daddy . . . '

'Say nothing to the master, miss, nothing at all. Do you hear? For we don't know, not for sure.' Yet in her heart she *was* sure; but she could only hope that the child would be born dead . . .

Two weeks later Ward learned that his daughter was carrying a child, but it was days before he reached a state of acceptance such that he could sit opposite his beloved daughter as she gazed out of the window, for straightaway he had again felt the urge to take drastic action. In any case, he could have done nothing more to the perpetrators of this evil, for they all had left the village; even Pete Mason, so he understood. The desire for vengeance was however more than ever terrible for it was becoming centred on his own child. For two nights running, while pacing his room, sleep being beyond him, he had thought she would be better off dead than bringing into the world a being bred of one or other of those beasts. Which of them was responsible would never be known. What lay ahead for the offspring? How would it face life when the knowledge of its creation was one day thrown at it, as undoubtedly it would be, either through tormentors or someone deciding it was time the creature should know why it was isolated, for isolated it would remain all its life in this place.

So yes, she would be better off dead, also the creature that was inside of her. But how to bring this about?

257

His mind grappled with the means. There were weeds and herbs that could kill cattle and were known to be dangerous to humans: there were the seeds of the laburnum; there was monkshood. These could be administered in her dinner drink; her fear of him had by now so lessened that she would take something from his hand.

When Annie had put him in the picture, for neither Patsy nor Jessie dared break the news to him, and had dared to say, 'It's God's will,' he had screamed at her, 'Don't be so bloody stupid, woman!' And when she hadn't retaliated, as she usually dared to do, but said quietly, 'I'll say it again, if it has to be it has to be, 'tis God's will; and 'tis said He works in mysterious ways. And I'm goin' to say this to you, whether it vexes you or pleases you, it has taken this happenin' to make you realise you yourself have a first-born, and it's only now she's come into her own when you need her,' her words had angered him further, and he had banged out of the room. But from then on he was honest enough to ask himself what he would have done over these past weeks if it hadn't been for Jessie, for she had not only comforted her sister, but in a way she had aimed to comfort him. But what of the future? Would she be able to cope with two children, for surely Angela would go on needing the constant attention of a child?

And it was at this point there came into his mind the thought that she must not be put to the test . . .

It was almost a week later when he forced himself to enter his daughter's bedroom. It was mid-morning and she was sitting by the window; and as he slowly approached her, she turned her head towards him and the expression on her face seemed to alter slightly. And when he took the seat opposite her, she actually leant a little towards him, and a strange sound issued from her opening mouth.

Jessie, who had been straightening the coverlets on the bed, rushed towards them now, saying, 'Daddy, did you hear that? She was trying to say your name.'

He shook his head. 'It was merely a sound.'

'But she has never . . . never made that sound before.' And she bent close to her sister now and said, 'Say it again, Angela. Say "Daddy".'

Angela looked at her, and her stare became blank for a moment. Then her eyelids blinking, she again made the sound, and now it was distinct: 'Dad . . . dy.' The word was drawn out, but it was certainly 'Daddy'.

Ward lowered his chin on to his chest and bit hard on his lip; then, his hands reaching out blindly, he picked up Angela's fragile one from where it was lying limp on her dressing-gown and pressed it between his palms, before laying it gently back on her knee; then rising from the chair, he made to go out of the room, only for Jessie to step in front of him before he reached the door.

Looking up into his face and with a sob in her voice, she said, 'It's a start. She'll come back now; and she'll be your Angela again. She will . . . she will. And she'll need you more than ever now, Daddy.'

Then her father made a gesture that brought the tears streaming from her eyes, for he put out his hand and gently stroked her cheek as he said, 'You're a good girl, Jessie, such a good girl.' And with this he left the room, and Jessie moved to the other window, where she pressed her mouth against the wooden casement in order to stifle the sound of her sobbing and in an effort to subdue her emotion . . . Her daddy had caressed her cheek; her daddy had spoken to her like that; her daddy had looked at her as he had never done before, with a deep kindness in his eyes. She was overcome. Whatever happened in the future, even though his whole devotion be again centred on Angela, she wouldn't mind; in fact, she would pray that it would happen, because from now on he would be aware that she was there: he had touched her; he had caressed her cheek, and looked at her as he had never done before.

Patsy stood in the little sitting-cum-living-room-cum-kitchen of Carl's cottage. She had just put the new print cover she had made on the biscuit pad of the two-seat settle that flanked the wall between the open range and the scullery door. The cover matched the pad on the seat of the armchair at the other side of the fireplace; the small wooden table in the middle of the room was covered with a chenille cloth much too large for it

259

so that the ends almost reached the floor; although, as Patsy thought, it gave a tone to the room, for it wasn't everybody who had a chenille table cover, and she'd always treasure it, for it was the combined wedding present from those in the Hollow; even the Protestants, her mother had said, had tipped up their coppers. On the wall opposite the fireplace was a small delph rack, and it held a full tea-set, besides four fine dinner plates with matching side plates. All this was a present from Annie: it had been her own wedding present many years earlier, but she had always felt that the tea service was too good to use, and so it had remained stacked away in a cupboard. But on a Sunday she had used the other two plates belonging to the dinner service. But when they were accidentally broken she had replaced them with cheap white ones from the market stall.

Patsy had been very touched by this gift, and she had dared to kiss the giver, being more than surprised when Annie had taken her into her arms and hugged her for a moment before roughly pushing her aside, saying, 'Now then, that's enough of that kind of palaver.'

She was now waiting for Carl to return after breaking the news to the master of tomorrow morning's event.

A few minutes later, when she heard his step on the path, she flew to the door and pulled it open, and when he stepped in he put his arms about her and hugged her tightly. Then when they were seated on the settle, still enfolded, she said, 'Well, how did it go? What did he say?'

Carl turned his head away and looked towards the fire. 'I'm so sorry for him, Patsy,' he said; 'he makes my heart ache, so much so that at times I think I could cry. I do. I do really.'

'Yes. Yes, I know. In a way I feel the same. But what did he say to you when you told him?'

'Well, he stared at me for some time without saying a word, and I didn't know what his response was going to be; and then it was surprising, for his voice was quiet and he said, "I can only wish you to be happy. I've always wished that for you. I think you know that." That's what he said. And when I said, "We'll just have the morning off; we'll be back about twelve," he said, "There's no hurry. There's no hurry. Annie will help, and I'll be there." And then, what d'you think? He went to a drawer and took out this.' He put his hand into his pocket and brought out a chamois-leather bag, and opening it, he poured ten golden sovereigns on to her hand.

As she looked at him, her mouth agape, he said, 'And that's not all: he's putting up my wage by five shillings a week, and yours by three.'

'*Never!*'

'Well, what am I telling you? Eight shillings a week in all. That's what he said.'

'And that means he's got no intention of letting us go then?'

'I shouldn't think so, my dear, because he needs you more inside than he does me outside.'

'Oh no, no. You're runnin' the place, as you have done for years. It would gallop downhill if you weren't here, and he knows it. But oh, I never expected him to be so kind.'

'Nor me; but at the same time, if anybody's worked for a raise, it's been you. Because who would want your job inside there? Fourteen hours a day, seven days a week, because you've never had your full time off for weeks.'

'Oh, that doesn't matter.' She now put her arms around his neck and said, 'Where else would I want to be but where my heart is? An' tomorrow my heart will be right in this house.' She moved her head and looked around the small room. 'This is my palace . . . our palace, an' I'll keep it as bright as such, even if I've got to take hours from the night.'

'That you won't.' He pulled her to him now, laughing down into her face. 'You'll do it some time in the day, but not in the night.'

Her laughter now joined his; but presently she said, 'Never in me life, Carl, did I think it would ever happen. I've dreamt of it a long time, while tellin' meself it wouldn't be my luck, me from the Hollow and you from here.'

'Oh Patsy. Patsy. Never look down on yourself like that.'

'I don't . . . not really, but others do. An' you know they do. And there's families down there, I know, who have already said I've got above meself. And there are others from the village who will think you're stoopin' very low in takin' Gibson's dairymaid, and her from the Hollow. I know what people think; I've been wide awake to it for years.'

'Now look here!' He had her by the shoulders, shaking her now. 'There's no real difference atween you an' me. I don't even know who my people were, brought up in a workhouse, then farmed out to a villain of a man. You know who your parents are, and your father's a decent fellow.' He made no reference to her mother, but went on, 'Tomorrow you'll be my wife, and that's all that matters to me—' then seriously, he added, 'If poor Parson Noble can stand up to it. You know, I'm worried about that man: he looks as though he'll not last much longer; he's never been the same since that night, for he blames himself and the lantern show. But' – he smiled now – 'he'll be there, never fear, to make you the mother of my children, and I want at least six, oh yes, and I want them mostly boys because they can claim better wages than the girls. And we'll start them off early in the fields . . . '

Her body shaking with laughter, she beat her closed fists on his chest: and then they were holding tight again, until of a sudden he almost thrust her from him, saying, 'Only one more night. Come, you'd better go back to the house.' And silent now, she let him lead her out of the cottage.

9

Carl and Patsy were married in the first week of June, and the following weeks were taken up with long hours and hard work, but no matter how tired they might be some part of the night was given over to their love for each other; and so they were content and happy, at least between themselves. But the atmosphere in the house could not help but impinge on their lives, as more and more work fell to Patsy's lot within the house, and more responsibility, besides the actual work, had to be taken on by Carl on the farm, for the master seemed to have forgotten that he owned the place and therefore had decisions to make. Carl was forever asking him if it would be permissible to take this or that step with regard to the rotation of the crops; or about the price to be charged for what they might be sending to market on a Saturday, for at the time prices of farm produce were very unstable indeed.

And then there was the feeling emanating from the village. This wasn't pointed so much at Carl, but at the men, the Irishmen from the Hollow, for it had been made plain to them that they were not welcome in either inn and, further, some of them were finding it not only difficult but impossible to get set on as casual labour on two of the other four farms hereabouts.

At one period, Carl felt he had to bring this to the notice of the master, and when he did so, saying, 'Can you do anything for them?' Ward had answered, 'Leave it with me;' then the following day he had said, 'The old barn wants renewing.

263

Give the first choice to Tim Regan, Mullins and McNabb. I'll be out there to see them myself but, generally, you keep an eye on them.'

The only regular visitor to the house was Philip Patten. Sometimes it would be twice a week, although he never missed looking in at least once. Angela had accepted him, but guardedly, for at seven months her belly was prominent and in a way grotesque, for her slight body did not seem strong enough to support it. On one particular day after she had indicated she was in pain by rubbing her sides with her hand, Patsy had spoken to the doctor about it.

Angela was in bed at the time and when Jessie had pulled back the bedcover and the doctor had gone to lay his hands on the mound covered by the lawn nightdress, the girl thrust out her hands like claws and tried to drag the bedclothes back over her, and staring wildly at him and shaking her head, she emitted loud sounds of protest.

He had, of course, been quick to reassure her, saying, 'It's all right, Angela. It's all right. I just wanted to find out where your pain is coming from. Don't disturb yourself, my dear.' And as he straightened up he looked towards the far window and intimated to her: 'It's lovely outside. The autumn leaves are turning. You could sit out today, couldn't you? Will you try?'

However, she made no response, and so he picked up his bag, and from the landing just beyond the open door he beckoned Patsy towards him; then said to her, softly, 'If she keeps rubbing her thighs and evinces any sign of further pain, send for me.'

'You think the baby might be coming, Doctor?'

'I don't know, but it's a possibility; she's seven months gone. It . . . it was early March, and this is the beginning of October: she's past seven months. But there . . .'

'It's to be hoped she goes the full time, Doctor, 'cos in any case, it's not goin' to be easy for her.'

They looked at each other as old acquaintances might, and by now they could be termed such, for he had spoken to her frankly during all his visits, more so than he did to Jessie. And now he asked, 'Where is Miss Jessie?'

It was a whispered reply: 'I made her take a walk in the fresh air, Doctor. She's never out of the house. The master's gone out this mornin' on his rounds. That's something an' all. He was examining the new barn – that's been made out of the old 'un, you know – an' then I espied him going over the fields. I . . . I told Miss Jessie which way he had gone. Just in passin' like, you know, Doctor? I thought it might be nice for them both if they could walk together in the air.'

Philip Patten said nothing for a moment. Then he put a hand on Patsy's shoulder, saying, 'You've got a wise and kind head on your shoulders, Patsy. Should everything else fail, these two qualities will always stand you in good stead.'

Her colour had risen; and she laughed gently, but then glanced quickly towards the open bedroom door as if to brush the compliment aside and said, 'That isn't a general opinion, Doctor. Even me ma's got a name for me.'

'What is that?' He was smiling as he leant towards her.

'The Black Vixen.'

'Oh . . . never!'

'Oh yes; when I wouldn't do her biddin' as a child, that's what she used to call me.'

'But no longer, I hope.'

'Oh, I don't know. There are still times when the stour flies.'

He flapped his hand at her as he went away smiling, thinking he well knew the reason why the stour flew, for her mother was one of the laziest women he knew of: the house was like the proverbial pigsty. Yet laughter was never far from the woman's face. But here was her daughter, solemn-faced mostly, yet beautifully solemn-faced. Oh yes; she was a bonny piece, and she was as clean as a new pin. That had likely been the result of her training under Annie, those long years ago.

In the kitchen, Annie enquired, 'Well, how do you find her, Doctor?'

'I'm not quite sure, Annie,' he replied. 'Only I've told Patsy if the child continues to have those pains in her side to let me know. I'll be quite close round about for the next couple of days, but on Friday I'm taking two days off. I haven't had any

265

leave for some time. It's to be the equivalent of a cowman's holiday spent helping with the harvest, for I'm going to attend a couple of medical lectures.'

'Oh. Well, what'll happen then, Doctor, say she comes on on Friday? Shall I have to send for his nibs?'

'Oh, I hope not. But if it should happen that someone is needed, well, you'll have to.'

'He's kept his distance all these months, hasn't he, Doctor?'

'Yes, I suppose he has, Annie.'

'Wanted to show the village which side he was on, I suppose.'

He could have replied, 'Not so much the village, Annie, but the gentry round about, at least those who were present at that special Sunday service.' But Annie spoke his thoughts for him by remarking caustically, 'He's like the vicar, frightened he'll lose his place at the big tables.'

He laughed now as he said, 'Perhaps . . . perhaps you're right. Well, I must be off. Something in the oven smells good.' He sniffed towards it, and she answered, 'Nothing more than usual . . . a bit of pork,' then added, 'onion sauce and a suet pudding. Workhouse fare, really.'

He chuckled as he went out of the room repeating, 'Yes, Annie, workhouse fare.'

He paid a brief visit on the Thursday afternoon. Jessie was with her sister, and her report was, 'Yes, sometimes she does rub her sides; but not all the time,' to which Philip said, 'Good. Good,' and went on to repeat to her what he had said to Annie previously, that he would be away on the morrow and Saturday; but should there be an emergency she must call Doctor Wheatley; and she answered that she too hoped nothing would happen to make her call on Doctor Wheatley, but that she also hoped he would enjoy his little holiday, to which he smilingly replied, 'I don't know about enjoy. If I manage to come away a little wiser, that will be satisfactory.' Then he pulled a slight face as he said, 'He is one of the great men from London, and I am very lucky to have been given a seat,' but immediately brought the subject matter back to her: 'Where is your father?' he asked. And when Jessie said, 'He's out on the farm,' he exclaimed, 'Oh,

266

that's good. I'm glad he's getting out and about again. I won't trouble to find him, but tell him everything's in order.'

'I will, Doctor.'

On returning to the bedroom, she said to Angela, 'Isn't Doctor Patten nice?'

But to this Angela made no reply; what she did do was to place her hands down her sides again, and her face twisted slightly, causing her to grimace as if she were experiencing pain.

Jessie peered down into Angela's face to make sure she was asleep before going round to the other side of the bed to turn the lamp down low and then taking her place in the bed beside her sister.

This pattern of childhood and youth had been taken up again some weeks earlier when it became evident that Jessie could no longer spend her nights dozing in a chair by the side of the bed and be expected to keep awake and attend to her sister during the day.

She hadn't slept in the bed from the start of Angela's illness because the girl herself had shunned close proximity with anyone at all, even with her. That Angela was aware of what was being said to her had been made plain one day when Patsy had spoken sternly to her, saying, 'You understand me, Miss Angela, don't you? you understand when I say that if you want to have Miss Jessie tend you during the day then you've got to let her sleep at nights, and in bed.'

Jessie lay on her side for some time gazing at the indistinct mound in the bedclothes and wondering, as she often did, what would happen when the baby was born. Would Angela act as a mother to it? And how would her father treat it? Would it be a boy or a girl? Whatever it was, she knew it would be strange to have a small baby in the house; and, further, the work shared between her and Patsy would probably be doubled. She wondered if she would be able to approach her father for help in the house. As it was now, but for himself in his room at the far end of the landing, she was alone: Annie was in her cottage, and Carl and Patsy were in theirs. This latter fact did not now disturb her. For the first week or so it had, when she would think of Patsy no longer sleeping above the stables, but in the cottage with Carl, and in bed with Carl. But gradually it registered in her mind that it was an established fact, and it registered, too, that they were both so very necessary inside and outside the house. And so she wisely came round to telling herself it was done. She had her father, and he needed her. Oh yes, he needed her. But when the baby came there would be broken nights, for babies had to be seen to during the night, and if Angela did not fully return to her normal self, then she would never be able to take charge of the child.

But now, she said to herself as her eyelids became heavy, there was enough to worry about without anticipating further trouble; she must wait until the child was born and take it from there . . .

She didn't know what time in the night it was when she was woken from a deep sleep by the sound of a groan. At first it seemed to be coming from some distance; then suddenly it was in her ear, and she sprang into a sitting position and dimly made out through her sleep-filled eyes that Angela was not only sitting up but bent forward, her hands clutching her stomach.

'What is it, dear? Are you in pain?'

For answer Angela just rocked herself from side to side; and Jessie sprang from the bed, turned up the light and was pulling on her dressing-gown as she went round the bed, exclaiming, 'It's all right, dear! It's all right.' But when her sister flopped back into the pillows and lay gasping, she had the horrified feeling that it wasn't all right and that there would be no time before the responsibility of the baby was indeed upon her.

She now went to the wash-hand stand and brought a wet flannel back to the bed, and with it she began to wipe Angela's sweating face.

When she was almost thrust aside by her sister's outflung arm as Angela again sat upright and began to rock herself, Jessie looked wildly about her for a moment, before she rushed from the room and along the landing to hammer on her father's door. And when she heard a sort of grunting sound, she flung it open, crying, 'Daddy! Daddy! Angela's in great pain. Come, please! Come!' Then she was running back to the bedroom again.

A few minutes later, when Ward looked down on his daughter as she cried out aloud, he turned to Jessie, saying, 'Go and get Carl. Tell him to ride for the doctor.'

'Yes, Daddy.'

She was at the bedroom door before she turned, saying, 'But Doctor Patten is away.'

He looked towards her, then seemed to grind his teeth for a moment before he said, 'Well, you'll have to get the other one. And fetch Patsy back.'

On reaching the hall she paused a moment before running into the clothes closet, where she pulled off a peg one of her father's coats which she flung around her shoulders.

In the kitchen she put a match to a candle lantern; and then she was out in the yard, the cold night air making her gasp.

At the cottages, she hammered with her fist on Carl's door, and in a loud voice she yelled, 'Carl! Carl! Come quickly. Daddy wants you to get a doctor. Come on, Carl! Do you hear?'

It was a full minute before the door was pulled open, and Carl, blinking down on her, said, 'What on earth's the matter? What is it?'

'The baby ... the baby's coming. Daddy wants you to ride for the doctor. Doctor Patten is away; you'll have to get Doctor Wheatley. And ... and he wants Patsy.'

Patsy had appeared at Carl's shoulder and Jessie said to her, 'She's going to have the baby. She's crying out.'

When Carl said, 'Good Lord! It's only seven months gone,' Patsy muttered, 'I'm not surprised,' and dashed back into the room, calling over her shoulder, 'I'll be there as soon as I get into me clothes, Miss Jessie.'

Carl now said, 'Go on back. You'll be frozen.'

When the adjoining cottage door opened and Annie appeared, enquiring, 'What is it, child? What's the rumpus?' Carl answered, 'It's Miss Angela, Annie. I think the baby is about to come.' And when Annie answered, 'I'll be over

269

directly,' Patsy's voice came from their cottage, yelling, 'You stay where you are, Annie!'

Annie made no retort to this, but, looking down on Jessie, she said, 'Get yourself back, dear, and into your clothes; you'll freeze,' and with this she banged her door; and Jessie was running again.

Back in the cottage Carl began to pull on his outdoor clothes as he said, 'I hate to go to old Wheatley's. It just would have to happen that Doctor Patten should be away the night.' Then hurrying towards the door, he called, 'See you, love,' and Patsy's answer was brief: 'Sure.'

Five minutes later he was on his horse, and within a further ten minutes he was banging on Doctor Wheatley's door. But he had to bang for a third time before a window was opened and a female voice called, 'Who is it?'

He stepped back and looked at the bulky shoulders of the housekeeper, and he called up to her, 'The doctor's wanted. 'Tis an emergency. The baby's coming . . . Gibson's farm.'

The head was withdrawn, but within a moment it seemed, the woman cried down to him, 'Doctor's in no fit state; he's heavy with cold. He shouldn't be taken out of his bed.'

Carl knew what he was heavy with, and it wouldn't be with cold, and so he cried back to her, 'You rise him up; I want a word with him.'

'He'll be no use to you, I tell you.'

'Nevertheless, woman, get him up.'

'Who do you think you are talkin' to? Don't you dare call me woman. And he's not this long in bed; he shouldn't have been . . . ' There was a pause before she added, 'He shouldn't have been out,' and these words were practically cut off by the window being banged.

It was some minutes later when the door was pulled open and the housekeeper stood grimly aside to let him enter; and there he saw the doctor shambling down the staircase, and having to aid himself by holding on to the banister.

On reaching the bottom, he stood swaying, a sign giving no satisfaction to Carl that his surmise had been correct: the man had not long been in his bed and had been indulging as usual with some crony or other. The man was a disgrace.

'What time of night . . . is this? What you want?'

'Mr Gibson's daughter's child is about coming; and she needs attention.'

'Well . . . why come to me? Where's your favourite scien . . . tific modern man and . . . '

The housekeeper was standing by him now, and she said something that was not audible to Carl, but the doctor seemingly understood, and he said, 'Yes . . . Yes. Playing the big fella.' Then looking at Carl, he said, 'I've . . . I've got a chill on me. I . . . I couldn't travel.' His words were becoming thicker.

Carl watched him turn an ear towards his housekeeper and nod; then he was speaking again: 'As . . . as this good woman says, there are two . . . two women there. They should . . . be able to handle it. 'Tis a farm, isn't it? Seen things born before.'

When his arm that had been around the stanchion of the stair-post slid slowly from it, and the florid bulk sat down with a plop on the second stair, Carl looked at the man in disgust, and he dared to say, 'You're not fit to carry the name of a doctor, sir.' And on this he turned and went out, and, having mounted his horse, he rode swiftly back to the farm.

When he reached the house it was to find Annie in the kitchen, the kettle bubbling on the hob and her busily cutting up a linen sheet into squares, and as she did so she greeted him with, 'These are things that should have been already prepared, yet even these have been under taboo. But nature will out, and it's shown it will out in this case . . . Is he coming?'

'No; he's as full as a gun, mortallious, I would say.'

'Dear God! Well, what's to be done?'

He looked at her in some surprise and said, 'Couldn't you see to her, Annie?'

She looked down at her work and did not speak for a moment; then she said, 'I've never had any childer of my own; and although I was in the room when the lasses were born, the doctor was there, and he did the necessary. Quite truthfully, lad, I'd be no hand at it. But your Patsy now;

271

she's helped bring calves into the world and a good few sheep, besides what she must have learned in the Hollow. She'll handle it all right.'

He looked at her in amazement, the while thinking that there were things about people you never guessed at. Annie, this motherly-looking woman who had spent her life on a farm was afraid of birth. And now she even shocked him by saying, 'And in this case, God knows what to expect. It could be a monstrosity, and I wouldn't bear look on it. I just couldn't,' and she looked up at Carl again, her expression seeming to plead for understanding; but he could say nothing except, 'I'd better go up and tell them.'

She nodded at him, then returned to her task of cutting up the sheet.

On reaching the landing, he was surprised to find the master standing there. He seemed to have been leaning against the wall; but now he was facing Carl.

'Well?'

'He won't come. In any case he would have been of no use, sir. He's drunk, heavily so. But I shouldn't worry; Patsy will see to her.'

When Ward made no reply, Carl asked, 'Will you tell her, sir?' Then after a moment, just when it appeared that Ward was thinking deeply about something, he answered sharply, 'Yes. Yes, I'll tell her,' and with this he turned about and went towards the bedroom. But as he opened the door there came at him a piercing cry, one which might have been wrenched from an animal in torment. He stopped dead and turned his head away.

When he again looked towards the bed it was to see Patsy endeavouring to pull a sheet over his daughter's knees.

Taking a few steps into the room, he beckoned to her, but before she moved from the bed she spoke to Jessie, and none too quietly, saying, 'Don't try to hold her arms down. I've told you, miss.' Then she turned to peer at Ward who was standing beyond the rim of light cast by the lamp; he leaned towards her, saying quietly, 'Carl couldn't get old Wheatley, he's drunk. Do . . . do you think you could manage?'

She drew in a deep breath before she answered, 'I'll have to, won't I? There's nothing else for it. I . . . I've never brought a child afore . . . animals, yes. Yet' – she moved one shoulder in a characteristic gesture – 'I've seen some bairns being born.' She nodded at him now, more reassuringly: 'Yes, aye, I'll manage,' she said. 'That is if things come straightforwardly. If it gets stuck . . . well, I don't know. We'll just have to wait an' see.'

During this exchange she had not once addressed him as master or sir, and it had not passed his notice, and somewhere in his mind was the thought that she was speaking to him in much the same manner as Annie did.

She was about to turn away when she said, 'How's the time going—' and now she did add, 'master?'

'Nearly one o'clock, I think,' he answered, as he watched her walk towards the bed in which his daughter was lying, comparatively quiet now except for her heavy gasping breath. He knew that he himself could bring the child; yet not for the life of him could he even approach the bed at this moment, for whatever she was about to deliver into the world would be obnoxious to him. And if it was a distorted body, well, he had already made up his mind what he would do about that . . . and even if it wasn't.

When Patsy heard the door being closed, she turned to Jessie, saying, 'I'd bring the big chair up, miss, and sit yourself down. There's nothing going to happen for a while; it could be a long night.'

Jessie's voice came in a startled whisper now as she said, 'But she couldn't go on like this all night, Patsy. She'd be worn out. She's tired already. It's dreadful . . . terrible.'

'It's natural, miss.'

'What!' Jessie screwed up her face. 'All that pain? her screaming with it? No, no; don't say it's natural.'

'I have to say it, miss: that's birth. That's how you came, and me an' all,' to which Jessie's reaction was in words which were long drawn out, spoken as she walked away: 'It's unthinkable. Well, I knew there must be some discomfort, having seen the animals; but . . . but not like this.'

'Look, miss. Sit yourself down for a time. She'll be all right. Don't worry. The quicker the pains come the quicker it'll be born.'

When, by four o'clock in the morning, there was still no sign of Angela's delivering her child, Ward ordered Annie into the room, saying, 'Those are both young lasses up there; go and see what you can do.'

And so Annie, eyes weary for sleep, her legs heavy with water, mounted the stairs and went into the bedroom. She knew it would be of little use telling the distraught man that she'd had no experience in such matters. And after saying, 'There, there, my lovely,' and patting the face of the heaving half-demented girl, she willingly sat in the armchair that Patsy indicated, and waited.

Annie was dozing when she heard Patsy's voice exclaiming, 'Aye, aye! Here it comes, miss. Another push. Another push. That's a good girl. Come on. Come on,' and she struggled to her feet as she watched the tiny body slipping out of the equally small frame, and heard the girl let out a great sigh before sinking deep into the bed.

'She's whole . . . bonny.' The tears were in Patsy's eyes and her voice was thick as she dealt with the cord before handing the tiny, yelling infant to Jessie, standing now holding a towel, her face awash with tears.

Patsy pointed to the basin of water on the wash-hand stand: 'Clean her eyes first; an' put another towel under her; then lay her on the wash-hand stand. She'll be all right. Go on: you can do it. I must see to Miss.'

Annie was now wiping Angela's face, and she turned to Patsy, saying, 'Can you deal with the afterbirth?' and Patsy replied, 'Yes, if it comes natural like. Otherwise, I don't know. We'll just have to wait and see. Poor little soul.' She stretched out her hand and touched Angela's cheek, encouraging her: 'That's a good lass. You've made it. You've made it.' Then turning to where Jessie was still attending the child, she said softly, 'Bring her here, and show it to her.'

Jessie gathered up the child in a towel, almost joyfully now, and moved hurriedly towards the bed, both Annie and Patsy

274

stepping aside so that Angela could see her child. And when she did, the response was so loud, so piercing that they both fell back in astonishment. Angela's mouth was wide as the screams issued from it, and her hands were flailing as if to throw the child from her.

'There now! There now! There! my love.' Annie was aiming to hold down the flapping hands when Patsy said, 'Out of my way! Annie,' and she took hold of Angela by the shoulders and shook her gently as she cried, 'Stop it! miss. Stop it! All right! All right! You don't have to see it. Only stop it!'

They were all well aware of the opening of the door, but no-one moved towards it until Jessie, who was standing in the corner of the room holding the small bundle to her, suddenly turned about to where the padded basket was standing on a low chair and, placing the child in it, she wrapped the towels well around it before covering it with the small quilt that lay across the bottom of the basket. Then she carried it towards her father; but she passed him and went into the corridor without speaking; but as he muttered, 'Wait!' he followed her, closing the door quickly behind him.

'She couldn't bear the sight of it, Daddy. It is dreadful . . . dreadful. And it is so lovely. It's a little girl, and she is quite whole . . . beautiful. And look, she's got quite an abundance of hair already.'

He did not look at the child, but at her, and said, 'I'll take it down.'

'It . . . it has to be kept warm, near the fire.'

She did not release her hold on the basket until he said, 'Yes. Yes, I know. Give it here.'

She stood watching him carrying the basket and holding it away from him until he disappeared down the stairs. Then she returned to the room, only to stand near the door, her hand tightly over her mouth, the tears running over her fingers, before she made her way towards where Patsy was seeing to something on the bed that looked very distasteful.

Becoming aware of Jessie, Patsy stopped what she was doing and turned quickly towards her and asked, 'Where's the child?'

275

Between sobs, Jessie said, 'Daddy's taken her down to the kitchen,' causing an immediate, unprecedented reaction from Patsy: she dug her elbow sharply into Jessie's arm, saying, 'Go down and see to the child. Go on now, quick!'

'But why? Daddy has . . . '

'Do what you're told, Miss Jessie,' Annie interrupted her, and the tone of her voice made Jessie turn and stumble from the room; but it wasn't until she was running down the stairs that she asked herself again, Why? and when the horrifying answer came to her she cried out inwardly. No! No! How dreadful of them to think he would do such a thing.

She entered the kitchen in a rush, and Ward turned from where he was standing in front of the fire, demanding, 'What do you want?'

She didn't answer but she looked towards the hearth and around the room. There was no sign of the basket holding the child.

'Look, go back upstairs. I'll be with you shortly.'

'*Daddy*, where is the baby?' Her tone was harsh now and she was no longer crying.

'Do what I say immediately.'

'*No! No! Daddy*. I won't. Not this time I won't. What have you done to the baby?'

'I've done nothing to the baby.'

'Well, where is it?'

'I've told you. Go upstairs and stay for a while. When you come back it'll be on the hearth waiting for you.'

She shook her head wildly, and then started to yell, 'I want the baby, and I want it now. Where . . . ?'

She stopped when she heard a whimper, and she looked towards the cold-store larder at the far end of the kitchen. This was a narrow room, marble-shelved and stone-floored, and cold enough to keep milk fresh for three days, even colder than the dairy. And now she flew towards it, thrust open the door, and there, on the stone floor and lying on the towel, she saw the child quite naked. The basket was on the shelf.

Grabbing up the child, she held it tightly to her breast and pulled her shoulder wrap around it; then she turned and confronted her father, who was standing in the open doorway

276

and the look in her eyes silenced him until, swinging his body around, he went to the table and beat his fist on it, the while growling, 'It was the best way.'

'No! No!' Her voice was as deep as his. 'The child is perfectly formed. It isn't a monstrosity.'

Swinging about again he cried back at her, 'What about its mind? Its mother is half-mad. You've got to face up to that . . . I've had to face up to it. And who can it claim as a father? Which one of the three? And each an evil, lustful, ignorant swine. Tell me, what kind of character is it going to have? What evil will it perpetrate, coming from such loins as those? *Tell me! girl. Tell me!*'

She could make no answer; she could only hold the child more closely to her.

And now he went on, 'And who's to care for it? Certainly not its mother. Certainly not Annie, who can hardly stand on her feet. And then there's Patsy, who will soon be creating a brood of her own. And that leaves you. Do you understand that, girl? Are you going to give your life for that thing?' – he was thrusting his finger towards her now – 'for she'll have to be guarded from her mother, and from me. *Yes, from me*, for I don't wish to set eyes on it. And then there's her growing. I guarded you both from the village, but there will be no-one to guard her from their tongues and their slurs. What name do you think they will pin on her, a child of three fathers, eh? an offspring of an unholy trinity.'

'Stop it, Daddy! Stop it! Please!' Her voice was low now but such was its unusual tone and authority that it silenced him. 'I'll never marry,' she said. 'The only one I wanted and I think I'll ever want is Carl. You offered me to him as a bribe in order to keep his services.' When she saw his eyes widen, she nodded her head, saying, 'I know all about it; and when he refused to take me the girl in me died. But I was left with one hope. Now that your favourite daughter was rejecting you, simply placing you among men, of whom she had become terrified, you would need me. And sure enough, you did notice me, because you needed me. But, like all second-hand things, it had no freshness: all your thoughts, in fact your whole being, is taken up with the tragedies that life has dealt you. And lately I have realised that your main concern is how things are affecting *you*. Not how they have affected Angela or me, or even Patsy and Carl and Annie. The tragedies that have touched you have rebounded on all of us, yet you can't see it.'

He stared open-mouthed at her. She was just eighteen years old but she could have been twenty-eight, in looks, in manner and in her thinking. Oh yes, in her thinking. And at this moment he could find nothing to say in answer to her sudden tirade, no reprimand welled up in him to chastise her for daring to speak to him in such a manner. But he was aware she had saved him from murdering the child, and it was murder he had intended. Oh yes; and if the cold hadn't done it, in the present state of things a hand over its mouth would have.

He continued to stare at her as he wondered what had brought her running in as she did. Some sixth sense? And then it came to him as never before that his first-born had inherited the character of his dear Fanny while her replica inherited only her stature and looks, and further, that she would have become frivolous. Appealing, yes, but wayward and frivolous.

As he turned from her and made for the kitchen door leading into the yard, it seemed to her that his shoulders had taken on a permanent stoop. But without dwelling further on this, she quickly stepped back into the larder, whipped up the basket and brought it to the fireplace and laid it on the end of the fender. Then with one hand she held up the towel before the fire, first one side then the other, before wrapping the child in it.

She was on her knees when the door suddenly opened and Carl entered. 'It's come then?' he said.

'Yes. Yes, Carl.' She did not look up at him. 'It's a girl.'

'I . . . I thought it had; the master's gone striding out of the gate.'

But she made no reply to this implication; and Carl was already bending over her and looking down into the basket and saying softly, 'She looks canny, but small.'

'Yes. Yes, she's very small.'

'She's whole?'

'Yes. Yes, Carl, she's quite whole.'

'Good.'

'Carl.'

'Yes, Miss Jessie?'

She had her face turned up to his. 'How . . . how does one feed a baby when . . . when the mother won't have it?'

'She won't have it?'

'No; she screamed at the sight of it.'

'Oh, dear, dear. Well, miss, it's er . . . I think they use pap bags.'

'Pap bags?'

'Yes. You just fold some linen' – he demonstrated now as if he was folding the linen round his finger – 'into about that thickness, you see, and tie it at one end. Then keep dipping it into the milk.'

'Is that all?'

'That's all for a time, until you can get a bottle. You can buy bottles now with, sort of, well, teats on the end, you know.'

She didn't know, but she nodded. 'How . . . how soon can you get a bottle?'

'Oh, I'd have to go into town, to a chemist's shop.'

'Would . . . would you get one today?'

'Aye. Yes. As soon as the chores are underway I'll get meself off.'

'Thank you, Carl.'

He slowly straightened up but remained looking down on her. A small fist had appeared over the edge of the blanket and was grabbing at the air; and when Jessie put her finger towards it, it was held, and after a moment she turned and looked up at him. Her eyes were bright with tears and her voice breaking: 'She's sweet, isn't she?' she said. He nodded at her, saying in a low tone, 'Yes. Yes she is,' while a wave of pity swept over him, not for the child but strangely for her, and even more strangely still he was wishing at this moment that things could have been different, for she looked so lost. And his feeling deepened as he said, 'You're going to have your hands full.' And she replied, 'I don't mind, Carl. I don't

279

mind in the least. I'll take full responsibility for her. And . . . and she'll give me an interest. Well, I mean' – she glanced up at him – 'one must have something in life and she'll be my something.'

He nodded, then stepped back from her and went quickly out of the kitchen. And when she turned her head towards the door she closed her eyes tightly for a moment and wondered why the old feeling for him should return at this moment in particular, when before her there stretched a life of service to this child, which would mean rearing her, protecting her, guarding her, not only from outsiders but from this house, where neither her mother nor her grandfather would own her presence.

PART THREE

I

The long cortège that had followed the last remains of Colonel Ramsmore to the cemetery on this bleak November day had dispersed, as too had those close friends of the family who had returned to the Hall for a warm drink and a light meal. And now, in the drawing-room, there remained only the sparse family, consisting of Lady Lydia's eldest step-son, Beverly, a man of sixty who had recently retired from the Army, and her own son Gerald, now twenty-nine years old, who had returned to his family home a week ago after a nine-year absence.

At this moment it was as if Colonel Beverly Ramsmore could contain himself no longer for, after draining his wine glass, he thrust it none too gently on to a side table; then rising to his feet he confronted his half-brother and, using the same tone as he might have done when speaking to a subordinate, he said to him, 'Am I to believe what your mother tells me, that if war did break out, and it is looming strongly on the horizon, let me tell you, you would not even enlist? I could never understand you turning down the Army; but not to stand up and fight for your country, should it need you, is to me atrocious, and coming from a member of this family . . . well, it simply astonishes me. We are an army family, have been for generations on both sides until' – he now pulled at his short moustache before ending – 'you came on the scene.'

'Beverly!' Although Lady Lydia's voice was firm there was a tired note in it, and he turned to her now, saying, 'It's no

283

use, Lydia, someone's got to speak out and tell him what we all think.'

'Beverly, I have already told you, you can save your breath.'

At this point Gerald put in, lightly, 'Yes; why don't you take Mama's advice and stop wasting your breath? Because you're getting short of it, you know.'

The portly figure swung round to where Gerald was lounging in a deep armchair and looking so utterly relaxed, and this seemed to infuriate the older man for now he blustered, 'You delight, don't you, in being different? But I'll put another name to you: you're a coward, a rank coward, have been since you were a little chap,' and then was utterly startled by the springing up of the reclining body, for Gerald was now standing within a foot of him and his finger was daring to stab into his chest as he cried, 'Yes! I'm cowardly enough not to go and shoot natives; I'm cowardly enough not to play God and laud it over men, those who in many cases have more brains and intelligence than either you or any other of your kind possesses. Yet you treat them as scum of the earth, cannon fodder. And I'll answer your question. Yes, I know there's every sign of a war coming. But do you know why? Do you read history? In fact, have you ever read anything in your life but army rules and regulations?'

When his hand was slapped hard down it did not silence his tongue, for now he went on, 'Greed! Greed! That's what makes war: the French and Germans at each other's throats to gain control of coal and iron; and the Russians, their greedy eyes on the Balkans; everybody out to take something from someone else. And what about our dear country? Oh, we only want to gobble up the whole bloody world.'

'*Gerald!*'

'Oh, let him go on, Lydia, let him go on. I've heard it all before from the ranters, the soap box politicians, the shirkers. You should amalgamate with the suffragettes.'

'Even your sarcasm is weak, Beverly, and as far back as I can remember, which is from when I was five years old, you've never had an original thought in your head. It's to be hoped, for their sake, that your sons take after their mother,

284

who, I recall, had a lively mind. Do you know something, Beverly? Neil and I are about the same age, I think he is probably a year older, but I know he was about sixteen when he said to me that he didn't want to go into the Army but that he was destined for it, just as Roger was, because Daddy was adamant. Do you know what he wanted to be? A farmer. But, of course, as he said, Daddy was adamant.'

He stepped back now and his lip curled when he said quietly, 'Daddy will be very proud of them if war comes and they are both shot to smithereens or bayoneted through the belly.' And with this he turned and stamped from the room.

With the banging of the door Lady Lydia closed her eyes tightly, and when the irate soldier demanded, 'Why on earth have you asked him to stay here?' her eyes opened wide and she exclaimed in a tone so like his own, 'Because someone must see to the place, the little that is left of it. And you, my dear Beverly, have made it plain you have no intention of leaving Hampshire and bringing your family to settle in this house. As you pointed out, what prospects would there be here for your grandchildren? And of course, there's your London clubs. And while I'm speaking plainly, I'm going to say that during the last four years you have been stationed at home, you have thought to come and see your father but once, to my knowledge . . . once. There is an excuse for your brothers, Arthur and William, they being stationed in India. Yet even they, on their leaves, came and went as if there were a plague attached to the house. It wasn't like that in their young days, when the place was running with servants to answer their beck and call. But when money ran out, yes, I will say this: that was helped considerably in seeing to your three careers and your generous allowances. The money flowed over all of you and your new families. But when my son needed an education, a cottage and a piece of land had to be sold, and his meagre allowance ended abruptly when he was barely twenty, as did his university education, for the simple reason he had the courage . . . and I object strongly, Beverly, to your daring to put the name 'coward' to him. I couldn't see you standing up in public defending a man who had been wronged, as my son did, and refuse to be silenced by his father and was therefore made to suffer for it.' Her voice now sank as she ended, 'There are different kinds of courage, and I may tell you my son has a great store of the right kind. And that's my opinion, and no matter what happens in the future, should he refuse to fight for his country, as he undoubtedly will, I shall stand by him. And you can convey that to your brothers.' And at this she pulled herself up from the couch and she, too, marched from the room.

They were walking up the weed-strewn path between the overgrown ornamental borders. They had been walking in silence for some time, seeming to be aware only of their breath visible in the cold air, when suddenly he said, 'It's a mess, isn't it?' And she answered, 'Yes, and has been for some time. But what can one man do? McNamara achieves miracles in his own way. I'm really amazed at times that he stays on. But he's very loyal. He came into the yard when you were about twelve, remember? He was fourteen at the time. It's a good job he never married else we should surely have lost him. One has to be thankful for his odd eye, in a way.' She turned, her chin moving over the rim of her high collar, and smiled at him, and he answered, 'He was always a good chap.'

She now thrust her arm into his, exclaiming, 'Oh! I'm so glad you're going to stay, Gerald. I'm so grateful.'

'It works both ways, Mama. Believe me it does.'

'But I thought you liked London and being in a publishing house, and . . . ?'

'Yes. Yes, I did; and honestly I'm going to miss it, not so much the work but the atmosphere of the place, those pokey little rooms. Mr Herbert and Mr Darrington. I'll always see them at their desks, practically back to back, surrounded by papers. Very odd, you know.' He nodded at her. 'It never seemed to me that they were actually reading books, checking books.'

'Well, that was your job, wasn't it?'

'Yes, I suppose so; but not until I'd been there . . . oh, three years. I was the dogsbody at first and glad, let me tell you, to be any kind of a body in a job where my main work was to read. But oh, some of those manuscripts. It seemed to me at times that the whole country was writing, yet more than half of them had never learned to write.' He paused now and said, 'And some of their accompanying letters were pathetic: will you please publish my book because I need the money. And it would likely be a love story full of fantasy; or as sometimes happened, a record of an awful childhood or marriage.' He looked down at her as he said, 'I received an education there, Mama, that showed me a way of life that we, as a whole, know nothing about. And not only working for those two dear, old-fashioned gentlemen, and Mr Herbert and Mr Darrington were indeed gentlemen and very particular about what they published; but at the same time they were from another world. Sometimes, I'm sure, they weren't aware of either Ronald or me . . . you know, Ronald Pearson, whom I told you about; they didn't know we were there. At other times, when they were aware, they would bawl the place down. Poor Ronald. When Mr Darrington called for him he would shout, 'Peasant! here.' And they would treat him as a peasant. One day they accidentally heard him referring to them as "Hell and Damnation". You see Herbert and Darrington were on their way out to lunch, and I couldn't shut him up for I was holding the door open for them, and I watched them turn away, both their faces showing surprise and amusement. And from then until we left the office at six o'clock I couldn't convince him other than he was in for the sack.'

They were now walking through the just-as-tangled flower garden and somewhat dolefully she said, 'You'll miss it all; and that funny lodging house where you were.' And he answered, 'Yes, I suppose so for a time; not the surroundings so much but the people, because they were so different. Especially the Cramps. Oh yes' – he was smiling broadly – 'especially the Cramps.'

'How on earth did you come to take lodgings in the East End of London? I mean, when you left, you had enough money to go to an hotel or, as I told you, to Beverly's cousin. He didn't like Beverly and I felt he would take to you.'

287

'For how long, Mama? Anyway, with the money you gave me and the bit I had saved I knew I could last out only about a month, and so I had to find cheap lodgings. Thankfully I found Mrs Cramp, or at least she found me . . . looking in a shop window where there were rooms advertised to rent.' He pulled a face. 'Erb . . . Mr Herbert Cramp and our Doug, Mr Douglas Cramp, and oh yes, little Glad, who was then really little but is now seventeen, and you could say from that day I was, in a way, happy ever after.'

'Oh, Gerald, you make the comparison sound as if your life here had been terrible.'

'I'm sorry, Mama, but they were such different people from those I'd been used to, so honest, so open and' – he now pulled a face at her – 'so wily, so crafty. The men, Mr Herbert worked in Covent Garden, had done since he was a boy, and Douglas followed in his father's footsteps. They also had a barrow on the side. Oh, the things I learned about commerce, you wouldn't believe. But what I enjoyed most was the house and the evenings spent there. It was a ramshackle place, dropping to bits in parts. It had originally been the home of some businessman or other, I should imagine, just as many others were in that quarter. Anyway, it had four habitable bedrooms and an attic. I had the attic. Oh . . . oh,' he emphasised now, 'from choice, for the attic space covered half the house and my books could sprawl all over the place and nobody bothered, least of all Mrs B . . . Bertha was her name. You know, Mama, she had the loudest voice I've ever heard issuing from any human being. You didn't need an alarm clock. Especially when she screamed up those stairs practically in the middle of the night, "You! Doug, get out of that bed or I'll dig you out with a fork!" ' He now began to shake with laughter as he said, 'I won't trouble to tell you where the fork was destined for, Mama.'

'No, I'm glad you won't, thank you, but I can use my imagination.' She, too, now was laughing.

'Erb . . . Herbert didn't need any calling. I think she pushed him out of bed the minute she got up. As for me, she would come to the bottom of those narrow stairs and bawl, "It'll be on the table in fifteen minutes, Mr G." And, oh, I would crawl out of bed, get into my clothes, all except my jacket and collar and tie, and down I would go into the scullery to wash.'

'Oh, Gerald, you had to wash in the . . . ?'

'It was very good training, Mama, and I, being a gent, as she openly stated to anyone who would listen, and that was most of the neighbourhood, I was given the privilege of using the large tin bath on a Friday or Saturday night. I had my choice.' This brought them both to a stop, and with her arm around her waist, she laughed loudly before she muttered, 'You're exaggerating.'

'I'm not. I'm quite serious, Mama. They all used the tin bath. And it wasn't too bad; there was a boiler in the corner of the scullery. The only trouble was the time limit given to your ablutions. You weren't allowed to relax in the, very often, almost scalding water she would ladle into the bath by the bucket. Then there was the possibility that either our Doug or our lad would put his head round the door, and more than once a neighbour, female, took the opportunity. Fortunately, I was either deep in the water or enveloped in a towel, which, I may say, seemed to be faced with sand paper. Yet in a way, they were very decorous, especially with regard to their womenfolk, and the women themselves . . . Glad always sang loudly when enjoying her ablutions. This was mostly on a Friday evening before she went to the . . . palais de danse. She was a very good dancer, so I was told. I'd never witnessed her display. Not that I didn't have constant invitations.' He now went into an imitation of Glad. 'Ah, come, Mister G. Do you the world o' good. Slacken yer knee caps . . . you'd be a wow down there, that's if you opened yer mouth." '

'Oh, Gerald.' Lady Lydia was looking at her son softly now and surprisingly she said, 'It might have at that. Am I right in thinking that you have no attachments? Well, I mean, you haven't made acquaintance with anyone . . . of a . . . ?'

He put his arm around her waist and pulled her to him as they walked on, the while saying, 'No, Mama, I have not made acquaintance of anyone of that class, which was what you were trying to say, wasn't it?'

'No.' She tried to pull herself away. 'Not really.'

'Yes. Yes, you were. You see, I have learned to study human nature. I've even written about it.' He paused now as if he had said too much, and she pulled him to a stop as she said, 'You have? I mean, you're writing, actually writing?'

'Yes, Mama, I am actually writing. And now I'll let you into a secret. I have actually been paid money for my writing, stuff that's come out of here.' He tapped his forehead. 'Fifteen pounds I got for my last short story. It was about the country.'

'Really? About what you garnered when you were . . . ?'

'Yes, what I garnered when I was young and lived here and about the people I knew.'

'Such as?'

'Well, the Gibsons.'

'You didn't . . . ?'

'Oh, no. No, no; I didn't touch on anything that happened: I wrote about farmers and the way they lived, what they did.'

'And you got fifteen pounds for it?'

'I got fifteen pounds for it.'

'That was kind of Mr Herbert and Mr Darrington.'

'Oh, Mama, Mr Harry and Mr David would not have given it a second glance. Trite, one would have said. Simple, the other would have added.'

'But if they saw your name?'

'They wouldn't see my name, Mama, because I used yours, at least your maiden name, Fordish. James Fordish, that was the name of my maternal grandfather, wasn't it?'

'Well, well.' Her face was beaming now. 'You are a strange young man, you know. You always have been unaccountable. But it could be a wonderful career.'

'Yes. Yes, it could be a career, if I ever get further than writing articles and short stories. It could be a career, but of sorts, a sideline.'

'Well, what do you really want to do, dear?'

'To tell the truth, Mama, I'm not quite sure, except—' he poked his face towards her now and whispered, 'I'd love to sit in the library, in there' – he pointed back towards the house – 'and read and read and read, and have someone to feed me.

290

And I would have a good wash once a week, but it would have to be in a tin bath.'

'Oh, Gerald!' She pushed him now. 'Be serious. Anyway, did your . . . Mrs Cramp know you were a writer?'

'Good Lord! no. Oh, no.'

'Well what about James Fordish and any correspondence?'

'Oh, I had an understanding with my publisher.' He now cocked his chin up in a pose, moving his head from side to side, and saying, 'It's got a nice sound that, hasn't it? My publisher. I really saw him only once. It was his editor I generally dealt with. But oh, as for letting the Cramps know I wrote anything and got paid for it, they would have had it out, they would have blazoned it all over the neighbourhood.' And he now struck another pose, his arms folded, his head nodding: ' "My gent writes. I told you he was different." I actually heard her say that one day to her close friend, someone twice her size and that's saying something, but with no wit. "Win," she said, "he's not just a lodger, he's a gent, like them along, you know, the West End." I won't recall, Mama, how she then described my further connections, not only with the West End, but with further along in the large stone house.'

'Oh, my dear, my dear.' Her gloved hand was gripping his now. 'You are very funny, you know. You could write funny things from the way you say them.'

'Mama, I'm going to tell you something. Talking and writing are poles apart. If any writer could write the way he speaks he'd be a millionaire in no time. You see it's getting the stuff from here' – he again pointed to his brow – 'down that arm, into the hand and on to the paper. That's the difficult part. It loses something in the journey.'

Her face straight now, she said, 'I love you dearly, Gerald. You are my only son, my only child, my only offspring. I've never loved anyone like I love you. But I've never been able to understand what goes on in that head of yours, nor from where you inherited it.'

'Well, my dear, there was always an odd one in the family. You said so yourself.'

'Yes, I know, but your oddness is different. Anyway, what did we come out for on this bitter morning but to see what could be done with the grounds. Isn't that so?'

'Yes, Mama, that is so. And I've been giving it a lot of thought. All told, we have about sixty acres left, and part of this is taken up with two woods and what you've always called the stone field, because of all the rocks in it that border the Gibson farm. Now that leaves, as it is, about thirty acres. Not enough to set up a small farm; and anyway the buildings down at Brook End are in an awful dilapidated state and would take quite a bit of money spent on them before they'd be of any use. So what do you think about a market garden?'

She screwed up her face as she said, 'A market garden? You mean, vegetables and . . . ?'

'Yes, Mama, that's what I mean, vegetables and fruit. And you know, if anyone knows anything about growing vegetables it's McNamara. And fruit, too. He's kept the house supplied for years, hasn't he, when there's been very little else? As you've admitted yourself, there's always been plenty of vegetables of every sort. And there's the vinery and the greenhouses. When you were to meet me in London last year, you offered to bring me a basket of grapes, and if you remember I had to refuse because that would have needed some explaining to Mrs C: her gentleman's people grew grapes. My! my!'

'But would it pay? I mean, you would have to engage another man.'

'Mama, there are farms all around us here and farmers are notorious for not bothering with flower gardens or wasting much land on ordinary vegetables. Oh, yes, potato fields, turnip fields, but for the rest it's dairy food and milk and beef they supply. Well, we could supply all kinds of vegetables, fruit and flowers. We have just passed through two large gardens which are now covered with a mat of dead flowers. It's worth a try.'

'Yes. Yes, dear, I can see that, but it's . . . it's labour.'

'Well, I've worked that out, too: with McNamara, one more hand and myself. By this time next year we could be in business; and this is the time to start clearing the land.'

She smiled now, saying, 'Have you ever wielded a pick or shovel, Gerald?'

'No, I haven't, Mama; but for experience I have spent a number of mornings in Covent Garden, humping boxes of fruit and flowers with Erb and Doug. And after a few mornings I got used to my aching bones, and when the fortnight was up – it was during my yearly holiday – I was not only paid handsomely for my assistance but I later received ten pounds for an article I wrote about it. So, yes, Mama, I think I would be capable of wielding a shovel and, through practice, could handle a pick.' He smiled at her now and patted her cheek as he said, 'Well, what d'you think?'

'Oh, I am with you. In fact, I am with anything you wish to do, Gerald, so long as I can have you with me. I . . . I have been so lonely.'

'Oh, my dear, my dear. Please, Mama, don't cry. Oh, don't, don't cry. You'll undo me if you cry.'

She turned away and they walked on in silence now until she murmured, 'I never cried over your father: love dies, and one asks oneself if love had ever been born. The only evidence lies in . . . well, what it produces.' She turned now and looked at him, and when she did not continue to speak he took her arm and pressed it close to his side.

They had entered the wood on the east side of the grounds and there, stretching before them, was a long meadow, studded here and there with crops of rock. And the immediate effect of it was to bring them to a standstill. After a moment she said, 'You'll never be able to do much here.'

'You never know. If we got the business going we could afford to engage a few navvies to uproot that lot. But look!' He pointed. 'It seems quite clear near Gibson's border. There's a long stretch there, not a rock to be seen.' He now led her forward, skirting the mounds of rock on their way, until they were standing near the five-foot stone wall that Ward had erected, the coping stones set in a serrated style.

They were actually standing close to the wall and looking over the frozen ridges of the ploughed field beyond, when a little girl came running up on the side of the field to their left. She had apparently caught sight of them before they had of her, but now she was coming round the corner and the curving of the high wall hid her from them for a moment. Then, there she was, standing below them, gazing up at them. 'Hello,' she said.

Gerald answered, 'Hello.' And he turned to look at his mother, who was already gazing at him questioningly; then they both returned their attention to the child who was saying, 'It's a cold day, isn't it?' She was addressing Lady Lydia now, and she, nodding down at the child, answered, 'Yes. Yes, it is a cold day, my dear.'

'What is your name?' Her attention was on Gerald again.

'My name is Gerald Ramsmore,' he said: 'and this lady is my mother.'

'Oh.' The child now took a step backwards before gazing up into Lady Lydia's face which seemed to be just topping the wall. And she kept her eyes fixed on her for a moment before she said, 'My mother is sick.'

'Is she, dear?'

'Yes; she doesn't walk about.'

'Oh. Oh, I'm sorry for that.'

The child now turned her gaze on Gerald as she said, 'My grandfather walks about, but he isn't well either.' And she lowered her head and was looking down into the ruts when there came the sound of a loud cry from the far end of the field: 'Janie! Janie!' it called.

But the child did not turn about and run; in fact, she took a step forward and towards the wall as she said, 'That is my Auntie Jessie.'

'Shouldn't you go to her, dear?'

The child didn't answer but remained with her head back, staring up first at one, and then at the other.

'I think we had better go,' Lady Lydia whispered.

'No' – Gerald did not move – 'Stay still, Mama. This could be interesting.'

'Janie! Janie! Come here at once!'

The woman was now taking a short cut over the ridges, holding her long skirt in both hands. And when she reached the child she was panting so much she could not speak for a moment. But after grabbing the child's hand she stared at the two faces confronting her.

That this woman standing there on the rough ground could be the one and same young girl who had flung herself on him in such frantic despair that night, the night which had seared a mark on his mind that he knew he could never erase and which in a way had stifled his natural emotions, Gerald could not believe. Was it only ten years ago it had happened? Surely not, for this girl ... no, this woman looked to be in her late thirties, not twenty-six or twenty-seven as she must be now. He heard himself saying, 'Good morning, Miss Jessie. Perhaps ... perhaps you don't remember me? Gerald Ramsmore; and this is my mother, Lady Lydia.'

He watched her eyes flicker from one to the other of them; he watched her wet her lips and say, 'Yes. Yes. Good morning.' Then looking down at the child she was holding firmly by the hand, she said, 'I'm sorry ... I'm sorry if she's troubled you.'

'I didn't. I didn't trouble anybody, Auntie Jessie. I only wanted to talk.' The child now looked up at them again and added brightly, 'I like to talk.'

'Come along.'

Before the child was tugged away she called to them, 'Will you come again?'

Neither of them gave any reply to this, but Lady Lydia muttered, 'Oh, dear me. Dear me.'

Gerald knew that his mother's head had drooped but he kept his gaze fixed on the woman and the child slipping and scurrying now across the ploughed field. And not until they had gone from his sight did he turn away and walk to where his mother was now standing some distance from the wall, and they looked at each other while she said softly, 'That's the child, the girl's child whom they say they keep locked away almost like a prisoner.'

Gerald, however, made no comment on this as they walked towards the wood; his jaws were clenched tight: he was seeing again the beautiful girl, her bare blood-covered limbs stretched wide. He could even feel the moan rising up through

295

his own body again. It was nearly ten years ago; he shouldn't still be feeling like this . . .

The child was standing near a stool at the side of the open fire in the cottage that had once housed Annie. Annie had been dead now for eight years. And this cottage and the adjoining one were now linked together through a doorway between the two kitchens, and they had been the home of both the child and Jessie ever since Carl and Patsy had moved into the house.

Jessie was bending over the child, saying in a harsh voice, 'I've warned you, haven't I? If your grandfather finds you roaming around there'll be trouble.'

'Why?'

'I've . . . I've told you why. He's not well.'

'He's quite able to walk about. He won't speak to me. He never looks at me.'

'*Child!*'

'I am not a child, Auntie Jessie. I am nine years old. On my next birthday I shall be ten years old and I think things already, and I feel things. And I would like to know why I cannot see my sick mammy, and why she doesn't walk about.'

Jessie straightened her back now and sighed as she said, 'I've told you, she never leaves her room and . . . and children, or a child like you, would annoy her.'

The girl stared up at Jessie before saying quietly, 'In the new book you got for my lessons there is a lady sitting with a little girl on her knee and . . . and she's reading to her.'

Jessie's whole demeanour now softened as it was wont to do at her child's need, for that's how she thought of her, as her child. Softly now, and putting out her hand to touch the cream-tinted cheek, she said, 'Don't I have you on my knee when I'm reading to you?'

'Yes. Yes, you do, Auntie Jessie; but you are not my mammy, are you? You are just my auntie.'

Jessie swallowed deeply. 'Yes, I may just be your auntie,' she said, 'but I have cared for you from the moment you were born, because' – again she swallowed – 'there was no-one else to care for you.'

'Patsy once said she had brought me into the world.'

Before she spoke Jessie thought, Oh, did she? That was stupid of her. But she said, 'Yes. Yes, she did, but she handed you to me straightaway, and ever since I've looked after you as my little girl.'

For a moment longer Janie stared at Jessie; then sitting down abruptly on the stool she looked towards the fire, saying, 'I . . . I get frightened at night now, Auntie Jessie. I . . . I have been having strange dreams.'

Immediately Jessie was on her knees by the side of the wide-eyed child, saying earnestly, 'But you never told me. You seem to sleep soundly.'

The little girl brought her gaze round to Jessie's again. 'Well, it's only this last few weeks or so, since I cannot help wanting to run, wanting to get out. I . . . I have no-one to play with. In all our books' – she looked towards the table – 'children are playing games: "London Bridge is Falling Down", "Ring a Ring o' Roses", skipping and such.'

'Well, you skip. You skip very well. And Carl and Rob and you and I have played ball together in the field.'

'Yes. Yes, I know.' The child nodded now, adding, 'But they are not little. I mean, they are not my size. And, oh yes, Mike remarked that I was growing up too quickly and would outdo my strength. What did he mean by that?'

'Oh, Mike says silly things. It only means that you will be tall when you are a young lady.'

'Will I ever be a young lady?'

The thought leapt the years and fashioned a young lady before Jessie's eyes, and the face it presented was not the bright shining countenance of this child, the long-lashed lids, the full-lipped mouth, and the luxuriant brown hair, so strong it had a life of its own and would stay neither in curl nor in plaits.

'Will I, Auntie Jessie, be a young lady some day?'

'Of course you will.'

'Will I marry a prince and live happy ever after?'

Jessie pulled herself to her feet, saying briskly now, 'That's a silly thing to ask. Where did you read that?'

'In one of the fairy tales, Mr Grimms.'

Oh yes, Mr Grimms, whose stories to Jessie's mind were either terrifying or silly . . . marry a prince and live happy ever after. She was about to turn away when she paused and, pointing an admonishing finger down at Janie again, she said, 'Promise me you'll never run off on your own like you did this morning.'

And now to her amazement *her child* stood up and dared to say, 'No, Auntie Jessie, I can't promise you that, because all the time I want to run, to run away outside the walls and the gate and the railings, everything that keeps me in. And if you won't take me out some time, one day I will run away and see the market where Carl goes, and the village where the men go and get drunk. And another thing I must say to you, Auntie Jessie: one day I must see Mama. I must, because she has never wanted to see me. I shall never love her as I do you, but I still must see her.'

Dear Lord in heaven! Her nine years of incarceration now appeared to be a most senseless thing, for from whomsoever she had inherited her traits, this child had a strength of will and a mind beyond her years. One thing was sure, she did not take after her mother in any way, nor after her grandmother, for she had never shown any inclination to dance as both she herself and Angela had done at a very early age. She had asked if she would ever be a young lady. Well, there was one certainty: she would grow to an age when that term could be applied to her, by which time the truth would assuredly have been revealed in one way or another. And what then would be her reactions? Only God knew. Yes, only God knew.

She turned to her now and said briskly, 'No more talk; there's your lesson on the table. I'm just going to slip across to the house. I'll not be more than five minutes.'

As she was taking down a shawl from the wooden rack attached to the inside of the door, she was startled when Janie's voice came to her, saying, 'Don't lock me in, please.'

'I . . . I mu . . .'

'If you do, Auntie Jessie, one day I shall climb out through the window.'

Jessie paused for a moment as she fumbled in her pocket for the key to the door with one hand while groping for the latch with the other, realising that Janie had meant what she said. Without answering her, she dropped the key back into her pocket and opened the door. Closing it behind her, she muttered to herself, 'Oh, dear Lord.'

As she made her way across to the house, she recalled how it had come about that only the kitchen now remained as it had been for years; and how, after Annie had died, alterations had been made to the rest of the house.

Up till then she had kept Janie in her bedroom and shared her time between her and attending to her sister, the latter task being shared by Patsy. But when, later, Patsy had had to take over the kitchen and the housekeeping and had become heavy carrying her own child, naturally she had spent less and less time upstairs. And so the complete burden of Angela's dumb but effective demands had been left to her to cope with. Until one day it had come to her that if her sister were capable of eating by herself and walking across the room to her chair, then she should be able to wash and dress herself.

The response from Angela had been a bout of tantrums, during which she had thumped the bedclothes, then gripped the head of the bed, causing her body to stretch out and to become taut and so provide the impetus for her suddenly to strike out at her and to push her almost on to her back, and with such a strength that denied her weak, apparently fragile condition.

It was then that her own pent-up frustrations had caused her to take her hand and slap her sister across the face, on both sides. And this had had the intended result, for when their father had come bounding into the room she had immediately cried at him, 'Now you can take over! I've had enough. She's quite capable of helping herself. She's almost knocked me on my back, all because I suggested she should wash and dress herself. So, there you have it.' And on this she had run from the room, leaving Ward looking from the screaming figure on the bed to the open door. But having realised at this moment that she had meant what she said, he had rushed after her and caught her just as she was about to enter her bedroom, and gripping her by the shoulder, he had swung her round, saying, 'You can't do this! You can't leave her! She's sick.'

'Well, you must help in seeing to her, Daddy, mustn't you? or get help in. And that's final. And another thing I'll tell you: if I have to stand this strain much longer I shall walk out of here and you will have *that* on your hands too.'

She had then pointed towards the bedroom door: 'And it will be too late to try to murder it this time, won't it?'

He had glanced hurriedly behind him, saying, 'Be quiet! girl. You don't know what you're talking about.'

'I know what I'm talking about, Daddy, and so do you,' she had come back at him. 'And I mean what I say. Now, you can go downstairs and get Patsy to see to her for as long as she can, and then engage a cook to take her place. Now there you have it.' And she had bustled away from him and into her bedroom, banging the door almost in his face . . .

This fracas had resulted in Ward having to do some quick thinking: Patsy would soon be having her child, and what then? Put his beloved daughter away?

No! No! Never! He couldn't do that. They would say it was retribution for having had the other one put in the asylum.

This had led to further pondering and harassed thinking, until he thought he had found a solution. And in a way he had. The next morning he had again called Carl into his office.

'You know what happened last night,' he had said; 'and this state of affairs can't go on.' And Carl had answered, 'I can see that, sir, and I don't know what's going to happen when Patsy is nearing her time.'

'I've thought about all that, so I've got a proposal to put to you. If you fall in with it then I will make a statement . . . an addition to my will . . . to the effect that you will become part-owner, complete in half, of this house and farm when I die. Should that happen before my daughter Angela goes you would promise to see to her until her demise. And my terms are these: you and Patsy take up your abode in this house. This room could be turned into a bedroom and next door, the dining-room, could be put to your use as a sitting-room; I myself would eat in my own sitting-room. We have too much furniture in the house anyway, but this would not go to waste, for I would install my elder daughter in the cottages. A communicating door between the two could make it into one. That would be her abode.' He did not mention who would go with her to that abode, but it was plain to Carl, whose face was showing no surprise. And when Ward asked, 'How do you see this?' he paused for a long time before answering, 'It could be done, sir.' But he did not add his thanks for the offer of the half-share in the house and farm, for he knew his own worth and that there would have been no farm left if he and Patsy had gone when they had first intended to. What he *did* say was, 'If that arrangement is to be made possible, sir, you will have to employ someone in the kitchen for cooking and housework. And someone to look after Miss Angela during Patsy's confinement.'

Ward had risen to his feet, but soon made his decision: 'I will engage someone for the kitchen and the house,' he said; 'but with regard to the attention my daughter needs, I shall put it to Jessie that unless she agrees to see to her sister during the necessary time that Patsy will need to be free of her duty, then I will not allow her to continue to live in the cottage, and, if necessary, I myself will do what has to be done.'

Carl had nodded his head but said nothing, for he was thinking: Yes. Yes, he would do what had to be done for his daughter rather than let a stranger in and note her condition. As Patsy had continually said during the years since the child was born, Miss Angela had become more and more trying and she felt that her mind was being affected.

'Well, Carl, tell me.' Ward's voice had changed now: he was no longer the master putting over his proposals and demands in stilted language; he was like a man seeking support as he had added, 'What do you really think? Will it work? And . . . and would you be happy to do as I ask?'

Carl had answered straightaway. 'Yes, sir. I'll do anything that will ease the situation, and I'm sure Patsy will see it in this way, too. And I thank you for your kind offer. I . . . I appreciate it, sir. And have I your leave to engage a woman for the kitchen?' And he had paused for some time before finishing: 'Of course it will have to be someone from the Hollow. Perhaps McNabb's wife or daughter. They are clean people.'

Ward had sighed and agreed. 'Yes. Yes, go ahead.'

And so it was that things had gone ahead. The house was altered, and just in time for Patsy's baby to be born in the room that had been known as the master's study. But unfortunately it lived only a few hours and this had heralded a further period of child-bearing anxiety, for over the previous years she had experienced three miscarriages. Her bright and kindly nature had strained to accept fate, but now it became somewhat embittered, so that she thought as her father did: had they been still living in the cottages this would not have happened. There was surely a curse on this house and all in it . . .

Patsy turned from the table as Jessie entered the room and said briefly, 'You found her?'

'Yes, right down by the far wall. And who do you think she was talking to?'

'I couldn't guess. But it could only be somebody from the village, and they'd likely appear to her as if they were from another country.'

'No, it wasn't anyone from the village; it was Mr Gerald and . . . and his mother, from the Hall.'

Now Patsy stopped placing an assortment of cooking utensils on the table as she said, 'Oh, aye? Well, me da said he was back for the funeral. So he didn't turn out like all the rest. It must be worse up there than it is here, for they've only got two inside the house now, I understand, the old cook and the maid. My! my! Even I can remember when the place was overrun with servants. But that's life.'

'What am I going to do with her, Patsy? I mean to . . . to prevent her roaming?'

302

'Well, if she really wanted to roam she could walk out the gates, couldn't she? It's the only place that isn't barred or walled. I've wondered she hasn't done it afore.'

'She's been warned not to.'

'Huh! She's also been warned not to roam.'

Patsy dusted her hands one against the other, and now looking on Jessie, as Annie might have done, and not unkindly, she said, 'Sit yourself down. There's a cup of tea in the pot.'

'I . . . I don't want any tea, Patsy,' Jessie said as she sat down. 'But what am I going to do with her? She has openly defied me. When I asked her to promise not to roam again she said she couldn't, and . . . and then she told me not to lock the door on her. She's only nine, but the way she's talking now she could be . . . Oh!' She shook her head. 'She's so intelligent, far above her age, so alive, so wanting to know.'

'Well, it'll get worse not better, you know that. She'll be asking real questions shortly. Oh my!' She turned to the table and picked up the rolling pin, then laid it down again as she said, 'You should take her away out of this altogether. He's got enough money . . . ' It was noticeable that her reference was to neither 'the master' nor 'your father', but to 'he'. 'He's got enough money to let you live comfortably somewhere else. You could ask him to advance some of your share in the place.'

Jessie was gazing down on her locked hands lying on her lap and she knew what Patsy said was the solution. But as much as the child wanted to roam away from this place, all she herself wanted to do was to stay here. This was her home: it had always encased her, and she wanted it to go on. And then there was Carl. The thought of not seeing him some part of every day was unthinkable to her. The fact that Patsy hadn't provided him with a family seemed, in a strange way, to have left him free. She rose abruptly from the chair, saying, 'Daddy would never agree to that. I doubt if he would give me a penny, even if it meant keeping me from starving. I have a feeling that he begrudges me my food because I share it with her.'

Patsy did not contradict her; all she said was, 'In that case, you'll have to keep a wider eye on her. But you won't do it by locking her up, for she's a determined miss if ever there was one.' She didn't add, 'I wonder from which one she's got it?' Rather, she thought, God help her.

2

It was on the evening of 28 July 1914, that Lady Lydia put down the newspaper and went in search of her son. She found him in the stables rubbing down their latest acquisition of the new venture, which was a horse.

'Gerald! Gerald!'

'Yes? Yes, Mama? What is it?' He turned to her, and when she thrust the paper at him, she said, 'You were right. It's come. Austria's declared war on Serbia and Russia is mobilising.'

After he had scanned the newspaper headlines, Gerald said, 'Well, they've waited a full month, longer than I thought, since they did their dirty work at Sarajevo, when they murdered the heir to the throne. Now we will just have to wait and see what Russia and Germany do. It won't be long; a matter of days, I should imagine.'

'Oh, dear me, dear me. What will you do?'

'Mama! Mama! Come along. Stop worrying.'

'I can't help it. Oh, Gerald, if you would only see things differently.'

'Now, now. You go in the house this minute and I'll join you after attending to my friend here. Betsy is hungry. She's had a hard day.'

'I . . . I don't know how you can take things so lightly, Gerald, when . . .'

'Get away, woman! Do you hear me? And take this rag with you.' He pushed the newspaper back into her hand.

When, a few minutes later, he returned to the house, she met him in the hall, saying, 'A meal is on the table.'

'Well, let me get some of this dirt off me and I'll be with you. Five minutes.' He held up a hand before her face, the fingers spread.

'That means fifteen to twenty; then it will be stone cold.'

'Look; get yours and put mine in the oven. Or I'll do it myself now.'

As he made towards the dining-room she caught his arm and said, 'No; no. Please! You know how cook can't get over you messing about in the kitchen; and if you start pushing her dinners back in the oven . . . Oh, dear! dear! Go and get your wash, and be quick. I mean it, mind, be quick!'

He was laughing as he ran up the stairs; but there was no laughter on her face as she turned towards the dining-room. The prospect of war meant trouble for him because he was so outspoken in his views. All this would happen, wouldn't it? when he was making such a go with his business ideas with regard to the smallholding. He and McNamara, together with the odd-job helper, had worked wonders in less than a year, aided by the new inhabitant of the stables, a horse, albeit neither a racer nor a hunter, but one that could certainly pull a cart. And it had pulled some carts of fruit to the market this summer. So much so, it had made her wonder what had happened to all the fruit in previous years. Of course, then there had been a much larger staff, and as Gerald had finickally pointed out, the staff at Buckingham Palace could not have gone through half the amount they had managed to sell this year alone. So he would give her two guesses as to what had happened to it. And then he had answered for her. It had likely found its way to the market but through different channels.

Oh, she knew there was always a kind of pecking order in all households such as theirs had been. And often the hierarchy among the servants would have their appropriate pickings from bonuses, depending on the size of orders. She remembered her father saying years ago that whatever was lost in that way was worth it to keep a happy staff. And he had added that the quartermaster's store should be left to the quartermaster, the implication in their case, she knew, meaning the butler. And her thoughts remained with her early days, those days even before she was brought out in London that were so gloriously happy; and she asked herself yet again, as she had done many times over the years, would she have married Bede if she hadn't still been feeling the hurt of breaking off her engagement with Raymond after she found out about his mistress? She doubted it, Bede being twenty years her senior and with a grown-up family. He had spelt security, a shield from a dirty world. She had been very naïve in those days, hadn't she? Yet what was a young girl to think when her future husband showed no intention of giving up his mistress, on the excuse that it was nothing to do with love; he loved *her*, he said, and perhaps after marriage things might alter. But couldn't she understand the situation?

No; she hadn't been able to understand the situation. And she still didn't. So perhaps she had remained naïve.

'You're a silly woman. Why have you not yet started on your meal? I have been seven minutes; I timed myself.'

When he sat down and took the cover off the plate he sniffed and said, 'It smells good. I could eat a horse . . . but never Betsy. You know, I'm very fond of that old girl. She has worked, hasn't she? She's been a godsend. Oh, my dear.' He put down his knife and fork and, leaning across the corner of the table, he placed his hand on hers, saying, 'Don't look like that. It may never happen. I mean, conscription. And it won't come about rightaway. There'll be dozens, hundreds of them flying to the Colours, all brave fellows dying to be butchered. Oh, I'm sorry.' He picked up his knife and fork again, and in a more sober-like voice now he went on, 'Anyway, dear, it's nothing new; conscription's been going on, well, practically down the ages in other countries. They used it in America during the Civil War, and it started in France sometime in the seventeen-hundreds, as far back as that. It's nothing new, I tell you.'

'I'm not thinking just about the actual conscription, Gerald, and you know I'm not. It's . . . it's what people will think because, knowing the position that your father held and your half-brothers do, it will be expected of you. And . . .

and when you don't conform, as I know you won't' – she stressed the last words – 'you'll be made to suffer in so many ways. People are cruel.'

Again, he laid down his knife and fork before asking her quietly, 'What would you have me do, Mama? Deny all my principles and do something that I abhor, such as shooting a man, or whipping off his head with a sword, or stabbing him in the guts?'

He sprang up now and stopped her as she was endeavouring to rise from her chair, and pressing her down again, he said, 'Mama, you forced me to talk of this matter, and I can't polish my words. I know your thoughts are with me – war is abhorrent to you as it is to me – so why do you want me to ignore my principles and . . . ?'

She twisted her body now and looked up at him, saying, 'Don't you see? Don't you understand I don't want you to suffer? And I feel you will suffer more through your opinions and open attitude than you would if you were taking up arms and, be it against all you think, making yourself fight for the cause of your country.'

He slowly moved from her and took his place at the table again, and after a moment he said quietly, 'Mama, I don't believe a word of it. But what I do believe is that if I were to do as you say I would lose your respect, and very likely your love. Whatever you say now you would feel deep and grievous disappointment that the one you loved most, and you have impressed this on me, could be swayed to do something that went against every fibre of his being, just because he was afraid of public opinion.'

A tap came on the door and Nancy Bellways entered carrying a tray and paused half-way up the room, saying, 'Oh, I'm sorry m'lady; I thought you'd be through by now.'

Lydia turned to her, saying, 'Oh, let us have it here, Nancy. We've wasted our mealtime in talking, but we'll soon be through. Just leave it there; I'll see to it.'

'Cook left it in the basin, m'lady, and the custard's in the tureen,' Nancy Bellways now added, 'in case Master Gerald was late.' And he, nodding at her, teased, 'You're insinuating, Nancy, that I'm always late.'

'Well nearly, Master Gerald, nearly.' She was now smiling broadly at him as she added, 'And you'll be pleased to know we've reached the hundredth jar of fruit s'afternoon.'

'*You have?* Marvellous! But carry on. And tell cook I love her – I love you both. I do. I do. And wait till Christmas when we take some of that lot to market; they'll dive on them.'

As Nancy Bellways who, after giving this house forty years' service, was afforded the liberty of what her mistress termed backchat, now said, 'Oh well, Master Gerald, cook says she's gona lock half that lot up in the cellar so you can't get your hands on any of it, and that'll see us through the winter.'

'Oh, does she? Well you can go and tell her that I'm coming out there shortly to have a word with her. Likely box her ears into the bargain. You tell her that.'

When Nancy went from the room laughing, Lady Lydia looked hard at her son as she said, 'You have learned a special way of dealing with staff, haven't you?'

'Have I? Well, perhaps it's because I served my time as an underling with Hell and Damnation.' He laughed.

'You know, I often think of them and the poor peasant, you know, Ronald Pearson, and wonder how he's getting on. I'd like to go up to town one day and look in on him. And, of course, the Cramps.'

'You liked that family, didn't you?'

'Yes. Yes, I did, Mama.'

'You never told me you kept in touch with them; I mean, wrote to them, until you got that letter.'

'Well, I didn't see the need. I just wanted to let them know how I was getting on in my new business. And you know yourself, you laughed at the letter, especially the end.' And he quoted: ' "I hope this finds you as it does me at present, half-stripped to go into the tub when Mam gets out. Dad's got a runny cold and has sewed himself into his vest, camphor block an' all. That'll take care of him for the winter." ' He smiled at his mother now as he said, 'And the last bit which expressed their warmth. You remember? "We'd all like to see you pop in one of these nights, Mr G." '

Again Lady Lydia stared at her son, who was now silent and staring down at his plate, and she said in a voice that held a mixture of sadness, and yet criticism, 'You always seem happier with that type of person. Don't you, dear?'

He looked at her and moved his head slightly, saying, 'It's just that I like people who act naturally. They had nothing to hide, they weren't playing a part: they hadn't to keep up any social class. In fact, they were proud of what they were. And don't think they were all ignorant slobs, as Beverly classes them. There was a bright intelligence running through the majority of them. They only needed the chance to widen it. And then I also enjoyed my days with the publishers; Mr Herbert and Mr Darrington were gentlemen, and so was Ronald Pearson. He, too, would have come under the banner of middle-class, upper middle-class. But being the tail-end of a huge family, he had to earn his living. I enjoyed their company. I don't like fakes, Mama.'

'Those you would call fakes, Gerald, are sometimes merely diplomats.'

'Oh, no, no. Anyway, my dear, let's start on cook's pudding and leave the future until it happens, eh? What about it? And by the way, I'm going to take another look at the woodman's cottage. You know, it could be made habitable again, and we could offer it to someone in return for a few hours of their labour.'

'It will take a lot to bring it into order.'

'Only the materials. McNamara and I could do it between us.'

'It was practically overgrown with scrub the last time I was down there.'

'Oh, the clearing of that will be the easiest part. And if I remember rightly, Trotter had a bit of a garden down there, grew his own stuff.'

'You couldn't remember Trotter, dear; he left when you were very small.'

'Not so small. I must have been about five. Anyway, I can recall what the place looked like, and if we can work another patch down there it'll all help.'

She smiled tolerantly at him now, saying, 'Given time, I can see you turning all the grounds into a vegetable patch.'

'And wouldn't that be good! Just think of the money it would bring in. You could go up to town, do the shows, get yourself seasonable rig-outs.'

She answered soberly now, 'If there was money to spend, I'd rather put it for help in the house.'

And he answered just as soberly now, 'Yes. Yes, that would be more sensible. But that's what will happen in the next year or two, you'll see.'

He finished his pudding and, rising from the table, asked, 'Will you excuse me, dear?' Then went round to her and kissed her cheek before going out.

But she sat on, thinking of the dread of going on living in this mausoleum of a house if anything should happen to him . . .

He was standing on the edge of what had once been a large clearing but which was now padded down with seasons of dank grass, with patches here and there of tall weeds. One such patch was obscuring the small window of the cottage. Then he noticed something odd: a patch of weeds near the door had been pressed to the side. The door, which for some long time, had been hanging half-open on one hinge, was pressed well back. It wasn't likely, he told himself, that a tramp had taken shelter in there, because the cottage was situated in the middle of the grounds and even now, although the acreage had become shrunken over the years, its situation was a good half mile from the nearest public path.

He had almost reached the cottage itself when he was startled by a combined screeching: a black shape just missed his face, cawing angrily as it went, and a small, screeching figure pelted herself at him before springing back and turning a terrified countenance up to him.

'Well! it was the bird. It . . . it jumped at me from the fire-place. I . . . I wasn't doing any harm, I was just looking.'

'Yes. Yes,' he said soothingly, 'I'm sure you weren't doing any harm, you were just looking.' He bent down to her now. 'You are Mr Gibson's granddaughter, aren't you? We have met before.'

She blinked rapidly before saying, 'Oh yes, yes. You were at the wall with your mother.'

311

'Yes, that's it; I was at the wall with my mother. But tell me, why are you roaming around here? How did you manage to find this?' He waved his hand towards the cottage.

'I was upset. I mean . . . Oh! dear me' – she put her hand to her head – 'that bird frightened me.'

He looked about him and to the side and said, 'There's a fallen tree. If we move the weeds we can sit down.'

After he had pushed the weeds aside and trampled on them, he pointed, saying, 'There you are.' And when they were both seated on the lying trunk he said again, 'Tell me, how did you manage to get this far? I mean, how did you manage to leave the farm?'

She now turned her face up to his and smiled widely as she said, 'It was quite by accident. It was the rabbits, you know. You see, I am not allowed to go out of the gates and I had told Auntie Jessie that I couldn't promise her that I wouldn't go wandering.'

'You told her that?'

'Oh yes. Yes. It was no good lying. Well, I mean it was no good telling her that I would do as she asked when I knew I couldn't help wandering. Well, I was at the wall, you know, where I saw you and the lady, your mother. And further along there is a mound and some bushes growing on the top and I saw a family of rabbits, baby ones. They were playing; but when I went near them they scattered. The men shoot the rabbits, you know, because of the crops. I don't like to hear them shooting. Anyway, I pushed between the bushes and the wall to see if I could look in their burrows. They don't have nests, you know, they have burrows.'

'Oh.' He nodded at her.

'Well, there were lots of holes and they had all disappeared down them. Then when I nearly tripped over a root of a tree, I noticed it had grown into the bottom of the wall and pushed a stone aside. It was quite a large stone; roots must be very strong, don't you think?'

'Yes. Yes, I do. Then what did you do?'

'Well—' A look almost of glee passed over the small face now as she said, 'I pulled the stone aside and then another one slipped out from above. I became afraid then in case the wall should topple down. It didn't, but just in case it did, you know what I did next?'

He shook his head.

She now held out her hands to him, saying, 'You see my nails?'

'Yes.' He nodded at her.

'They're very dirty, aren't they? Well, you see, I did what our dogs do before they bury a bone, and the rabbits do it and the foxes. I scraped the soil away with the help of a piece of wood. But I really couldn't go very deep. Although I kept away from the big root there were smaller ones criss-crossing. Anyway, I must have managed to dig for about three to four inches and it was enough to make the hole large enough for me to crawl through. I had to lie flat, of course. It was quite an adventure. I did think at one time that the wall might suddenly drop on me, but it didn't. The stones are usually placed very firm against each other, I understand from Mike. He is the cowman, he helps to mend the walls. But that big root had certainly oozed them out.'

'Won't your aunt be looking for you and be worried again?' he said.

'Yes, I suppose so; but she knows I will come back. I promised her only yesterday that if I roamed round the farm I would always come back.'

'But you didn't say anything about roaming outside the farm, I suppose.'

She stared at him for a moment, as if thinking, then said, 'No. No, I didn't.'

'I should imagine she will be very worried, perhaps annoyed.'

'No doubt. No doubt.'

He had the urge to laugh, for she sounded so old-fashioned. How old would she be now? Yes, he remembered she had said before that she was nearly ten. Dear! Dear! and not allowed to go to school. Not allowed to mix with other children. It was a crime against youth.

He watched her now looking straight ahead, her hands joined tightly between her knees, and this caused her long dress to ride up above her black shoes and white socks. And he was on the point of saying, 'Come along; I'll take you back to your rabbit hole,' when she turned to him quite suddenly and asked, 'What is an unholy trinity?'

'A what?'

'An . . . unholy . . . trinity.'

It was a moment or so before he said, 'Why do you ask?'

'Because I want to know.'

Well yes, of course, that's why she asked. But where had she heard that? 'I realise you want to know,' he said, 'but tell me why and where have you heard that?'

She was looking away from him again; it was a moment or two before she said, 'There's the village over there.' She pointed in front of her, but then let her arm travel to the right before adding, 'It's somewhere in that direction, I think. But I wanted to see it. And there is a school. You see, I don't meet many children. In fact, I don't meet any children at all except in books, and so when I got through the hole the other day I didn't come this way, I walked by the wall on your side and I came to a wood. And when I came to the end of it there was a ditch; but the railings on the far side were broken here and there, and so it was easy to step on to the pathway. And I walked up the pathway and I heard children . . . children's voices. And when I got nearer I saw some buildings and from the end one children were running. They were coming out of a gate in twos and threes and they were running, not towards me but away. I suppose to their homes. But there were three girls: one was just my size and the others were larger.' She paused here as if thinking, and he remained silent, looking at her, until she went on, 'When I went up to them they stared at me. Then one said, "Who are you?" And I said, "I am Janie Gibson. Who are you?" And she laughed at me and giggled, and she looked at the taller girls and now one of them turned to where two ladies were coming out of this building. And when they got to the gate they stood behind the girls and they, too, looked at me. One was, I suppose, young, and the other seemed old. Then one of the girls turned, reached up to the older woman and whispered something. And what she whispered was my name. I have very good hearing, you know. "Her name is

Janie Gibson," she said; and the older woman stared at me before she said to the girls, "Go along! Get along home." And when they didn't obey her at once she raised her voice to them and then they ran off. Then she said to me, "Go home, dear." Just like that, very quietly, "Go home, dear." And I turned and I had taken some steps when I heard the younger woman saying, "So that's the result of the unholy trinity." And then the older woman said something to her that sounded harsh, but I couldn't hear what it was she said. So, that is why I am asking you, sir, what is an unholy trinity?'

He said, 'That . . . that wasn't meant for you, it's . . . it's just a saying.'

'Then why did she say I was the result of it?'

'People say the oddest things. There's a lot of ignorant people in that village.'

'But she was a woman, and perhaps she was a teacher; I think she was. The older woman was, because she sent the girls home. Are you telling me the truth when you say you don't know what it means?'

He drew a deep breath into his chest before he lied, saying, 'As far as I can gather it has no meaning, not really. But people make bad meanings out of simple words.' And now he took her hand as he added, 'I would ask you to forget it; and you know, you do realise that if your aunt knew that you had been outside the perimeter of the farm she would be very upset, especially if she knew you had been talking to people from the village, because many of them in that village are not nice people.'

She stared at him wide-eyed until he became almost embarrassed. And he was embarrassed when she said, 'You are a very kind man.' Then she asked, 'How old are you?'

He smiled now at her before answering, 'Very old. Twenty-nine come thirty.'

She nodded at him. 'Yes,' she agreed; 'that is very old. Auntie Jessie, too, is old. She's nearly twenty-seven, I think.'

'Yes' – he was laughing now – 'age is a dreadful thing. But one day you will be twenty-seven or even twenty-nine come thirty.'

'Yes. Yes, I shall.' There was a brightness to her voice and she now sprang up from the tree-trunk and, her face on a level with his, she said, 'And then I shall be able to go where I wish, to travel the world. I have a globe of the world. It is very big, and one day I shall go round it.' She made a big circle with her finger, ending, 'Right round it.'

He again took her hand as he said, 'Yes, my dear, I'm sure you will. Yes, you will, you will travel the world. But now I think you had better travel to your rabbit hole. Don't you?'

She hunched her shoulders and laughed gently as she answered him conspiratorially, 'Yes, I think so. But . . . but may I come again?'

He hesitated; then pulling himself to his full height, which to her made him appear very tall, and gazing over her head, he said in what he imagined to be a stern voice, 'I have no say in the matter, miss. I don't know anything about rabbit holes or little girls escaping through farm walls. And if I saw one here again I'm sure I wouldn't recognise her.'

She now flapped her hand up at him and actually laughed out aloud. It was a high tinkling sound as might come from a young child, not one with an old head that had been forced on to her shoulders. And then she said, 'I like you. I like you a lot, and I shall come again when you can't see me.' And at this she tugged at his hand, and he led her through the labyrinth until they came to the wall; and from here she led him to the hole which was hidden by the bushes on the mound. And as he watched her lie flat and crawl through it, he wondered how she was going to explain her soil-dabbed dress as well as her dirty hands.

3

Apart from the front door and the kitchen door, there was another entry to the house: a door from the yard to a back stairway leading up to the attic rooms, but with a door, half-way up, on to the main landing. The attic rooms had at one time been used for winter storing; but the door had been locked for many years now. Janie was very aware of this door for she had more than once tried to open it. But this morning she had a key; at least, she had a bunch of keys, seven in all, most of them rusty.

She had first noticed a very old horse collar hanging in the corner of the harness-room, and on investigation had seen the keys on the nail driven into the wall at the collar's centre. A few days previously she had been passing the front of the house, when her attention was caught by an indistinct figure standing in front of one of the upper windows. One minute it was there, the next it was gone. She knew immediately that the figure could be no other than that of her sick mother. But if she was sick, why wasn't she in bed?

The glimpse she'd had of the person had suggested someone very small. But she had reasoned that having seen only the upper part of her, she might perhaps have been sitting on a chair.

However, that glimpse had been enough to stir her determination to see her mother. Why not? And her mind did not take her further than 'why not?'

317

Shortly after this sighting, the bunch of old keys caused her to plan a way of bringing about the encounter. First, she told herself that even if one of those keys fitted the lock it would not turn because it was rusty. So when the opportunity occurred, she took down the ring and dipped the whole of the keys into the oil bucket, then let them drain for a while before hanging them back on the wall. The oil would need to soak in, she told herself.

However, it was to be some time before she could bring her plan to fruition, for it was on that same day she had met the nice man, and as a result of this meeting she had been confined under lock and key.

After returning home with a soiled dress and dirty hands and refusing to explain how this had come about, her Auntie Jessie had said there was no alternative: she must be kept in. And she was until the day there was great excitement in the yard, all because war had been declared somewhere. Even her Auntie Jessie was excited. And so she was let out and left to her own devices. It was then that she decided there was no better time to try the keys in the lock of that door.

And this she was now doing.

It wasn't until she tried the fourth key that she felt it click as if it had dropped into a socket. And when she turned it half-way round and the door moved under her hand, she was so overcome by trembling excitement that for a moment she didn't push it open. When she did, she saw a flight of stairs with cobwebs hanging from the sloping ceiling. One step at a time she mounted the stairs, to be confronted at the head by another door. But this opened easily. And now she was in a small hallway where more stairs went off to her right. But opposite was a large landing and she stepped cautiously on to it, only to jump back when she heard a door opening. She waited, her head turned to the side, so that she could see part of the landing; but then stiffened when there emerged from a room the figure of Patsy carrying a slop pail.

She held her breath, wondering which way Patsy would go, for were she to pass this way she would certainly see her. And there wasn't time now to scamper down those stairs.

But she sighed with relief as Patsy's figure disappeared from her view.

After waiting some minutes, which she gauged would give Patsy time to reach the kitchen, she stepped on to the landing and noticed there were doors on both sides. But she knew now which one she must go to.

At the door, she paused for a long moment before tapping on it. But when there was no response she opened it and, lifting her feet as if she were about to tread on something fragile, she entered her mother's room. And what she saw was a large bed – she did not take in other pieces of furniture, only the bed – and standing at the far side of it was a very small . . . she hesitated to think lady, and woman didn't fit either. The only way to describe the person she was looking at was 'a young girl'. She was fat; even under a loose dress it could be seen that she was fat. But it was the head that Janie stared at, for this wasn't the face of a girl and her hair was almost white.

Unaware that she had closed the door behind her and that she was standing with her back to it, she knew only that the small person had walked down by the side of the bed and that she could now see all of her where she was clinging to the iron frame of the foot of the bed. And what the complete sight of her conveyed to Janie was that there must be a mistake. This little person could not be her mother, for she was not much bigger than herself. And she didn't look the kind of person to be a mother.

She wanted to get out of this room and with this in mind she stepped away from the door and opened her mouth to say 'I am sorry', but instead what issued from it was a high scream as she found herself flung back against the door. And now the room seemed to echo with screams.

The bouncing of her head against the door made her feel dizzy for a moment, although this did not prevent her from letting out another scream when she saw the small woman lift the lamp from the bedside table with a very obvious intention. She sprang to the side, but not quickly enough to evade the splintered lamp-glass splattering the back of the hand she had put up to shield her face.

Still screaming, she groped blindly for the door as more objects were hurled against it. But then she was out on the landing, so terrified that she didn't know which way to run until, looking to the right, she saw her grandfather appearing at the top of the stairhead. He was running, but at the sight of her he paused for a moment, his mouth agape. Then as he came at her, she sprang back towards her exit; and she actually fell down the last three stairs and tumbled through the door into the open again. But once on her feet she began to run.

Philip Patten stood by the bed, looking down on the contorted face which, like the rest of the body, was gradually relaxing. And now he turned towards Ward, who stood at the foot of the bed, and said, 'That should keep her under for a few hours. I'll come back later and give her another shot.' He bent now and closed his black bag and was making for the door when he stopped and looked back at Ward, saying, 'I warned you some time ago, you know, how she would react and matters won't improve. All right, she was provoked this time, but there have been times when she hadn't been provoked . . . well, let us say nothing that would provoke any sane person. Oh, yes, I know, Ward.' He put his hand out as if in protest. 'You don't like that word, but you've got to face it. Her mind is deranged. It has been from the beginning. She'll have to be put under control – I've said so before – or you must engage someone to do that. I'm warning you; Patsy can't put up with much more. As for Jessie, she's had to cope with more than any human being should be asked to do. She's got her hands full as it is; and this last event has proved that. Now, I'll say no more at the moment; except that she has to be sedated and . . . yes, I'll say it, guarded. Just imagine if this had happened during the evening when that lamp was lit; the whole house would have gone up. From what I see here, even since it's been tidied up' – he looked around the room now – 'it must have been a shambles. It seems that not even your presence or Patsy's could stop her wreaking havoc. She should have been tied down. It's no news to you that Patsy has voiced this again and again when she's had to deal with her alone.'

'She doesn't often deal with her alone; I'm always on hand.'

'You're not always on hand; you can't be. Anyway, you have my opinion, and I don't think, on this occasion, that you want a second one, do you? But I'm telling you, if this is allowed to go on as it is now and you don't have her restrained in some way, there will come a time when there will be a second outburst, and perhaps at night; and I'm putting this plainly to you; it isn't far ahead.' But then, his voice softening, he said, 'I know this must be affecting you, Ward. But in your heart you've known for years how things were with her. Well, I'll be off, but I'll see you shortly.'

When he reached the kitchen and before he had time to say anything to Patsy, she confronted him, saying, 'I'm not standing much more of this, Doctor. Not for all the bribes in the world. And I've told Carl, and him an' all' – she thumbed towards the ceiling – 'there's got to be more help up there, night and day, and somebody experienced. D'you know, you wouldn't believe it, but she's got more strength when she's in one of them turns than me and Carl and him put together.'

Her voice sinking, and with it her whole tense frame, she asked, 'What's to be done, Doctor? Things can't go on like this, can they?'

'No, they can't, Patsy; and I've just told him so; it's either one thing or the other. I've put it plainly to him. The first suggestion I know he wouldn't hear of, and that's having her put away. So he'll have to engage more help. But don't forget that'll mean more work for you down here.'

'Oh, I don't mind that. I don't mind that. It's the running up and down; and her, she's become more thankless with the years. It's funny; she can't speak, yet she can demand. Oh, aye, she can demand. And scream. Oh, my God! her screaming.'

He put in, 'What happened to the child? Where is she?'

'Don't ask me, Doctor. Miss Jessie's out hunting for her now, and Carl an' all, 'cos Rob said he saw her flying across the lower field, and he swears there was blood on her. Where's it all going to end? Can you tell me that, Doctor, where's it all going to end?'

'I can no more answer that than you can, Patsy; only time will tell.' Then he lifted his hand as she went towards the teapot. 'Nothing for me this morning, thank you,' he said; 'I've got a very busy day ahead of me. I must be off, but I'll see you this evening.' And with that he left . . .

It was in the afternoon when, sitting beside the bed on which lay his beloved child, as he still thought of her, Ward came to a decision. The doctor had given him two options. One he would never condone; having her put away would give the village two bells to ring. The first: it was only justice that his daughter should end up in the same place as Daisy Mason; and secondly: God would not be mocked: He was making him pay for His desecration through his daughter. No, that had always been out of the question. And as for the second option, having a day and night warder in this room, the image presented to him was of big strong, hefty women handling his child. Never! Never!

He now put out his hand and stroked her hair back from her brow. Her face was relaxed; she was his little girl again, so like her mother, at least her countenance was, for her inactivity had bloated her body.

He rose now and, gazing down on her, he murmured, 'When you join your mother you will be so happy, and then together you will wait for me.' Then he bent and kissed her, a long slow kiss, before going out of the room.

Jessie was nearing the farm gates when she saw Carl riding in from the other direction, and when he pulled his horse to a stop she could see by his expression that he had no news. Without her enquiring, he said, 'Not hilt nor hair of her.' Then she asked, 'Did you see the blacksmith?'

'Yes. Yes, and nobody gets past him. I went to the Newberrys too, and to the Holdens, and to Mr Wainwright's. He's the Methodist minister at the far end of the village, you know, and his wife's ailing and sits in the garden a lot, and she said no-one had passed there. They were very kind in their concern for her. Lastly, I went right through to the

322

other end and made it my business to go to the school, because I've always said she's been starved of her own like and age and' – he nodded down at her now – 'I did find out something there, but not touching on today. Apparently, some time ago she turned up at the school gate.'

'No! At the school gate?'

'Aye. Yes. That's what Miss Pratt said, and ... and she apparently told her to go home because there were some children around and she thought it was better that they didn't get to talking, although Janie had already told them her name.'

She said now, 'There's nothing for it but to tell the polis.'

'Not yet.' He bent down towards her. 'The state that things are in, your ... well, I mean, your father would be more upset. You know what happens when they arrive on the scene; they're always followed by newspaper men.'

'Well, where can she be?'

'She could be hiding somewhere quite close.'

'I've been through the wood.' She now paused a moment before she asked, 'You don't think she could have got in the Hall grounds? I can't see her climbing the walls, and certainly not the fences. And she knows she mustn't go out through the gate.'

'After what happened this morning,' Carl said tersely now, 'I think she would have gone straight through a blank wall.'

She was silent for a moment as she looked around her, as if searching for some clue, and then she seemed to get it by saying, 'You remember when she came back that day with her dress and hands all soiled and she wouldn't tell me where she had been or what she had been doing? She could have crawled through some place, couldn't she?'

'Yes. Yes, I remember. But you know,' and he was shaking his head now, 'we went all round those walls. She'd have to be a badger to get underneath that wall, wouldn't she?'

'Yes, but she had been crawling somewhere. Carl' – she put her hand up to him now – 'would you go to the Hall, and ask if you could look through the grounds?'

'Yes. Yes.' He nodded down at her. 'The young master up

323

there is very amenable, I hear, and Lady Lydia always has been pleasant. Yes, I'll do that, although it's a faint hope; if she kept running in the direction that Ron saw her, it wouldn't have led her towards the Hall. She would have to go out of the gate for that. Anyway—' He now turned the horse about, saying, 'It's a long shot.' Then he galloped off leaving her standing, her arms tight about her waist now as if trying to squeeze out the anxiety that was filling her body. If anything had happened to the child she wouldn't be able to bear it, she just wouldn't. She had done wrong in disobeying her orders, but then, what could you expect? She knew she had a mother, and now what could she think of her mother? Only as a mad woman; for it had to be faced, and her father had to face it, too, his beloved Angela was mad, and craftily mad: what sweetness remained in her she expressed only when her father was present, but her manner towards both herself and Patsy was demanding and aggressive, and it had worsened with time, so much so that she had to make a big effort not to hate her.

What if anything had happened to her child! And Janie *was* her child: she had reared her, cared for her, loved her; and yet in doing so she had imprisoned her; but only for her own safety. With what result? Yes, she knew if anything had happened to Janie she would scream her loathing at her sister, and at her father, too. Oh, yes, at her father, who cared for nothing, nor for no-one but the replica of his wife.

As she turned away she was surprised by the fact that she could think of her mother just as her father's wife . . .

Carl had dismounted from his horse, which was now holding up its head as it answered the neighing of another in a stable along the yard; then he turned to meet Lady Lydia's approach.

Her greeting was warm: 'Hello, Carl,' she said. 'Dear! dear! it's such a long time since we met, but . . . but it's enviable how you carry your years because you don't appear any older than when I last saw you.'

'Thank you, Lady Lydia.' He nodded at her as he smiled. 'I would like to believe that. You're very kind, as always.'

She asked now, 'Can I help you in any way?'

'We've had a little upset back at the farm, and the child – you know, the young girl, Janie – has been missing since this morning. And Miss Jessie wondered if you would allow me to look through your grounds to see if she might . . . well' – he shrugged his shoulders – 'it's a faint hope because I don't know how she could have got into your place. But as I said, Miss Jessie thinks she might be hiding somewhere. It's a sort of last straw before we apply for further help from . . . the polis. And I . . . well, you can understand Mr Gibson wouldn't take kindly to that.'

'Oh no; I can understand. And of course you are very welcome to search where you like. My son is out at the moment. He's on some business in the town and McNamara, our gardener, is with him. They were killing two birds with one stone, so to speak.' She smiled before adding, 'We run a business now, you know, called a smallholding.' She poked her face forward, an amused expression on it, and he said, 'Yes. Yes, I've heard, and also, m'lady, that it's doing well.'

'Yes. Yes.' Her eyes widened now. 'Surprisingly well. My son seems to be a genius with a pick and shovel, which, too, is very surprising when he doesn't appear to be . . . well, to have a manual temperament. Books are more in his line.'

Carl smiled at her now, saying, 'Yes. Yes, I recall that was his line, m'lady. We had a talk now and again when he came home from the university, and he recommended one or two books to me that were good reading. Yes, yes, that was his line.'

'Would you like to leave your horse here' – she pointed . . . 'there are plenty of empty stables – while you look around?'

'Thank you, thank you. I'll do that.' Now his smile widened: 'And he won't be lost for company, as he's already made evident,' he added.

He turned now and led the horse into a stable towards which Lady Lydia was pointing; then after closing the half-door on his animal he bade her goodbye by saying, 'Thank you for your kindness, m'lady.' And to this she answered, while shaking her head, 'Oh, 'tis nothing. If we can be of help in any way, you must tell us.'

It was a full hour later when he returned to the yard, and there being no-one about he knocked on the kitchen door; and when it was opened by a maid, he said briefly to her, 'Will you please give her ladyship my thanks?' He did not add, 'I haven't found her,' for, as he knew only too well, maids' tongues rattled, and not only inside the house. So he turned and retrieved his horse and rode away, leaving Nancy Bellways asking herself, 'And what has he got to thank her for, I wonder.'

It was not fifteen minutes later when Gerald entered the house and, having been informed by Nancy that his mother was in the sitting-room, he went straight there, making a dramatic gesture as he opened the door: flinging his arms wide, he cried, 'Success! Success! Another avenue has opened: fruit, flowers and vegetables, they'll take as much as we can supply.'

He allowed his arms to drop, then moved quickly towards her, asking, 'What's wrong?'

'Nothing here,' she said. 'And I'm so glad about the new orders. But Carl from Gibson's farm called in. The child is missing, you know, the daughter of the young girl. Something must have happened at the farm this morning because they've been searching all day, and he came to see if he could look through the grounds. Of course I said yes, but I didn't see him when later he left. He gave only a brief message to Nancy, and didn't say whether or not he had found her. Well, I didn't expect him to. Likely, if the child was running away she would have come here, wouldn't she? She would have made for a house, surely? Yet, I don't know.'

'How long ago was this?'

'Oh' – she thought for a moment – 'since Nancy told me, I should think some twenty minutes or so. Anyway, our place seemed to be the last resort for them before they went to the police. But come; sit down and tell me all your news. Nancy's just brought the tea in.'

'I'll just have a cup, Mama, then I'll go and have a look through the woods and thereabouts.'

'But Carl has already done that, dear.'

326

'Yes, I know, but' – he smiled at her – 'he doesn't know this place as I know it. Don't forget, I used to hide in the woods when father was on the rampage looking for me when I had yet again refused to play toy soldiers.'

'Don't be silly, Gerald. Your father never wanted you to play toy soldiers.'

'Well, the equivalent during my vacs: riding hell for leather over the fields as if we were in tournaments, lances pointed – I'm sure he imagined he was doing that half of his time – then yelling at me when I purposely missed shooting the rooks. What was that but soldier practice? Anyway, I knew some good hidey-holes. Now, I won't be long, and I'll tell you all about our latest rise in the business when I come back.'

He heard her tut-tutting as he left the room; then he was hurrying through the yard and into the labyrinth of garden beds that still hadn't been cleared. As he approached the near-derelict woodman's cottage his step slowed, and at the door he stopped and called in a low voice, 'Are you there? It's only me.' Then there being no answer, he went on, 'I'm the man that knows about your rabbit hole.'

When there was still no answer he pushed past the hanging door and passed through the first room and into the second. And there, about to rise from the mattress that he knew had housed a colony of field mice, he saw her. And he stared at her in amazement and pity for her chin and neck were covered with dried blood, as was one of her hands. She was blinking at him as she said, 'I . . . I must have fallen asleep.'

'Oh, my dear!' He was sitting on the mattress beside her now. 'What on earth's happened?' And when he went to touch her hand, she jerked it back from him, saying, 'There's . . . there's pieces of glass still in it.'

'What?'

'She . . . she threw the lamp at me.'

'Who did?'

'The . . . the—' She had to swallow hard now before she could go on and say, 'The woman, or person who they say is my mother.'

His eyes stretched, his mouth dropped into a gape, and he asked softly, 'But how did it come about?'

'I . . . I wanted to see her. I oiled the rusty keys and got in the back way. When I went into her room—' She now screwed up her eyes tightly, then did a strange thing: she put her tongue right out and brought her teeth down on it as if to stop herself talking. And when he said, 'Come, dear; we must get you home,' she shrank back from him, saying, 'No! No! Auntie Jessie will keep the door locked on me forever now.'

'Oh no, she won't. No. No, she won't. I promise you.'

'How . . . how can you promise me; you don't live there.'

'No, I don't.' His voice was stern now. 'But I shall see . . . I shall make it my business that no-one locks you up again.'

'Will you?'

'Yes, I will. And that is a promise.'

'I feel very tired. I . . . I heard Carl calling me.'

'Didn't he come in here?'

'I wasn't in here then, I was lying in the thicket, but I didn't let him know. Then I felt very tired and I remembered the bed.' She turned her head and looked behind her and said, 'The mice all ran away. They were only small. I am not afraid of mice.'

He took out a handkerchief now, but when he went to wipe her face she pulled her head back, saying, 'I think my neck is cut.' And when he looked closer he could detect a long scratch covered with dried blood. He didn't know how deep it might be, but he did know he must get her back to her home, and that she must see a doctor, for there were still pieces of glass in her hand. Good God! It was unbelievable that her mother, who had once been that beautiful, fragile young girl, was capable of wreaking such vengeance on her offspring; but then it was her offspring that had wrecked her life. What a tangle! What a dreadful, dreadful tangle!

'You're a very sensible little girl,' he said more gently now, 'and you must know that you cannot stay here. It will soon be nightfall and the animals' – he moved his hand as though he knew of their whereabouts – 'they'll come roving round here and frighten the life out of you.'

'I'm not afraid of animals.'

No, she wasn't afraid of animals, it was people she was afraid of, and with good cause. He said, 'Now listen, my dear. Nothing bad is going to happen to you when you get back home. I shall make it my business to see that you are in no way punished for—' What word would he give to a child for wanting to see her mother? The only one that came to mind was escapade, and that is what he said – 'for your escapade.'

She shook her head slowly now, then asked him a question that he could not answer: 'Why are things at the farm like they are?' When he made no reply, she went on, 'Other children can get out and run about. I saw them, lots of them. Were you ever locked up when you were a boy?'

'Yes' – he could smile at her – 'and apart from some water I had nothing to eat or drink for a full day.'

'What had you done?'

'Well . . . I had kicked one of the yard men; then I had thrown a bucket of' – again he paused – 'not too clean water over him.'

'Why did you do that?'

'Because' – he had to think here of his next words – 'he was treating some animals as I thought he shouldn't.' He couldn't go on to say he was drowning a litter of unwanted puppies.

When she moved her hand and winced, he got up, saying firmly, 'Now you must come back with me. I've already told you, haven't I? and I promise you again, you won't be locked in.'

'How can you stop me being locked in? You don't live there.'

'There are ways and means, my dear, ways and means. Now, come along.'

When she stood up she swayed slightly. And when he went to take her hand she said, 'Oh, don't touch that hand, please, it's very sore.'

'I wasn't going to touch your poor hand; but give me your other hand.'

She gave him her hand; but when they were outside the cottage he stopped her and, looking down on her, said, 'Now you know you can't crawl back through your rabbit

329

hole because you mustn't get dirt in that hand. If you were to do so, well . . . I don't know what would happen. So we'll go by the road.'

To this she made no objection; and so he now led her through the grounds and to the actual ditch she had jumped on the day she visited the school. And after helping her across, he stamped down the broken railings with his feet, making note that this part of the boundary must be seen to. But they hadn't walked very far towards the farm when her step slowed and she said, 'Can we sit down for a while? I am feeling very tired.'

He looked down at her, then along both sides of the road before saying reluctantly, 'There is nowhere to sit here, my dear, except on the verge.' But when she suddenly leant her head against his arm he shook his own as though for the moment he was perplexed, but then, bending down to her, he said, 'I am going to lift you up and carry you. Now I won't hurt your hand. Just hold it out away from me.'

She made no protest. But when she was in his arms and leant her head against his shoulder, it came to him that on their walk here she had not chatted at all and that the child might not only be tired, but ill, and not only from her injuries but from shock. And further, as he approached the farm gate, he was thinking it not only strange but somewhat weird that he had once also helped to carry the child's mother through these gates, and now he was carrying the child herself.

He was greeted with a loud shout: it was from Hamish McNabb, crying, 'Mr Carl! man. Look! Look!' as he dashed, not towards Gerald, but to the kitchen door, from where there now appeared not only Carl but also Jessie and Patsy.

'Where did you find her?' Jessie ran quickly to meet them.

'God! Look at the sight of her.' This remark came from Carl and was mixed up with other exclamations.

But it was to Jessie that Gerald addressed himself, saying, 'Where does she sleep? And . . . and I think you should get a doctor as soon as possible.'

Jessie had stepped quickly ahead of him, one hand stretched out as if to guide him to the cottage, but now turned and called, 'Carl! get . . . get Doctor Patten.' Then she was pushing open the cottage door; and when they stepped into the room she guided Gerald further, saying, 'Through here. Through here, please.'

They were in the bedroom now, and gently and thankfully he laid the child down on the bed. And when Jessie exclaimed tearfully, 'Oh! the blood. I . . . I'll get a basin,' he stopped her, saying, 'I would do nothing until the doctor comes. I think there are splinters of glass still in her hand. I don't know about her neck.'

'Where . . . where did you find her?'

'In my wood.'

'But Carl searched there not long . . . '

'Yes, I know. But Carl belongs to this house, and I must tell you it was to this house she was afraid of returning.' He watched her stiffen as he went on, 'And, too, I must tell you, Miss Jessie, that her freedom must not be curtailed to the extent of her being locked up.'

'Mr Ramsmore, this . . . this is our business. She is my responsibility.'

'I am aware of that, Miss Jessie. But I repeat, she is to be given the freedom due to a child.'

'Sir, you are interfering in something that is none of your business.'

'It may not have been in the past, but I can inform you that it certainly will be in the future.'

'My father is the head of this household and he can do what he likes.'

'To my knowledge, your father ignores the child, and if I am to go by rumour, he cursed the day she was born. So your father wouldn't care if she roamed the country and was picked up by the gypsies or run down by a horse.'

'Sir! You are taking advantage.' She choked on her next words but brought out, 'You have no right at all.'

'I think I have, Miss Jessie. Remember I found her mother and I helped to carry her back into this house. And it is that very mother who has denied this child her rights to a mother and who, I would imagine, made an attempt to kill her. Look at her.' He now turned about and pointed down

331

to the still and apparently sleeping figure of the child, then said, 'Whether or not you like it, I have been forced through circumstance to take an interest in the child. Today isn't the first time we've met. And if I don't happen to meet her in the near future then I shall know that you have continued to incarcerate her. That might seem a strong word, but the child is of a very lively nature and to be locked up in this' – he looked from one side to the other, as if encompassing the whole room – 'rabbit hutch, can be described as nothing else but incarceration.' And almost bouncing his head towards her, he turned about and stamped from the cottage, leaving her gasping, one hand clutching her throat, the other her bodice.

A movement from the bed brought her attention back to the child, who had raised heavy lids to look at her for a moment before she brought out slowly, 'I'm sorry, Auntie Jessie.' And with only the plight of the child filling her mind now, Jessie said, 'It's all right, dear, it's all right. Lie quiet, the doctor's coming.'

But when presently Janie said, 'Where's the nice man?' Jessie had to force herself to say, 'He . . . he has gone home.'

'Will he come back?'

'Er . . . perhaps. Go to sleep now.'

'Auntie Jessie?'

'Yes, dear?'

'I know now why you didn't want me to see her. She isn't nice, is she?'

Jessie didn't question who wasn't nice, but after biting down on her lip she said, 'Lie quiet now, dear.' Then bending closer to Janie's face, she asked, 'What did you say?' and almost a look of horror came on her own as she heard the child say, 'She was in disorder like the bull.'

When, last year, they had to shoot the bull that had suddenly gone mad, the child had been a witness to the men's efforts with pitchforks to corner it in the barn, and she herself had explained that it was some disorder in its mind and it would have done serious harm if it hadn't been destroyed. And now she had likened her mother to the bull.

She hadn't said mad, just disordered, yet she must have heard the men in the yard discussing the animal as mad. She turned away from the bed, saying to herself, 'Hurry up, Doctor, please, so I can get her cleaned and into bed.'

It was a good hour later when Doctor Philip Patten arrived. And he stood looking down where the child lay fully dressed and just as Gerald had brought her in. Then turning to Jessie, he remarked, 'Well, this should clinch the matter, shouldn't it? whatever your father decides. I shall want a bowl of warm water.' Then turning to the bed again, he said softly, 'How do you feel, Janie?'

'Very tired, Doctor; and my hand is paining.'

'We'll soon put that right, dear. Now this might hurt just a little.' He lifted her hand and moved his finger in between the blood stains, and each time she winced so his eyes met hers. And then he said, 'Ah, well now, you have four splinters in there, Janie, and I'll have to take them out, won't I?'

'Yes, Doctor.'

'Well, now, I'll be as gentle as I possibly can, but in the meantime we will get it nicely cleaned up. Ah, here is your aunt with a dish of nice warm water. Now I want you to put your hand into it and keep it there while I look at your neck. Ah, that's right. Now can you move it backwards and forwards? Oh, that's a clever girl.'

After examining her neck, he said, 'Just a long scratch, no glass here.' Then he turned and pointed to his bag, saying briefly, 'Cotton wool.' And after Jessie had handed it to him he showed it to Janie, saying, 'I'm just going to wipe your hand very gently;' and as he did so she did not wince.

As he extracted the first sliver of glass she cried, 'Oh! Oh dear!'

And by the time he had extracted the fourth sliver she was lying gasping, and her face was wet with perspiration.

After he had carried out the cleansing of her neck, he put his hand on her forehead before taking her pulse; then patting her cheek, he said, 'The quicker you get into your nightie and into bed the better, eh?'

When, a few minutes later, he was standing in the other room facing Jessie, his tone had an edge to it as he said,

'She has a temperature. It is some time since this morning when this incident occurred – I understand Mr Ramsmore found her lying in his wood. Well, the result of that delay, if not of the shock, will likely result in a fever. I will leave a mild draught to settle her down, but I'll be back first thing in the morning.'

He sighed deeply as if he were tired of the happenings that called for his attention in this household; and when he left without bidding her goodbye, she had much the same feeling as when Gerald Ramsmore had departed, and she muttered to herself, 'Men! Arrogant men!' And lining up with these two was the figure of her father . . . but not Carl. No; not Carl. Carl was the only male in her life whose tone had never been other than kind.

It was four days later. Janie had developed pneumonia, and Jessie's and Patsy's time was taken up attending her. And every spare moment Carl had would be spent assisting them. A steam tent was erected and this necessitated a continuous supply of kettles full of steaming Friar's Balsam.

Ward was left almost entirely on his own to see to the needs of his daughter, which however were now very simple: the draught the doctor was giving her was keeping her quietly subdued. In fact, she seemed to sleep all the time; only when her father would raise her head and say, 'Drink this, dear,' which might be milk or tea, did she rouse herself. At first she had protested, but he had put one strong arm around her, so pinning her hands, and forced her to gulp at the liquid. But now on the fourth day she was making no effort to refuse; the only effort she made was when she was sick. And it was on this fourth day that Philip Patten came into the room unannounced and to witness her vomiting.

'How long has she been like this? I mean, is she often sick?'

'No, not often,' Ward replied. 'I made her eat some dinner. It was cold food as usual, for you can imagine we have no attention from downstairs, and I think that's what she's bringing up.'

When Ward took the dish from the bed, Philip Patten noticed the colour of it, and it wasn't, he thought, much like the eruption of cold mutton. It had a dark greeny tinge, which could very well be bile.

After taking hold of her wrist he turned for a moment and looked at Ward as if he was about to say something. Instead, he first laid the hand back on the coverlet and paused for a moment before announcing, 'I'm going to stop the draughts. I think she's had enough; she should come round now. And may I ask what you have decided to do?'

'Yes. Yes.' Ward was washing his hands in the basin on the wash-hand stand, his back to the doctor, and he repeated, 'Yes. Yes, I have decided. We'll get someone in.'

'Good. Good. I'm glad of that. Well now' – Philip Patten gave a half smile – 'I've no need to open my bag tonight. By the way, there's a good nursing agency in Newcastle. It's just off Northumberland Street. I've forgotten exactly the name of the street.'

'Oh, I know it. It's Cranwell Place; at least, so I found out yesterday. I looked it up. It was advertised in the paper. I'll go in today and make arrangements.'

The doctor turned and looked at the bed. 'She'll still be quiet I think. Yes. Yes. What time did you give her the dose last night?'

'Oh, not till rather late, about eleven, just before I lay down myself.'

'Oh well, I suppose that will do it.' He did not add, 'I must go and see your granddaughter,' for he knew what would make this man happy was the thought that the child could die. And so he left the room saying simply, 'I'll see you tomorrow.'

Half an hour later Ward once again lifted his daughter up from the pillows and, forcing her head back, poured most of a glass of milk down her throat, then put the glass on the side table before he wiped her mouth and arranged her hair. Finally, bending over her, he kissed her twice and, his head deep on his chest, he muttered, 'Goodbye, my darling.' Then he went out of the room. He entered the kitchen to see Patsy scurrying around. She was throwing roughly-cut vegetables

335

into a pot in which already there was a piece of lamb. As she pushed it on to the hob she remarked, 'You'll have a hot meal by dinner time.'

'I won't be in to dinner. You'll be pleased to hear I'm going into town to engage help . . . nursing help, for both night and day.'

She stood looking at him for some seconds; then she nodded once, saying, 'Yes. Yes, master. I'm pleased to hear that.'

As he turned to go back into the hall, he remarked, 'I'll have a bite in town; and she won't need anything, she's still under the doctor's draught.'

'Very good.' Patsy nodded towards his back. The kitchen to herself again, she thought, none too pleasantly, that'll mean two of them, night and day I suppose. Well, they won't have me waiting on them. Meals, yes: but that's all. And this decision made, she left the kitchen by the back door that took her into the yard, there to see her master mounting the trap. Carl was standing to the side of it and the master was saying something to him. And she watched her husband wait until the trap had disappeared into the lane beyond the farm gates before he turned towards her, and she to him, and her first words were, 'He's going to get help, night and day people.'

'Yes.' He nodded at her, then enquired, 'How's the youngster?'

'Oh, we won't know until tonight, I suppose, but she's holding her own. You know, I think Miss Jessie will go as daft as her sister up there' – she thumbed towards the house – 'if anything happens to that child. You know, she looks upon her as if she had given birth to her.'

'Well, she might as well have; she's seen to her since the minute she was born.'

She looked at him closely now, saying, 'What's the matter? Something wrong?'

'No. No, nothing.'

'You look more thoughtful than usual.'

He smiled at her now, saying, 'Do I? Well, I've got a lot to think about.'

'Yes,' she said somewhat tartly, 'about this bloomin' place. It's never about us, ourselves.'

'Oh, that isn't fair, Patsy. You know it isn't.'

She folded her arms tightly now before saying, 'I get tired of it at times, Carl. We have no life of our own. And I'm at the beck and call of that one up there.'

'Well, you won't be any longer, will you, if he's getting help?'

'No; but I'll have other work. I'll have more cooking, won't I? And Mrs McNabb can only do the rough.'

'But, you know, dear, we took it on, and we will be half owners of the place . . . '

She turned quickly to interrupt him, saying, 'Yes, but when? When? When he dies, the master? He could live for another twenty years. And so could she. But just imagine if he went and we're left with her. I know what I would do with her, and I've heard the doctor say the same on the quiet. Perhaps not in so many words, but I know what he thinks.'

'Yes. Yes, you're right, Patsy. But that's the last thing the master would do. He'd never let her be put away, you know that. He'd go to any lengths, yes, any lengths' – he nodded now as he looked to the side – 'before he'd put her in an asylum.'

'Well, if she has another turn like she had the other morning, that's where she'll end, because she could have killed the child. Her poor little hand is swollen up twice the size, and it was only a scratch on her neck, so Doctor Patten said, but it's going to leave a mark. It started to ooze blood again yesterday. To my mind it should have been stitched.'

'Well, I suppose the doctor knew what he was doing,' and then as if to dismiss the matter, he said further: 'I've got to get on now.' But as he went to walk away, she called after him, 'Carl, the master said he wouldn't be in for dinner – he's going to have a bite in town – and that she would sleep. But I can't leave her all day up there by herself, can I? And yet, at the same time, I'm not going to go in that room by myself. I've never ventured in, unless the master's been there, for some time now. So will you come on up with me?'

337

'Yes. Yes, of course. But she'll likely scream the place down when she sees me.'

'I don't suppose so; she's been under those sleeping draughts for days now. But I must warn you, you'll see a difference in her. Since you last saw her she's become like an old woman.'

'I could never imagine her looking like an old woman.'

'Just wait till you see her. She's a vixen of an old woman at that.'

'Well, give me a shout when you need me.' And with that he went across the yard, and she made her way to the cottage . . .

It was almost three o'clock when she called to him as he was weighing out the meal in the corn room: 'I'm going up now,' she said.

'Righto.' He left what he was doing and walked towards her, clapping his hands and dusting down his clothes. And as he crossed the yard he smiled at her as he said, 'I don't suppose she'll notice I'm not spruced up.'

'I don't suppose she'll notice you're even there. But, of course, you never know; I haven't seen her for days. I really don't know how the master can stand looking after her day and night. He's even been sleeping on the sofa in the room. But then, he's always been as barmy about her as he was about her mother.'

They were in the kitchen when he put an arm around her waist and said, 'Aren't you still barmy about me?'

And now she looked at him softly and seriously as she said, 'Yes, Carl. I'm still barmy about you, and always will be. But at the same time I'm filled full of guilt, because I can't rear a family for you.'

'Now, look . . . look, I've told you, it doesn't matter one jot to me. I want you and not a family. I've told you, dear.'

'Aye, you could go on telling me for the rest of your life and I would try to believe it, all the while knowing that I can't. Every man wants a family. But . . . but look, I don't want to start and bubble here; I've done enough crying in me time. Let's get upstairs.'

338

He kissed her before he let her go; then they were climbing the stairs together.

She entered the room first, and he hesitantly followed. She went and stood near the bed and looked down on the still form; then she turned towards him, whispering hoarsely, 'Carl! Carl! Come here. Look at her.'

Quickly and quietly he went and stood by her side, but said nothing as he looked down on the face that now had a young appearance. The eyes were wide open, the lips apart. He was seeing the young girl again as she was before the night of the magic lantern show.

'Oh, my God! My God!'

'Be quiet!' he said. 'Get out of the way.'

He moved close to the head of the bed and put his hand tentatively on the white nightdress and left it there for some seconds. Then Patsy's voice expressed the futility of what he was doing as she hissed at him, 'She's dead! She's dead! Look at her eyes, she's dead.' She backed from the bed now, whimpering, 'I should have come up before. I should. Yes, I should.'

'No, you shouldn't!' His voice was firm but quiet. 'Look; go down and get one of them. It better be Rob, as he can ride the horse. Tell him to go for Doctor Patten as soon as possible. I'll stay here. Go on now.' But he had to press her as she walked backwards towards the door.

He looked about him, and presently muttered something to himself, then said aloud, ' 'Tis the best way. And he knew what he was doing.' And with the thought he went over to the side table on which stood a glass with about half an inch of white liquid left in it. This he lifted and smelt, then held it up to eye level. There was some sediment at the bottom of the glass. His suspicions had been right. Yet, he wouldn't believe it when he had seen him at the tin. It was the dim light of a covered lantern that had attracted him to the store-room. He had been unable to sleep, and he had lain listening to the dogs growling in the yard. It was when they stopped abruptly that he had risen and gone to the window of their bedroom, the room that used to be the master's study and which looked on to the end of the yard. It was from there he had seen the light

339

in the store-room. This had puzzled him. If the light had been next door in the harness-room he could have understood it, for then somebody would have been after a harness or horse's accoutrements of some kind. But who would want to be in the store-room, where only empty sacks, boxes, or tools and such were kept?

He had pulled on a coat and gone quietly outside and made for the window, and there, to his amazement, he had seen the master with a tin in his hand. After watching him put the tin back on the shelf on which were kept rat poisons and such, he had scampered back into the house. But the next morning, early on, he had examined the tins. There was a dust of powder against three of them: one contained rat poison; a second, arsenic; the third a kind of jellied liquid which they diluted for spraying.

He now put his hand tightly across his jaws. But when he heard footsteps running on the landing, he turned towards the door and there was Patsy again. She was breathless, and she said, 'Doctor's behind. There was no need to go, he was just coming in the yard to see the child. He's . . . he's here now.' Her face was wet with tears, and again she said, 'I should have come up earlier. I should, I know I should.'

'Be quiet! Be quiet!' He turned and looked towards the glass on the table, but there was no time to remove it, for there stood the doctor.

Philip Patten looked down on the woman whom death had transformed into a girl, and slowly he did what Carl had done earlier; he placed his hand on her chest. Then he felt her wrist. Then, just as slowly, he closed her eyelids and drew the bed-sheet over her, before turning to the two people who were standing staring at him. And now he spoke, saying, 'When did it happen? I mean, when did you find her?'

'It was me, Doctor. Just . . . just a few minutes ago. I was scampering downstairs to send for you and . . . and, well, there you were. I know I should have come up earlier. But when he left, I mean the master, he said she would be quiet after the draught you gave her, and that he was going into town to hire some help.'

He nodded, then said, 'She's had nothing to drink today?'

340

'No. No. I should have brought something up, but I was afraid of her on me own, the way she's been. Well, he said she would sleep for some time. And then I went and got Carl to come up with me.'

'It's all right. It's all right, Patsy. Look, go downstairs and make us a pot of tea.'

'Yes. Yes, Doctor.' She looked from one to the other, then turned and hurried out.

Philip Patten now looked around the room, taking in the glass on the side table holding a small amount of white liquid; and he resisted the urge to go near it. This room was impregnated with tragedy and sorrow and he asked himself, Was he going to add to it? He knew full well that the sedative he had left to be given to her each day in no way would have caused her demise. Anyway, if more proof than was already in his own mind were needed, he had only to go by her pupils, and the fact that her father had definitely made up his mind what was going to happen to her. He had taken advantage of her being rested under the sedative and then had thought he was being clever in showing that he was apparently agreeing to the lesser evil: either she went into an asylum or he got competent nurses to see to her. Oh, Ward had thought it all out. But what was he himself to do about it? Accuse him? There was that accusing white sediment in that glass. He had slipped up there, hadn't he? He had only to test it himself and find the slightest trace of a poison and that would be proof enough. And what then? The man could hang, or, if compassion came into the judgment, be imprisoned for the rest of his life. And how old was he now? Early fifties?

He went past Carl and stood near the window looking down on the garden, and he asked himself where he stood in this. What was his duty? Oh, he knew what his duty was all right. But could he carry it out? And who was to know if he didn't? Who was to ask questions about the death of one demented woman, when the whole country was at war? Even the village was caught up in the excitement. The fact that Ward Gibson's daughter had died would cause nothing but a flutter.

341

He turned briskly from the window and, looking towards the bed, he said, 'I think I have missed something. I had better examine her again. There are signs that she may have died from a blood clot on the brain. As I recall, her mother went the same way. Look, slip down and bring me a cup of tea up, will you?'

'Yes. Yes, Doctor.'

As soon as Carl had left the room Philip Patten picked up the glass, swirled the contents round, dipped his finger in it, then tasted it. As he placed the glass back on the table his jaws met tightly together for a moment. Before grabbing it up again he emptied the contents in the china slop bucket standing beneath the wash-hand stand; then he half-filled the glass with water from a ewer, did some more swilling, then poured this into the bucket, after which he took a handkerchief from his pocket and wiped the glass clean, paying particular attention to the bottom of it. He had only just managed to pull the sheet down from over the still face when the door opened and Carl entered carrying a small tray with cups of tea on it and by its side a bowl of sugar.

As he laid the tray on the side table, Carl noticed the clean glass, and he stared at it for a second. When he looked up the doctor had turned from the bed and their gaze linked and held for some seconds with the unspoken knowledge they both shared . . .

Philip Patten did not return to the house until six o'clock that evening. Ward was sitting in the room that he used also as a dining-room. He rose to his feet as Philip came up the room, and his head was slightly drooped and his eyes cast down as he said, 'I came back to a shock.'

When there was no response to this he raised his head and looked at Philip, and added, 'She was resting peacefully when I left her.'

There was a war going on in the doctor's mind. The man's attitude was making him regret that he had washed that glass out: he must think him an idiot. Had Ward's wily brain not taken in the fact that there would be a post-mortem? He hated to be thought the doctor who didn't know his business; but he knew he must go carefully; if the man thought that his

342

doctor was condoning a poisoning, he could hold it over him. Not that he thought Ward would do such a thing. Yet one never knew how a man's mind could be turned, given the circumstances. The next moment he only just prevented himself from speaking the truth, bawling it, when Ward said, naïvely, 'How do you think it came about, and ... and so quickly?'

Philip had to turn away. And it was some seconds before he was able to say, 'I ... I think her heart must have given out, or she had a blood clot on the brain.'

'Oh. Well, well!'

Philip swung round to see Ward now walking towards the fireplace, where he put one hand up and gripped the mantelshelf and stood looking down into the fire as he said, 'Isn't that strange: her mother went in the same way. Well, she's at peace now. God rest her soul. Yes. Yes.' He turned now from the fireplace and looked at Philip, saying again, 'She's at peace. But what I must do first thing in the morning is get word to the agency in Newcastle. I'll be able to prevent one of the nurses coming. She was due at the week-end. But the other, the day nurse, she was to start in the morning.'

Philip could stand no more. He made his way towards the door, saying, 'I must go and see your granddaughter. She's in a very bad way. By the look of her she may not last the night.' He was half-way down the room when he swung round and in a loud voice said, 'And don't say that you hope she joins the others! Just don't say it!'

And now he witnessed the real man again, not the actor, as Ward yelled back at him, 'Don't say that she will join the others, for she never will. She's not of this house. There's none of my daughter in her.'

For a matter of seconds they glared at each other across the distance, until Philip turned about and, on leaving the room, banged the oak door so fiercely behind him that it actually shook the architrave.

Janie recovered from the pneumonia. But the illness had so sapped her small strength that it was not until the end of September, seven weeks later, that she was able to walk alone

343

in the farmyard. And there she was greeted by McNabb, who cried, 'Well, you're a sight for sore eyes, I'll say that, Miss Janie. And look at the height of you. You've sprouted. You'll soon be as big as meself. Where've you got that height from? You were a little striplin' the last time I saw you.'

She smiled at him now as she said, 'That must have been many years ago, Mr McNabb.' And at this, his head went back on his shoulders and he laughed as he said, 'Well, it's many weeks ago, but it must have been years to you lyin' there. By! it is nice to see you again.'

'Thank you, Mr McNabb. It is nice to be out. I'm . . . I'm tired of sitting.'

'Oh.' He bent down to her and in a loud whisper he said, 'If only they would let me sit a bit. Oh, if only; I'm on me feet mornin' till night. D'you think you could see Mr Carl and ask him to let me sit?'

She was laughing into his face now, and what she said was, 'You are a funny man, Mr McNabb.'

Now she turned to watch Carl approaching across the yard, and to hear McNabb cry at him, 'She says I'm a funny man, Mr Carl. That's what she said, I'm a funny man.'

'And you'll look funny, too,' Carl admonished him, 'if you don't get about your business, and this minute!'

'There you are, miss. You see what I mean about sittin'?' And the tall Scot turned away laughing, and Carl, taking Janie's hand, said, 'You going for a walk?'

'Just a little.'

'You're looking grand.'

'Mr McNabb says I've sprouted. That's what he said, I've sprouted. Am I much taller than I was?'

'Yes. Yes, you are. My! I would say you have sprouted. I didn't notice it so much when you were in the cottage. But here, now' – he drew away from her and looked her up and down – 'you must have put on six inches. Yes, I'd say you've put on six inches.'

'Is that a lot?'

'It's a lot at your age,' he said, but then quickly asked, 'Where're you making for? I wouldn't try the fields; there was a lot of dew in the night.'

'No, I wasn't going across the fields. I was going on to the road, nice and flat. Auntie Jessie says I may go through the gate.'

'She did?' There was a note of surprise in his voice. And she nodded at him, saying, 'Yes. But she also said' – and now she looked up at him – 'that I mustn't be a nuisance. And that means, should I meet my grandfather I am not to speak to him. Can you tell me why, Carl? I've asked Auntie Jessie, but what she says is, that he . . . he is still suffering the loss of—' She paused and swallowed: she could not say, 'my mother', but tactfully added, 'his daughter. But I told her, or I reminded her, that he hadn't spoken to me when she was alive. I cannot understand it, Carl.'

Carl asked himself how he could answer this one. However weak the illness had left her, it hadn't weakened her thinking or probing. She would get to the bottom of it one day. But it shouldn't be now. She was too old for her years. But what could you expect? she'd had no ordinary babyhood or childhood. She had been among adults all her life and she had listened to their prattle. And her thinking must have been heightened by her sharp ears and taking in what wasn't meant for her, with the result that things had left her puzzled.

'Can I ask you something, Carl?'

'Anything, Janie.'

'Well, did the nice man call when I was ill?'

'The nice man?' He screwed up his face, thought a moment, then said, 'Oh, you mean Mr Gerald from the Hall?'

'Yes, from the Hall.'

'Yes. Yes, he came a number of times, and brought you nice big bunches of grapes. Didn't Miss Jessie tell you who the grapes were from?'

'No. She only said a visitor had brought them. She does not like me speaking . . . of him. When I first mentioned him she said she didn't want to hear anything more about him, as he was a very rude man. But I found him very nice.'

'I'm sure you did. And he is a nice man. He carried you home, you know, on that particular day.'

'Oh, I knew he brought me home, but I don't remember him carrying me.'

345

'Well, he did.' He now bent down to her, saying, 'You were so drunk you couldn't stand.'

She pushed him with her hand, laughing, as she exclaimed now, 'Oh, it is nice to be out again, Carl, and to be able to walk. I mean, on my own.'

Looking down on her, he thought to himself, Yes, and you've got the nice man to thank for that an' all. He recalled Gerald's second visit and the talk they'd had in the barn there. It had been very open on both sides. And he believed what the young fellow had said he would do if the child was locked up again. Oh yes, he certainly meant business about that, and this was the result. The only obstacle to this new freedom, as he saw it, was a big one: what would happen should she confront the master and in her forthright way ask him why he wouldn't speak to her or recognise her person . . . Well, sufficient unto the day the evil thereof. Today was bright and the child was happy. In fact, it could be said the whole atmosphere of the place had certainly lightened from the day they had buried Miss Angela; yet he knew it hadn't for the master: he had become more morose than ever.

Carl had imagined that now Ward didn't need to give most of his time to his daughter, his old interest in the farm would have returned. But it hadn't. In fact, he walked less, and spent most of his time either in the sitting-room or in his bedroom. Could it be that his mind was affected, too?

However, the work inside the house was definitely lighter, and Patsy was in a better frame of mind. At first, the war had troubled her in case he should be called up: being thirty-six he was still within the age limit. But then he was running a farm and food was wanted, and so it was a special job. He had no fear for himself, but they might take Rob. The first spate of patriotism seemed to have died down somewhat, only to have been re-awakened by rumour of German atrocities, especially that of sticking babies on the end of bayonets. Unfounded, but it had brought a fresh surge to the Colours. It also brought, and soon, three heroes into the village, but they were all dead ones. And Mike had reported the strong village feeling that was growing against Mr Gerald, because he had openly said that in no way would he take up arms and fight. Apparently

346

he had made no bones about it. This, Carl thought, was a daft thing to have done; he should have kept his mouth shut. He had surely lived long enough in the vicinity before he went away to know how the villagers reacted to individual opposition. Of course, he was well aware of it, for hadn't he had to leave his home because he dared to stand up for the truth that day in the church? Nevertheless, he still thought he was a fool for making his opinions so plain, because as far as he could gather, conscientious objectors were being given hell one way or another.

They were outside the gate now, and he said to Janie, 'Which way are you going to walk?' And she pointed along the road: 'That way,' she said.

He bent down to her and, quietly, he said, 'That leads, after a long walk, to the village. But you won't go that far, will you?' And she looked at him and said, 'No. No, I won't, Carl. I don't want to go to the village. The people there are not nice. No, I will just walk a little way, then I will come back. I promised Auntie Jessie that, too.'

Watching her walking away, he thought: there goes an old head on young shoulders. And he wondered if the old head would be strong enough to face the future and what lay in it, particularly for her.

BOOK THREE

1916–1921

PART ONE

I

It was in February 1916 that War Office form W.3236 came through the post. It stated that the recipient was required to join some section of the armed forces. And that if this was not complied with the recipient would be regarded as a deserter. Also the recipient was expected either to present himself at the local recruiting station or to send documentary evidence entitling him to exemption. But the exemption, it stated, had to be accompanied by a certificate from the local tribunal before which he would have appeared.

In November 1915 Gerald had appeared before a tribunal, made up, he recognised, of local businessmen of supposedly assumed varying standards, from the bank manager down to the butcher. There were women members, too, and their questioning he found virulent when he truthfully owned up to being a conscientious objector. However, he had pointed out that he was supplying a great deal of food to the community. And he felt it was only because of this and the particular sympathy of two members of the tribunal, that it ordered suspension of the verdict for three months.

He knew that his suspension had, in a way, been a matter of luck, for his objections to his conscription had not been pleaded on religious grounds, for there were many doing so solely to save their own skins. It was reasonable to suspect that no conscientious objector was objecting solely on his principles.

And this he had strongly pointed out to his mother, to

which she replied, 'I don't blame them. And I beg of you, Gerald, do what I ask, please. Do this for me, or else I can see you, too, landing up in prison.'

'I fully expect to, Mama.'

'Oh, don't say that.' She closed her eyes tightly, then swung round. 'You've already told me what some of your company, as you call them, are going through in prisons. I couldn't believe it, but since that acting soldier wrote to the papers about it . . . well, you've got to think there's some truth in it.'

'There's all truth in it, Mama. Some of the Army and the prison warders are treating these men of conscience much worse than any German would do. They claim that the Germans are barbarians; they haven't got a look-in where our brave Englishmen are concerned. Yes, it *is* true that they are being manacled, beaten into insensibility in some cases, and degraded in such a way that is hardly possible to imagine, because they refuse to do work of any kind to enable this barbarous business to go on. These men, to my mind, Mama, are heroes.'

'So you want to be a *hero*, do you?'

'*No, I don't*. I'm not made of such stuff.'

'Well, why don't you do what I'm asking? You said yourself, some time back, that you wouldn't mind driving an ambulance and going into the thick of it. So what's the difference in signing up with the Friends' Ambulance Unit? because you said there were Red Cross units that wouldn't look at a conscientious objector.'

Gerald emitted a long drawn-out sigh before he flopped down on to a chair, saying, 'It . . . it seems too easy a way out.'

'Easy? If I'm to go by what Arthur says, they are given the most menial tasks possible and sent to France and all over the place.'

'What does Arthur Tollett know about it? and he being in the Army all his life.'

'Yes, Arthur's been in the Army all his life, but he's got very broad views. And . . . and although it's like betrayal, I must say that he saw things differently from your father.' She went to him now and dropped down on her knees beside

354

him and, gripping his hand, she said, 'Do this for me, please. I'm worn out with worry about you.'

He leant towards her and took her face into his hands and said softly, 'And I'm worn out with worrying about me. And what will you do if I go now? McNamara will never be able to carry on by himself.'

'I'll . . . I'll help him. I'm much stronger than I look. As long as I know you aren't in prison and . . .'

He sighed deeply, saying now, 'Hush. Hush. All right. Let me have a look at that form again.'

She now almost sprang up from the floor, rushed over to a sofa table, and returned with a sheet of paper.

Sitting back now, he read aloud: 'I, so and so, and so and so, and so and so, of the so and so, so and so, so and so, in undertaking service with the Friends' Ambulance Unit, hereby agree to comply with the conditions which entitle me to the protection of the Geneva Convention and to observe the rules, regulations and orders issued by the officer commanding or by the committee, provided that I am not called upon to enlist and that my conscientious objection to military service is respected.'

He now looked upon his mother, saying, 'It's a Friends' Ambulance Unit, yet they go on to say that you must conform to all military etiquette when wearing the uniform, which you're expected to provide yourself, as well as your own kit. Now, I think that's a bit thick. They give you your food and lodgings and travelling expenses. How kind of them.' He again looked up at her; then read on, 'You are expected to serve for the duration of the war but with the right to leave after six months' – he nodded his head at her now – 'which I take to mean I'd be drafted into the armed forces after all . . . Oh, Mama.'

She stared at him now and her look was so pitiful that he said, 'All right, all right. I've given you my word; I'll do it. And you know something? You're worse than any tribunal. I could face them and defy them, to the last breath, but there's you with that plaintive look on your face.' He drew her up and, putting his arms about her shoulders, said, 'I'm not worth all your trouble, dear. I really am not. Inside myself

I know I'm not worth twopennorth of copper. The only real, strong bit about me is my so-called principles, which just means I don't like sticking a bayonet into another fellow's belly. All right! all right! My conversation tends to be coarse even before I get into the army or corps or whatever.'

She smiled at him now, saying, 'Unit, dear, friendly unit.'

'Friendly unit? My!' He shook his head, then said, 'How much time are you giving me before I sign my name on the dotted line?'

'No more than twenty-four hours, dear.'

'*You're joking!*'

'No, I'm not. From what I gathered from Arthur, you could be up before another board, and this time not the local one, and this one wouldn't let you off for three months. And, oh, dear me! The very thought of it makes me . . . '

'All right, all right! dear. I have twenty-four hours. What shall I do with them?' He turned from her, walked over to one of the long windows that overlooked the terrace, and after a moment turned around, saying, 'I'll get drunk, simply blind, paralytic drunk.'

'There's not enough wine left in the cellar for that, dear.'

'Who's talking about the cellar? I'll go out and paint the village red, give them something to remember me by, and likely land up in a cell and you'll have to come and bail me out.'

She smiled at him tolerantly, saying, 'Do that, dear, but not before dinner; it's Nancy's night off and cook's legs won't carry her back and forth from the dining-room to the kitchen, as you know; so leave it until after we've had dinner.'

She now put her hand to his cheek in a gentle gesture and smiled at him before leaving the room. And he turned to the window again and his gaze roamed over the balcony, the drive, and that part of the flower garden they had cleared and which now looked bare, but actually was full of seeds, bulbs and young plants which, come the spring, would have given him a good harvest. And he looked beyond that, over the tall hedge to where lay the work of their main labours, now showing rows and rows of bright green heads of winter cabbages and brussel sprouts. Then on to the store-house where stood boxes of carrots and parsnips and such ready for Saturday market. And he felt a weakness in the bottom of his stomach, and it rose to his chest, then into his throat. Only the feeling that it might spring from his eyes in the form of tears turned him about.

He had never, up till this moment, realised how he was going to miss his work on his land, and this house, and his mother. And yes, the little visitor who came occasionally, not only to the woodman's cottage but also to this house, for she had become a kind of responsibility, a responsibility that worried him; at least her future did.

The calf was motherless. The cow, having died shortly after giving birth, had left a sickly calf which, if she were to survive, had to be fed four-hourly; and Janie had taken on to herself part of this nursing.

The calf was housed in a small partitioned area at the end of the long byre: Carl had told her that it would be comforted there by the sound of the others' voices. It was lying now in a bed of straw and, in order to give it a constant body warmth, two lighted lanterns were hanging close by on the end of the byre wall.

Janie was sitting with her back to the partition, and she talked softly to the small animal, which was lying quite inert: 'Come on now, you'll like this,' she said.

When it moved its head away from the teat she squeezed some milk out on to her fingers and put one to its mouth and rubbed its lip gently. And slowly now it began to suck; then with a deft movement she inserted the teat into its mouth and, tilting its head a little back, she said, 'There now. Drink it all up, then you'll grow up to be a big girl, or' – she smiled down on it – 'a big cow.'

It was when the bottle was half-empty that she heard Mike come into the byre, and he was talking to someone. 'You see,' he was saying, 'look at the length of this place. There's plenty to do an' this is just half of 'em. So, what we need here is more hands, not to lose any.'

And now she heard a voice, one that she didn't recognise, reply, 'Well, I should say you're safe enough.'

'And so are all the others, mister.'

357

'I understand you have a son working for you.'

'Aye, you've been well informed. Me son does work here, but he's on forty. So, I should think it's been a waste of your journey trying to recruit round here.'

'Oh, not entirely, not entirely. I got four from the village yesterday.'

'Huh! I bet they were half canned.'

Janie now heard the stranger's voice turn to laughter as he replied, 'Well, not quite, but it helps, it helps. By! that's a funny village of yours down there.'

'It isn't my village, mister, never has been.'

'No? You don't seem to think much of it.'

'You're right there, you're right there.'

'Well, if one believes only half of what that lot get talking about in the inn there's no love lost. By! they can spin the yarns like fairy-tales. But I suppose there was something in it, for they say all the mischief started when your boss jilted a lass in the village and went and married a dancing piece from Newcastle. Is there any truth in that?'

'There's truth in part, mister. She was no piece, she was a lady.'

'Oh! But did he jilt anybody?'

'I don't know so much about that. I can only repeat what I've said: his wife was a lady.'

'Well, is it true that the supposed jilted one set fire to the place?'

'She didn't set fire to the place, just a field.'

'Oh, just a field. Well, as I said they spin the yarns down there. They even said she killed the wife, I mean . . . dancing lady, with a catapult. I laughed at that, but they swore it was true.'

There was silence in the barn for a moment; then the stranger's voice said again, 'They say he had her put away in an asylum, and there she is to this day.'

Still Mike made no reply until the stranger said, in a low tone now: 'If what they said next is true, I'd put them down as a rotten spiteful lot of buggers, for they said that three of the village blokes raped his daughter, and her but a lass of fifteen. And she had a child and the lass is of an age now . . .

Well, I gather by your silence there was some truth in it. By God! All I can say is, I would have helped that lass's father to strip those buggers, as they said he did, an' pin 'em up on the church screen. By! I would. And I would have helped to flail them an' all. They deserve to be shot. And you know something? I didn't like the village when I came into it. I'm a recruiting sergeant, right enough, an' I take all I can get me hands on, because that's me duty, but as I said, I never liked that village from when I first smelt it; and I've been in lots of villages. They're all peculiar in their own ways. Give me the city any time. And it's true what I said, mister, I didn't believe half of it. But I can see now, as I said, by your still tongue, I didn't know the half of it. That child will never find out from where she sprang, will she? And they talk about the atrocities of the bloody Germans and what they did to the Belgian women! Well, I would say you couldn't go much further than this village. Anyway, we'll be leaving it the night and I won't be sorry. But thank you, mate, for showing me around. And I'll take your word the whole place is run by old codgers.'

There was the sound of laughter now, then the byre door closed, and the empty bottle dropped out of Janie's hand on to the straw. And she sat staring across the calf at the wall opposite . . .

How long she sat there she never knew, but she didn't seem to come to herself until Jessie's voice said, 'Have you gone to sleep, dear?'

She turned to see Jessie standing in the opening to the little byre, and she gave her no answer but tried to stretch out her legs, which had gone into cramp. And when Jessie's hands came under her arms and lifted her up and her voice said, 'Did you fall asleep?' she muttered, 'Yes. Yes, I must have.'

Jessie now stooped and picked up the empty bottle, saying, 'It drank it all. And oh, it looks more lively. Come along.'

As they walked up the byre Jessie, bending down to her, said, 'You must have fallen asleep; you look dozy. Are you all right? You're not feeling tired?'

Janie shook her head slowly. 'No,' she said; 'it . . . it was warm in there.'

'Yes. Yes, and you must have dropped off to sleep. Come and have a cup of tea. I've made some of those scones you like.'

Janie drank a cup of tea and forced herself to eat a scone. 'Must I have my history lesson this morning? I . . . I could do it later on today.'

Jessie looked at her closely. 'Well, you have done your English and geography,' she mused. 'Yes, I suppose you could have your history lesson later. But what do you wish to do instead?'

'I . . . I would just like to take a walk.'

Jessie remained silent for a moment. She had just checked herself from saying, 'You won't go over to the Hall again, will you? I mean, you mustn't trouble them.' But she knew if she voiced those words a look would appear on Janie's face that she had come to dread. The only name she could give to it was withdrawal; and oh, she didn't want her child, as she still thought of her, to move away from her again, because lately, through not penning her in any way they had become close. Nevertheless she was worried about the association with that man, who had outrageous ideas and was said to be a conscientious objector. Oh, how she wished they would force him into the services, so that his absence would break his self-imposed responsibility for her.

'You won't go far, will you? You get tired so easily, you know.'

'I won't get tired, Auntie Jessie. I'll walk slowly.'

'Well then, you must wrap up well. Come and put on your thicker coat and your woollen hat.'

She now helped Janie into her outdoor clothes, and lastly she put a woollen muffler around her neck before handing her her gloves. Then stooping, she kissed her cheek, saying, 'Don't be long now, dear, because it will soon be dinner time.'

Without giving her aunt any response other than a smile, Janie turned and left the cottage, walked across the yard and into the road; then along it until she came to the stile. Having crossed this, she walked half round the perimeter of the field, pulled herself up into a sitting position on top of a low stone wall, then swung her legs over and walked across the meadow and into the wood. Beyond this, she skirted another field before arriving at the edge of the smallholding, and from there she made her way towards the first of the long greenhouses; but seeing Gerald apparently in serious conversation with McNamara, she stopped. But presently McNamara pointed towards her; and then there he was . . . her nice man, standing before her, saying, 'Where have you sprung from? This is a coincidence. I was just on my way to visit you.'

'You were?'

'Yes. Yes, I was. I . . . I wanted to tell you something. Come along; come into the house.'

She did not move, but said, 'Could . . . could we go to the cottage first?'

He looked down on her for a moment before saying, 'Yes. Yes, of course, if you wish.' And so they walked side by side along a roughly hewn path until they came to the cottage. The outside had been cleared of dank grass and weeds and the door was now upright on its hinges. He pushed it open; then when they were both inside and he had closed the door, he shivered and said, 'Well there's one thing: we can't remain long in here, it's enough to freeze you. But come and sit down a minute.'

They went into the next room, which no longer held the bed. Its window had been mended, and the presence of a number of large wooden crates showed it had been used as a store-room.

She sat down on one of the crates, and he pulled another in order that he could sit opposite to her. And now, bending forward, he said, 'Something wrong?'

'I . . . I don't know. What I mean is, yes, there is something wrong. But it must have happened a long time ago. A lot of wrong things happened a long time ago. And that's why I am—' she stopped now and shook her head, then said, 'me.'

His voice was quiet when he spoke, saying, 'You're beating about the bush. What has happened?' He now watched her bend forward and put her joined hands between her knees, and this, as always, indicated her troubled mind. Then she

361

started: 'I was in the cow byre,' she said, 'we've got a sick calf; I was feeding it. No-one could see me; it's partitioned off. Then Mike came in. I recognised his voice but not the man's who was with him. From what I know now, he is one of those men who go around gathering recruits. Well, he was in a public house in the village and he heard things that he didn't believe or only half-believed. And he asked Mike if they were true or not.'

She lifted her head and looked at him, and she said, 'Now I know what it's all about: why . . . why I am lonely, always have been lonely; and why, when I once asked Auntie Jessie if my mother was upstairs ill, and where my father was, and why wasn't he with her, she screamed at me and yelled, "He's dead. He's dead! Do you hear? He's dead!" And now I wish he *was* dead, because I don't know who my father is, do I?'

The words that were passing through his mind could have been considered blasphemous. He continued staring back into her eyes, when all the while he wanted to turn away from her, or yell in much the same manner as Jessie had done: not 'He's dead! He's dead!' but 'It doesn't matter who your father was. You are you, yourself, and you are a wonderful little girl, one growing rapidly into a tall big girl.' Oh, my God! what was he going to say? This shouldn't be happening to him. That stiff-necked individual should in some way have broken it to her.

Yet, how could anyone break such news to a thinking child? But no; she was no longer a child; she had never been a child. They had never allowed her to be a child. She had a mind and she used it. A mind that had been cultured in an adult school without love, or with such love that was frustrated through fear. He put out his hands now and gathered hers into them. Then, his voice cracking on the words, he said, 'It makes no matter who your father was' – he could not say which one was your father – 'you are yourself, someone very special; and not only to your aunt, but . . . but to me. Yes, to me.' He nodded at her. 'Always remember that.' And now feeling he had found a way to take her mind off the present situation by enlisting her sympathy

362

for him, he added, 'I may not see you for a long, long time after today. I . . . I'm leaving in a few hours.'

'*No! No!*' She was on her feet now, her knees touching his, her hands still between his, pressed against his chest; and again she cried, '*No! No!* Oh, please, please don't go. You are the only one I have.'

'I've . . . I've got to, my dear. I am not going into the Army because, as I think I told you, I'm against killing people, but . . . but this is a kind of job that others don't like doing, you know.'

She closed her eyes and shook her head from side to side in a despairing fashion as she said, 'I will have nobody. Nobody.'

'Look at me. I shall write to you and you will write to me; and in the meantime you must continue to come over and see my mother. She's very fond of you, and you can keep her company now and again.'

'She's not you. I can't talk to her, tell her things like I can to you. You're the only one I can talk to. And now I know this dreadful thing, I won't be able to speak about it to anyone else.'

'Well, that's as it should be: it is all past and finished with; you now have only yourself to contend with. By that I mean . . . '

Shaking her head impatiently, she interrupted him; 'I know what you mean,' she said, 'I know what you mean. You mean that I shall never get rid of this . . . well, what I know.'

'I mean nothing of the sort. I mean, as you grow older your common sense will tell you that it is something you've got to accept. You cannot change yourself. You are what you are' – he paused – 'a very beautiful person.'

When she fell against him he put his arms about her, but when he felt her body shudder he pressed her gently from him, saying, 'Now, now. No tears. I don't want to remember you with a wet face.' When her eyelids blinked rapidly he leaned forward and put his lips gently on her brow. But when her arms came around his neck he bit tightly on his lip and pulled himself to his feet. His own lids moving rapidly now, he looked down on her, saying,

363

'Come along. We'll go and see my mother.' But when she said quickly, 'No, no. Please not now. And anyway, I promised I wouldn't be long. But I will, I will come and see her soon. Yes, very soon, because she will tell me what you are doing. And . . . and you will write to me?'

'Oh yes, I will write to you. And I will expect long letters back mind.'

'I have never written a letter to anyone, but I can write well.'

'Then you must practise your letter writing on me.'

They were outside the cottage now and when he said, 'I will see you to the stile,' she answered quickly, 'No. No. I'll leave you here. I . . . I would rather. Yes, I would rather I left you here because this is where we first met. I don't count the time by the wall.'

He held out a hand now, saying, 'Goodbye then, my dear.' And she, placing hers in it, said, 'Goodbye,' then she turned and walked away from him. And he watched her until she had disappeared into the thicket.

Slowly now he made his way back to the Hall, and there, after telling his mother what had transpired, he said, 'Keep an eye on her, will you, dear? Make her welcome. Try to get her to talk' – he smiled – 'if it's only about me.'

As she kissed him she said, 'Let her be the least of your worries. I shall see to her. And perhaps we shall comfort each other for your loss.' And when she added, 'Oh, my dear, what am I going to do without you?' he replied, 'As I've told you before, dear, it's more a case of what am I going to do without you?' to which his mind added, 'and her'.

The first letter he wrote was neither to his mother nor to Janie, but to Jessie. He wrote it that night, before he left the house. It was brief, stating that her niece had found out the facts of her beginning through overhearing one of the men and a recruiting officer talking while she was attending to a sick calf. And authoritatively, he ended, 'If she does not mention this to you herself, it would be very unwise of you, at this stage, to make her aware that you know. No doubt the opportunity will occur some time when she's more able to handle the situation.'

He knew that this letter would undoubtedly anger Jessie, but he had little patience with her and condemned her for her treatment in keeping a child segregated for years.

The next letter he wrote was to his mother, and this was from Birmingham, telling her he was stationed in a camp near a village and undergoing training. The letter was quite cheery. He sent a similar, shorter one, to Janie. And this he ended on a light note, saying that the kind people in charge were thinking of sending him to London on a holiday, but that he wouldn't be given any spending money.

The next letter his mother received from him was from a hospital in Richmond, and in it it was evident that he could not contain his feelings, for he was angered at the purposeless suffering of the men there.

Gerald had known well from the beginning that he would go through the mill, even though he was under a certain protection, being a member of the Friends' Ambulance Unit. Yet it wasn't the way he was received and treated, nor the menial tasks imposed on him and the others in the same corps, but the number of mangled bodies filling the wards. He was sickened and horrified by the agony endured by the limbless and mangled remains of men, and rent inside himself by the nameless courage that sustained many of them with the desire to go on living. But there were equally as many who gave up the ghost, and for these he was thankful that their crucifixion was over. Yet, covering all his emotions was an anger at the senseless waste of human life and the feeling of frustration at being unable to do anything about it. Here he was cleaning latrines, his hands burnt with the use of so much chlorine. And he was sickened further with the habits of men *en masse*.

They were camped outside in unheated huts and he had made friends with a couple of like minds in his section. But he had also discovered there were some weak knees within their company when one day he was warned by a young fellow that it would be well for him if he kept his mouth shut and his opinions to himself, else the lot of them would be landed overseas before they knew where they were.

Gerald had asked in mock enquiry, 'Do you happen to be a conscientious objector?' And the answer he got was, 'Oh, to hell with you!'

One day, when he was on his way to the theatre to wheel out blood-stained sheets and parts of human anatomy to be consigned to the incinerator, and seeing a visitor whom he had noticed once or twice before now making her way towards a ward door, he stepped forward and was about to open it for her when the side of her hand came like a chisel across his wrist, and in a deep throaty voice she said, 'Your courtesy doesn't hide your cowardice. My son is back there, his body mangled just to protect the likes of you. I know what I would do with the lot of you if I had my way. But this is what I think of you.' And then she spat in his face.

He remained still while the door was opened and then closed on her. He felt as if all the blood had been drained from his body. They called cowards white-livered, and that's what he felt at this moment, white right through. Nothing seemed to be working inside him. Even when he turned away he found that his legs didn't actually obey him; it was as if he were drunk.

This incident attacked the sensitivity in him. Not only did it increase his awareness of who he was, and why he thought as he did, but also the knowledge of how the action of one person, that might cover merely a matter of seconds, could affect the life of another, as it was to do in his case for the next three years.

3

〰

It was towards the end of July 1917 that Janie received a letter from Gerald telling her he was in France, and so glad to be there, for now he felt he would be of some real help. And when she next wrote to him to the address he would leave at the bottom of the page, she must tell him how the smallholding was going, because his mother didn't give him many details. And was she really all right and not ill? But he had finished on a light note, saying, 'Before I make myself of some use I think I'll just pop over to Paris tonight and have dinner, somewhere along the Champs-Elysées; then perhaps go to the opera. Or on the other hand, I may prefer a lighter entertainment. It all depends upon my mood. Be a good girl, and one day I shall bring you over to France, that is after I've shown you all the beautiful places in London.' And he signed himself as always, 'The "nice man" Gerald.'

Jessie had watched her reading the letter, the while pushing from her thoughts the hope that they might suddenly cease, for terrible things were happening in this war. As McNabb said, the papers were just one big cover-up. He had proof of it, he said: his grandson, minus a leg and half an arm, had recently been sent home from a hospital where they had endeavoured to make him walk; but the mutilations being on both sides of his body, he found himself unable to balance. And now his life would be spent in a wheelchair, and what pension he got would scarcely feed him.

But Jessie resisted the thought that there was still hope. Yet she knew if that man survived nothing she could do would change her child's attitude towards him. It would be only the man himself who could change it, and he had become her father figure, which he could well have been, having been twenty years old when she was born.

Seeing Janie raise her head from the letter as if about to speak, she put in quickly, 'No, you can't miss your lessons this morning, dear. It's becoming a habit.'

'Oh, it isn't, Auntie Jessie. I don't often ask in the mornings, I go over in the afternoon. You know I do. And I know what's the matter with Lady Lydia; it's because the house is full of soldiers and she hasn't told Mr Gerald about it. And they are noisy; some of them are quite rude. Although she's had most of the furniture packed away there are some things she can't move, of course, such as the big bookcases in the library. And one of the men in the last lot pulled out illustrated plates from the big books. And when she went for him he was rude to her. The sergeant said he was sorry and had him moved ... Some people are very ignorant.'

'And you will be one of them if you continue to miss your lessons.'

'I don't miss my lessons, Auntie Jessie. You do exaggerate, you know. And when I don't have to do the lessons, I still read.'

'Yes, but not the things you should. Poetry won't get you very far in this world.'

As Janie looked at the thin, tight-lipped face of her aunt, she thought she knew why her nice man and her aunt didn't like each other. Yet how could she put it into words? Only that one was light and the other was heavy. Yes, she understood the heaviness that was on her Auntie Jessie's shoulders, and that she herself was a big part of that heaviness.

Of a sudden she sprang up and with an unusual display of tenderness put her arm around Jessie's shoulders and kissed her on the cheek.

Jessie was much taken aback by this unexpected gesture, for what kissing had to be done she did herself, and then with a peck on the child's brow or cheeks at night. But as it was now, she had the urge not only to cry but also to hold the child tightly to her, as she used to when she was small and manageable. The embrace, however, ended as quickly as it had begun, with Janie, laughing and saying, 'Let's away to the grindstone, for if the corn is not turned to flour, there'll be no bread and then we'll all be surprised when we find ourselves dead.'

Jessie had been about to turn away to go into the other room, but now she swung around and looked at the laughing girl, saying, 'Where on earth did you hear that?'

Janie seemed to think for a moment, then said, 'I've never heard it. I mean, it just came out.'

Jessie sighed. Rhyming. Another result of her association with that man, and so she remarked tartly, 'Well, in future I think what you let . . . just come out should have a little more sense to it. Come along.'

Janie sighed. There was no fun with her Auntie Jessie, whereas Lady Lydia, although she was very worried about Mr Gerald, could always laugh and see the funny side of some things. Oh, she wished this afternoon was here. She seemed to be always wishing these days: wishing the war was over, wishing her nice man was back again, wishing she wouldn't keep growing so tall, wishing she was older. Oh yes, a lot older, seventeen or eighteen, wishing . . . Here, her wishing came to a full stop and she answered herself, No, she didn't wish any more that her grandfather would speak to her. Her grandfather hated her and she hated him. Oh yes, she hated him.

Well before reaching the main gates she could see that the old lot of soldiers must have gone and a new company had arrived, for behind the line of trees on the right side of the drive, tents had been erected right down to the lodge. But she saw no soldiers until she was about to ascend the steps leading to the balcony and the front door, when she was hailed by a voice behind her, saying, 'Ah, now, what 'ave we here? A spritely young miss who 'as come to see the lord of the manor and asked to be taken into his service. Eh?'

Janie turned on the bottom step and so her face was almost on a level with those of the two grinning soldiers; and when one looked at the other and said, 'She has lost her tongue,' she quickly came back at him, saying, 'It's a great pity you haven't lost yours, too, if you can't make it say anything sensible.'

The smile slid from the man's face whilst the grin on his companion's widened; and in a very changed tone the first man said, 'Now, now! missie! there's no need to be cheeky.'

As she went to turn away from him, he added, 'And where d'you think you're off to?'

'That's my business.'

'Oh, but it isn't, madam. Let me tell you it isn't. This house has been taken over.'

'Yes, and it's a great pity.'

'Look' – he had quickly placed himself one step above her now – 'it's my business to see who goes in and out of here.' He pointed to the single stripe on his arm. 'And now I'd advise you to get yourself away. There's a notice on the gate that this is private property. Weren't you checked there?'

'No; but you will certainly be checked if you don't let me pass.'

'What is it?' The voice brought the man round to see Lady Lydia coming across the balcony to the top of the steps, and he was about to say, 'This 'ere girl,' when she said, 'Is there anything the matter, Janie?'

She was coming down the steps now and the man looked up at her, saying in a tone that could only be called smarmy, 'I was just enquiring, m'ladyship, what her business was. We've just come in, as you know, and not used to the run of the place yet.'

Lady Lydia stared at the man for a moment, taking in his type; then she held out her hand to Janie as she said to him, 'Then the sooner you recognise members of my family, the better, Corporal.'

'Yes, ma'am, your ladyship.' He stepped aside, then watched the two figures mount the steps, cross the balcony and enter the house through the front door of the hall, before he muttered, 'Bloody upstarts! One thing this war'll do will be to put an end to that lot.'

'And perhaps your lot an' all.' As his companion turned away laughing, the man demanded, 'Whose side are you on?'

Still holding Janie by the hand, Lady Lydia crossed the empty hall, passing the uncarpeted stairs, to the broad passage where new notices had been attached to the doors, and so to the far end to a door on which the notice said, 'Private. No admittance'; through this and into a further passage that led into a largish room which had been the servants' hall but was now fitted out as a sitting-room. Next to it, what had been the housekeeper's sitting-room was now Lady Lydia's bedroom. The butler's pantry, the silver room, the housekeeper's office and various other small rooms in this quarter, with the exception of one which held a bed for Nancy Bellways, were filled with silver and china and relics of family history, besides small pieces of antique furniture.

In the sitting-room Lady Lydia said, 'Come, warm yourself.' Then she pointed, 'Look at the big lumps of coal. We've got a coal-house half-full.'

'Really? Where did you get it?'

'Well there was a soldier in the last lot, they really were a nice crowd altogether . . . well, he and one or two of them went out with a lorry yesterday, apparently, and did some foraging, all in the name of the Army, of course.' She bit on her lip now and shrugged her shoulders as a young girl might. 'And just before they left, and it was quite early, quite early in the morning, they handed me a great big key. And they said, "We've left a present for you, ma'am. It's in the coalhouse. And hang on to that key. Anyway, that lock'll take some getting off." I didn't know what to say. Having said it was in the coal-house, I thought it must be wood, because, you know, they've been chopping down a lot of trees. Oh, Gerald would have been so angry if he were here. Anyway, after they left . . . and you know, they waved me goodbye from the lorries – it was as if they were going on holiday. And, oh dear, dear' – her tone changed now – 'they're all for France, all of them, and they know it. And some of them don't want to go, from what they said. But anyway, I was telling you' – she shook her head – 'when I opened the coal-house door I couldn't believe my eyes. You've never seen our coal-house, have you? It's enormous, like a small room, and there ... there was a hill going up from it and all beautiful big lumps of coal, what they call roundies here. And another thing – of course we've had to store it in here: we daren't leave it in the kitchen cupboard – but look at that!' She pulled open the doors of a large Dutch press, and there on one shelf was an array of tea, sugar, butter, bacon, and some eggs. On another shelf was an array of tins, some of jam, others of bully beef. 'Isn't that marvellous! The only thing is the butter won't keep. But that doesn't really matter because your aunt is always kind in sending me both butter and cheese. But wasn't that sweet of those men? And you know something? When they brought the stuff in, it was late last night, they said, "This, ma'am, is with the quartermaster's compliments." Nancy had let them in, and when she saw all that stuff and heard what they said, she answered, "Like Jimmy McGregor, it is." And at that, one of the soldiers burst out laughing and pushed her, and she pushed him back. My dear, I've never seen such goings-on in this house. I couldn't help but laugh.' She paused now as she closed the door and said, 'It's good to laugh at times, isn't it, Janie?'

'Yes, Lady Lydia, I think so, too. But the only ones at the farm who seem to laugh are the men, and mostly the Irishmen. McNabb – he's a Scot, you know – he rarely laughs but he says funny things. And you can laugh at them, although he never really laughs. Yet Mike – you know, Patsy's father – says the most comforting things at times. Some of them may be a bit mixed up. I remember the other day he said to Patsy: "God helps those who helps themselves," but then added, "And God help those who are caught helping themselves; it'll be three months' hard labour." It was funny, wasn't it? The Irish people talk very mixed up. But other people's talk is nearly always about war, don't you think?'

'Yes, I suppose so, dear. But, come and sit down.' She drew her towards the fire, and when they were seated, she said, 'A lot of warm things happened to me yesterday. There was the coal, and all that food, but most of all there were those words that a soldier spoke to me. He was just a private, and during the weeks they've been here I've noticed him once or twice looking at me as I walked across to the greenhouses. In fact, it was he who, when the unit first came here, said he was sorry that the vinery had been stripped the way it had, before the fruit was really ripe. I was so angry at the time I didn't take much notice of him. But then yesterday he made a point of coming to me and asking me if he could have a word. And he started with, "We'll be leaving here tomorrow, ma'am, and there's something I want to say to you, and it's just this." And he went on to say that he was, as he put it, dead nuts against conchies. At least when the war had first started, he was. To him they were simply just a lot of cowards. But after he had joined up, or was enlisted, or, as he put it, was pulled in, and himself now saw how men of conscience were treated, with the lowest type of work being put on them, he had had to change his opinion. He was now seeing for himself. And having recently heard from the village that my son was a conscientious objector, he felt that he wanted to say to me—' Here she stopped and, taking out her handkerchief, she wiped her mouth hard with it before going on, 'He wanted to say to me I should be proud of my son.'

When Janie caught hold of her hand and in a breaking voice said, 'You've always been proud of him, and I have, too. I . . . I wish he had been my father,' Lady Lydia leaned forward to touch her, saying, 'Oh, my dear.' Then she was holding the sobbing body to her and comforting her: 'There, there. And I can tell you something, my dear, he looks upon you as if he were your father. He feels he has a responsibility towards you. If he'd had a daughter he'd have wished for one just like you. There, there now. Dry your eyes; here comes Nancy with some tea. You can hear her feet a mile off. And oh dear me, she's had to be on them such a lot since cook left. But, of course, cook was getting very old. It was the soldiers in her kitchen that she couldn't put up with. But Nancy doesn't seem to mind.' She now took her handkerchief and dried Janie's eyes, saying in a whisper, 'She gets very skittish with them. They tease her and she loves it. Poor Nancy. But why do I say poor Nancy? She could have been married years ago but she didn't want it. She's of a happy and contented nature. All she wants is to look after me. Don't you think that's wonderful? I should be so thankful, and I am. Oh, I am. Every day I'm thankful for her. And for you, dear. Oh yes, and for you. Ah, here it is.'

The far door of the room was now opened by a bump from Nancy's buttocks and she came in carrying a laden tray, saying, 'Oh, ma'am, we've got a lot 'ere; I feel as if I want to run after the others and bring 'em back. The sergeant's as snotty as a polis. Wanted to know how many hours I was allowed in the kitchen, and I told him it was more a case of how many hours I was going to allow him in my kitchen.' She now put the tray down none too gently on a side table, adding, 'The officer came in. He wasn't too bad, but young, ma'am, just out of the cradle. How he'll ever give orders to that lot beats me. But there, it's them pips on the shoulders that does it. Will I pour out, ma'am?'

'No, Nancy; Janie will do it. Thank you.'

Nancy approached Janie now and, bending down towards her, she whispered, 'Did you see our gold-store?' She jerked her head back towards the cupboard, and Janie whispered back, 'Yes, and I won't split.'

'You'd better not, you'd better not, 'cos I'd cut off your retreat.' And with this she went out, leaving them both smiling now, and Lady Lydia saying, 'What she means by that last bit I don't know. But look' – she was pointing to the tray – 'she's managed to make some scones and a fruit tart. Come on, let us tuck in. You pour the tea and I'll cut up the tart and butter the scones.'

It was an hour later when Janie left the Hall. It was then spitting rain mixed with sleet, but before she was half-way to the farm she was enveloped in a downpour of hailstones. They stotted off her hood and stung her face, causing her to slow her running. But she was still running when she reached the farm gates. She bent forward, and through the hail she thought she saw Patsy going into the dairy, and so, keeping to the shelter of the buildings, she was making for it when someone stepped out of the harness-room, and she bounced into the figure, only to bounce back again and stare up, gasping, into the face of her grandfather. She was standing in such a position that she was blocking his way forward, and when the voice growled at her, '*Out of my way* you!' she screamed at him, 'I hate you! Do you hear? I hate you! You're cruel! ugly, horrible! I wish you were *dead. Dead!*'

She did not know that the arm going round her was Patsy's, but she knew it was Patsy's voice, louder than her own had been, that was crying, 'Don't you dare hit her!' And then it seemed they were both sent flying into the air as his forearm hit her shoulder, while at the same time Patsy was lifted off her feet.

For the next minute or so all Janie seemed to be aware of was the shouting, everyone shouting in the yard. And then, as someone picked her up from the ground another voice shouted, 'You'd better get Carl, Patsy's dead out.'

Janie was also aware now of Jessie being on the scene and of her saying, 'What happened? What happened?' and a voice answering, 'All I know is he knocked them flying. And the slush didn't help.'

'Father?'

And the reply in the Scottish accent was curt: 'Who else? Now, who else?'

Her head had cleared by the time they reached the cottage; and now Jessie was plying her with questions. And when, for the third time, she said, 'Look, tell me what happened,' she shouted back at her, 'I couldn't see through the hail-stones and I bumped into him. He lifted his hand to strike me.'

'He would not do that, child.'

'He did! He did! It was not to push me away. I know the difference. I am not a baby or a child. No, I am not a child, Auntie Jessie. And I tell you again I am not a child and I know what he meant to do. And so did Patsy, and with his whole forearm. And . . . and I told him what I thought.'

'You . . . you mean you went at him?'

'Yes, I went at him. I told him he was cruel and ugly and a beast. And you can close your eyes like that, Auntie Jessie, but he is. He is. He always has been to me. He's never wanted

376

to own me and I don't want to own him. Do you know something?' She now stood up and her voice rose to almost a high scream now: 'I would rather have had one of those other men who made me than him for a . . . '

When the hand came across her face and stung her, while knocking her backwards, they both became silent. And when Janie now began to cry, Jessie made no move towards her; instead, turning about, she went towards the door and grabbed up the coat that she had thrown off as she entered.

There was no-one to be seen when she reached the yard, but seeing Rob emerge from the door into the kitchen, she called to him, 'Where is Patsy?' And he answered, 'On her bed, miss; and Mr Carl is sending me for the doctor.'

'Has she not come round?'

'She's come round all right, miss, but . . . but she's hurt her back.'

Straightaway, she hurried to Patsy's room, and there, bending over her, asked, 'Where are you hurt, Patsy?'

'I'm . . . I'm not sure, miss. At the present moment I feel I'm hurt all over,' and she tried to smile; but then said, 'The bottom of me back pains, the more so when I move me legs.'

'You can move your legs?'

'Yes. Yes, thank God, I can move me legs.'

Jessie raised her eyes to where Carl was standing at the foot of the bed, and when he said, 'Your father will be the death of all of us before he finishes, miss,' the bitter note in his voice being such as she had never heard him use before, she turned from him and looked again at Patsy, and asked, 'How . . . how did it happen?'

'Well, as far as I could see, miss, I had just stepped out from the dairy when I heard her screaming at him. He must have been coming out of the tack-room and she dunched into him. He was about to raise his hand to her and I just got to her in time; at least I thought I was in time to pull her away when his arm knocked us both flying. He really meant to swipe her. Oh yes, he did. But it caught us both. If she had got the full force of it and hit the ground with her head instead of me hitting it first with me backside, her brains would have been knocked out. Because

377

it was no light blow, oh no, not with the forearm. And the force of it! It was like a chop.'

'Oh, Patsy, Patsy, where's it going to end?'

'You tell me, miss, just you tell me. But what you've got to face up to, miss, is Janie's no longer a child. She's thirteen years old and an old thirteen at that, and it's this place that's put the age on her. She's never had a child's life. So you shouldn't blame her because her mind thinks beyond her age. And let me tell you something, she's not afraid of him, not when she could scream at him, "I wish you were dead!" '

'She said that . . . ? No. No.'

'Oh yes, yes, and more than that, judging by the bits I caught before we were sent flying. Anyway, we must get down to brass tacks, mustn't we, miss? Because I can't get up for a while. As I said, I can move me legs but the pain's hellish when I do that. Anyway, it's about time there was some help in this house again. It was cut off needlessly after Miss Angela went. So, for the time being, if you don't want to have it on your own hands, you should get McNabb's wife in again. She was quite good and she's clean.'

'Yes. Yes, Patsy. I'll do that.'

She nodded now at Carl, then went out; and he, going to the bed and sitting on its side, bent over Patsy and said, 'I've wished it many a time, dear, and not more than I do at this minute, that we had up and left when we had first made up our minds. Even with the circumstances as they were. I could have said to hell with the bribes of a half share. What life have you had here? Working morning, noon and night. And now this, knocked flat on your back, and we don't know yet what damage has been done. Backs are funny things. I feel like going to him this minute and giving him, not a piece of my mind, but the whole bloody lot of it. I no longer feel, as I did years ago, that I owe him my life. He's had more than the best part of it.'

When her hand came on his cheek, she said, 'As long as I've got you, I'll consider me life all right. And I've given you very little in return for what you've given me. Now, now' – she tapped his cheek smartly – 'don't start. I know, I know what you're going to say: as long as you have me you're all

378

right. Well, for once I'm going to make meself believe it and you can believe it when I say, as long as I have you I'm more than all right. And now, you know what I want?'

'No, dear, no.'

'A cup of strong tea with four spoonfuls of sugar in it. Really strong, thick enough to keep a knife standing up in it, and helped with a wee drop of the hard.'

He smiled, and when he bent and kissed her, she said, 'You know something? You're too bonny for your own good.'

Now he pushed her face to one side, at the same time clicking his tongue, then left her.

But when she was alone the smile went from her face and she bit tightly on her lip. Her back felt bad; the pain was gripping her waist. She hoped to God there was nothing wrong and she'd be able to get on her feet in a day or so . . .

The doctor's verdict was that she might have cracked a bone at the bottom of her spine: she must lie still for at least two weeks, by which time she would likely be able to get on to her feet again.

Later, not for the first time in his career, Philip Patten had to admit to himself that his diagnosis had been wrong. It was to be many months before Patsy could get on her feet, and then it was with much effort and a great deal of pain and only with the help of crutches.

4

~~~~

Trains, trains, trains. Stretchers, stretchers, stretchers. Bodies, bodies, bodies. Blood, blood, blood. That's what the wheels were saying. That's what all the train wheels said. They never speeded up the rhythm: they slowed it down, they stopped, but they never speeded it up.

He was tired. His body was crying out for rest; but more so, his mind pleading for it.

How many ambulance trains had he travelled on over these past months? When did he come here anyway? May? Yes it was May, when the Arras affair was on. God! God! That was an introduction. They were shovelling them in then, those who got back across the Somme at Abbeville. And many of those that were left were wishing they had never got back.

How many times had he thrown up? If it hadn't been for Jim Anderson and David Mayhew he might have joined the mutineers or the absconders and risked being shot. Jim had said he had suffered from diarrhoea for the first three months. 'But you get used to it,' he had said. David was more laconic, less sensitive. 'It's what you asked for,' had been his comment. Yet it was David who had taken him aside and said, 'We've been put here because we're needed. I've asked God time and time again, why is this happening? Why is He allowing it? And the answer is, as the answer always is, man's free will. It's a paltry answer and I've told Him that. But He's also reminded me that His Son was crucified for doing good and that we and fellows like us are in the same boat. And then David had added in his usual manner, 'And it's no good crying out like His Son did, "Why hast thou forsaken me?" because we'll get the same answer, "You asked for it, so you've got to see it through." '

Yes, it was David that had been his prop really, and still was. But if they should ever have a quiet minute together again, and God only knew when that could possibly be, he'd ask him if he, too, had this whirling repetition in his brain that woke him out of sleep, repeating everything three times.

David's voice came to him now, saying, 'Have a word with Geordie at the far end there, will you? because if he starts ranting again he'll wake the whole lot up. And as long as we're stuck here they might as well get a little sleep, those who can.'

Gerald repeated to himself, 'Those who can,' as he looked along a double row of stretchers flanking each side of the long railway carriage. This carriage was supposed to take only twenty-five in some kind of comfort, but there were over forty on this trip. How many had been left behind altogether? He didn't know. What he did know was that by the time the next train arrived, some of them wouldn't need to be lifted up.

He stepped cautiously down the narrow, dimly lit aisle. The place was hazy with breaths that took a little of the chill off the atmosphere. Suddenly the carriage shook violently and a voice to his side said, 'A couple of inches more and it would have been goodbye, Blighty.'

He looked at the man whose stretcher was on a rack to his shoulder and he uttered a platitude that was beginning to wear thin in his vocabulary: 'A miss is as good as a mile.' And then he moved on to where the voice could be heard above the mutterings and groans; but before he reached the source at the end of the carriage, the train shuddered again and he had to thrust both hands over a platform stretcher to steady himself against the blacked-out carriage window. The man whom he was leaning over and whose whole face was bandaged, as was one arm, muttered through a slit where his lips were, 'Why don't they get their aim right and finish with it?'

He could give no answer, and especially not a quip, and so moved on to the man who was doing the talking. He had pulled himself up over his pillow, with his head now resting against the partition that divided this section from the rest of the train, and he greeted Gerald with, 'How much longer are they gona dither here? A sitting bloody duck, that's what we are. Nobody seems to learn a bloody thing in this war. Keep moving. Keep moving. That's the thing to do.'

Gerald dropped down on to his hunkers and he said quietly, 'Arty, isn't it?'

'Aye, that's me name, Arty Makepeace. And that's a hell of a joke, isn't it? Makepeace.'

His voice only just above a whisper now, Gerald said, 'There's one or two along the line there not too good. They're trying to sleep it off.' And the man's voice now was even lower as he said, 'For the last time, you mean.'

'Could be. Could be.'

'Aye, well, join the band.'

'Oh, you'll be all right.'

'Think so?'

'Yes, once you get back to base; and after that it won't be long before you're on the boat.'

The man's voice had become really quiet now when he said, 'Funny thing, you know, this is my third bloody year out here. Aye. Aye, end of '14 I joined. And I'd begun to think nothing could touch me, all because me wife always finished her letters with, "I'm praying that God will protect you." And, you know, I had got to believe it up to this.' He now pointed down to where the blanket sank below his left knee. 'Went through a lot, I did, and not a scratch. Bullets going through me cap, an' the seat of me pants, but not a scratch. Even *this* bloody year, when I was in the counter-attack at Arras. Aye, I was, and we thought we were away. Oh, aye, we did. After having been pushed back across the Somme at Abbeville. Oh, we were all cocking our snooks, when it happened again. You know summat? The lot that they're sendin' over now are like bloody boy scouts. Some of the buggers couldn't tell their arses from their elbows. Trained. Aye. By God! they call it training!'

His voice was rising again, and so Gerald interrupted the threatened flow, whispering, 'What's your regiment?' And thankfully a whisper came back to him: 'Tyneside Scottish. We were with the Tenth and Eleventh Battalions, you know. Eeh! the commander. He was a bloke. A leader all right; he ferried us across in little boats. But what did we meet, eh? Air attacks, tanks, and their bloody infantry.'

'Shh! Shh!'

'Now don't you Shh! me, lad. Anyway, you just sound like me old man. He always used to say, "Shh! Shh thy gob!" And, you know, it's a funny thing, I'll tell you somethin'. I've been more frightened of the bloody mud than the bullets, crawling in it, being choked by it, gulping it down. If we lose the war, an' it's a penny to a pound that we will, it'll be the mud that's done it. But the funny thing is, I was brought up with mud. You see, me old man always had an allotment, kept our bellies full many a time mind, but workin' on it he would sometimes put the fork through his boot or get a cut in his hand. What did he do? He stuck mud on it. Aye. If the ground wasn't wet he would wet it, you know, then stick mud on it. That was when he was outside the house. Inside he went for salt. So—' He now pointed down towards what was left of his right leg below the knee, and he went on, 'When I was lyin' in that bloody shell-hole, half covered in water, I thought of me da an' the mud. And when I came to meself an' saw what'd happened, well, that's what I did. I packed the stinking thing with mud an' I'd like to bet that was why I lived to reach that stinkin' station. How long did we lie on that stinkin' platform eh . . . ? For how long?'

Gerald didn't give him an answer. But he knew some of them had been left there for twenty-four hours and for many it had turned out to be just four hours too long. And the rest of them, those who had been picked up with this lot, would now probably go the same way if this bombardment went on much longer.

The man now lay back on the pillow, but as Gerald was about to move away he found his wrist gripped, and the voice, now quite low and solemn, said, 'You have my respects, lad, and all your gang. As that bloke across there said' – he now jerked his head towards a stretcher at the other side of the aisle – 'you lot were the heroes of this bloody senseless game. That's what he said after your mate got it just afore we pushed off. By! that was a quicker do: here the day an' gone the morrow. You know, he was an 'ero; he could have been picked up on the last train, but he gave way to a bloke that was in a bad way.' He suddenly paused. 'I'm sweatin' like a bullock now. I was freezin' a minute ago.'

Gerald put his hand on the man's brow. It was wet. Here was the answer to his jabbering; he was in a fever. He now pulled the blanket up under his chin, saying quietly, 'Lie still. I'll be back in a moment.' Then he exclaimed, 'Ah now! Listen! We're moving off, and we haven't got all that far to go.' He did not add, just another five hours, that was if they weren't held up again.

He had got only half-way down the carriage when he had to stop and help David Mayhew hold down a burly sergeant. The poor man was back in the trenches giving orders and yelling: 'Over! Over! Over! Come on! Lift it! Never mind the bloody moonlight. If they can see you, you can see them. Over! Over! Over! Hell! move it.'

As they pressed the man down, David, gasping, said, 'This is where we need Arthur and that damn needle of his.'

Yes indeed, Gerald thought. Arthur the hero. Arthur Sprite had almost completed his training as a doctor when he had joined their ranks and become such an asset to them. Yet strangely, he hadn't been liked. Perhaps it was because he had aimed to show his superiority from the beginning. That he was brave, there was no doubt; but there had always been the question as to the reason why he was one of them. Was it on religious grounds? Political? Personal morality? Or what? Strangely, he could never be drawn.

Anyway, he was dead now, killed while carrying out an apparently brave act. As David had pointed out, there had been no need for him to dash along the road to the two wounded men supporting each other. Having got that far, they would have made it the other few yards to the station and the Red Cross vans. But no, he had to be spectacular and he had raced along the road and right into the bomb that had not only killed the three of them, but also blew the last van to smithereens. Daily he was asking himself

384

what drove people to do the things they did. What had driven him into this hell-hole? Principles? What were principles but the sparks of one's ego? Variety? No. No. No. Don't start again, he told himself.

It was two-thirty in the morning when the train drew slowly into the base. There was no need for lanterns for the moon was shining, transforming the night almost into daylight. And now there was a scramble to get the wounded from the train and into the field hospital.

He and David had laid the last man of their section in a sort of outpatients' tent, waiting their turn for a doctor's attention, when a nurse, coming by, looked at them and said, 'You're late as usual.' And they both said together, 'Hello there, Susie.'

'You've packed some in this time.'

'Not one half of what we've left behind,' said David. 'And we've had to crawl most of the way, so slowly at one period that we picked up some stragglers, six of them, three of them in a bad way. They had become separated from their unit. But who hasn't! Well, here I'm off for something to eat.'

'You'll be lucky. Oh, I forgot, you've got a kitchen of your own; half of ours got it.' Her voice sank. 'And two orderlies with it.'

David said nothing to this, but he sighed and turned away. And the nurse, looking at Gerald, said softly, 'You look all-in.'

'Me, look all-in? I could go for another . . . full ten minutes.'

'How long have you been on this trip?'

'Since the beginning of the year.'

'Don't be daft.' She pushed at him, then added, 'But it must feel like that at times. It must be twenty-four hours, at least.'

He sighed now and said, 'Well, I've got a forty-eight coming. And you know what I'm going to do in it?'

'Yes. Yes. Sleep.'

'Right on the dot, Susie. Right on the dot.'

'I'd like to take a bet with you.'

'Yes?'

'You won't sleep for twenty-four hours; you'll hardly sleep for twelve.'

'Perhaps you're right . . .' He knew she was right. You got past sleep. You might be lying on your bed, and there you were, your eyes wide open, staring straight ahead into the past . . . you were on orderly duty, running here and there. Then quite suddenly there was Dunkirk and the ambulance train, and the sickness in his stomach mixed with anger by the sight of more mangled men.

It had been in Dunkirk that he first saw Susie, during the bombardment. The Germans were firing their long-range guns on the town from Dixmude. And he could even hear her now saying, 'If you don't want to have to lie on a stretcher, lie on your belly, man.'

It was a brief meeting in the mud; he was not to see her again until some three months later, and that was in Rouen.

Then they had met in this medical outpost that seemed to be part of no man's land. That was two months ago. Since then, now and again, they had exchanged a few words, as they were doing now.

'Part of your billet got it, but your kitchens are left. That's the main thing.' She smiled her impish smile as she added, 'You can sleep standing up as long as your belly's full. And by the way, thank your mother for the cheese; that was real cheese. You're lucky. I hope there's another parcel waiting for you.'

All he could manage was a short laugh before he turned from her. But he was thinking, I must put a stop to those parcels. They're really worse off over there than we are here. Janie must be sending the butter and cheese from the farm . . . But then, if he stopped the parcels, he'd miss the fruit-loaf. Good God! Fancy thinking about fruit-loaf after the experiences of the last twenty-four hours. Just let him get into that bunk, that's all he wanted right now. Sleep. Sleep . . .

But he wasn't to get straight into his bunk, for he was stopped by Jim with the order that he was to report to the officer in charge, one William Haslett.

386

William Haslett told him what he already knew: he would not be on duty for the next twenty-four hours. When, however, he added, 'After one more train run you'll be due for seven days' leave. I bet you'll be glad to see home again,' the man was not a little amazed when Gerald said, 'I won't be going that far.'

'You . . . you won't? Why not?'

'For the simple reason that if I got there I'd not come back.'

Gerald had delivered this with a wry smile, as one might a joke. But it was no joke, for he knew that once home he would never return to this hell-hole. He also knew that he could not possibly take that risk for he wasn't brave enough to stand the result, a term in gaol. He was sure, too, he would even be unable to face the reception he understood still awaited the conscientious objector in England.

He could not believe that it was just on a year since he left the Hall; and yet all his life beforehand now seemed a hazy dream. Sometimes he could not visualise clearly even his mother's face. As for Janie, her letters were perky enough but did nothing to bring back the real picture of her.

William Haslett had been staring at him and his mouth opened twice as if he were searching for words; and then he said, 'It was dreadful about Sprite. He's going to be an awful loss,' to which Gerald nodded, saying, 'Yes. Yes, indeed.'

'But there,' said Haslett now, 'you're all well acquainted with first aid and I'll get Doctor Blane to have a talk with you and advise you on' – he stopped – 'well, anything that you might be able to do . . . further, I mean when it comes to handling drugs.'

When there was no comment on this, and taking in the blank look on Gerald's face, he ended quickly, 'Ah, well, we'll see about it. All you want now, I suppose, is your bunk.'

'Yes, you've said it,' said Gerald. 'That's all I want now,' and turned away, leaving the man thinking: stiff-neck. Odd fellow. Surprise me if he lasts out.

David was waiting for him outside the hut, and his first words were, 'Seven days. Think of it laddie, seven days.'

But Gerald did not comment on this particular statement; instead, he said, 'You talk quite a bit to him' – he jerked his head back – 'why don't you suggest he takes a ride along with us on the next trip? And the one after that . . . And the next . . . '

David surveyed Gerald for a moment before he said gravely, 'If you had put that question to Jim, him with his kind heart, he would have said, "Oh, well, he does good work here." There's a lot of organising to be done one way or another. We're quite a big unit, you know. But since you ask me, I'd say simply it's got something to do with his guts.' Then his voice changing, he said, 'But anyway, let's forget our dear organiser and think of Blighty.'

'I won't be going across, David.'

David looked at him for a moment in disbelief before exclaiming, 'In the name of God! why not?'

'Well, I must say to you as I said to him' – he now thumbed towards the hut – 'once over there I wouldn't come back.'

'Oh, you would, lad, you would.'

'*No, I wouldn't. I wouldn't come back.* No! No! I couldn't, and because of that I know I must not go over, for there would be worse in store once they caught up with me. So, I ask myself, why do I criticise old William? Because if the truth was known my guts are in a worse state than his.'

'Never! You'd come back because you would know you were needed. That's what keeps you going here. Quite candidly, I've always thought you've got more compassion in your little finger than I've got in both hands. Come on. Come on, lad, make up your mind. I mean . . . you needn't go home. We could have a good time in London. Come to my place. I've a mother who's as skittish as a kitten. She's kicking fifty. The last time I saw her she was holding dances for our "dear boys", together with Lady this and the Honourable that. She'd introduce you to some piece who would assuredly make you forget . . . '

Now Gerald pushed him none too gently, saying, 'You're wasting your breath. Anyway, get yourself to bed. I'm telling you, if you keep me standing here talking any longer, you'll have to carry me to my bunk . . . See you in twenty-four hours' time, boy.' And with this he went to his bunk. But as Susie had predicted, he did not sleep for the full twenty-four hours.

It had been seven in the morning when he lay down, and he woke up at six in the evening. After a good wash, he had a meal, then returned to his hut and wrote to his mother and also to Janie.

They were not long letters now, just terse notes telling them he was very busy, and that he didn't like moonlight nights. He made a joke about this. And he asked his mother how she was putting up with the soldiers she now had in her house.

In his letter to Janie, he thanked her for being such a companion to his mother. And he ended it, saying, 'Don't be as generous with your butter and cheese et cetera. We get enough to tuck in here.' Which was far from the truth.

Having made the letters ready for the post, he then put on his greatcoat, his cap and a muffler, and went out for a walk. The air was cold and bracing and the moonlight was hazy.

He went down what had once been a village street but which now, apart from two houses, both roofless, had nothing to indicate anyone had ever lived there. Where the road led beyond the village it was bordered on both sides by fields, which no longer held crops but were pock-marked with craters, black-holed craters. Further along stood a farmhouse, intact except that part of the roof had slates missing, and also seemingly quite untouched was a barn, from which came the sound of cattle mooing.

At the sound, Gerald made a small motion of disbelief with his head, as he had done a number of times before, wondering how they had escaped, not only the bombs but the butcher's knife. There was no sound of cackling hens, which was understandable: hens were easy target for the pot. He recalled that he had once been put on guard at night to protect their meagre stores from a new company of soldiers that had just arrived. What he would have done if a few of them had set about him he didn't know, because, of course, he didn't carry a rifle. Food seemed to be the priority of everyone these days. It didn't matter about the sameness of it as long as it filled you up.

389

He had walked some distance when the moon appeared again, and he told himself he should turn about and make for the camp: it was the sort of night those fellows over there might make full use of; even so, the influence of the moon set his mind singing:

The moon has raised her lamp above
To light the way to thee my love . . .
To light . . . the way . . . to thee . . . my love.

However, the Dictator, as he thought of that inner voice that was constantly getting at him these days, suddenly said, Enough of that!

He was passing by the farm again when he saw a figure coming out of the farmhouse door he instantly recognised as Susie. She was carrying a can.

Having heard his footsteps, then recognised him, she shook hands with the small round figure of the farmer's wife, before hurrying towards him. He greeted her with: 'Been on the scrounge again?'

'She's been very kind. Guess what I've got in my pocket? But don't come too near me.'

He said, 'A chicken?' well knowing that it couldn't be.

'You're getting warm.'

'Never!'

'Well, not a chicken but a couple of eggs.'

'I thought they hadn't any fowl left.'

'She's a wise woman. She's got half a dozen penned up in the back of the house.'

He laughed. 'And you found out so she's had to bribe you.'

'No, I didn't find out. Well, I mean, after she gave me two eggs and I looked at them in amazement, she took me by the hand and into the back place, and there they were, six females, and very contented, even though their husbands had been polished off some time ago. But nevertheless, they were singing to themselves . . . Have you ever heard a hen sing? They do, you know.'

He made no further comment, and they walked on in silence for some moments before she said, 'I wish I'd laid some money on my bet. It wasn't even twelve hours, was it?'

'No; but nearly. Anyway, I feel a little more like myself; although that is no credential for saneness.'

'You really were all in, weren't you? You've hardly had a full night's sleep in the last three or four trips.'

Another silence ensued before he said, 'How do you stand it out here, Susie?'

'Oh, well, I stand it the same as the others do: it's got to be done. And anyway, with all the muck, misery, blood and gore, I'd rather be here than back home, because I look upon most of the fellows I handle as heroes.' She paused then added, 'I mightn't if I had known them when they were whole and had to listen to their inane jabber. But when they are helpless and suffering, and when you hear a man crying below his breath for his mother . . . They all say it in different ways: or Mam, or Mammy, or just Ma. Some of them jabber their wife's name. And then they come round a bit and say, "Oh, nurse, was I chattering?" Ashamed of their weakness. Sometimes I want to put my arms around them, or even' – she now pushed him to one side – 'get into bed beside them,' and her laughter rang out; and he joined her, saying gallantly now, 'I'll have to get myself in a mess,' to which she made no rejoinder until they had walked on further steps when she said, 'I was going to give you an answer to that, but I won't.' Then she added, 'How would you like a cup of real coffee, and a boiled egg and toast?'

'Who but an idiot could refuse such an invitation?' he said.

'Well, come on, put a move on, because you know what might happen if the maiden' – she now pointed up to the moon – 'keeps on doing her stuff.'

Reaching the camp, they skirted the back of the hospital, then crossed a hard mud-ridged area that led them towards a line of low brick buildings which at some time must have housed an assortment of animals. Here, at the end door, she took a key from her pocket and still in keeping with the mood of such an evening, said, 'Step in, sir.'

Compared with the moonlight outside, inside it was dark. He heard her strike a match and when she had lit the hanging

391

lantern, he looked around him in some surprise, saying, 'Well, well; you're nicely ensconced, aren't you?'

'I'm privileged. I'm one of the old hands; in fact, next to matron who, by the way, and thankfully, is off on her forty-eight. So you don't need to fear someone knocking on the door and crying, "Nurse! you know the rules." '

'You've got a fireplace, too.'

'Yes, it must have been some sort of boiler house, likely for pig food, because . . . look!' She pointed to the pot-boiler in the corner of the room.

He looked around the rest of the hut: a single bed stood against one wall; there was a dilapidated armchair to the side of it, and beyond that what looked like a folding card-table.

On the other side of the room, and looking grotesquely out of place, was a single mahogany wardrobe; also, and more in keeping, four large boxes, forming two open-fronted low cupboards. In one he could see odd pieces of crockery and a kettle; in the other what he imagined must be pieces of food wrapped in paper, a tin of jam and one of bully beef.

'Home from home.'

'Sit yourself down,' she said. 'But don't flop in that chair else you'll go straight through the bottom.'

'Can't I help you?'

'No. Do as you're told; sit down.'

So he sat down gently and found himself sinking into the broken mesh of the chair seat; nevertheless, it was comfortable. He now leant his head against the back, stretched out his legs and sighed. But then he said, 'How are you going to boil a kettle and your eggs on that fire? It's enclosed and it looks to be on its last legs.'

'Be quiet.'

She went to the far corner of the room to another cupboard and took out an oil burner. And after she had lit it and set the kettle on top of it, he remarked, 'You're set for life here.'

'You know nothing yet.'

He sat looking at her. Without her overcoat and hat now, and in her blue print uniform with its big white apron, that wasn't very white any more, he thought, She's comely; only to ask himself why he had used such an old-fashioned word to describe her. Perhaps it was because of her shape. Everything about her looked round: her buttocks, her bust, her face; yet she wasn't fat. She was a comforting person, was Susie.

Sister Susie sewing shirts for soldiers
and soldiers sending missils they would rather
sleep on thistles.

Oh why did his mind prattle on so? And he didn't know the words of the song. Why was it taken up with such trivialities? And the answer came, Because you don't write any more. And the voice yelled back at him: What the hell will I write about in this madhouse! A thesis on the anatomy of spilled brains, rivers of blood and guts? For God's sake! shut up. Look at Susie; she's frying the eggs.

'I thought you were going to boil them,' he said.

'I changed my mind. We can have them on fried bread with butter this way. Anyway, I thought you were asleep.'

'I wasn't asleep.'

'No? Likely, musing as usual. What do you think about, anyway? I've often wondered. Is it true your mother's a lady? David says she is.'

When he started to laugh, half remonstrating him, she said, 'Well, what's amusing about that? Is she?'

'Yes, I suppose so. But what do you mean by a lady?'

'Well, one with a title.'

'There are lots of ladies without titles, and my mother would be a lady whether she had a title or not.'

'Is she nice?'

'Lovely. Beautiful in all ways.'

'Have you ever been married, Gerald?'

He chuckled now as he said, 'Only to a smallholding.'

'You had a smallholding?'

'Yes. Yes, I had a smallholding.'

The bread sizzled as it went into the hot butter, and she turned it over on to the other side before she asked, 'Been engaged?'

'No, I haven't been engaged, or anything like that.'

'Never had a girl then?'

'Oh, yes, yes. I've got a girl back home.'

'Oh.'

He was amused now, and so he said, 'She's rather lovely, too; different.'

'Well! Well! a beautiful mother and a beautiful girl.'

'Yes. Yes, I'm very lucky, and I'm sure my girl will grow more beautiful every day.'

He saw her turn a sharp look towards him, her face now unsmiling. And his tone became lighter, a little teasing, as he went on, 'She was always very bright and her letters show this. The only thing is she writes too often; I can't keep up with her. What she'll be when she grows up I don't know.'

'What? When who grows up? Who?'

'My girl.'

She lifted the eggs off a plate where they had been standing on the hob of the dying fire, slapped them on to the bread, then took them to the small table, pulled out some cutlery from a box to the side, then said, 'Come and get it. No! Stay where you are. I'll lift the table round and I'll sit on the bed,' and she continued to contain her feelings, at least until they had started to eat, when she said, 'What did you mean, when she grows up?'

'Just what I said. She must be ... well ... oh, twelve, thirteen, going on fourteen now.'

'Oh you! You're a funny fellow. You know that, Gerald?'

'Yes, I've been told that before. By the way, this tastes marvellous.'

It was some time later. The meal had been finished with a cup of milky coffee. The greasy plates had been put into an iron pan half filled with water and placed at the front of the boiler fire, which prompted him to ask, 'Won't it put it out completely?'

'No; it will still be on in the morning. I'll just have to give it a blow.'

Again he remarked, 'You are well organised, aren't you?'

'Just some parts of my life.'

When later he was about to sit again in the chair, he hesitated, saying, 'My next effort will find me through on the floor. You sit there.'

'No; I prefer the edge of the bed.'

And that's how they sat; and when she leant against his shoulder, he put his arm around her. And after a moment of holding her so, he said, 'You're a very nice person, you know, Susie.'

'How is it you've just found that out?' She didn't turn to look at him as she spoke, but nestled her head closer to him.

'I haven't just found that out; I've thought so all along.'

'You've been rather backward in telling me then.'

'Have I?' There was a surprised note in his voice. 'I've always talked to you. I found you easy to talk to, comforting in a way.'

'In a way? You're lost, aren't you, Gerry? I've always wanted to call you Gerry, but that would be classing you with them over there.' Her head moved under his chin. Then she went on, 'This is not your scene. It staggers you. I can see that every time you come back. You take things to heart too much. You put me in mind of a fellow that used to be on the trains just before you came. He was always spouting poetry. He'd be speaking ordinary to you, then he'd come out with a quotation or other. But when he started to go up and down the ward . . . oh well,' she said with a small hunching of her shoulders, 'they took him back home.'

'And you think I'll go the same way?'

'Oh, no.' Her tone was emphatic now. Yet she added, 'It's the look of you at times, and you keep things bottled up. David says you do.'

He brought her head up from his shoulder, saying, 'Then I'm discussed between you and David? Why?'

'Oh, we have a natter at times. He's very fond of you. Well, he thinks you're great, your principles and all that. Quite candidly, I think all you fellows in that unit, in all your units, are great because of your principles. But you haven't got to let them get on top of you, not out here.'

She now put her hand up and stroked his cheeks and her touch sent a quiver through him. She began to unloosen his tie and the last button of his coat that hadn't been undone, and he did not stay her hand. And when a few minutes later they were both standing up and her last piece of clothing fell to the floor, she stood looking at him for a moment before, stretching her hand behind her, she rolled back the blanket on the bed. And then they were both lying side by side, and when she whispered, 'You hadn't to get wounded,' he made no answer, but as his lips passed over her face he wasn't seeing it.

After rising from her side, he got into his clothes before, bending over her again, he kissed her on the brow and said, 'Thank you, Susie. Thank you.'

She was half asleep as she murmured, 'You're welcome any time, sir.'

There was no longer any moonlight as he stepped out into the night, but he stood looking at the stars in the sky. He was feeling greatly relaxed, changed somehow. Would anybody believe that had been his first night with a woman? No, he could hardly believe it himself. And now the question he asked was, why had he put it off for so long? Why? For it had been the most marvellous, most wonderful experience. He could face the morrow now and the days ahead on the train, for there'd always be Susie to come back to. And what about the seven days' leave? Yes what about it . . . ?

As it turned out, she wasn't able to get seven days off, but was given a forty-eight hour pass. And they spent it in a little village some long way behind the lines. And he experienced a feeling of comfort and ease that was like a soothing salve on his mind.

5

Things were going from bad to worse. They all knew this and it was being voiced in many quarters: where were the bloody generals who were ordering them forward only for them to be thrown back on all sectors again and again? Exacerbating comments but, in truth, very telling when voiced by the wounded crammed now like sardines in the trains. Why didn't they come up to the front? No; they were sitting in their comfortable billets and drinking their bloody port after dinner, toasting the Royal Family . . . England . . . the Flag.

And the officers. Who did they think they were anyway? Young snots, hardly able to wipe their own noses. When it came to leading men . . . leading men, huh! Doing it in their pants, some of them, but they still looked down their noses at you.

Yet in the trains there was no distinction of rank, no officers and men, only a bloody mass of mutilated bodies. Even so, here and there, a voice would rise in defence of a particular officer, or even a sergeant who had perhaps risked his own life and in doing so had enabled a speaker to be on that particular train.

He had stopped writing so many letters home. Although he had the occasional comfort of Susie whenever she was free, the horror of the war seemed, at times, to be turning his brain: as David described it, the world had turned into a slaughter-house and the abattoir was very messy. And to the comment of their latest addition, one Sydney Allington, 'God made the back to bear the burden,' David immediately retorted, 'Yes, Mother Shipton,' a reference which the young man did not understand, but nevertheless one which simply strengthened his growing opinion of Gerald, David and Jim as being strange company, and further made him question why any of them were there at all, at least in their capacities as non-combatants. And he continued to address them formally.

It was in March 1918 that three outstanding things happened, two of which were to propel Gerald's mind into the oblivion for which he would often crave in order to escape the horror of the everyday scenes he was forced not only to look upon, but to deal with.

The first took place when again the train was making slow progress back to base. They had taken on four sitting passengers, now propped up against the end partition of the carriage.

While entraining, he had noticed that two of these men had helped each other, one using his only usable arm to help his companion hop. And now bending down to the nearest man, he asked, 'How's it going?'

'Not too bad. But Lawson, my friend here, I think his leg's giving him gip.' And the tone of the man's voice made Gerald look more closely at the mud-covered uniform. Then he leant across to the man Lawson and said, 'Feeling low?'

'Not too bad, sir. I'm all right, thanks to the captain here.'

Gerald turned his attention back to the other man, saying now, 'Rough show, sir?'

'Yes, you could say that.' He was about to speak again when Allington, the odd man out of their particular team, tapped him on the shoulder, saying, 'Mr Ramsmore, you're needed further down; Mr Mayhew requires your assistance.'

After nodding at the soldiers, Gerald turned away, thinking to himself, Requires your assistance. That fellow got on his nerves more than did the war. He had almost said, bloody nerves and bloody war, and he must stop that: he was becoming as bad as the others in using such expletives with every other word.

He found David having trouble with a delirious and very ill man: 'Get the needle,' was David's greeting, and inclined his head further along the carriage to explain his call for assistance: 'Jim's got his own hands full.'

Gerald knew it was no use saying, 'What about Allington?' because David couldn't stand the fellow. How odd that one individual could mar a team. Yet if they were to go into it, Allington's motive for being here at this moment was purer than theirs, for in his case God had come into it.

It was more than an hour later when he made his way back to the men propped up at the end of the carriage. The train had gathered some speed, and he could see that the private was dozing. The officer had his eyes wide open, and, on seeing him he put up his good hand to beckon Gerald down to him.

'Ramsmore?'

'Yes. Yes, that's my name.'

'Strange coincidence, so is mine.'

'Really? Well, well, it's a small world, as they say.'

'May I ask if your Christian name is Gerald?'

'You may, and it is.'

Gerald straightened up a little; then bending again, he peered into the young officer's face and said, 'Don't tell me your father's name is Beverly?'

There was a small chuckle now as the young man answered, 'No, but my grandfather's is.'

'Good Lord!'

'I've heard a lot about you.'

Somewhat stiffly now Gerald answered, 'I bet you have.'

'Oh, not in the way you're inferring.' The words had been rapidly spoken. 'Oh, no; I mean, along this route. Those over there know damn all about it. I'm . . . I'm very pleased to meet you.' And when the hand came out Gerald shook it warmly.

'My name is Will. We must get together and have a crack after this. Are you on the same run all the time?'

'Most of it.'

'My God! You chaps certainly have had your bellyful of war and no medals. How long are these runs?'

'Eight, ten hours; it all depends.'

The young officer peered at his wrist-watch and remarked, 'We've been going for five and a half hours. Good Lord!' And the next moment he asked, 'Have you been home lately?'

'No; not since I came out here last year.'

There was a pause; then peering up at Gerald, the younger man said somewhat thoughtfully, 'You know, I have never seen my step-grandmother, or is she my step-great-grandmother? Yes, she would be, wouldn't she? They say she's a very nice lady.'

'Yes, she is. And you must rectify your omission when you get back. She would be delighted to see you. Although, as I understand it, most of the house has been taken over by the military.'

'My grandfather often talked of the Hall where he was brought up. But he seemed to think you had lost all the land.'

'Not quite; there's still a few acres left. I ran a smallholding, you know.'

'You didn't!'

'Yes.'

'Good for you. You must be longing to get back out of this hell-hole.'

Gerald did not answer but straightened up. Was he longing to get back? He'd had a strange thought in his mind of late that he would never get back, that he would never live in that house again. It had become an obsessive thought about which he could do nothing other than aim to ignore it.

There was a commotion further down the carriage: a man was crying out, not for his mother or father, but for someone called Little Jackie, perhaps a son.

He intimated that he must go, and the young man nodded and said, 'We mustn't lose touch,' in answer to which he himself nodded and muttered, 'No. No . . .'

He saw his distant relative twice while he was in the base hospital prior to his being moved on down to the port when they had shaken hands and promised to meet up again. Will had also said he would go and see his step-great-grandmother.

The second thing that occurred shocked his system more than even war scenes and the ambulance trains had done.

400

The last stretcher had been passed over to the hospital orderlies, who had protested loudly as to where it was expected it should be put. 'They're hanging from the ceiling,' said one. 'And if they don't soon clear some of them to the boats, you can put off your next run, for they might as well lie outside where they are, as lie outside here.'

David and Jim had heard it all before, and they gave as much as they got, but Gerald had turned away. He was now making for the showers and his bed. But having to pass the nursing staff kitchen and day quarters, he stopped a nurse who was coming out of the door and asked, 'Is Susie about?'

She glanced behind her into the room, then closed the door; and now, looking up at him, she said stiffly, 'She's gone.'

'What do you mean, she's gone?' He turned and looked about him. There was no evidence of a bomb having been dropped overnight.

The girl now said, 'She left yesterday. She's been posted.'

'Posted! Where to?'

She shrugged her shoulders; and when it seemed she was going to walk away, he said, 'Well, do you know where she's been posted to?'

'Not quite. I hear it's back home . . . sort of training job or something.' She now smiled and bit on her lip before walking away, leaving him standing perplexed.

It had been three days since he had seen her, and then only to have a quick word. Surely, she must even then have had an inkling it was about to happen. Why hadn't she mentioned it to him? Why? She had been a bit . . . well, offhand lately. He swung about to go hurriedly in search of David.

He met him emerging from the bunkhouse, and without any lead-up he said to him, 'Do you know anything about this? Susie's gone, they say. Well, the nurse seemed to think that she might have been sent home.'

'Yes.' David glanced away before looking back at him, then said, 'Yes, that's what I understand, she's been sent home. I think she's going into a training job there.' He smiled now, rather sadly as he said, 'She'll be a great miss, will our Susie. She was a great comforter. Oh yes.'

401

Gerald's eyes narrowed and he moved his head slightly to the side without taking his eyes off David. There had been something in that tone he hadn't liked, that he wished he hadn't heard, that he didn't want to understand. Still he pursued with his questioning: 'What do you mean by a great comforter?'

'Well, she was, wasn't she? Great girl, Susie. I knew it would come as a bit of a shock to you. It was to me, I can tell you. And not only to me. Oh, Susie's little grey nest in the West will be sadly missed.'

He was seeing the room now: the boiler, the table, the oil lamp, the frying pan, the bed. Oh, yes, the bed, and the comfort of that bed. There wasn't much room in the bed . . .

David's voice seemed to come to him from a distance. Although it was in an undertone it was very loud in his head, for he was saying, 'Don't look like that, man. You must have known. God! You must have known. And you know, you were favoured: it lasted a long time compared . . . '

When Gerald's fist shot out it was warded off painfully by David knocking it aside. But when he repeated the action, he felt the impact of David's fist on his mouth. And he not only tasted his own blood but smelt it, and it smelt as strong as a carriage full of mangled flesh. He knew he was now being pinned against the hut wall by David's thick stubby arms and chest and, with his face close to his he was spilling words over him: 'All I can say, chum, is you're a bigger bloody idiot than I thought. Couldn't you see she was one of nature's bedwarmers? And I say, thank God for it. She knew what she was doing all right, and she enjoyed it. There are women made like that. And we knew what we were doing, too, the risks we ran with any of them . . . and what they ran an' all. Anyway, you're not an infant. You know what's going on. Why did you think she was any different when she came so easy, as she did? It should have told you.'

David slowly eased himself off Gerald's shoulders, muttering as he did so, 'Sorry. You'd better have your lip seen to. Funny, but you're the last person on God's earth I expected to battle with in this bloody war. The only thing I can say is, I didn't start it, and I'm not going to say now that I understand

402

your reaction, because I just don't. I was always under the impression that you knew what you were doing and you knew who you were doing it with. Anyway, I know the matron's been on her track for some time. She was giving her girls a bad name. You know, some of them in there' – he jerked his head back towards the hospital – 'are wearing chastity belts. Of course, I don't blame them, nor do I blame the Susies of this world, for God knows what we would do without them. The alternative, as I see it, has always left a nasty taste in my mouth.' He now leant forward and looked into the white, stiff-drawn face of the man whom he liked and called a friend, and he said, 'In spite of our high-falutin' moral stand against this wholesale slaughter, we remain men with the needs of men. There's no bloody saints among us. Some heroes mind, those who are back in the English prisons. Oh yes, those back there in the English prisons are the real heroes for you. Only yesterday I heard about the treatment meted out to a couple of them, and it's unbelievable that Englishmen are torturing Englishmen. Give me the Germans any day, rather than such individuals.' He paused now before again leaning forward and saying, 'Come on. Come on, old fellow. Say something. Let's forget about this. Come on.'

But Gerald couldn't say anything. He pulled himself from the wall, wiped the back of his hand across his blood-ied chin, then turned and walked away. And David stood looking after him for a moment, then he bowed his head and muttered, 'Damn and blast!'

He was no fool. He was no simple-minded individual; he was an educated, highly intelligent man. Without being swollen-headed, that was how he saw himself. He saw the futility of war and the greed and the insensibility of those who created it and of those who kept it going. Like drovers driving their herds of cattle to the slaughterhouse. But then, not quite: they sent in their cattle, their battalions, but they did so from quarters well behind the lines, some even from as far away as London.

Yet being knowledgeable in this way, why hadn't he the insight to realise that first night that, unlike himself, she

403

was well practised in the art of so-called loving. As she had admitted, she had wanted him for a long time, but then she hadn't said, as she could have, that he wasn't like the rest of her clientèle.

Clientèle.

My God! What had he just thought? He wasn't just a fool, he was an idiot; and more so, for marriage had crossed his mind. He had gone as far as to wonder if his mother would take to her. He did, however, recall the doubt there. But why should there have been a doubt? He had never gone into that, for he knew the words to describe her that his mother would have used: cheap and slightly common. But would that have deterred him, the way he was then feeling about her?

How had he felt about her? Had it been love or just body hunger? Were you capable of distinguishing between the two when you were in that state?

During the following days different members of the unit remarked on the change in Ramsmore. He had never had a lot to say, unless you could get him into a conversation on books or poetry. But now he scarcely ever opened his mouth. That was, until around the 17th of March, when a long section of the front was pinned down for two days and nights by gas shells. And this was the third and final thing that sent him into oblivion, albeit not right away.

First, he had to experience the results of the gas attacks. The cases were horrifying: a choking, throttled mass of humanity. For two solid days and nights the Germans had bombarded the great stretch of the front with gas shells. And this was soon commonly recognised as being the prelude to their making a big push. The Red Cross and its orderlies, their own Friends' Unit and its orderlies, everyone available was mustered to cope with the influx, which soon developed into a mêlée. Even so, it became evident to many and was remarked upon that Ramsmore was not just talking, that he had taken to much swearing and blaspheming. And David made it clear he preferred the dour man, that to him the present pattern had all the signs of an approaching breakdown.

From this particular stretch, the trains ran every day to Rouen. If they left in the evening they didn't arrive there till about five the next morning. But what was worse, they had to pass several stations this side of Amiens and see hundreds of stretcher cases lying on the ground and hundreds on hundreds of walking wounded waiting patiently to be loaded into some vehicle or other.

When it was rumoured that the Fifth Army had been routed, spirits could not have been lower, and everyone waited for the end, telling themselves that whatever the outcome it couldn't be worse than this.

The end didn't come quickly. Nor, to David's surprise, did Gerald's final collapse; for not only through April and May did he continue to be very voluble, but at every available moment he could be seen scribbling in his notebooks.

It was on the 2nd of June that Gerald sent a batch of hand-written material to the War Office in London, and with its despatch his mind closed down on him. That night he lay in his bunk and a voice from a great distance told him not to get up again, and of a sudden, he was enveloped in a great peaceful silence.

So Gerald Bede Ramsmore, the conscientious objector, was called up before not a military court but a medical one, after which he found himself in hospital, where he lay quite content as long as no-one tried to get him back on to his feet, for then he became aggressive.

He arrived in England on a stretcher and heavily sedated. He was taken straight to hospital. And he knew nothing about the Allies preparing to advance again and doing so in August, and nothing whatever about the armistice on the 11th of November.

PART TWO

I

'Where are the men?'

'I've let them go. Rob will be back later to give me a hand. There's a Victory Tea in the Hollow.'

'It's three o'clock in the afternoon.'

'I'm well aware of that.'

'You're taking too much on yourself.'

They were both standing in the doorway of what had been the old barn. And now Carl stepped into the open as if putting distance between himself and this man. And after taking in a deep breath, he said, 'Yes, perhaps I am, but that wouldn't be necessary if you hadn't left the whole of this place on my shoulders for years now. When, may I ask, did you last turn a hand in this yard? You walk through it only when the fit takes you.'

Carl watched Ward's colour deepen into an almost purple hue, and his voice was a growl as he said, 'You forget who you are talking to.'

'No, I don't forget who I am talking to. I only know that ten years ago I wouldn't have dared to address you in this way. But now, when you don't give a damn for man or beast, I consider it my right to speak my mind. And I've been wanting to do it for a long time, and there's no time like the present. I've been working for you for over thirty years and not only have I kept this farm going, I've turned it into a profitable business. Oh, yes,' – he made a wide gesture with his hand as if throwing something off, as he said, 'There is the carrot

409

of the half-share. Well, I don't give a damn for that, let me tell you, because I could leave here tomorrow and start up on my own, and the men would come with me.'

'Huh! Start up on your own? Don't make me laugh. What would you pay your men with? Eh? . . . *My* men . . . with rabbit skins?'

A number of seconds passed before Carl, his voice low but his words steely, said, 'The agreement was that I had a part of the profits over a certain amount. Yes; on top of this I had my wage and Patsy had hers, and we've saved.'

'Huh! You've saved. I know what you've got over the profits and your wages. And what would that amount to? You couldn't run a house and allotment and one man on it, never mind livestock.'

Carl's jaws were tight. He knew that this was true. However, it would be a start, and he knew he could rely on Mike and McNabb; they would go along with him, small wage or no. Then a thought struck him. He did not know from whence it came, unless it was perhaps from Janie's talk of the prospects that lay in the Hall acres when the young master was well enough to come home. And now he heard himself say, 'I certainly wouldn't have to start at the bottom for land. There's an offer open to me from the Hall. There's land there and buildings that would house stock; all it needs is labour. And as I warned you, the men would be with me. So what d'you think of that?'

What Ward thought of it had silenced his tongue for a moment. He knew only too well what would happen to this farm if Carl left. But he couldn't bear to be downed in this manner. So he answered, 'Talk. That woman hasn't enough money to hire a couple of servants, never mind stock a farm. And this is the gratitude I get. You forget what I took you from. You owe everything you are to me.'

'I owe nothing that I am to you, sir, for from that boy that you took in, I worked for my keep, and more. But you owe me a lot, for you crippled my wife. Yes. Yes, you did.'

'I did no such thing. It was the other one I was thrusting away. I did not cripple your wife, and don't you dare say that again.'

410

'I'll say it, not only again, but with my dying breath.' And now he leant forward and growled into Ward's face, 'You crippled my wife. You could have murdered her, and the youngster, but in a different way from that you did your daughter. Oh, you can look like that, but I know what I know.'

Ward now stepped back into the doorway as he muttered, 'No! You're out of your mind. You're mad. You could be brought up for even suggesting such a thing. Do you know that?'

'I'd be quite happy if you did bring me up. I saw you taking the poison from the tins. You made one mistake, though: you left the milk glass on the wash-hand stand and there was sediment in it. And I'm not the only one who knows.'

After saying this he realised he might be incriminating the doctor and so he added hastily, 'I took it to a chemist and had it analysed.' And then his imagination took him further when he added, 'He put his findings in writing.'

Carl now watched Ward put his hand out as if to support himself on the stanchion of the door, but felt no pity for the man, for now he was speaking his mind. 'You became obsessed with your daughter, as you had been with your wife,' he went on. 'You could do nothing wrong. Your love for them became a mania. But for the child that your daughter gave birth to, and no matter who the father was she was the daughter of your child, and you are her grandfather, what have you done for her? I'll say what I've thought for years. It's a damn good job she didn't inherit any trait of either your wife or your daughter, else her mind would have been turned years ago under your treatment. But what she has inherited, God knows where from, has stood her in good stead and given her the strength and the power to stand up to you, because she doesn't fear you. As she herself said, she only hates you. And you're the one to know what hate can do. You had your first lesson from the village. But that first wave did nothing to what they felt for you after you ruined three families, one of them for the second time.'

He stepped back quickly as he thought Ward was about to strike him. But when the hand left the stanchion of the door

411

and was lifted forward like a blind man groping his way, he did feel a sudden pang of mixed guilt and sympathy.

He stood where he was and watched the older man walk across the yard and round to the front of the house. He never entered these days by the kitchen door, not since Patsy took to crutches.

He, too, now felt in need of the physical support of the barn wall, and he stood there for a full minute, his head back against the overlapping slats, his eyes tightly closed. And then he actually jumped as a voice to his side said quietly, 'Carl.'

'Oh! Miss Jessie. You startled me.'

'Carl, is . . . is it true? I heard . . . I heard it all. I was just at the corner coming round.' She could have added, 'as clearly as I heard you and Patsy through the slats of what was the old barn years ago.' But when he bowed his head and made no answer, she muttered, 'Oh dear Lord! What next? This house is indeed doomed. But . . . but Carl' – she clutched his arm – 'about you leaving and going to Lady Lydia's. Oh, please! Please, don't do that. Never leave . . . I mean, I just couldn't bear it.' Her voice was breaking now and she didn't say why she really couldn't bear it, but she added, 'To be left here with him alone. No! No! I would have no-one. Janie, I have lost her. I know I've lost her already. I lost her years ago, first to . . . to that man in the Hall, and now to his mother. And if you went . . .'

'There, there. There, there.' He patted her hand where it still lay on his arm and as he looked into her tear-stained face he felt an ache in his heart for her, for he well knew of her feelings and her awareness of the hopelessness of them. And so by way of comfort he said, 'I'll . . . I'll not go as . . . as long as I can stick it out. And anyway' – he forced himself to smile – 'where would I find anyone to help Patsy as you have. You've been wonderful with her and she appreciates it. As for me, I'll never be able to thank you enough.'

'Thank me enough?' She turned away now from him, her lips rubbing one over the other. 'You to thank me when, as you said, Patsy's accident was due entirely to Father?' Turning slowly about and facing him again, she asked, 'Has this ever been a happy house, Carl? Can you remember?'

He seemed to consider for a moment, then said, 'It was a long time ago, shortly after your mother came, before things began to happen from the village. But when she died . . . well, I think all happiness went with her, at least for him. And yet there were times in your early childhood when you and Angela romped and played with him.'

'I . . . I can never remember romping or playing with him. Angela used to, but not me. All I can remember of my childhood is feeling lost. Needing someone, wanting someone to love me.' She brought her eyes fully on to his now, and in a very low voice, she ended, 'But you know all about that, don't you?'

She turned away and walked briskly along by the barn and retraced her steps to the cottage, and there, to her surprise, she found Janie. And she expressed her surprise by saying, 'Well! that was a short visit.'

Janie was bending down warming her hands at the fire when she said, 'Lady Lydia was away. She won't be back until tomorrow. She's gone to see Mr Gerald.'

'I thought she only went once a month, and she visited him last week, didn't she?'

'Yes. Yes, she did.' She straightened up now and turned and looked directly at Jessie as she said, 'Perhaps they've sent for her to bring him home. Perhaps he's well enough.' She stopped herself from adding, 'And you wouldn't like that, would you, Auntie Jessie?' Why, she was always asking herself, did her Auntie Jessie not like Mr Gerald? She knew that she had been disturbed when she heard that he was being brought back from France. She also knew that she had been relieved when she found out he was to be kept in a hospital, not for wounded men, but for those that were sick in the head. She herself could never imagine Mr Gerald going sick in the head. To her, he had always appeared so sensible and wise.

Jessie said now, 'I'll have to go over shortly and help Patsy with the meal; Mrs McNabb has gone to the Victory Tea in the Hollow.' Then she added in a querulous tone, 'They've all gone mad with their Victory Tea. I'll leave your meal out for you.'

'I can see to it myself, Auntie Jessie. You know I can.'

413

'Very well, very well, see to it yourself.' She half turned away, then paused a moment before she said, 'By the way, what's this talk about Lady Lydia turning the place into a farm?'

As this was absolute news to Janie, she just stared at Jessie, which only made her aunt snap, 'All right! All right! If you've been told not to say anything. But don't tell me you don't know anything about it, when Carl says he's been approached. I think it's very bad of her ladyship, anyway, to try to take another person's men . . . staff. And I would tell her that if I met up with her.' And on this she flounced round and went into the kitchen.

Lady Lydia starting a farm, and asking Carl to go and man it? Lady Lydia hasn't got any money. They had talked about it only yesterday. She herself had suggested how good it would be if they could engage two or three men to get the land back into shape for when Mr Gerald came home, and what had Lady Lydia said? Her income was just enough to keep the house going, pay its rates and Nancy. What money she had received from the military for housing them she had put away for Mr Gerald, because he had been given no actual pay, no money for the work he had done during the war years, which had struck her as being very odd, because even the wounded men in the Hollow got some kind of a pension. And in a way Mr Gerald had been wounded. She must get to the bottom of this. She must see Carl.

She waited until she knew that Jessie would have reached the house, then she bundled herself into her coat and woolly hat and went out.

She found Carl in the cowshed; and now, leaning towards him where he was lifting a pail of milk away from a cow, she whispered, 'Can I speak to you?'

Laughing at her, he whispered back, 'Any time, any time. But it'll cost you.' Then straightening up, he said, 'Come on into the dairy. What is it?'

She didn't answer him until he had finished pouring the milk into the cooler, and then she said, 'Auntie Jessie has just said something very odd to me. It is that you have been approached by Lady Lydia to start a farm.'

414

She watched him now take his broad hat and pull it slowly down over his face; and then he said, 'Oh dear me!'

'Is it true?'

'No, my dear, it isn't true' – he was bending down to her and whispering – 'you see, I got so mad with your . . . grandfather' – he always hesitated when naming the man's relationship to her – 'that I threatened him I would walk out. And when he pooh-poohed the idea that I could ever make a living outside this place, I thought of you and your chatter about the smallholding and what could be done there when Mr Gerald came back . . . that was before he . . . well, went into hospital. And it just came out. I said I had been approached. And you know something?' He wagged his finger at her. 'They've got enough land there and facilities to start a little farm of their own. I've thought that time and time again. A few men and a bit of money behind them and I wouldn't mind doing it.'

'It's a pity Lady Lydia hasn't got that kind of money, for then you could start. But . . . but then what would become of this place? Everyone knows it's really your farm.'

'Oh, no, no. I've kept it going. I give myself that much credit. But it isn't my farm. And as you know, I'm supposed to have a half-share in it when he goes. But I'd give that up tomorrow if . . . if I could work, if we could all work under happier conditions. You know what I mean?'

She stared at him for a moment before she nodded her head, saying, 'Yes, Carl. Yes, I know what you mean.'

He shook his head and then said softly, 'Of course, of course. I know, lass. Yes, I know. Your years here have been tough going too. You know, when I look at you I can't believe you're still only fourteen. You've got a head on your shoulders that many a one hasn't at twenty. It isn't fair.' He put his hand on her cheek now, then patted it as he added, 'And it isn't fair either, no, it isn't, that you've had no childhood, no girlhood.'

'I don't mind not having any childhood. As for girlhood, I don't feel like a girl, Carl.' She turned her head away now as she said, 'I passed some girls on the road a while back. They were chatting and talking and laughing before they came up

415

to me. Apparently they had left school; they looked fourteen, but they sounded so silly. They were like . . . well, I really hadn't anyone to compare them with, but I knew they weren't like me, or me like them. And . . . and as I passed them they all stopped and stared at me as if I was something strange.' She shrugged her shoulders. 'I suppose I am. Yes, I suppose I am.'

'Don't say that, dear, don't say that. *Now don't say that.* You're a normal, lovely-looking girl, and, with another few years on you you'll be a spanker.'

She smiled at him now, saying, 'You know what I did when they stood like stooks? I stepped past them and then turned quickly and went, "Boo! boo!" And they scattered like frightened rabbits. And you know—' Both her expression and her tone now altered: 'I should have laughed, but I couldn't. I just felt sad, like I did, you know, when I told you last year about that old man whom I'd seen standing by a stile a number of times. And . . . and when he came up to me he looked as if he was about to cry; then he said, "Hello, dear." You remember?'

'Yes. Yes, I remember.'

'You still don't know who it was?'

His tongue moved in and out of his mouth before he said, 'No. No. I never found out. And anyway, he wasn't there any more, was he?'

'No, I never saw him again.'

No. No, you wouldn't, he thought. Poor old Mr Mason, the man whose family had been torn asunder by this child's grandfather. His daughter was still in the asylum, his eldest son was God knows where, and his wife had died of a broken heart, and he was left with one son on a farm that had once been prosperous. The old man had likely wanted to see the child who could be his granddaughter: it was more likely that his son, not one of the others, would have been the first to take her mother, for his feelings for Ward Gibson had been those of real hate.

He said now, 'Is there any news of Mr Gerald coming home?'

Shaking her head, she said, 'Not this year anyway. Perhaps next, Lady Lydia says.'

'Do you know what is really wrong with him?'

'No; only that he is not wounded; he won't talk. And you know, that's very odd because he used to like to talk, as I do.' She smiled at him now. 'I always want to jabber, but I never really do until I get to the Hall.'

'And you jabber a lot there?' He was smiling widely at her.

'Oh yes. Lady Lydia seems to like me to jabber. But—' Her tone altered, as did her expression, as she said soberly, 'But I like to jabber sensibly. You know what I mean? When I once said that to Lady Lydia she laughed until the tears ran down her face, and she said, "Never stop; never stop jabbering sensibly." I . . . I like Lady Lydia,' and she immediately added emphatically, 'More than like her.' And on this she turned and walked away.

And again Carl stood thinking, Yes, the girl had to more than like someone, and someone to more than like her in return. Jessie undoubtedly loved her but she couldn't like her because she didn't really know whom she was liking; in fact, whom she was loving: to her, the child must always have been a triplet of evil.

2

‘How's the pain, love?'

‘Oh, I hardly feel it when I'm lying down. My chest's worse than any other part of me.'

‘Well, that's your own fault. You're stuck in that draughty kitchen.'

‘Don't be silly.' She slapped at his hand. ‘Draughty kitchen indeed! What about the draughty dairy. That's where I got it in the first place.' Then, drawing in a painful breath, she said, ‘It's going to be some Christmas.'

‘Never mind about Christmas. Mrs McNabb has every-thing in hand in that quarter, and Miss Jessie will see to the rest.'

‘There's another one that should be in bed. She looks utterly tired.'

‘Well,' said Carl, ‘it isn't with work so much as with worry.'

‘Do you think there's any truth in what Rob says, that he's sure he saw Pete Mason?'

‘I don't know, but I don't think so. Anyway, would he recognise him after nearly fifteen years? There'll always be rumours about him and his whereabouts. Remember, he was supposed to have been killed in the war – a good way of getting rid of him. Then, just a few months ago, that he had absconded from the Army. Anyway, from what Mike said, Rob was tight on the night he was supposed to have seen him.'

'It's a terrifying thought. I can understand Miss Jessie worrying because of Janie.'

'Oh, I couldn't see him doing anything to her . . . well, you know—' He lifted his hand expressively; then changing his tone, he said, 'Never mind them; it's you that's worrying me. Now you've got to make up your mind to stay there, not for a few days but, as Doctor Patten said, for a couple of weeks or more.' Then bending over her, he added, 'Why don't you do what he says, love, and go to one of those hospitals. They do wonders. Well, the war has given them practice. They've got fellas walking who thought it would never be possible to put their feet on the ground again. And anyway, they could rig you up with one of these corsets,' he said.

'Yes. Yes, dear, I've heard of them, and what I've heard I don't think I'll bother. Now listen to me. I'm all right. I'll . . . I'll do what I'm told.' She gasped again, saying now, 'I have no other choice. Anyway, I was managing fine on my wooden legs until this hit me.' She stabbed her chest. 'I've had bronchitis before but never as bad as this. Now get about your business, Mr McQueen, and leave me to mine, which is reading the paper. By!' She flicked the newspaper that was lying on top of the counterpane, saying, 'The way they're preparing for Christmas in some places, you'd think there had never been a war. They seem to have forgotten half the houses will have no man to play Santa Claus, or to see in the New Year. Oh yes; it'll be merry and bright, but just for some.'

'Well, you cannot undo the past. There's a new generation coming up. They'll want their fling, and those who are lucky enough to come back alive, they'll have it. But talking of generations, I've got a few in the cowshed waiting to start another one, so I'll go and see if they've arrived yet.' And with the back of his closed fist he punched her gently under the chin, then went to do the cows' bidding.

In the kitchen Mrs McNabb greeted him with, 'Look at that!' as she pointed to a tray. 'He's hardly eaten a bite; well, just a mouthful of bacon and a bit of toast. He's not taking his food, Mr Carl, at no time. And I set it out well enough.'

'Yes. Yes, of course you do. But don't you worry, he'll eat when he's hungry.'

419

'I don't know, Mr Carl: he won't get very hungry sitting about in that room most of the day. He hardly moves until night-time. D'you know' – she leant towards him – 'McNabb said he saw him leaving the cemetery again last night, and it was almost on dark.'

'Well, he often goes to the cemetery.'

'Oh aye; but not like he's been doin' lately. McNabb said he shouldn't wonder if he's found dead there one day,' to which remark Carl only nodded before going out, but he could not restrain himself from thinking: that wouldn't be a bad thing either. He might even take with him the confounded curse that seemed to be on the place, because let him face it, that village would never forget or forgive Ward Gibson, at least while he was alive. It remained so strong that even he, when forced by the weather to drive the cart through rather than skirt it, would feel, even smell the fear his master must have engendered in it.

When he entered the yard it was to see Jessie and Janie crossing swords again. Jessie was saying, 'There are plenty of things here to keep you occupied. We need all the help we can get, you know that.'

'I've told you, Auntie Jessie, I shan't be long. I just want to catch Lady Lydia before she leaves; I have Mr Gerald's Christmas present.'

'Well, see that you aren't long. I'm . . . I'm becoming tired of this running backwards and forwards . . . Something will have to be done.'

Janie had moved a couple of steps away from Jessie when she turned and said defiantly, 'Yes. Yes. Something will have to be done. It could be my staying over there altogether. And I would like that. Yes, I would. *I would*.' And on that she turned and ran from the yard, leaving Jessie looking at Carl and saying helplessly, 'What am I going to do with her?'

'Just leave her alone. She'll grow out of it.'

'Oh, Carl!' Jessie tossed her head now as if throwing off the inane reply; then she muttered, 'Grow more into it, you mean,' and flouncing about, made for the kitchen, whilst Carl drew in a gulp of the icy air, shook his head, and went back to the byres . . .

420

When Janie actually burst into the Hall, which had now taken on a semblance of its old style, with some of the smaller pieces of furniture having been brought in and set in their familiar places, she came to an abrupt halt and looked up the stairs to where Lady Lydia was about to descend. And she cried, 'Oh! I was afraid you'd be gone.'

'No; the taxi isn't due for another fifteen minutes. You're out of breath, child.'

'Well, I wanted you to have this to give to him.' She now held out the brown paper parcel. It was tied up with narrow grey-silk ribbon, and she pointed to it, saying, 'Men don't like fussy stuff, but it's better than string.'

'Oh, I'm sure he won't notice what it's tied up with. But come into the drawing-room, it's a bit warmer in there. May I ask what the present is?'

'I've knitted him a scarf. I hope he likes it. But I'm not a very good knitter. I mean, the stitches are not even, you know. Sometimes they're slack and sometimes they're tight; it's according to how I feel.' She laughed, a sound that, with her growing taller, was becoming more and more attractive, and which drew Lady Lydia into laughing with her and to put her arm around the girl's shoulder. And as she pulled her down on to the couch that was set at right angles to the fire, she wondered what she would have done these bleak years without this child. She dreaded to think how bare her life would have been.

'Are . . . are you going to ask if I may come with you next time?' The question was put very softly, and as softly Lady Lydia answered it, saying, 'Yes. Yes, I am, dear. And I'll put the question straight to him.' But even as she said this she could see the response: silence and that blank look in his eyes. Yet she would feel that he knew he was pleased that she was there, even though he might show no sign, not even the movement of a hand. Her heart was always heavy with love and pity for him, but it turned to lead in her breast whenever she sat beside him.

'Will you be back tomorrow? or are you staying longer this time?'

'Oh, I think I'll come back tomorrow. The weather is very

uncertain and, as I've told you, the hospital is some way out in the country and I wouldn't want to be snowed up there.'

Oh, no, no, she couldn't bear that. Although she loved him so dearly she could only tolerate the pain of seeing him in such a state for a few hours at a time.

And then there were the others, the poor others. Was there any God in the heavens that allowed men to go on living with only bits of their bodies and minds left?

They had said that if Gerald got even a little better they would move him, perhaps to Highgate; she would then be able to see him every week. But would he ever get better? Some of those men had been there since the first month of the war . . .

But the dear child was chattering again. 'What was that you said, dear?'

'I said, I've been working on an idea. It's about the small-holding and putting it into shape again and getting it ready for when he comes home. He'd like that, wouldn't he?'

'Oh yes. Yes, I am sure he would. But . . . but you know, we talked about this before and . . . '

Now Janie patted the hand that was resting on her knee and said with some excitement, 'But this is different. It wouldn't take a lot of money. Well, just a little, and you said you had a little that you were saving up for his return. Well, it won't do much good lying in a bank, will it?'

Lady Lydia threw her head back now and laughed; then, hugging Janie to her, she said, 'You know, my dear, one day I can see you ruling a big company or some big house. Really ruling it, and all on your own.'

'Huh! Huh! I don't see anything like that, Lady Lydia, not for me. Although' – she now pulled herself slightly away and affected a pose – 'I wouldn't mind ruling over the gardens and telling men what to do, like Carl does. Carl's very good at telling men what to do. He doesn't demand: he doesn't say, do this and do that; he always says, We. "I think *we* should do this. What do you think?" '

'Oh! Janie.' She was laughing again.

'Do you find that very funny?'

Lady Lydia coughed, almost choked, then managed to say,

'I'm more positive than ever, child, that one day you will be saying *we* would like this done, and *we* would like that done, and not only to gardeners, mind,' and straightaway rose to her feet, pulling Janie up with her. But Janie did not immediately leave go of the holding hand; she slowly looked around the room as if contemplating, then said, 'I'll never want to run a big business or do anything like that. You know what I would like to do?'

'No, my dear, I don't.'

'Well . . . really and truly—'

'Well, tell me what you would like to do, really and truly.'

'Live here for the rest of my life, with you.'

'Oh, my dear. My dear.' Lady Lydia bowed her white head, and as the tears ran down her lined cheeks Janie put her arms around her, saying, 'Oh. Oh, I didn't mean to make you cry. And . . . and I wasn't being what you call—' She searched for the word before saying, 'presuming. It is just that . . . well, I feel more at home here than I do—' Her voice breaking now, she muttered, 'I'm very sorry.'

'My dear child, you have nothing to be sorry for. My tears were really of gratitude. It's wonderful to hear you say that. But now look at me.' She stepped back, dabbing her eyes with a fine lawn handkerchief. 'Here I am about to go on a journey, and if I'm not mistaken there is the taxi man's hooter telling me he has arrived. Dear, dear! Where are my gloves? Oh, there they are. And my parcels. Come on, come on. Is my hat straight?'

Smiling now, Janie said, 'Your hat's always on straight, m'lady, and you always look lovely. Will you tell Mr Gerald that . . . that I love him and ask him, will he come back soon?'

'Yes, my dear, I'll tell him that.'

It was four hours later when Lady Lydia was ushered into the matron's room with some ceremony. And the matron, rising from her chair, held out her hand, saying, 'You must have had a very tiring and cold journey, m'lady. Isn't the weather dreadful? Do sit down.' Then turning to a nurse who was standing by the door, she said, 'Bring Lady Lydia

423

a coffee, please. No, bring two. I know I've just had one but I can always drink coffee.' She smiled widely now; then she resumed her seat and from across the desk she said, 'We're all getting ready for Christmas.' But seeing the expression on Lady Lydia's face, her own changed and she said, 'Yes, it does sound silly, doesn't it? It's ludicrous really, but, you know, a number of them do appreciate it.'

'May I ask if there's any change?'

It was the same question on every visit and the matron said, 'I'm afraid not; but it's early days. It's amazing how the change comes about in cases like that of your son. You know, I often think of the first two lines of psalm 130:

Out of the depths have I cried unto Thee, O Lord.
Lord, hear my voice,
Let Thine ears be attentive to the voice of my supplication.

Sometimes it's as if the Lord's ears are open to the prayers and pleadings and supplications because quite suddenly something happens. Ah, here's the coffee.'

Ten minutes later the matron passed Lady Lydia over to a nurse who, smiling, then led her along a corridor made up entirely, so it seemed, of a great number of doors. She had been down this way before and she knew to where it led, and she dreaded going into that room.

When the nurse opened the door a strange buzz of sounds assailed her ears. She sometimes likened it to an aviary of birds, cockatoos, mocking birds, parrots. It wasn't loud, just an overall hum, and as usual she concentrated her gaze on her son, who sat in the far corner of the room, because the faces looking at her created such a sadness it was unbearable; not the faces that were twisted up as if in pain, nor those of the disfigured or limbless, but those that smiled at her with that soft appealing look, like a child at its mother. The look always said: come and hold me. Please! come and hold me. Put your arms about me.

Sometimes hands would go out to her and it would take all her will-power not to jump aside. Sometimes she would

424

take hold of one and pat it, and sometimes the nurse would have to loosen its grip on her.

Then she was with her son. He was sitting in a comfortable chair, a small table to the side of him. But this, she had noticed the first time she had come into this room, was fastened to the floor, as were all the other pieces of furniture.

'Hello, darling.' She took the limp hand from the knee. 'How are you feeling?' Oh, if she could only think of something else to say. But what?

'I've brought you some presents.' She pointed to the table, but there was no response whatever from him.

She sat for some minutes stroking his limp hand while gazing into his thin blank countenance. His eyes seemed to have sunken deeper into his head each time she came. After a while she allowed her eyes to wander around the room. Nurses were to be seen here and there. They all seemed very cheery. One was sitting at a table showing a patient how to make paper chains, and the man was laughing as his fingers fumbled under her guidance.

And this is where her beloved son would have to spend the remainder of his life. It was unbearable, unbearable. She suddenly reached out to the table and, picking up Janie's present, she put it on his knee, saying, 'Guess who this is from? She's knitted it for you.' And as if she had received an answer to this she undid the ribbon, then unfolded the paper and took out the blue- and white-ribbed scarf with its tasselled edge. And now, putting it across his hands, she said, 'It feels lovely and soft. You must wear it when you walk in the garden. She must have spent a long time over it because she's no knitter. But I must tell you she's full of ideas about getting the smallholding ready for your coming home. Anyway, she wants to come with me on my next visit . . . '

When his hand lifted suddenly and thrust her aside she could not help but cry out. But it did not drown the sound that came out of his wide-open mouth, like a wail from some injured animal, as it emitted one long drawn-out word: 'Noo . . . o! Noo . . . o!'

Immediately two nurses appeared at his side, trying to

restrain him. But when suddenly his head flopped and he coughed so much that she imagined he was going to choke, all the while clutching at his throat, she stood aside speechless. Then she watched the nurses lead him from the room, and as she went to follow she stepped on the scarf and the parcel she had brought, and, stooping, she grabbed them up and together with her handbag she clutched them to her before running from the room. When she reached his room the nurse said, 'He'll be all right. He'll be all right. Would you like to go to the waiting-room?' and as if following some invisible signal another nurse appeared and, taking her arm, led her along the corridor and into a small, cosily furnished room. 'Just rest there awhile,' she said. 'Matron is on her rounds with the doctor. Would you like a drink?'

Lady Lydia looked at her but did not speak, and the nurse said, 'A cup of tea, eh? I'll get that for you. It always helps.' And on this she went out.

She did not know how long she had sat there: she thought it was for hours, but it was only twenty minutes later when the matron and doctor entered the room and they were both smiling. And the doctor said immediately, 'Well this is good news. A definite breakthrough. How did it happen?'

'How . . . how did what happen?'

'I mean, did you say something to him that caused him to react? or do something that all our gadgets have failed to do?'

She thought back for a moment, then said, 'No; nothing startling. I just made small talk as usual, and I was talking about a present a young friend of his had sent him. She had knitted him a scarf and' – she paused – 'it was just as I was saying she wanted to come and see him and would he like that, that he . . . well, a change came over him. He yelled something that was like, "No! No!" '

'It was indeed, no, no.'

'But then he seemed to choke. You . . . you said he wasn't gassed, but . . . but it looked as if . . . '

'He wasn't gassed, Lady Lydia. We've talked about it before: he went through a very bad time, being so long on duty on the ambulance trains and then with the sudden huge influx of gas victims, and he saw their suffering . . . well, that

426

was the breaking point, I'm sure. And deep inside himself he is still suffering with them. Although he made a great effort to go into oblivion, and has succeeded for some time, nevertheless the suffering in his mind is still there. But—' And with a small toss of his partly bald head the doctor added, 'It is the best news I've heard today. His has been a stubborn case, you know, and it really looked as if it were set in. You can go home with a lighter heart, today, Lady Lydia, for from now on we know that he is capable of thinking rationally. But' – he now lifted a warning finger – 'everything must go slowly; don't expect miracles straightaway. And who knows, in time you will have him home.'

Lady Lydia looked up at the matron. She was smiling at her and she could hear her saying:

'Out of the depths have I cried unto Thee, O Lord.
Lord, hear my voice,
Let Thine ears be attentive to the voice of my supplication.'

He had been attentive to her crying.

When she looked back into the smiling face and murmured something like, 'Voice of my supplication' before bursting into tears, the doctor said, 'That's it. There's no easing of tension like a good cry, especially over good news. You can go home happy now.'

Quickly she dried her tears. His talk was just patter. He was talking as if she could walk out of here now with her son when he had previously said it would be a long job. But she should be grateful. Oh, she was. But what she wanted now was to be home and tell Janie. Yes, tell Janie, but not that he didn't want to see her, and that the very thought of the sight of her had brought him out of the depths. Oh no, not that.

427

3

It was about seven o'clock in the morning of the 2nd of January 1919, that a farm worker, taking a short cut across the cemetery, almost tripped over a prone figure lying across a grave. His flashlight showed that the man was lying with his blood-soaked head on the nine-inch ornate rim of marble that bordered the grave.

The farm-hand rushed to the vicarage and raised Parson George Dixon, successor to Parson Tracey, but of a different calibre, from his bed.

There was so much blood on the victim's face that neither the parson nor the farm worker could recognise him: so therefore, the parson had sent post-haste for the police. He had no doubt but that the man was dead and had lain outside in the bitter night for some long time, as the blackened and congealed blood showed.

It was broad daylight when the police arrived; just the one constable at first, but he immediately sent for his superior, who came accompanied by another policeman, by which time Doctor Patten had arrived on the scene. And there was no doubt from the first moment Philip Patten saw the figure and how it was dressed that he knew who the victim was, if the word victim could be put to it. This would become evident, he told himself, only when he examined the body, which he did some time later, in the church hall, when his assumption was confirmed. It was later still when the police doctor, accompanied by an inspector, arrived,

428

although his findings were not as quickly given: Philip had to wait until the man had examined the stonework surrounding the grave, when he commented, 'He is a heavily built man, and he must have slipped and come in contact with that.' He pointed down to the marble surround. 'It certainly could have done the damage, but he might have survived if someone had been with him. He must have lain all night for he's as stiff as a ramrod.'

'You say he's a well-known farmer?'

'Yes; Ward Gibson. Farm's just a mile or so away,' Philip said.

'Likely as drunk as a noodle,' was another cursory conclusion.

'He must have been visiting his wife's grave.'

'Oh? . . . Oh, yes. Gibson. Very odd situation. Yes. What do you think?' But Philip added nothing further, and the man seemed content to return to his surmising. 'Well, his fall certainly did some damage to his skull. And there's no evidence of any other marks on his body that could indicate he might have been attacked. Apparently the search of the surrounding area shows no sign of a struggle. The footprints are all precise and still imprinted with a covering of frost.' He nodded down to the grass around his feet. 'If there had been any sign of a skirmish the ground would have been churned in some way. Well now, I suppose his people will have to be told.'

'They've already been sent for.'

As they walked back towards the church the police doctor said, conversationally, 'You've been here some time then? You took over from old Wheatley?'

'Yes, that's so.'

'By! he was a walking hogshead, that one.' The man laughed. 'I met him, you know, a couple of times. He really could carry some.'

'Yes,' Philip Patten agreed with the man, 'he could carry some.'

Just before they entered the church hall the man turned round and surveyed the cemetery to his right and the drive to the church on his left. He could see the lych-gate and part of the street beyond, and he remarked, 'It's got a bit of a name, this village, hasn't it? if anything can be made

429

of the old wives' tales, and they can't all be wrong.' But receiving no comment he said caustically, 'This business should have turned out to be a murder, for then it would have fitted into the picture, eh?'

And now Philip did speak, and there was bitterness in his voice that was not lost on the police doctor as he said, 'Yes, yes, it would have fitted into the picture, indeed it would.'

Carl and three of the men had come from the farm to take the body home. Jessie had come with them. It was her business to identify the dead man. And it was after they had gone and there was only the vicar and Philip left that the vicar said to him, 'Can you spare a few minutes, Doctor?'

'Yes. Yes, of course,' said Philip.

'It . . . it's something that no-one has commented on. But I wonder what you think, because truthfully I don't know what to make of it. If you'll come back to the cemetery I'll explain.'

They were again standing by the grave, and, pointing to the headstone, the vicar said, 'Do you see anything peculiar there?'

Philip looked at the writing on the stone, and then he said, 'It says at the top quite plainly, "Remember me".'

'Yes. Yes,' put in the vicar quickly now. 'It is quite plain. But can you make out the rest of the inscription?'

Philip bent forward now and peered at the moss-covered stone, and what he read was

Remember me.
Agatha Hamilton,
aged 49 years,
left this cruel world
and took her pains to the Lord on
May 2nd, 1872.
R.I.P.

'Well?'

Philip repeated, 'Well, all that strikes me is that "Remember me" is very clear to read whereas the rest is not.' He now leant forward again and looked at the two words heading the stone, and he said, 'It looks as if these have been roughly scraped clean, or at least just the surface. A bit of emery paper or such could have done it. But then' – he turned to the vicar – 'every now and again you have the headstones cleaned up.'

'Not often in this old part; it must be two years ago since any cleaning was done here. Anyway, you know yourself, Doctor, he was a most hated man for many miles around. He had brought tragedy not only on his own house but . . . but on others. And this village, I have found to my dismay, is very prone to superstition, and somebody's just got to recognise that these two words have been made clear and the rumours will start again.' He looked down at the old grave, at the frozen weeds, and pulling at one he managed to loosen some earth about it. Then taking a handkerchief out of his pocket, he put it around his fingers and scooped up some of the soil and rubbed it quickly over the two words. And the thought that crossed Philip's mind as he watched was, If this man had been vicar of this village the day Ward Gibson had come to him and asked to have the banns of marriage read, half the events that had happened since would not have come about. Oh, there would always have been Daisy Mason, but he was sure her actions would have been condemned in many more quarters and the knowledge that much of the village wasn't with her would surely have curtailed her venom. And now this kindly man shook out his handkerchief, rolled it into a ball and put it into his pocket, and, turning to him, said, 'It may be just a coincidence, but when I earlier read the name Hamilton on this stone, I remembered it had been recalled to my mind some time earlier, and I wondered why; and I'm of such a nature, Doctor, that I always have to follow things to their source, if you know what I mean. So I have just looked up the name in the church register, and there I find that Mrs Mason's maiden name was Hamilton.'

'No! Never!'

'But we'll let it rest there, eh? Shall we, Doctor?'

Philip twice nodded his head slowly as his mind pictured two fiercely strong hands banging Ward Gibson's head against that stone. And whoever had done it, he couldn't have been alone, for as had already been noted, there was no sign

431

of a struggle. He must have been knocked insensible before being carried to the grave. And whoever had done it had planned it.

Seth Mason was the only one left of the Masons, and he was a weakling, at least he would be on his own. And Pete was dead ... Or was he? Every now and again there had been a rumour of his returning home and being hidden, and this was since the War Office had written him off as 'missing, believed dead'. And that was in France. If he had absconded, how on earth could he have got here? But hate, like faith, could perform miracles. And it wasn't unknown that men could feign loss of memory and be shipped over with a crowd of wounded, only to disappear.

It was all very strange and rather terrible. Anyway, Ward was dead, and all that was left of his family was Miss Jessie and the girl. He did not know really how Miss Jessie would feel about her father's going, but he knew that the child would be released from his tyranny and could not help but be glad.

As the two men walked back to the church, the vicar said, 'I don't often see you at the services.'

Philip turned to him, a wry smile on his face as he said, 'I don't often have much time. As you know, it's a busy job. But I'll try to squeeze a visit in now and then ... in the future.'

'Do that. Do that. I'd be pleased to see you.'

They parted at the church door, knowing that they understood each other.

4

It was said in the village that the day Ward Gibson was buried should be celebrated with another Victory Tea; for God, having seen fit to strike him down in the cemetery, was pointing out his final destination.

There was relief, too, among the families that had been for him, although perhaps with the exception of Fred Newberry. His comment was that Ward had been a fool to himself from the beginning in letting his fancy stray to Newcastle.

It had been said that on the farm, too, there was permeating a feeling of relief. It was as if the dark oppressive shadow that had been hanging over all their lives had been swept away. Never more so was this feeling evident as Carl and Jessie sat by Patsy's bed discussing the future.

The will had been read. It had not been altered from the time Ward had struck the bargain with Carl. That Carl was now the legal owner of half this house and its prosperous business seemed at the moment more unreal to him than when it had been just a promise that might never be kept. It certainly wouldn't have surprised him if Ward had changed the will after his outburst on that particular day at the barn.

What was being heatedly discussed now concerned Jessie and where she should reside in the future. She was saying, 'We are quite comfortable where we are. Anyway, Patsy, I ask you, just think what it would mean if you went back there. You'd need someone with you all the time, you know you would. Here, there's Mrs McNabb at hand and me, and

433

you're within call of Carl from the yard, whereas . . . '

Patsy turned her face away on the pillow, at the same time raising her hand to stop Jessie's flow, and what she said was, 'This is your rightful place. Even the two cottages put together make no more than a box. And then there's Janie, she . . . '

'Yes, there's Janie. And let me tell you, if I was dying to come back in here tomorrow, I couldn't do so, and because of her, for she absolutely refuses even to talk of the possibility of our living in this house. Do you know, she's been in it only once since the time I moved us to the cottage, and you know when that was. But—' and now she drew in a long breath and shook her head as she said, 'believe it or not, she has given me an ultimatum: if you and Carl were to come back to the cottage, she would go and stay at the Hall, and nothing would stop her. I couldn't. It seems impossible to admit it, but she is past me, I cannot believe I'm just dealing with a fourteen-year-old girl. Anyway, she's just waiting for an excuse to be able to stay over there. She's obsessed with that place and those two. Thank God that madman isn't there.'

For the first time Carl spoke, and now harshly, saying, 'Oh . . . oh, no, he's not that. Well, what I mean is, it's something like shellshock he suffers from. God help him.'

'Shellshock!' Jessie was indignant. 'He was never in the war really; he was a conscientious objector.'

Carl dared to say, 'Don't be silly. From what we hear some of them had the rottenest jobs imaginable. They were in the thick of it out there, stretcher-bearing and such.'

Patsy turned her head and was smiling at them as she said, 'That's it, have a row. It'll make a good start.' Then looking pointedly at Jessie, she said, 'You know, you should be grateful that she found something to hold her interest. What life had she here as a child? It really broke my heart to see her locked up in that cottage every time you came out. And in this house it was the same; in fact, worse, for she only saw the bedroom.'

Jessie looked down at her fingers where they were plucking imaginary threads from her skirt, and she muttered, 'I know, I know, but what else could I do? Have her run in here and

434

bump into Father? It was bad enough when they crossed paths outside.' She did not add, 'And you're lying where you are because of one such encounter.'

But Patsy did not pursue this trend in their discussion, except to look at Carl and say, 'You know that piece of fancy talk you often come out with, which means let things be, leave them as they are? Well, that's what you want to do now.'

Carl laughed and looked at Jessie and said, 'Status quo?' And when Jessie, with raised eyebrows, nodded and smiled at him, he knew that she had as little understanding of the term as Patsy. Her reading likely didn't touch on the daily papers, whereas his own got no further these days. And so he said briskly, 'Well! to business. I'll leave you two to get on with your jabbering but I must get back to work. Somebody must do it.' He pulled a face, turning from one to the other, and then went out.

It would appear that Janie had been waiting for him to come out of the house, for she was there by the door, requesting straightaway: 'Come into the tack-room a minute, will you, Carl?'

In the room and with the door closed, she immediately excused her request: 'I don't want Auntie Jessie to see me talking to you,' she said. 'She'll want to know what I'm saying, as always,' and she wrinkled her nose, then astounded him: 'How much do you pay the farm-hands?' she asked.

'How much do I pay the farm-hands? Oh well, it varies. They get good money now, you know, since the war.' He pushed out his chest in explanation. 'We're the feeders of the nation, you know. So we're being recognised at last. Well now, you want to know what they're paid. Mike and McNabb get thirty-five shillings a week each. Rob gets thirty-three. Then of course any extra male help in the summer in the fields is paid by the hour.'

'Do women helpers in the summer get the same?'

'Oh no.' The shake of his head was emphatic. 'Women never get paid as much as men, because they don't do the heavy work.'

She thought for a moment, then said, 'In the summer they do, lifting the stooks and all that, and they rake with the men.'

He tapped her cheek gently, saying, 'Now we're not going into politics. Why d'you want to know all this?'

'Oh.' She shrugged her shoulders, but she didn't answer his question: what she said was, 'I didn't think they got all that. How about if they slept in; I mean, had a place to stay and got their food; how about it then?'

'Oh then, well, a pound a week or perhaps a little more, a little less, according to their experience.'

'As low as ten shillings?'

'Oh no, you couldn't offer a man ten shillings a week, even with bed and board. Anyway, what's all this about?'

'Well, I can tell you. I was thinking about . . . well, I put it to Lady Lydia about employing someone, or perhaps two, to clear the ground and get some of it set for a crop or such. I'm going to pick all the fruit this year . . . I might need a little help. We'll bottle it, and it could be sold like they used to do when Mr Gerald was at home. But during the war and the soldiers tramping over everything, and then those village children coming in and scrumping, there wasn't much left. But it will be different this year, because now they can't get in since the Army mended the fences and the walls. Well, they went through them, didn't they, with their trucks? So that part's all right; it's just clearing the ground and getting it into shape again.'

He now placed his hands on her shoulders and looked into her face as he said, 'You're taking something on, aren't you? And, you know, you should still be at school?'

'Oh, Carl, I'm at school every morning. History, geography, arithmetic, English. She . . . she keeps me on such childish things, Carl. If she knew of the books that I look at in the Hall library, she'd have a fit.'

He laughed now as he asked, 'What kind of books?'

'Oh, all kinds, about gods and goddesses. And then there's stories, marvellous stories. You could spend days reading the stories. But I hardly ever get one finished, because I can't stay long enough.' She now turned from him and walking towards a saddle hanging on the wall, she stroked the leather for a moment as she said, 'I'll never live in that house across the yard, Carl. Although he's gone I feel he's still there. You

436

know what I'd do with it?' She swung round to him. 'Set fire to it and make it into a sort of funeral pyre like they used to do in Egypt and put it on his grave.'

'*Oh. Oh, Janie,* you shouldn't think things like that. Oh, my dear.'

'I do think things like that, Carl. I hated him when he was alive and I can't stop hating him now because he's dead. And another thing, whichever one was my father he couldn't have been as bad as he was, not so cruel, so cold. He hated me because of what those men did to my mother and I was the result. But they only did that to my mother because he'd had a woman put in an asylum, the sister of one of them.'

'*Shh! Shh!*' He had her by the shoulders again. 'You shouldn't think about it. You shouldn't talk about it. And anyway, she was put in the asylum because she had done very wrong things to your grandfather. She had, in a way, killed your grandmother. Now there's two ways of looking at this matter. You should try to see the reason for your grandfather's actions.'

'I . . . I experienced his reactions, Carl. I . . . I knew there was something wrong with me right back when I was a child and had to be locked in the cottage. And . . . and I wanted to be loved and' – she now bit on her lip – 'Auntie Jessie's love was a different kind. I can't explain it. She was always saying she loved me then doing hard things.'

'She had her reasons, too, dear; she was trying to protect you.'

'Oh well' – she now flung her arms wide – 'it doesn't matter any more, well not much. I'm me, and I've known I'm me for a long time. I'm . . . I'm different from others. I know I am. Yet—' Her expression now changed to one of slight pleasurable surprise as she said, 'One of the girls from the village spoke to me the other day. Do you remember me telling you about the ones I went boo! to? Well, she was the tallest one. She was by herself on the road when she half stopped and spoke to me.'

'What did she say?'

'She said, "Hello", and I was so surprised that I didn't answer. And then she said, "Isn't it cold?" And I said, yes, it was. And then she said, "Goodbye", and I said, "Goodbye".'

'When was this?' His voice was low now.

'Oh, the day before yesterday.'

Well, well! Could it be with the passing of the thorn in the villagers' flesh that their attitude would change towards the child and she would be finally accepted? But would she want to be accepted? Did they but know it, they were dealing with someone as strong-willed as ever her grandfather had been; only there would be no vindictiveness in her strength.

She was saying now, 'If . . . if Lady Lydia decides to take on a man, would you . . . on the quiet, come and check him over for her? I mean, to tell us that he was capable of hard work and was of good character?'

He now put his two fingers to his forehead and flicked his hair back, saying, 'At your service, ma'am. Any time, at your service, with no charge.'

As she laughingly pushed at him so he put his arms around her and held her tightly for a moment; and he, laughing too, said, 'Any time you want help, my dear, you come to me, and it won't cost you a penny.' And now they were pushing at each other, their laughters mingled. And Mike, passing by in the yard outside heard the laughter and, as he remarked to the others, he had never heard such a gay sound in this yard since he first came into it.

438

5

〜

'We've made seventy-four pounds out of the fruit and jams this year, and there's still a month to go to Christmas.'

'Yes, my dear.' Lady Lydia nodded at Janie. 'But that's only because Carl has been so kind as to loan us his transport and a driver. And we can't expect to take advantage of him again at Christmas and . . . '

'It isn't taking advantage, and he likes helping. It takes his mind off . . . well, Patsy's going. He's still mourning her, I think, and it's now over seven months. Anyway, he said we've just got to ask him. And so with the money that you've got, you could take this man on. It would be a start.'

'It would mean buying extra food, my dear, and men eat a lot. And then he'd have to have a wage, and I read that some of them are demanding two pounds a week.'

'I think this one would be glad to take anything. And anyway, as Carl once told me, it comes down by practically half if they have bed and board.'

'But where's the bed, my dear? Those rooms above the stables have never been used for years. They are dank and . . . '

'If a man has been a soldier he's used to sleeping on anything, I should say. In any case, we could soon fix that up; in fact, he would fix it up himself, I think. And this one's young and strong-looking, not like some of the older ones that come begging. But his shoes are in holes. They must be because one sole is loose. I noticed that.'

Lady Lydia sighed as she said, 'What don't you notice, my dear? But there is another thing: I don't think I would be able to cope with labour; I mean, giving orders and seeing that they do their work. And, you know, I'm away a day or more in every week now that Gerald is closer to home.'

'Well, I'm not afraid of giving orders.'

Lady Lydia chuckled as she said, 'No, you certainly are not. But you are still a very young girl for all your height and all your' – now she wagged her finger at the tall girl standing at her knee – 'for all your height and for all your talk you are still a young girl. And that's how men would see you.'

'Not for long they wouldn't.'

Lady Lydia's chuckle became louder as she said, 'You're an awful child, you know.'

'I know I am. But, Lady Lydia, I don't feel a child. I can't remember ever feeling a child.'

The smile went from the older woman's face and her voice was soft as she said, 'That is a great pity.'

'No, it isn't, because I'm able to see things that so-called girls don't. I mean . . . well, I'm not silly.'

'No' – there was a chuckle again – 'you're far from that. Well now, to get back to the business that I don't want to take on. I think we had better take advantage of Carl once more and ask him to come and vet this applicant of yours, because he's not mine.'

'Well, you'll have to pay him.'

'Yes, I'll have to pay him, but you will have to oversee his labour. You say you have stopped your lessons in the mornings?'

'Oh yes, some time back. Well, ever since Patsy went, because Auntie Jessie is taken up with re-doing the house inside.'

'But she still lives in the cottage? I mean, you both live in the cottage?'

'I told you, didn't I? I would never live in that house. She might. Oh, yes' – she nodded now – 'she might sometime.'

'Well, away with you! and ask Mr Carl if he can spare the time to come and see me; then, if he finds that the man is suitable, you will have to take him and show him where he's

440

supposed to sleep, and that will likely turn him away.'

'Not by the look of him, it won't.' She bent slightly forward now and placed a light kiss on Lady Lydia's cheek, whispering as she did so, 'I love you.' Then, as any young girl might, so she acted and ran from the room, with Lady Lydia sitting shaking her head as she wondered, for the hundredth time, what she would have done without her. And yet, she thought, if it hadn't been for Janie, Gerald would have come back with her two months ago. During that visit, while she sat talking to him, she had happened to say that Janie now practically lived in the house, except that she didn't sleep there, and that her bright personality lit up the whole place.

For some weeks up to then he had been talking to her slowly and sensibly. But on that day, as they were sitting in the garden, he had one of his choking fits. It wasn't one that would need attention, but it was a signal that he was distressed. And when later he had calmed down he had said to her, 'If . . . if I ever come back, it . . . it won't be to the house. I . . . I don't want to see anyone.' He had then brought his face close to hers to say slowly but somewhat aggressively, 'Do . . . you . . . understand, Mama? No one! When . . . when I come back it will be to the cottage . . . the woodman's cottage . . . alone, or else . . . I don't come . . . at all.'

So vehement were his words that they were still imprinted on her mind.

When, later, she had spoken to the doctor about him, he had said she could take him home at any time. He might still be withdrawn and not want company, but it would be better if he had an occupation of some kind. And yes, there was no reason why he should stay any longer, unless he wanted to. He wouldn't press him either to go or to stay. And then he had smiled as he said, 'You could say he is one of our successful cases. Would there were more like him.'

But the very thought of putting Janie out of her life was unbearable to her, as was the thought of her son existing in the woodman's cottage that was again entangled in the undergrowth.

Dear, dear! She felt old and tired. She would be seventy next year, and what had she done with her life? Her marriage of convenience in order to have a child; and what a child! one who had been driven out of his mind because of his sense of moral right.

The house seemed dead. Yet since her father's death she had worked on it daily, returning it to something like its former state and even better: replacing curtains and covers, moving furniture around, even getting rid of some, such as the bed in her father's room and the one in the room which she had once shared with Angela. She hadn't replaced either bed. Carl slept in one of the two spare bedrooms. She herself still slept in the cottage; and that simply because of Janie's stubbornness.

At the moment the kitchen was empty, for Mrs McNabb left with the men at five o'clock, at least in the winter. However, one or other of the men would return at half-past six to help with the last of the chores. But now it was six o'clock and there was nobody here in the house, or in the cottage, or on the farm. Carl had gone across to the Hall to look over a man her ladyship was about to engage, a man to do the clearing, so went Janie's garbled story.

Jessie walked into the hall, at the moment lit by the hanging gas lamp, then made her way along the corridor to the room that had once been her father's study, then later Patsy's and Carl's bedroom, but which was now a small and comfortable sitting-room. The fire was low in the grate but she did not immediately tend to it. She stood with her hands on the mantelpiece and gazed at her reflection in the mirror. It was long, white and drawn. She was thirty-three years old and she told herself that if she were to meet a woman who looked like her reflection, she would say she was forty at least. She had never been beautiful. Carl had once promised her beauty when she grew up, but that was only through kindness. All the beauty had gone to Angela, only to be marred, broken and wasted. Her life, too, had been wasted.

When there was no hope of her ever having Carl, she had grabbed at the child who had been born of cruelty as something on whom to shower her love and to receive love in return. But it hadn't happened like that. The measures she had had to take to confine the child had killed the

442

return of love that she might have had from her. And now she had lost her. Oh, she had lost her a long time ago: to that man first, and then his mother, and now to the house itself ... And what about Carl? It looked as if it was going to be the repeat of her father's story, for he had hugged his mourning to himself as if all the while embracing his lost love. And Carl seemed to be following the same route, for he never spoke of Patsy. He was civil and kind to her, but so were the paid hands.

She had a terrifying thought of him going into Newcastle and seeing a poster of a dancer on a billboard, as her father was said to have done, and falling madly in love with the girl it represented, maniacally in love with her, just as her father's loving had not been sane. Yes, the same thing could happen to Carl, for twice during the last three weeks he had been into Newcastle and never mentioned the errand he had been on.

If he were to take another wife she would go mad. Yes, she would, she would go mad. She nodded into the mirror. She would go back into that cottage and lock herself in and she would go the same way as Angela had.

The gas mantle on the bracket to the right of her went plop, plop, plop, and the glass shade seemed to shiver, as did her reflection in the mirror, only this was shaking its head and its mouth was open, denying her last thoughts, saying, No! No! What was she thinking?

When the tears spurted from her eyes she looked upwards for a moment and whispered aloud, 'O Lord, I am so lost, so lonely. Whatever happens, don't let me do anything silly, please.' She could no longer see her reflection in the mirror and her throat was full; and she was about to turn away when she heard footsteps coming along the corridor, and almost in a panic now she dropped on to her knees, grabbed the tongs up from the hearth and began to take lumps of coal from the brass helmet bucket at the end of the fender. And when the door opened she did not turn around as Carl said, 'Oh! There you are. I've just taken Janie to the cottage. She'll make a farmer one of these days. Anyway, the fella seems all right and he was more than willing to take on the job for a

443

pound a week and his grub. He didn't turn a hair when he saw the condition of those rooms above the stables, even seeming to like what he saw and said that he would soon have one shipshape. And he kept thanking me, and I told him it wasn't me he should thank but the young lady.'

He stopped now and watched Jessie plying the bellows until she had kindled a flame among the coals again. And when she still didn't speak or turn round, he bent over her, saying, 'What's the matter? Are you all right?'

He could just make out the mumbling, 'I'm all right.' But when she pulled herself up from the hearth and did not turn towards him, he took her arm and pulled her gently round to face him. And he stood staring at her bent head, her face awash with tears and it was some seconds before he said gently, 'What is it, Jessie?'

She now pulled herself away from his hold and, grabbing at the lawn waist-apron she was wearing over her woollen dress, she rubbed her face vigorously with it, but still she didn't speak.

Again he took hold of her, both shoulders this time, and made her face him; and when, looking up at him, she mumbled, 'I'm sorry. I . . . I can't help it. I . . . I just felt so lost, the house, everything. Nobody here. Lonely. I . . . I seemed to have been born to be lonely. I . . . I have lost Janie and . . . ' She couldn't bring herself to lie and say, 'Patsy, too,' because she had known for a long time that Patsy was nearing her end, and although she had grown fond of her over the years, she could not help but think and hope what her going would mean: she would have Carl once more. He . . . he would be bound to turn to her, if only for sympathy. But he hadn't, he didn't need her sympathy. And now she blurted out, 'You . . . you hardly ever speak . . . you . . . you don't know I'm alive.'

'Oh, Jessie, Jessie.' He brought one hand now and cupped her wet cheek and his voice was thick and low in his throat as he said, 'I know you're alive, dear. I know you're alive, only too well. But . . . but it's early days . . . I mean . . . well, you know I cared deeply for Patsy and . . . and I have missed her. But I've known of late you can't live with the

444

dead for ever. And she . . . she wouldn't want that, she told me she didn't. The last thing she said to me was' – his own voice was throaty now – ' "Be happy and don't be lonely. No . . . nobody should live alone," she said.' He did not add, 'She knew how you felt for me and always had done,' because he had immediately reacted by saying, 'Never ever! I'll never put anyone in your place.' And she had smiled at him and said that her mother had a saying: the heart has a number of rooms.

He went on now, saying, 'It's seven months. I . . . I would have made it easier for myself if I had been able to talk about her to you, but somehow I . . . I couldn't make an opening. D'you know what? Twice lately I've been into Newcastle and got blind drunk, but it didn't help.'

The tears were still running down her cheeks but more slowly now, and he took out a handkerchief, and as he wiped her face he said, 'We'll take it from here, eh, Jessie?' to which she answered, 'Yes, Carl.' Then the meaning of his words and the tender look in his eyes as he had said them acted like the bursting of a dam.

And now her whole body was shaking and her sobbing was audible and he was holding her to him, and it was as if he was back in that bedroom all those years ago and asking if he could hold her. In some strange way she had belonged to him from then on. Even the beautiful Angela couldn't displace her in his affection, although she was never convinced of this. But then there came Patsy. Dear, dear Patsy. But now Patsy was no more, and he was holding that woman that had been the child, and he knew that he must go on holding her, for she had indeed been his from the day she was born.

6

⁓

Lady Lydia looked at the tall young girl standing before her. She was wearing a long, mole-coloured velour coat, with a fur collar. A green velour hat completed the outfit, the whole seeming to complement the face and the two deep brown eyes set in wide sockets and outlined by curved eyebrows. The nose was small in contrast to the wide mouth, and the hair framing the whole and covering the ears held a deeper tinge than the eyes, and it was drawn back and lay in a bun under the rim of the hat. The face had no claim to beauty nor could it be called pretty, but it was arresting. The eyes alone would hold the onlooker, as would the rest of her: the way she stood, the pose of her head, the chin tilted forward, created a picture that would draw the eye and hold it, for the whole expressed a vivid personality.

'Oh, my dear, you look lovely. How did it go?'

'Fine. Grand. They looked happy.' She nodded now. 'Yes, they both looked happy. And Auntie Jessie . . . well' – Janie gave a small laugh – 'she looked so young. I've never seen her look like that before. And Carl looked . . . oh, so handsome. I went with them to the station. McNabb drove us. He and Mrs McNabb are going to look after the place for the week.'

'And they're going to Devon for their honeymoon?'

'Yes; and it will be the first time in their lives that either of them has been more than a few miles from the farm. And . . . and the place will be so different when they come back . . . I mean . . . well, happier. But,' she added now with a

446

straight face, 'I'm still not going to live in the house with them. I've told them I can manage by myself in the cottage. Anyway' – her smile returned – 'I'm not often there, am I? Auntie Jessie says that by being so stubborn I'm keeping the McNabbs and Rob and his family from good housing. Well, I said there was a solution, I could come and stay here, couldn't I?' Her smile was wide again.

'But what did your aunt say to that?'

'Well, up till now, you know, it's been because I'm all she's got. And that is a silly saying, isn't it? because nobody belongs to anyone, not really.'

'Oh, my dear.' The older woman slapped at her now, saying, 'You're far too young to think things like that. But you do think she might change her mind now that she is married?'

'Yes. Yes, I think she might, because she will have someone else, someone she's always wanted. I think she has been in love with him all her life. Apparently he held her when she was born and so she claimed him, as I did. I used to follow him around. He became, in a way, my father, until I met up with . . . the nice man.' The smile sliding slowly from her face now, she said, 'How did you find him yesterday?'

'Oh, really very well. He's . . . he's talking much more now, in an ordinary way.'

'Then why can't he come home?'

'I've . . . I've told you, my dear, it's . . . he can't stand being in the company of people.'

'But he's with lots of people in the hospital.'

'Yes. Yes, you're right, but they're different. They don't bother him. They . . . well, I suppose they don't want to talk to him or him to talk to them. The orderlies, I suppose, don't count. He's become used to them.'

Janie now pulled off her hat and threw it on the chair, and with definite impatience said, 'Well, is he going to spend the rest of his life there?'

'No. No, dear, I don't think so. But look—' Lady Lydia smiled now, saying, 'I know what you're going to do next. You're going to throw your coat on top of that lovely hat, aren't you? Now take them both and put them in the hall closet, and then tell Nancy she may brew the tea.'

With the coat over her arm and the hat on top of it, Janie turned once more to Lady Lydia, saying, 'Have Arthur and Billy finished that patch?' to which the very quick reply was: 'Oh no, dear. They've been in the loft lying on their beds; they can't work unless you're standing over them with a whip.'

At this, Janie, tossing her head, walked quickly from the room, followed by her ladyship's laughter. Within a few minutes she was back and picked up the conversation as if it had never been interrupted by saying, 'That could well be in Billy's case; Arthur would be willing to work all night if you let him. He said he knew Billy would, too, for Billy had been in the Army with him. But Billy is not the same as himself, and now that there are dozens of men on the roads begging for work, I'm going to tell him he'd better watch out.'

'Oh! my dear; he does a good day's work.'

'He doesn't, Lady Lydia. You know he doesn't. He gives us what he calls our pound's worth. He forgets about his bed and board, and there's many on the road, in fact, many have knocked on the door, who would gladly do what he's doing for good meals and a place to sleep. He thinks he's still scrounging in the Army. And I can tell you this, Arthur's disappointed in him, too. Anyway,' her voice changed, 'I shouldn't be a bit surprised if he ups and goes one of these days. I hope he does.'

Lady Lydia looked at the slim figure of the girl who already had a woman inside her, and she said to herself, it shouldn't be. It shouldn't be. And looking back she thought that at her age, all she would have thought of was what dress she should wear for the coming ball; and would John Cook Mortimer be there? Or Jim Harding or . . . ? 'What was that you said, dear?'

'What I said, Lady Lydia, was, if things improve the way they've done this year and we can send vegetables to the market as well as the fruit, then we'll need a horse and cart, just a small one.'

Lady Lydia closed her eyes as she said, 'My dear, I've dipped into the funds so much.'

'You won't need to dip into the funds any more, Lady Lydia. What we make next year, even without the vegetables, now that we've got the orchard cleared and the vinery and the hothouses all going, there'll be more than enough profit to buy a horse and cart. Carl would pick an old one out that had still a lot of work left in it. You can get carts at any of the sales; and if you're in a position to buy at any time, there'll always be a cheap one. It would more than pay for itself, and quickly. I'm sure it would.'

Lady Lydia stared at the girl sitting by her side. Was she only sixteen? In her day, a girl of sixteen . . . What was she thinking? The girls of her day were long, long past. They had passed before the war; nowadays they were a new generation. They were different beings. She had encountered them of late on trains and buses. They were flamboyant; their youth had age to it. And this girl here . . . well, she had never known youth, not with her upbringing. And then there was the questionable mixture inside her. Yes, yes, that mixture. Did she ever think about it? Oh, being who she was she would think about it. Perhaps that was why she was so different, even from the youth of today. She was beyond them. Her heritage, whatever it was, had forced her into adulthood.

'Nancy's a long time with that tea. You haven't been listening to what I've been saying.'

'Oh yes, I have, dear. Oh yes. I always listen to what . . . you . . . say.' She stressed the last words then added, 'How could I do anything else?'

Now Janie leant her head against Lady Lydia's shoulder and, laughing, she said, 'Do I always appear so forward?'

'Yes. Yes, you do, dear; you always appear so forward.'

'But does it annoy you?' She was now sitting up straight.

'My dear' – Lady Lydia took her hand – 'I couldn't imagine you ever annoying me. Surprising me, oh yes. Amazing me, oh yes. Yes, that, too, but never annoying me. What you are, dear,' her voice dropped, 'is a comfort. You always have been and I hope you always will.' But as Janie went to embrace her, she exclaimed, 'Oh! Ah! Ah! At last. Have you been to China for that tea, Nancy?'

'No, ma'am; I didn't get as far as that, only to Newcastle. And I hadn't me tram fare back so I had to walk.' And Janie,

449

jumping up to take the tray from her, laughed loudly, saying, 'Well, you should have had enough money for the tram; what have you done with your bonus?'

'There you are, ma'am.' Nancy was nodding to Lady Lydia, who sat smiling tolerantly on the sofa, 'She'll not let me forget that bonus. And by! I had to work for it. I nearly lost me fingers pickin' an' bottlin'. I pity those fellas outside, I do that.' Then looking Janie up and down, she said in a more appreciative tone, 'I saw you coming in with your new hat an' coat on. You looked lovely, you did.'

'Thank you, Nancy. Thank you.'

But when, looking towards her mistress, Nancy bantered again, 'She looked like a young lady for once, which is a change,' Janie cried, 'Oh, you! You would go and spoil it, wouldn't you?' and Nancy made for the door laughing, only to stop abruptly, saying, 'Oh, I forgot, ma'am. That bloomin' telephone thing, bell, kept ringin' and when I got to it there was nobody there, and I shouted, twice I shouted, "Hello! Hello!" '

'When was this?' Lady Lydia had risen to her feet.

'Oh, when you were upstairs restin', ma'am. If anybody had answered saying, "It's me," or some such, I would have come up for you, but there was nothin'.'

The telephone was a new addition to the house and she'd had it installed because, earlier in the year, she'd had to miss two visits to Gerald because of his suffering from a severe cold, and she had said to him, 'If another time you are not feeling well, would you phone me?' And he had nodded at her before saying, 'Perhaps.' So she'd had the instrument installed. But he had never used it; and the only other call she had received was from her stepson Beverly's daughter-in-law, the mother of the young officer whom Gerald had attended on the hospital train. The young man himself had written to her a few times and had commiserated with her on Gerald's breakdown, and always he had spoken highly of him. And a year later, after he died from his wounds, his mother had informed her and then taken up the correspondence. And it had been she who had phoned that once.

450

'Whoever it was, they'll ring again,' said Janie, now handing her ladyship a cup of tea. 'It could be someone from the market. I gave them your number.'

Lady Lydia did not say, 'I wish you hadn't,' but she listened to Janie going on, saying, 'Mr Potter in the fruit shop said that's how business is done today.' She smiled now as she added, 'He was very funny. He said, all you had to do was to lift that thing, and he pointed to the phone, ring to the source, say what you wanted, and they put it on the carrier cart if it was for in the country, and Bob's your uncle.'

The cup rattled in the saucer. It was impossible, Lady Lydia told herself, not to laugh or to be happy in this child's company. Yet why did she still think of her as a child when she kept telling herself that Janie Gibson had never been a child?

The sound of a bell ringing sent the teacup and saucer clattering on to the table. And when Janie cried, 'I'll see who it is,' Lady Lydia checked her quickly, saying, 'No, no! I'll see to it.'

In the hall she took up the receiver from the wall and said, 'Yes? Hello.' There was no answer for a moment; then the voice said, 'Mama.'

'Oh. Gerald, Gerald. Hello, my dear.'

'Mama. Will you put a single mattress down in the cottage and . . . and a few cooking utensils?'

'Oh, Gerald . . . Ger . . . '

'Mama, I am not coming to the house. Either I go into the cottage or I stay here.'

She had to draw in a long breath before she could say, 'All right, dear, all right. When . . . when are you coming?'

'I . . . I don't know. Perhaps tomorrow or the next day. When . . . when I feel you've done as I asked.'

'Yes. Yes, my dear, I'll do as you ask. Oh yes. Hello, hello, Gerald.'

There was no answer. She replaced the receiver; then stood gripping the edge of the small table on which lay a telephone directory. Her eyes were tightly closed; but then she started when a voice behind her asked, 'Are . . . are you all right?'

She turned and leant against the edge of the table. Her body was shaking slightly and she put out a quivering hand and gripped Janie's as, her voice seeming to come from high in her head, she said, 'He's . . . he's coming home.'

'*Oh! Oh, wonderful. Wonderful!*'

'But' – she pulled herself from the support of the table – 'not here, not into the house.'

'No? Why not?'

'He . . . he . . . Oh, my dear, let me sit down.'

Janie supported her across the hall and to the drawing-room again and seated her on the couch, where she lay back, then said, 'What you must understand, Janie, is that he doesn't want to see anyone. Those are his conditions. If he is not left alone he will' – she gulped in her throat – 'well, go back to the hospital. He said as much. He wants a mattress and some cooking utensils put into the cottage. But' – she now shook her head – 'it is in a dreadful state, so damp. But there it is, we must do something.'

Janie remained silent for some time before she said quietly, 'Not even me?'

And Lady Lydia could have answered, 'You in particular, dear, because even the very mention of your name seems to make him retreat even further into himself.' She couldn't understand this because he had been so fond of Janie. Hadn't he taken it upon himself to go to the aunt and threaten what he would do if she was locked in again? And he had been her confidant. She could have been his daughter, so close were they.

'Oh, dear, dear!' Lady Lydia put her hand to her head. 'Now we'll have to get the men to help clear around that place, and take a bed down and put a fire on. The next thing is, it will be all over the village and they'll say he's . . . ' She stopped.

'They'll say nothing of the kind,' said Janie. 'And I'll talk to those two and tell them what will happen to their jobs if they open their mouths down there. Anyway, Arthur won't jabber and he'll keep a watch on Billy's tongue. Now don't you worry.' She leant towards Lady Lydia. 'I'll go now and put my old coat on and change my shoes, and I'll see to things.'

452

And this is what she did. In the hour that was left of daylight she had the two men clear a path to the cottage. She herself built a fire and swept down the cobwebs and the floor. Then the following morning, by daylight, she had the men at it again. They brought a single bed from the house and a small couch, an easy chair, and a straight-backed one, also a wooden table. She herself collected all the utensils needed for cooking and eating. And lastly, the men took down a double-doored cupboard in which food could be stored in one section and utensils in the other.

It was that afternoon when the things were in place that she thanked them both, while reminding them: 'You know what I said about not talking about Mr Gerald in the village?' And Arthur Fenwick replied, 'There'll be no gossip from us, miss. But what about leaving a stack of wood outside the door?'

'Oh yes, yes. Thanks, Arthur. Yes, do that, please.'

It was Billy Conway who now said, 'What kind of a fella is he, miss?'

Janie thought for a moment, then said, 'When I last saw him he was tall and thin, and very nice looking. And he wasn't a fella, he was a gentleman.'

'No offence meant, miss, just a manner of speakin', like. But . . . but 'tis funny him wantin' to live down here when he's got that fine place up there.'

'He . . . he stayed down here a lot before he went away. This is where he used to . . . write.'

'Oh. Oh, he was one of them writers? Oh, I see. Well, that explains it,' which brought another reminder, this time from Arthur Fenwick on a laugh: 'Well, he won't be able to write if he's frozen, Billy. So let's get at it.' And Janie, too, laughed, then left them to it, and walked back to the house, thinking to herself, Yes, he used to write, and he might again.

She met Lady Lydia descending the steps from the terrace; she was muffled up against the chill wind, and over one arm she was carrying a greatcoat and a woollen jumper, and in her other hand she was holding what looked like a large brief-case. Nodding first to the coat, she said, 'He'll need this. And this is the writing case he used before.'

Janie didn't say, 'That's odd, I was thinking about writing materials;' instead, she suggested: 'Let me take these and you go back indoors, it's so cold.'

'Well, you can take the case.' And Lady Lydia handed it to her. 'It's rather heavy. But . . . but I'll carry the coat. And I want to see how it is down there.'

'But it's very rough going. Although they've cleared a path, it's all ruts and stones.'

'Well, if I fall, my dear, you'll only have to pick me up.'

'I won't do any such thing,' Janie said, taking her arm. 'I'll let you lie there and I'll say, "It serves you right. I told you so." '

'Yes, I'm sure you'll do just that.'

So, exchanging light chatter, Janie helped her along the pathway; and when they were standing inside the cottage, which to Janie looked quite habitable compared with what it had been when she had first pushed the door open, Lady Lydia looked aghast for a moment, saying, 'Oh, dear me! Dear me!'

'I . . . I think they've done very well. You should have seen it before.'

'Yes. Yes, I know, my dear. I know you've done wonders, and the men too. But that he should choose this. Oh!' She gave a shuddering breath, then said, 'I should be grateful that he wants to come back at all. But, my dear—' She turned to Janie now and, putting her hand on her shoulder, she said, 'You won't—' She stopped as if searching for a word to substitute for 'pester', then went on, 'I mean, you won't come down here? He won't mind Arthur bringing what is necessary, but . . . '

'You were going to say that I mustn't pester him. Well, if you say I mustn't come down here, I won't. Although I still can't see why not. We got on splendidly before, like a house on fire. Why doesn't he want to see me?'

'My dear, it isn't only you, he doesn't want to see anyone.'

'You mean females?'

'No, no; I don't mean only females, because there were nurses in the hospital as well as the orderlies. It's just people.

454

He wants to be alone. He . . . he tolerates me, and that's about as far as he can go at present, but he may change.'

Janie swung about and went towards the door, saying tartly, 'Well, I hope he does, for your sake, if not for his own, because he's got you worried to death.'

'Oh my dear, don't talk like that.'

'I can't help it, Lady Lydia, because it's true. You can hardly eat for worry, you're all skin and bone.'

'Ho! ho! Look who's talking. If I'm all skin and bone I would describe you as two lats.'

'Yes, you might,' said Janie now, her head bobbing; 'but there's a chance that I'll develop in places, at least I hope so. But you'll just fade away if you're not careful. Then what will he do? Come on; you look frozen.'

'Yes, yes. And he'll be frozen in here.'

'No, he won't. That fire gives out a lot of heat. And if it's on night and day the place will soon be snug, and many a one would be glad of it, let me tell you.'

'Yes, I suppose you're right, dear. Those poor men on the road. The war was going to make all the difference. But what has it done? Turned this country topsy-turvy, with young men who had commissions in the Army now having to do menial jobs, door-to-door salesmen, and glad to do it. It's unthinkable really. The world will never be the same again.'

As they walked back to the house Lady Lydia exclaimed, 'Something will have to be done to this path; you could break your neck on the ruts.'

'Well, we'll have to see about that later,' said Janie, again tersely. And then she added, 'Because if Mohammed can't go to the mountain, the mountain should come to Mohammed. And let's hope it happens.'

'Yes, my dear, yes.' Lady Lydia could not help chuckling. 'Indeed, let's hope it happens. But until it does, my dear, I must ask you to promise me not to go anywhere near the cottage. As I said before, Arthur will take down what is necessary.'

For four days Arthur visited the cottage, only to report no-one was there, and that he had replenished the fire. But on the fifth morning he came hurrying into the kitchen and

455

asked Nancy to inform her ladyship that he had found the cottage door locked and that there was smoke coming from the chimney.

On her way upstairs Nancy had met Janie coming down, and excitedly she had said, 'He's back! He's back! Arthur found the door locked. He's back!' And as Janie made her way slowly down the remainder of the stairs and to the kitchen, she thought, for all the change it's going to make to me he might as well be still in the hospital. But what I'd like to know is why he doesn't want to see me. She could understand him not wanting to see people. But she wasn't people, she was Janie, his Janie, and he was her 'nice man'. At least that's how it had been before he went away. But now no more.

7

It was now May 1921, and Gerald had been ensconced in the cottage for seven months, and Janie hadn't seen a sight of him, even though she was now living permanently at the Hall.

This arrangement had been amicably made after Carl and Jessie's return from their honeymoon. It was Carl who had suggested tactfully to Lady Lydia that Janie's Auntie Jessie was concerned for her future career and was urging that Janie take up a course of some sort or other, such as nursing, that would provide her with a livelihood later on, because she didn't want to stay on the farm. However, he wondered, would Lady Lydia consider taking her into a partnership, for the girl seemed to be adept at managing labour? He said he was aware that she, Lady Lydia, was giving Janie a generous portion of the profits, but again he pointed out that her aunt was concerned with her future security, and at the moment the part of the profits she was receiving did not suggest future security.

The thought that her protégé would leave her to start on some trifling course or other filled Lady Lydia with dismay, and so, 'Yes, yes, of course,' she said. But as for a partnership, she herself did nothing towards the business: the men did the work, but it was organised by Janie, who seemed to have great plans for extending the smallholding.

From this, Carl went on to say there was just one more point: perhaps she knew that Janie had refused to live in the farmhouse, and they didn't like her staying alone in the cottage, so would her ladyship consider Janie living at the Hall with her? Yes. Yes. Her ladyship was only too delighted to agree to this: and so it had come about.

As it had also come about, and you could believe it, that her ladyship had adopted 'that one' and 'that one' was running the place, ordering this done and that done. And the latest was a horse and cart, all out of veg and fruit . . . I ask you!

Then there was the son living in a broken-down cottage in the wood. He was still round the bend in his head. And this latter was the cause of another division between the patrons of the two inns. Some said he was still barmy, and some said he wasn't, that he was writing, and writers had to be on their own. He'd be doing a war story. He was at it every day . . . But what did he know about the war? it was questioned.

He was a conchie.

So the village gossiped as usual, and the recluse stayed in his fastness in the wood, seeing only his mother and a man called Arthur. Meanwhile, Janie went on building up the business of the smallholding and defiantly riding through the village by the side of Arthur on a Saturday morning, when they attended the market in Fellburn where, more and more, she was greeted with smiles and kind encouraging words.

She had never allowed herself to question Arthur about what happened when he took the stores down to the cottage, until this particular Saturday morning. It was when passing through the village and after the second unknown person had looked towards her and smiled and brought the remark from Arthur, 'There now, people aren't as black as they're painted, are they? Things are changing, I understand, from what they used to be.' It was then she asked, 'Have you found any change in Mr Gerald since he came?' And after a moment he said, 'Yes and no. He's always civil and we have a word now and again.'

'What kind of a word? What do you talk about?'

'Oh, the weather and the crops.'

'Does he ask about crops?'

'Well, not exactly. I mention them with the weather, you know.'

She now forced herself to say, 'Does he ever speak about me and . . . what I do? I mean with the business?'

'Oh no, miss, no, nothing like that. He doesn't touch on the house, just the weather an' that.'

Just the weather and that, she thought, and not without some bitterness. Why didn't he get himself out of that place and clear the shrub? He had started chopping his own wood, but that was about all. If he could do that he could cut the undergrowth and use a shovel. The more she thought about him the more mad she got at him. And Lady Lydia had to go along that path because it was impossible to cut back all the roots of the trees. That way was never meant for a path. The only reason why the men had made it was that it was a straight run from the front of the house, over the sunken lawn, through the shrubbery and into the wood. One of these days she would blow up, she knew she would.

And the day wasn't far ahead.

It had been a hard winter. There had been a heavy and unexpected fall of snow at the beginning of May. It was then that Lady Lydia caught her chill. And after a week of taking linctus which did nothing to alleviate her cough and the pain in her chest, she took it upon herself to ring for the doctor. When Philip Patten came, he ordered her to stay in bed for at least a week, threatening that otherwise her bronchitis might develop into something more severe. And when he finally said to her, 'Now we understand each other, don't we, your ladyship?' she had said, as in an aside, 'Yes, Doctor.' And when he insisted, 'You won't disobey my orders, will you?' and she had answered, 'I can't promise you,' he said nothing more. But when going downstairs with Janie, he remarked tersely, 'If she goes out into the cold I won't be answerable for the consequences, so see she stays in bed. And by the way,' he added, smiling at her, 'I hear very good reports of you as an excellent businesswoman.' Then he added further, 'You don't miss the farm?'

'Oh! no.' The two words were emphatic, and he said, 'No, no, of course you wouldn't. But it's a happier place now, you know.'

'It would have to be, wouldn't it, Doctor?'

'Yes, my dear, it would have to be. And . . . and how is the other patient?'

'I don't know. He keeps to himself. He does a lot of writing.'

'So I understand. Anyway, he doesn't need a doctor, that's something.'

'Yes. Yes, that's something.'

'Now do what I say and keep an eye on her ladyship and don't let her get out of bed.'

'I'll do that, Doctor.'

She did that for a week; but when her ladyship said she felt better and able to get up a while, Janie was emphatic: 'No, you can't! If you attempt to, I'll get on the telephone to Doctor Patten straightaway,' a threat to which Lady Lydia seemed to accede, for she now asked Janie, 'Has . . . has Arthur said anything?'

'No, he hasn't. But the person in question must know you are not well, and if he can't see fit to take his legs along that path just for once, then I feel he wants . . . ' Oh dear me. She closed her eyes and turned away. She had nearly said, 'Somebody's foot in his backside,' a threat she had often heard Mike use to Rob, a threat that worked. 'If you don't get on with that you'll have me foot in your backside.'

'What were you going to finish on, my dear?' said Lady Lydia with a smile.

'Something that would have shocked you, I can tell you that.'

'No doubt, no doubt. Well, I promise you I'll stay put for the next two days. The weather has changed, and I'm so much better now, I've hardly coughed at all today. Just two days more and then I'm getting up.'

As Janie went out of the room she remarked to herself, 'That's what you think.' Then downstairs, she pulled on her old field coat and a woollen hat and actually marched out of the door and thence along the rutted path. But when she came in sight of the cottage she stopped. Her heart was beating against her ribs. Why it should, she didn't know, only perhaps, she thought, it was with temper. Who did he think he was sitting in there all day? Even if he *was* scribbling.

When she reached the door she hesitated a moment; then determinedly lifting her hand, she knocked twice.

She heard a movement inside the room and she knew there was somebody now standing just behind the door. When there was no reply, she knocked a further three times; and when again she received no answer she put her face close to the door and yelled, 'If you're afraid to open the door, I'll give you the message through it! Your mother is ill in bed, and you must know that, else she would have been along to see you. And why she should the Lord only knows, because you've still got two legs and you could walk. But no! you've got to hide yourself away. Well, there you have it. She's been ordered to stay in bed, but she's not going to because she has to come along here and see how you are. And to my mind you're not worth bothering about. You're cowardly . . .'

The door was pulled open with such force that she staggered back. And there he was, this tall, thin, spare-looking figure that gave her no semblance of the 'nice man'. He was glaring at her. His eyes looked black, whereas she remembered they had been grey. But now, like his face, they seemed ablaze. She didn't know this man. He was like no remembered image that she had retained of him and that she had conjured up during the years since she last saw him on the day she learned of her beginnings through the conversation in the cow byres. The 'nice man' she remembered was all gentleness, whereas this man looked like a demon; and she stood gulping, her hand gripping the top of her coat, too terrified to turn and run now. Then she saw the man seeming to melt away and the figure lean against the stanchion of the door and close its eyes. And when his voice came low, saying, 'Go away,' she still stood. And when, in a croaking whisper, she said, 'I'm . . . I'm sorry,' he said again, 'Go away, please.'

She went to turn about but something stopped her. What, she didn't know. Whatever it was it made her take three steps towards him. And now in a trembling voice, she said, 'I'm . . . so sorry. I shouldn't have said all that. I didn't know.' She did not add, 'you were still ill,' or that, 'I should not have called you a coward.' Perhaps it was that word, because Carl had told her and explained to her about the conscientious

461

objectors, and it would seem not one of them could be called a coward.

When she put her hand on his arm he jumped backwards as if he had been stung, and again she said, 'I'm . . . I'm sorry.' Then she watched him almost stagger to the easy chair and drop into it and lean his head back while his eyes stared straight in front of him.

She stood within the doorway now, saying softly, 'I . . . I just came to ask you if you would come and see your mother. There's . . . there's no-one there after five o'clock. I mean, the men finish and . . . and go upstairs above the stables, and then out. You could come in the back way. There's only Nancy in the house, and you know Nancy. I'll . . . I'll leave the back door open for you . . . shall I?' She saw him now close his eyes and she could see a vein standing out on his left temple. It was throbbing. She said softly, 'Shall . . . shall I make you a cup of tea?'

'No!' It was as if he were about to spring up from the chair again; but all he did this time was grip the arms. She had stepped further back, and now he said, but in a normal-sounding voice, 'Please go away.'

She stayed for a moment or two longer; then she backed out of the door and pulled it closed, and on the sound of it he opened his mouth wide; then gripping his chin, he muttered, 'No, no,' and slowly his mouth closed again. No more gas attacks. No, no. That part was finished with. But that she should appear at the very moment when he had just finished writing of that first night with Susie and how her face had turned into the child's, and in what followed he had felt the purity of the child in Susie. It had been the most wonderful experience. Nothing he had thought of before had ever come up to it. He had been glad he had waited for that ecstasy that hadn't ended in a moment but had gone on and on. And then to learn . . .

He now flung an arm wide as if throwing off the child who had become defiled, and he was the defiler, just as all men were defilers.

It had been following the shock of Susie and while on a forty-eight-hour pass that he saw them, a line of them, laughing, joking, going from one foot to the other while they stood in the queue waiting their turn. It had come to him in that moment the unfairness of the saying that man acted like a beast: beasts would never act like man; they were selective and there was a time arranged by nature to satisfy their needs. In that place there hadn't been much chance of selection. So they had lined up. To what? To a victim, or another Susie? The sight had created a stench in his nostrils that remained with him, a stench that was stronger than any of the blood-soaked, mutilated, gangrenous limbs that he had handled on the trains. And then he had asked himself if he was less of a man because he thought this way? He had wanted love, and to love, and to feel the essence of love, but it had ceased to be clean. It had become dirtier than the war had become, on a par with gas. *Yes, gas. Oh, gas.* That had been the end. *Gas.* The blind eyes, the choking throats, and agonised hands. The bursting lungs spewing forth.

But why had she to come at that moment? the moment he had dreaded to face up to and then to write about; and that word she used to him. He could have struck her. And she had looked so frightened. And yet where had the child gone? Where had the girl gone? She now looked a young woman. How old was she? Sixteen, seventeen? Oh yes, she must be that. She was so tall. Yet her face hadn't changed, nor had her voice. But why had she come? Oh, yes, yes; his mother was ill. Well, hadn't he known something was wrong with her, else she would have been here? Why hadn't he gone to see her? She did not represent civilisation, nor people, and chatter, and daily papers, lying daily papers covering up the faults of old men. But they couldn't cover up the graves, could they? Nor the numbers, hundreds, thousands, millions that would look upon the stars no more. Were they all looking down from heaven? The padre used to say that they were at rest now in heaven. Were they standing up, or laid out in rows, the hundreds, thousands, millions? Why weren't they falling through the clouds?

He sprang from the chair, put his hand on his head, drew in a long, long, slow breath and said aloud, 'Stop it! No more! Get rid of it! Go on writing it out!'

463

He went into the other room and was about to sit down at the table on which, at one side, lay his writing case and a pile of papers, all sheets covered in a close spidery hand, and at the other books and loose-leaf folders. He didn't sit down, but he said, and again aloud, 'Do it now! Don't put it off. You must do it now!' And with this he went to the door, took his greatcoat off a hook, pulled a cap on to his head, and left the cottage.

During the following week Gerald visited his mother three times, and each time Janie had been aware that he was in the house simply by going to the side entrance and finding the door closed; she always left it ajar until she was about to go upstairs to bed. But in no way did she show herself during his time in the house.

On his third visit he sat with his mother for almost an hour. In order to keep him by her side a little longer, she felt she could ask him about his work. Was he, for instance, going to compile his writings into a book?

Yes, he said, that was his plan.

And was it all about the war? she dared to ask him.

Yes, but the war of a conscientious objector. The title would be 'My Conscience, My Cross'.

'Oh. Oh.' They looked at each other for a moment before she asked, 'Has it helped you? Will you publish it?'

'Yes, definitely it has helped. But no, I won't have it published, because that would mean—' he moved uneasily on his seat before going on, 'Well, you know what it would mean, and I couldn't bear . . . well, publicity . . . people.'

'You could use another name.'

He smiled wanly at her. 'And this same address? Just imagine what would happen. The things that I've dared to say and . . . and expose would cause questions to be raised in Parliament and stir up the white-feather gang again.'

'Oh, my dear, I don't think there are many white-feather individuals left, not now.'

'O . . . h,' the word was long drawn out, 'you don't know, Mama. There was a young fellow in the hospital, he was one of us; in fact, we were the only two among soldiers and we

464

were accepted by them. But this young fellow didn't break down until he returned home, when he was actually attacked by a herd of women from the street in which he lived, because they had lost husbands, or sons, or brothers in the war, and there he was, to them, whole and hearty. They smashed the windows and beat him up. The fact that his mother had to shield him finished him. It's unbelievable, yet women can be more fierce than men . . . or animals.'

They sat in silence for a time, and then she dared to bring up another subject. She did it very diplomatically. 'I . . . I am sorry that Janie disturbed you the other day. I told her that I should be all right in a day or two.'

'It's . . . it's all right. She didn't disturb me. Well, at least . . . well, she surprised me. I . . . I thought I recognised her voice and then when I saw her, I didn't recognise her at all. She . . . she has grown . . . very tall.'

'Yes, she is tall. I hope she doesn't keep on, she is five-feet six already. But then, she'll soon be seventeen and one stops growing after that, I think. Yet,' she smiled, 'I don't remember what age I was when I stopped. I only know at the time I was glad I did, because very tall women were looked upon as oddities in my day. But Janie will never be looked upon as an oddity. She . . . she's such a charming girl. I don't know what I would have done without her during these last . . . Are you going, my dear?'

'Yes. Yes, I mustn't tire you.'

'Oh, you could never tire me, but I must tire you with my chatter.'

'It's good to hear you, Mama. Yes.' He bent over and repeated, 'Yes, it's good to hear you. Goodnight, my dear.' As he kissed her softly on the cheek, she put her arms around his neck and held him to her for a moment, and it seemed to her he might be about to return the embrace, but then his body jerked away from her and he was standing straight, saying, 'Goodnight, my dear.'

'Goodnight. Wrap up well. It's . . . it's still chilly out.'

He had backed a little way from the bed and now he nodded before turning abruptly and leaving the room. And she lay with her hands tight pressed against her chest, and she prayed, 'Bring him back, dear Lord. Bring him back to what he was.'

The raspberries had followed the strawberries and had given them a real bumper crop. And now it was the end of August and they had finished clearing the bushes. Arthur had gone into the town with fifty-pound punnets and there were still four large and two small baskets on the kitchen table. And Nancy, surveying them from her stool at the end of the table, said, 'I thought I'd seen the last of them lot. D'you mean to bottle them all?'

'Well, I think we'll do three baskets, and' – Janie turned to Lady Lydia – 'I would like to take one over to the farm and,' pulling a face, she added, 'get some cream in exchange.'

'Yes, that's an idea,' said Lady Lydia, nodding her head, her eyes sparkling their amusement, and Nancy put in, 'A bit of butter when you're on.'

'I brought a pound back the day before yesterday.'

'Oh, what's a pound, miss, when those two hogs outside cut into a loaf?'

'You should give them some of your dripping.'

'Now you know why I don't, miss, 'cos it makes better pastry than your farm butter. I've always said that, an' I always will.'

'Well,' Janie retorted, 'as you say yourself, people say more than prayers and they whistle them.'

'Oh! Janie.'

And to this laughing reprimand Janie said, 'I only repeat what she says, Lady Lydia. Anyway, I'll take this basket and we'll have one of the small ones for tea . . . with cream.'

'Oh, get yourself away.' Lady Lydia now pushed Janie gently in the shoulder, 'And give your aunt and Carl my thanks for the eggs and their kindness.'

As Janie made for the door Nancy called to her, 'What do you want doing with the other basket then?'

'I want it kept to one side. That's for Mr Gerald. I'll see to it when I come back.'

'I'll take it down.'

'You'll do no such thing.' She had turned on Lady Lydia.

'You nearly twisted your ankle yesterday.' Then muttering, 'Something will have to be done,' she lifted the none-too-light basket and went out . . .

When she entered the farmyard she was sweating profusely and Rob, seeing her and taking the basket from her, said, 'Coo! I could just do with a basin of those. By! they're big 'uns. The missis has just gone into the kitchen.'

A moment later, Jessie, too, was exclaiming over the size and freshness of the raspberries, and she said, 'I'll get a good few bottles out of that lot. But why didn't you tell Carl, and he would have come over and carried that basket? It's an awful weight. Sit down and I'll make you a cup of tea.'

'I can't stay long.'

Jessie sighed. 'That's always your cry, you can't stay long.'

'Well there's so much to do over there.'

'You're still happy doing it?' Jessie turned from the table where she was spooning some tea into the teapot, and Janie said, 'Yes, couldn't be happier. Well . . . I mean.'

'What do you mean? Something else you want?'

She could have answered, Oh, yes, there's something else I want, and I mean to get it on my birthday . . . my seventeenth birthday, which is only a few weeks away. But were she to give Jessie an inkling of what she meant to do, she would see her aunt flying across to the Hall and confronting Lady Lydia; and then everything would be spoilt. And all under the heading of 'I'm doing it for your own good'. So she answered, 'Yes. Yes, there's umpteen things I want. Anyway, you're happy, aren't you?'

'We're not talking about me, we're talking about you. Because . . . because I'm concerned for you, always have been and always will. I want to see you happy.'

'Oh, I'm happy enough.' Janie got to her feet now, adding, 'Am I going to get that cup of tea or not? There's more raspberries waiting to be bottled.'

It was noticeable that she never mentioned Gerald nor did Jessie refer to 'that man down in the cottage'. So fifteen minutes later she left the farm carrying the basket, now laden with butter, cheese, cream and eggs. And when, back in the Hall, she picked up the smaller basket, Nancy protested,

'He won't get through all of them on his own,' and Janie answered, 'With the help of half this cream he will.' . . .

When Gerald saw the raspberries, he said, 'You're still picking?'

'This is the last, thank goodness. My fingers are sore.'

'Well—' he smiled wryly as he said, 'that's your own fault. You should take on extra hands at this time.'

She was standing near the table, and now she swung round and stared at him, and the look on her face caused him to say quickly, 'Don't say it. Don't say it.'

'Well!' She turned from him, her shoulders shrugging, and when she muttered, 'Well!' he repeated, 'Well!' Then she looked to the end of the table. It was clear. Usually it was littered with paper and books, but now it was clear, and she said in surprise, 'You . . . you're not writing? You're finished?'

'For the present, yes.'

'Are you going to send your book away?'

'No.'

'Why?'

'Just because I've decided that the past is best left in the past.'

'Then why did you go on writing it?'

His voice rose now and his words were rapid, 'Just because I wanted to get things out of my system, and I prefer to write them down instead of jabbering.'

She now faced him squarely, saying, 'Well, don't you bark at me.'

And his answer to this was, 'I'll stop barking at you when you stop acting like a woman.'

They were staring at each other, their bodies stiff. But then she said, 'I . . . I am a woman, a young woman.'

'You're nothing of the sort. You're a girl, a young girl.'

'I'll be seventeen in October.'

'Huh! Seventeen in October. You haven't started to live yet. You know nothing about life.'

'Oh, don't I!' Now she was yelling, 'I've known about life since I found there were locks on the doors, let me tell you. You think because you were in a war and it didn't suit you, that you're the only one who has experienced life, as you call

468

it, and the things it can do to you inside. Well, let me tell you, you needn't go any further than this village to suffer all the pangs of life and none of the joys. That woman back there' – she thumbed towards the door – 'she said years ago that I was the result of an unholy trinity. Carry that around with you in your mind. Do you remember the day when I asked you what an unholy trinity was? Well, almost every day since, I've asked myself, am I doing this because that one fathered me? or, because that one fathered me? or, because that one fathered me? You said stop being a woman. I was a woman before I was a girl. You and your conscientious objecting and your moral protesting. I've been protesting all my life and it's been a long one, and I don't have to wait until I'm seventeen to be a woman.'

When he moved a step towards her and said, 'I'm . . . I'm sorry,' she moved swiftly back from him, her voice still loud as she cried, 'You're not sorry. You're not sorry for me, you're only sorry for yourself. If you were sorry for anybody else you would stop your mother having to trail over here to see you, wet or fine. And she's an old lady, you seem not to have noticed that, and she's very fragile. And if you were really sorry you would do something about it.' Now she flounced out of the room, across the other one and to the door. And when she had pulled it open, she finished her tirade by yelling, 'And instead of sitting on your backside moping on your wrongs, you want to get a shovel in your hand and start digging outside here. So there, you have it! and I've been wanting to tell you that for a long time.'

She left him standing outside the cottage watching her march away, and his whole body was yelling, 'Janie! Janie! Come back! Please! I need you!' But he knew he must never say that. And now he turned back to the doorway and leant his brow against the stanchion. And his mind told him there were all kinds of crucifixions, and he was suffering another now as he faced the knowledge that had always been buried deep with him. But he saw no end to this form of torment: look at him, what was he? A middle-aged man, bewildered and still sick in his mind.

8

A week passed without Janie visiting him; nor would she tell Lady Lydia why, except that they'd had a few words. And anyway, she was too busy, and didn't Lady Lydia think it was time that he did the walking this way? 'He's still not quite himself, my dear,' Lady Lydia still maintained, only to be slightly amazed when her dear girl, who was so sympathetic in all ways, came back with, 'Well, it's about time he was. And if people didn't run after him he might pull himself together.'

It was half-way through the second week, after one of Lady Lydia's hazardous journeys across the rough, root-strewn path that she brought a letter from him. And it took Janie quite some seconds before she could open it, and there on a rough scrap of paper were written the words: 'Please come back. I have something to show you.' She now handed it to Lady Lydia, saying, 'Why couldn't he come and say that instead of writing it?'

'Be patient, dear. You have got him this far; don't let him go back.'

'Me? Me! got him this far?' There was definite surprise in her voice, to which Lady Lydia responded and said, 'Yes. Yes, only you. With that sharp tongue of yours and that bossy manner, and you'll do it my way or else; of course, the latter softened by your own form of diplomacy.'

'Oh, Lady Lydia.'

'Oh, Miss Gibson.'

Janie had to bite on her lip to prevent herself from laughing outright; then she asked quietly, 'Am I like that?'

'Yes. Yes, dear, you are; together with being so honest, and true, and kind. Oh, my dear, don't cry.'

'I'm not crying.' She blinked her eyes rapidly. 'And anyway, there's no time for that.'

'No, of course not, dear. But . . . but will you go along today and see him?'

'Perhaps; after I've had a talk with Arthur. He broached a very good idea yesterday. It's about the bottom field: if a few huts could be put up there, he says, we could keep up to a hundred hens. And there's the pond at the bottom of the field. It's fed from the ditch and, as he pointed out, it only wants some of the silt clearing and there you have a place for ducks. Eggs are always a good market sale.'

'Oh, my dear, my dear. I wonder what next?'

'I wonder, too, and among my wonderings I thought about your friend that you phone, the one who's asked you up to London. Now there's enough money in the coffers to give you a holiday anywhere you like, and you said you loved London and the theatres, and so . . .'

'Oh, my dear, I'm too old to explore London and do the rounds of the theatres.'

'You're not at all. Anyway, I've settled in my mind that you're going to London. And I haven't time to waste talking,' which left her ladyship gasping as usual and telling herself that the child was right: she wasn't too old to go to London and see a play. No, of course she wasn't. In fact, she was feeling better now than she had done for a long time. And that was because her dear boy was so much better . . . proof of which was to show itself that day.

It was four o'clock in the afternoon before Janie made her way to the cottage. And there he was, washing his hands and arms in a sawn-off tub of rain-water supplied by a spout at the end of the cottage. When he saw her he pulled a coarse towel from a hook in the wall and rubbed himself briskly before approaching her. 'Hello,' he said.

'Hello.'

'Feeling better?'

471

'I've never felt bad.'

'No. No, of course not. The . . . the kettle's on. Would you like some tea?'

'I don't mind,' she said and he made to go into the cottage, but as he stood aside to allow her to enter, he said, 'Wait a minute. The tea will taste better if there's some sugar in it. Come here.' He did not put his hand out towards her, but motioned her to follow him, then led the way to the back of the cottage to the small stone-walled yard. The gate leading from this had been overgrown with weeds and here and there low shrubs had embedded their roots in the wall. But now, to her amazed gaze, the yard stood out clear amid a largish piece of ground which had not only been cleared but also tilled.

As she stood surveying it, he pointed silently to the spade leaning against the wall, and he was smiling as he said, 'You provide good medicine.'

'Oh.' She bowed her head now and muttered something like, 'I'm sorry. I shouldn't.' But he came back at her quickly, saying, 'Oh you should. You should. The time was ripe. The pen gets rid of some things but there's nothing like tired limbs to give you dreamless sleep . . . now and again. Thank you, Janie.'

She flung round from him now, saying, 'You're making me feel awful, you know. Lady Lydia said I was . . . ' She hesitated.

'Was what?'

'It doesn't matter.'

'I know what she would say, and that would be that you have been such a great help to her; she doesn't know how she would have got through without you, but,' he added now, 'at the same time you are inclined to be bossy and expect to get your own way.'

'I'm not and I don't!' They were standing beside the cottage door now. 'I am not bossy. I . . . I just know how things should be done, and I always ask and politely. I am not bossy.'

'Well, that surprises me.' He shook his head, at the same time directing his arm as if ushering her into a drawing-room. And like any annoyed young miss, she now flounced in before him only, immediately she was in the room, to point to the fire and declare, 'It's nearly out! How do you expect the kettle to boil on that?'

'Oh, undoubtedly it will take a little longer. But in the meantime, madam, would you mind sitting down and stop acting . . . '

Her arm was already thrust out towards him and she was saying, 'Don't you say that to me again. You know what happened the last time.'

'You don't know what I was going to say.'

'Oh, I do, I do. Acting like a woman.'

'I wasn't.'

'Well, what were you going to say?'

'Oh—' He gave a little shrug now, saying, 'I've forgotten.' Then he took a seat at the opposite side of the table and looked across at her, and as she looked directly at him for the first time since he had returned home, she saw the semblance of the 'nice man': he had smiled more during the last few minutes than he had done during all the past months she had seen him.

He stared at her intently for some minutes until she said, 'What . . . what's the matter?' She put her hand up to her hair. 'I'm . . . I'm a mess? Well, I've been at it all day.'

'You're not a mess. You're a beautiful young girl. Always remember that. Now I'm going to ask you something.'

'Yes?' She waited.

'Can we, from this time on, become friends, as we were, I mean, before I went away?'

She swallowed deep in her throat, then said, 'I'd like that.'

For the first time his hand came out to her and she placed hers in it. She watched him bend his head for a moment; then he said, 'Let us take it from here.'

'Yes.'

It was he who now let go of her hand and, rising from the chair, he said briskly, 'If I don't put the bellows under that kettle it'll never boil tonight.' And as she watched him she thought, I don't care if it never boils. Never, never, never.

*　　*　　*

473

It was her birthday, and she was seventeen. Lady Lydia had given her her own gold fob-watch and a ring that she had worn when she was a young girl. Nancy had given her half a dozen handkerchiefs with drawn-thread hems and her initials hand-worked on them. And the men together had presented her with a bunch of roses and a pound box of chocolates.

Now she was in the sitting-room at the farm and there, facing her, were her Auntie Jessie and Carl. And she had just opened their present, at least one of two presents, and was exclaiming aloud as she held up in front of her the lovely pale blue taffeta dress, saying, 'It's beautiful. It looks too good to wear.'

'It could be a party frock.' Carl was smiling widely at her. And she looked at him for a moment with a look that didn't exactly hold disdain, but something they both understood, for it said: what party?

'And the pearls will go with it.' Jessie held up a double strap of necklet pearls.

'Yes. Yes. Oh, thank you both.' And impulsively she kissed Jessie, then Carl.

And now Jessie said, 'But these aren't all. You should see the lovely cake that Mrs McNabb has made for you. She thought she would keep it till tea-time and we'd have a little party on our own.'

'Oh, Auntie Jessie. Oh, I'm sorry. I . . . I won't be able to come, I don't think, not today.'

'What! Why not?' It was Carl asking the question now. 'Surely they can get on without you for one afternoon?'

'Yes. Yes, I know, but . . . well, I must tell you something and . . . well, it's this.' Before she went on she turned and picked up the dress from where she had dropped it on a chair before she had embraced them, and she laid it carefully over the back. Then turning to them again, she said, 'I'm . . . I'm becoming engaged to be married today.'

They stared at her blankly, then glanced at each other. It was Jessie who said, 'What! Engaged . . . who to? Who are you engaged to be married to? What are you talking about?'

'Just what I said, Auntie Jessie. I could have told you before, weeks ago, but I promised myself I would wait until

474

my seventeenth birthday and then you couldn't say, Don't be silly, you're still a child or some such, as you always do. I'm seventeen today, Auntie Jessie, and I feel I've been seventeen, eighteen or nineteen for a long time. And as you know, I've been doing the work of someone older for a long time. And I know my own mind, I always have, always, for years and years.'

'Who are you becoming engaged to, dear?' Carl's voice was quiet.

'Well, need you ask? To Mr Gerald.'

'No! No!' It was almost a scream from Jessie. '*No! I won't allow it.* You're mad, girl, as mad as he is.'

'He's not mad. Never has been mad.' Janie's voice was quiet but each word was emphatic. 'He went through so much in the war that his mind closed up against it and all those people who perpetrated it. He is no more mad than you or I. But speaking of me, there's more chance of my going mad with my background than of his.'

'He's old enough to be your father.' Jessie closed her eyes tightly at this. What had she said? But Janie picked it up, saying, 'But he didn't happen to be one of the three, did he, Auntie Jessie? He was, though, the one who found my mother, so I understand, and carried her back here. And he was the only one, let me tell you, who showed me any kindness, apart from you, Carl; because you didn't, Auntie Jessie, you were my gaoler, and I was just something to fill up the gap in your life. You see, the way I'm talking is not as a young girl would, Auntie Jessie; someone who doesn't know her own mind. Now, no matter what you say or what you do, you'll not stop me in my purpose.'

'Has he asked you to marry him, dear?' The question coming from Carl was again quiet.

Janie looked away from him for a moment before answering, 'No, he hasn't, and I know he never will. But what I do know is that he loves me. And I'm going to tell him today that I love him and we are going to marry. Not straightaway, but we are going to marry.'

'Oh my God!' Neither Carl nor Janie went to Jessie's side as she slumped into a chair; but Janie looked at her, saying now, 'You never liked him, did you, Auntie Jessie? For the simple reason that he told you your treatment of me was wrong. Well, there it is. I'm sorry I won't be over today, but if you still want me to, I will come tomorrow. And very soon' – she now turned to Carl – 'if you'll allow it, Carl, we'll walk over together to see you . . . because, in a way, I've known he's always looked upon you as my guardian.'

Carl said nothing.

But when she turned to look at her Auntie Jessie again she saw her actually shudder. Slowly she picked up the dress and the string of pearls, saying, 'Thank you so much for the pearls.' And then she added, 'I suppose I may keep them?' which brought a grimace from Carl as he said, 'Don't . . . don't say things like that.' Then she walked out.

The minute the door was closed on her, Jessie sprang from the chair and, going to Carl, she said, 'You . . . you've got to stop it! It's indecent. That man must be forty or near it.'

'My dear' – he put his arm around her shoulders – 'I can't stop it, and I wouldn't if I could. In fact, I've known it would come about some day. Yet, I must admit it was a bit of a shock, especially today and the way she put it over, when she implied he would never ask her. And what he says when . . . she proposes to him will never be known, I suppose.'

'But he'll take her.'

'If he's wise, yes he will, dear. She's loved him from the beginning, I know that; and that man had a most protective feeling for her as a child, which must have grown with the years, especially of late.'

'Oh dear Lord!' She turned from him now. 'More fodder for the village.'

'Damn the village!' She almost jumped at the sound of his voice, and he repeated, 'Yes, Jessie, damn the village. That village is not going to impinge on my life or on this farm any more. And she being who she is, it won't impinge on hers. I'll take a bet on that. So damn the village!' And on this he, too, walked out of the room, and she was left exclaiming to herself, 'Oh, that girl! That girl! She's been the bane of my life. And now this. Is it ever going to end?'

The bane of her life was standing at the farm gate and Carl was saying to her, 'I understand, dear. Yes, I understand.'

'And . . . and he's not forty, Carl, he's thirty-seven or perhaps thirty-eight.'

He smiled at her now, saying, 'What does a few years matter? The main thing is that you love him. But how do you think he's going to take your proposal?'

'Not quietly.' She smiled at him. 'He'll argue a lot, put up more obstacles than Auntie Jessie would ever dream of, and . . . well, I'll take it from there. Whatever he says I'll point out to him that I consider myself engaged and . . . and that next year we could be married.'

He suddenly pulled her to him and said, 'You're one in a million. You always have been.'

When she put her free arm around his neck and said, 'Thanks for everything, Carl. Next to him I love you best of all. And oh my!' – she pressed herself from him – 'my dress will be all crushed,' she said, and she made motions of smoothing out the dress, then said, 'Bye-bye, Carl.'

'Bye-bye, love. Come over tomorrow. I . . . I want to hear the end of the story. No, no, not the end, the beginning.'

'Yes, Carl, I'll do that . . . and the beginning.' . . .

It was an hour later when she reached the cottage. The weather had turned sultry, the sky was low and it promised rain. He was standing outside in his shirt-sleeves and he greeted her with, 'Hello. I think we're going to have a storm.'

'Yes, yes,' she said; 'we could have a storm.'

'Happy birthday, Janie.'

'Thank you.'

'Do you feel any different?'

'Yes. Yes, I feel twenty-seven.'

He laughed his gentle laugh. 'You have a long way to go, my dear, before you come to that. But come in. Look, it's spotting rain.'

'Have . . . have you been working?'

'Yes. Yes, ma'am, I've been working since early on. I should say that I have a quarter of an acre ready for planting. So watch out, I might beat you at your own business.'

'It isn't my business, never was my business. It's your business. I've just been carrying it on for you.'

'Now, now, now, don't start, it's your birthday. Look, I've got a little present for you. Stay there.' He pointed to the couch, and she sat down. When he returned to the room he dropped a parcel on to her lap, saying at the same time, 'I'd better light the lamp. It will soon be dark in here.'

As he lit the lamp she undid the paper and looked down on what, if it had been bound, would be the flyleaf of a book, and the heading was, 'Conscience Crucified'. And underneath was a pen and ink drawing of the Three Crucifixions. She looked up at him and said, 'You're . . . you're giving this to me? You're not having it published?'

'No. No, I told you I wasn't having it published. And, although I am giving it to you, I would urge you not to read it for some time. Put it aside as one of those useless Christmas boxes that one gets, say, for about another year.'

'Why?'

'Why?' He looked up towards the low smoke-dyed ceiling and repeated again, 'Why? Well because I don't want your emotions to be torn to shreds by the wailings of a conscientious objector.'

'They've already been torn to shreds by the wailings of a conscientious objector.'

'Huh! Huh!' He was chuckling now. 'I've never known anyone in my life to come back with answers to a statement that asks for further questioning. But in this case I am not going to ask you the question about your emotions.'

'No, because you're afraid to.'

'Now, now, Janie, don't start. We made a pact some time ago. Remember?'

'Yes, I remember, and that pact was we were to be friends. But friends can talk plainly to each other, otherwise they are not friends but just acquaintances who have to be polite and probably lie while doing so. Anyway, it's my birthday and you've given me a present. I . . . well, there's something else I want.'

'Something else?'

'Yes, something else.'

478

'Well, what is it?'

'I want to be engaged.'

He screwed up his face. 'Engaged? Engaged in what?'

She was on her feet now and actually yelling at him, 'Don't be so damned stupid! I want to be engaged to you!'

'*What?* You must be . . . this is romantic nonsense, girl. You are seventeen years old and I'm nearing forty. *Stop it! Stop it! Stop it!*'

'I won't stop it, and you don't want me to stop it; you are just covering up again. You'll marry me some time, so it might as well be soon.'

'I'll . . . I'll not marry you some time.' He now held both hands up before his face, though not touching it. It was as if he were putting a shield between them. And when she grabbed them, saying, 'You know that our ages have nothing to do with it. You love me, you always have. And I look back and I cannot remember the time when I started to love you, nor the time when I will ever stop.'

It sounded like a whimper. 'Out of the depths have I cried unto Thee, O Lord, Lord . . . '

'What are you saying?'

'Nothing! Nothing! Only remembering something that someone said, and I'm appealing to Him now to keep me sane, or, what is more important, to bring you to your senses.'

When she stepped back from him his hands slowly dropped to his sides and, looking at her, he said, 'You'll never know how much I . . . I am more than honoured, but I can't let you throw your young and clean life away.'

'Will you stop talking like some character out of a book? We're standing facing the truth in this awful little cottage.' She now flicked her hand to the side. 'I am seventeen and you are thirty-seven and you love me. And what's more, you need me. And I love you and I want you, and it will come about some time. I know it will. And you in your heart want it to come about. And now, please, please, Gerald, hold me, just hold me.'

He did not raise his arms towards her until she lay against his chest, her head under his chin; and then he was holding her, every fibre of his body shaking as he pressed her to him. And then he kept repeating her name, 'Oh, Janie! Oh, Janie! My Janie! Oh, Janie!' And when her brow became wet she looked up at his face to see it aflood with tears, silent tears. And now she beseeched him, 'Oh, don't cry. Don't cry, my love. Please, please don't cry.'

But he went on crying and now taking her with him, he stumbled towards the couch, then dropped on to it. And when his crying became audible, she beseeched him, 'Gerald! Gerald! Listen to me, it's all right. I'm sorry. Please!'

But between loud agonising sobs he gulped out, 'Let me cry, my love, let me cry. I . . . I have never cr . . . cried, never. Hold me tight, Janie. Hold me tight. Don't ever leave me. And let me cry.

'Oh, let me cry. Let me cry, my love.'

THE END